# HIS PERFECT POISON

LEE SAVINO

*To the wild woman inside all of us. May we always remember that she is unstoppable.*

# PLAYLIST

Listen to the Belladonna's playlist here: https://geni.us/
perfectpoisonplaylist

# BLURB

**She'll be my captive, my bride, my perfect possession.**

From the moment I saw her, I knew she'd be mine.

She looks so sweet and innocent, just my type.

Her father owes Fraternitas a debt, and she's the one who will pay.

And then she poisons me, and I realize... this won't be so easy. This manic pixie murderer is no one's possession. She's not going to submit without a fight.

I've been fighting all my life. She was meant to be my reward.

I will have Belladonna Bosco as my wife or die trying. And my psychotic bride makes it clear she would love to be the death of me.

This is one fight I cannot lose.

But she's my perfect poison. One taste and I only want more.

Content Warnings:

Stalking, edge play, death of a parent (past), enslavement (past), illness

# PROLOGUE

B*ella*

I BOUNCE up the driveway to the big brick mansion I now call home. Papa's black Rolls-Royce is parked in front of the door. I didn't know he was going to visit; he must be here to see how I'm settling into school.

I pause on the stoop to check myself over. I'm covered in powdered sugar from my visit to the bakery. Papa says I shouldn't eat donuts for dinner, but I love the sugar high.

I brush the powder off my cute white top and pink plaid skirt. My shoes are white, so the sugar blends right in. I make sure the bakery bag with the rest of the donuts is hidden deep in my backpack before barging into the house.

"Honey, I'm home." My voice echoes across the polished wood floors. Papa bought this place because it's close to the university. It was partially furnished, but we really should buy some rugs.

I swing my backpack down and toss it on the couch, then head through the dining room towards my father's study.

And stop short when I see the three masked men surrounding Papa with scary masks covering their faces.

"It's all right, Bella," my father calls before I can scream. He's standing by his desk, with two of the three men towering over him.

I swallow my scream. My heart is thumping.

"Papa?" I should be freaked out that these sinister-looking men are here. And I am, but I've met some scary people in my life because of the business my dad does with them, so I'm a bit more used to it.

Or at least better at hiding my shock.

So on a scale of one to ten, one being chill and ten being "so scared I pass out and pee myself," I'm at about a five.

Maybe a six.

Okay, seven.

*FOCUS, BELLA!*

Papa is a small man. He looks meek and mild, but he's badass in his own way. But right now he looks defeated. His sober expression sends alarm bells ringing in my head.

"What's going on?" My dad is the only family I have left, and he looks like he's been told he only has three months to live.

The men standing over him look like executioners. One is tall and slim in a gray suit, wearing a skull mask, but I can't make out the details because he's positioned himself in front of the window, right where the light blazes in and blinds me.

My eye moves to the man in the middle. His mask is shiny and black with short devil's horns and covers his entire face. He's sitting behind my father's desk, and that's almost worse than the scary costume. He's acting like my father's office belongs to him. It's a power move that takes my breath away. "We had some business to discuss with your father," the man in the devil's mask says. "And now you."

"Me?" I suppress a shudder.

I'm definitely at a seven.

"It's okay, Bella," Papa says, but his voice is soft. A little sad.

RED ALERT.

"You're lying," I say in a small voice. Because Papa lying to me... is the scariest thing of all.

He says nothing. Doesn't take it back or try to reassure me. Nothing.

My sugar high is turning on me. I'm gonna puke.

The third guy moves in front of me, and my stomach flips over. He's bigger than all of them. Huge with bulging muscles. I stare up at him, taking in his wavy blond hair and the dark map of his tattoos.

"Calm down," he says, and his voice is familiar.

Slowly, he leans down. His mask only covers the bottom half of his face. It isn't smooth and shiny like the others; it's just a black bandana with a skull design.

Dark blue eyes meet mine. His hair is pulled back into a ponytail, exposing his misshapen ears. Cauliflower ears, I just learned they're called.

"You," I gasp.

"Me." His voice is as deep as I remember. The way he's looking at me is strangely intimate. Tingles spread through my body.

"What are you doing here?" I ask. I'm still freaking out, but I lean closer to him.

He smells like burgers and French fries. Because this morning he ate at the diner.

Sitting across a table from me.

Now he's here. To threaten me? I know Papa and I are in danger, but my focus is entirely on the man before me and the strange pull between us. This moment feels familiar. Inevitable.

Slowly, I reach out. My fingers float toward his face, slow enough that he could stop me. He could grab my wrist and overpower me easily.

But he doesn't.

He lets me reach out. His stormy eyes hold mine as I pull the bandana down and expose his face.

His familiar face.

It is him. Mr. Muscles. The man from the diner. The man who helped me in the garden last week.

The one who's been stalking me.

"I'm here to sign this." He holds up a sheaf of papers I didn't notice in his hands. "A marriage contract between me and you."

*What?*

I stare at the papers. The printed words blur together. I'm too shocked to focus enough to read what he's showing me.

But I can read the satisfaction radiating off of him as he continues, "The deal is done. You're going to be my wife."

1

———

T*wo weeks earlier...*

*BELLA*

IN THE YEAR of our Lord 2025, I decided to embrace my destiny and become a supervillain.

Step one: enroll in Unitas University. These beautiful, hallowed halls spawn the worst of the worst. And I look forward to becoming one of the best.

The best of the worst. Ha.

Unitas University is the most exclusive college you've never heard of. Most of the world doesn't know what goes on behind these walls. The alumnae keep its secrets well-hidden.

The college doesn't do any recruiting. It doesn't need to. In some circles in New Rome and Metropolis, it's the only college worth attending. All the big mafia families send their children here and had for over five generations.

Most of the students are legacies, but a few of us who aren't slip through the cracks.

I'm one of them. A crack-slipper-inner. Or whatever. Pretty supervillain of me to infiltrate a criminal spawning zone, right?

I'm cackling as I skip past the gorgeous fountain at the university entrance, on my way to orientation. It's late summer and the air is heavy with heat and humidity. In the sunny beds outside the main administration building, the bees are browsing over the cone flowers and bergamot. I wave to them and trot up the steps.

According to my research, most colleges have a welcome week. Unitas is slightly different. Non-legacy first years are invited to move in early June in order to take a semester-long orientation class that will teach them about Unitas's unique academic environment.

It's perfect, since I've been homeschooled for the past couple of years. My only experience of high school comes from binge-watching *Vampire Varsity*, my favorite show. Papa and I decided that this orientation would help me acclimate, so I moved from our city home into an ivy-covered house within walking distance from campus.

So here I am, bright and early for orientation, carrying a box of cronuts fresh from the bakery. I pause before the white columns of the Greek Revival building. It's so grand, I feel transported to another time.

This place is awesome!

But I also feel like someone is watching me. I turn and scan the line of hundred-year-old oak trees, but other than a few students and robe-wearing professors hurrying down the paths, there's no one around. Everyone's focused on their destination or their cell phones. No one is watching me.

I must be imagining things.

I head inside the admin building, where it's blissfully cool, and my sneakers squeak on the marble floor.

I slow down and try to stuff down my excitement. The hall is full of students like me. Which is perfect for my plans. No, I'm not about to go supervillain on these poor defenseless first years. Today, unlocking full-blown villain status will have to wait because I have another goal in mind.

I'm going to make a friend.

I pick up my welcome packet, find a seat to dump it and my pink backpack, and survey the room. Who are my prospects?

There's a group of young women in the corner. They're a bit preppy in white tennis skirts and pink tops.

I like pink. I wouldn't pair athleisure attire with a pearl necklace the way all these women have, but I'm willing to overlook a few flaws in a potential friend.

I grab my box of cronuts and head over there, holding the pastries as bait.

"Hi," I say to the nearest one. She's tall and thin with warm brown skin and perfectly glossy black hair. A huge tennis bracelet sparkles on her wrist. She glances at me as I launch into my spiel.

"I'm Bella. I'm starting school here in the fall. Would you like a cronut?"

"Ugh, no," she wrinkles her nose like I offered her a box of dog poop. "I'm off carbs."

"Me too," adds a pale brunette across from her. The rest of the women look at me with disgust. Then the dark-haired beauty turns her back, blocking me out.

I can hear them murmuring about me. After a moment,

they start laughing. The tips of my ears heat, but I keep cool. Guess I've just met some mean girls, like the cheerleader ghouls in *Vampire Varsity*.

That's okay. Onward!

I move away, heading toward the back of the room. There's something beyond this room that looks a little like a library. Before I can enter, a college employee blocks the way and shakes his head at me. "No food in the reading room." Okay, denied again.

I find myself near a grand arched window. A young woman stands there, bathed in sunlight. She looks spotlit from above, as if the hosts of heaven have conspired to be her lighting team, her hair set in perfect curls that frame her lovely profile.

She's so gorgeous, if she walked onto the set of *Vampire Varsity*, they'd cast her as the lead on the spot.

She also looks a little lost. There's a longing in her gaze as she looks out over the immaculate grounds.

She startles and turns, catching me staring.

"Hey," I say, trying not to be a creepy weirdo. "Uh, I like your outfit. I've never seen a pink suit before."

"Oh. Thank you." Her long eyelashes flutter. Her makeup is flawless, highlighting her light brown eyes and golden brown skin.

My heart sinks. She's so gorgeous and put together, she's probably a mean girl, too. No diamond tennis bracelet, but she's wearing large silver hoop earrings and a silver chain around her neck. The necklace holds some sort of charm on the end, but I can't see it because it disappears below her neckline.

"Didn't mean to bother you."

"No, you're too kind," she says. "I'm Honey. Nice to meet you." She holds out her hand in a formal, practiced move, and then freezes when she realizes I have to juggle the cronut box to shake it. "Uhhh…"

"It's okay." I free a hand and shake hers as best I can.

"I'm Bella. Do you eat carbs?"

She blinks. "Um." Her eyes dip to the box of cronuts. "Yes. Definitely, yes. Are those from Pane P's?"

"Yes!" She could probably tell these are from Panetteria Principessa, or Pane P's, by the signature pink box.

"They're my favorite." Her eyes light up, but she keeps her voice modulated, soft and polite. But that's fine; I'm loud enough for the both of us. "May I?" She gestures to the box. Even her hands are perfectly manicured in a classic French style. She's the best dressed in this room, and now that I think about it, that might be a sign that she's overcompensating.

She's nervous about being here.

"Yes, please." I hold out the box and watch her select a cronut to enjoy.

I sidle up next to her and look out the window. "Beautiful here, isn't it?"

"Yes." Her melodic voice is full of wonder but also touched with worry.

Hmmm. Something's on her mind, but I don't know her well enough to pry.

So I fill the silence.

"The landscaping is pretty good." I point out the usual colorful annuals planted in pretty patterns. "Those are native plants over there, though." I point to the beds under the eaves of this old building. "And that's a rain garden. I also like how they've mixed in herbs and perennials, like the lavender and catmint over there." There are shade plants like ferns and hostas in beds under the hundred-year-old oaks. "It's not just a boring grass lawn. They get points for their attempt at biodiversity."

"Wow, you know a lot about plants."

"They're my favorite. I'm here to study botany. They have an amazing department here. Have you heard of the poison garden?"

"No, but the place I'm staying is down by the labyrinth."

"Ooh, I want to see that. I'm living off campus, so I haven't explored it yet."

"I'll show it to you."

*Squee!* I cock my head. "Are we friends now?"

She pauses. Oops, maybe that was too presumptuous.

"I'd like that, Bella. I could use a friend."

YAY!

"I don't have many friends," I say. "I was homeschooled through high school. It was fun, but my closest classmate was a *Nepenthes × ventrata.*"

Honey blinks. "A what?"

"It's a type of carnivorous plant." I start to tell her all about my greenhouse collection, and unlike most people who glaze over when I talk about flora, she seems intrigued. At least, she listens, nodding and murmuring responses at appropriate times.

A few shouts interrupt my flow, and I turn to see that a bunch of guys in sports gear have wandered into the hall.

As soon as Honey sees them, she mutters a curse and whirls back to face the window. She looks flustered. Her hand rises to fiddle with the long chain around her neck.

I check out the guys. Their voices bounce off the wooden walls. They must be upperclassmen with the way they act like they own the place. First-year students scuttle out of their path.

"Who are those guys?" I ask.

"The lacrosse team," she answers stiffly.

Their leader is a tall, leanly-muscled guy with a set of dimples and floppy hair. Grade A trust fund himbo. He shoves his way through a group of freshmen.

I narrow my eyes. "What a tool."

The lacrosse team guys head straight for the ladies in tennis skirts, who turn with smiles to welcome them.

"Those are the girls who are off carbs." The mean girl rises onto tiptoe to kiss the head himbo.

"Yeah," Honey grimaces. "That's Sailor. She's dating the lacrosse team captain, Radley."

One of the other guys turns, like he's a shark scenting blood in the water. "We should go," Honey mutters, keeping her head down. She's uncomfortable. Because of the PDA? Or those guys?

"Let me just grab my bag." I leave her with the cronuts and hustle to grab the rest of my things, but I take too long. By the time I've returned, the guy and three of his lacrosse buddies have cornered Honey.

"Hey, freshie," one of them says. "I thought I'd find you here. You left too early last night. Running away?" He leans in, brushing the curls back from her face. She recoils from his hand, her hand rising to slap it away, but he just laughs. Her eyes dart around, looking for escape and gauging the situation, but there are more of them than her.

Except now she has me. "Leave her alone," I say, using my bag to shove through the group and get to her side. "She's my friend."

He scoffs. "Hey, Radley," he calls. "Pinkie's got herself a bodyguard."

Radley and Sailor look our way briefly. I notice that his eyes fall right to Honey's large breasts. She's not showing cleavage, but the suit showcases her hourglass curves.

Sailor notices her boyfriend staring at Honey's chest, and her lip curls. She tugs his shoulder, calling out to the guy harassing us. "Penn, quit slumming with the scholarship kids."

"But they're so much fun," Penn protests. He eyes me. "Hey, kid, when did you escape from daycare? Who'd your daddy have to suck off to get you enrolled?"

The lacrosse guys all laugh. I'm short and young-looking, but it doesn't matter that these guys are a foot taller than me. It won't take many bites of a death cap mushroom to destroy their liver and send them into convulsions.

"Fuck off." I bare my teeth at him, channeling Duffy, the prom queen werewolf on *Vampire Varsity*.

"Fucking feral," he mutters, but he backs off.

The other guys wave at Honey, leering. "See ya around, Pinkie," one of them says.

"Tool," I mutter loud enough for him to hear.

"Thanks for standing up for me."

"Of course."

"Let's get out of here," she whispers. She's clutching the charm on her necklace, her knuckles white.

She's really freaked out. I think escape is our best course of action, so I let her lead the way out of the hall. Unfortunately, we have to pass right by the tennis skirts to get to a side door.

"Slut," Sailor hisses at Honey.

I'm tempted to stop and shove a cronut in her mouth, but I keep moving. Why is she being so mean to my new friend? Something's going on, and I don't want to make things worse for Honey.

I wait until we're in a quiet corridor to ask, "Are you okay?"

"Yeah. This way." We slip through another side door and hurry over a black and white tiled floor to a locked door.

"This is a secret," Honey tells me and tugs her necklace out of her bodice. She shows me the charm—an old bronze key. She inserts the key into the lock on the heavy wooden door, and a thrill goes through me when I hear the snick of the lock.

The door swings open with a gust of stale air. Beyond it is a set of small wooden stairs, like the sort that might lead to an attic. It smells of antiques, too, old wood and lemon furniture polish.

"This way." Honey leads me up, and we get to a gallery overlooking a reading room. The place is quiet and empty except for the odd employee. In the corner is a man studying a large book that's in a display case. He's wearing robes. Black with a cinnamon brown velvet stripe.

"A professor," she whispers. "Professor of history. You can tell by the colors on his hood."

We can hear the lacrosse team's laughter echoing through the building. They're loud as fuck. The professor looks up and frowns but doesn't make a move to do anything about it.

I follow Honey's lead and sink into a worn leather armchair across from her.

She exhales. "Sorry about that."

"You have nothing to be sorry about. It was all them. They're just like the ghouls on *Vampire Varsity*."

Honey still looks stressed, but her mouth twitches like she's close to a smile. "I love that show."

"Me too."

She sobers. "I should explain."

"You don't have to." I pause a moment, though, in case she wants to.

"No, it's fine. I went to a party at the sports dorm last night. I thought the air conditioning would make it chilly, so I wore a light sweater." She's rubbing her arms now, an almost unconsciously soothing motion. "I must have drunk too much, or the punch was stronger than I thought, because I ended up in a room with a bunch of those guys and... I got really overheated. One of them suggested I take off my sweater, and I forgot I was only wearing a bra underneath." Her brows knot again, and she looks at the floor, sad and ashamed.

My body grows cold. My friend was taken advantage of. That's what this story is going to be about. And it's not like the storyline from *Vampire Varsity* season two with the succubus demon. This really happened.

"Somehow, I ended up on Radley's lap. Sailor came in and got pissed that I was 'taking her man' and kicked me out. Probably for the best. I don't know what those guys would've done. And I was too out of it to say no."

I don't know what to say. I wrack my brain and finally figure out what I want to know first. "Are you okay?"

She sighs before answering. "I'm okay."

She's not okay. Fuck. The back of my throat gets tight. I want to do more than throw cronuts. "Do you think they drugged the punch?"

"Maybe? I don't know. It was my first college party. That'll teach me."

"It wasn't your fault." I briefly rest my fingers on her arm. It might be overreaching, but I've noticed that touch comforts some people.

"Thank you."

"Thank you for telling me," I say solemnly. She trusts me. She really is my friend. A real-life human friend, not a carnivorous plant.

She opened up and told me a painful thing. Like a real friend would. I feel a connection with her, and that means a lot. It also means I've got her back.

Anyone who hurts my friend is my enemy.

And they will pay.

"Someone should teach them a lesson," I say, testing the waters. Honey doesn't know about my supervillain tendencies yet. She seems like a kind, sensitive person, but I'm sure I can convince her to join me on the dark side.

We have cronuts.

"I just want them to leave me alone."

"They scared you."

"They're scary. I can't believe you stood up to Penn like that." I shrug. I don't get scared. I get angry.

Honey blows out a breath. "Karma will get them. It's summer, so they can pretend they're kings of the campus. They're just drunk with power right now. But their reign will end soon."

"It will?"

"Yes," Her face grows shadowed with a mixture of the worry and wonder I saw on her face earlier. But then she tilts her head, and the lost expression takes on a touch of malice. "When the fall semester starts and the mafia kids get here, they won't be the biggest bullies on campus. Not even close."

**2**

———————

# B _ella_

I LOVE my new best friend. Hanging with her is better than attending orientation. We're learning some interesting facts about Unitas University in our first year class, but Honey knows all sorts of extra facts about the university's history and the four mafia families that helped found it. And she has a key that will unlock any door in the school. "All doors but one."

After she told me about her night of horrors with the lacrosse team, she didn't want to talk about it anymore. So I didn't bring it up again. Better to keep her out of my plan for payback so less suspicion falls on her.

Which is why, when I return to campus on Saturday, I go alone. I'm carrying a big basket full of a special surprise for Penn and Radley and all their friends. I also dressed in a sexy cheerleader outfit with heavy makeup to disguise my face. Plus, I added streaks of pink to my hair to match my pink and black pom poms and put it up in high pigtails on either side of my head.

I look like I'm ready for Halloween, several months early. And a bit deranged.

YOLO!

The point is, no one will recognize me.

*Supervillain Rule #1: Your best offense is a good disguise.*

Anonymity is a weapon. Anyone who's suffered second-degree burns after mistaking a giant hogweed flower for Queen Anne's lace knows this. Nature hides the deadliest poison in the prettiest bloom.

I'm almost to the sports dorm where the lacrosse team lives when I sense someone following me. I turn, and no one's there. But I can feel myself being watched.

Weird. Maybe I'm just being paranoid. I am about to enact an evil plan. It's good to be wary, but I don't think the lacrosse team has any idea what's coming.

"Mwahahahaah," I try out my evil laugh. It needs work.

I still feel someone watching me when I reach the sports dorm, but I ignore the sensation and focus on the two guys loitering by the door. Their eyes widen as they take in my costume. "Hey," one says while his friend checks out my boobs. "You here for the party?"

"Yes," I lie.

"You're a little early."

I hold up my heavy basket. "I have these gifts from the athletic department."

Snacks and an energy drink with a special surprise. "Good luck at your big game tomorrow!" I give them each their gift and thank them when they hold open the door for me. "See you at the party!"

"Should we tell her it's not a costume party?" one asks,

and the other shushes him and says something crude about how my pigtails would make great handholds.

I smile to myself and continue down the hall. Two players down, eighteen to go. By Sunday, I'll be that much closer to unlocking supervillain status.

And the lacrosse team will learn to never fuck with my friend ever again.

3

K*aiser*

IT WAS A SIMPLE JOB: shadow the Poisoner's daughter. Monitor her every move. Don't engage, unless one of the Poisoner's enemies tries to harm her. Then, protect the asset.

It should've been easy. She's eighteen and freshly enrolled in Unitas University.

Sure, her father has powerful enemies, but none of them have made a move yet.

It's a piece of cake to stalk someone who isn't expecting it. Most people live comfortable lives. They never had to sleep with one eye open in case someone tried to stab them in their sleep. They move through life, oblivious.

This girl is more oblivious than most. She hasn't just been sheltered and protected for most of her life; she's been kept in a bubble. Locked down. She's been homeschooled for years and barely has any friends. Barely any contact with anyone other than her father. And now she's living in a big house near campus, all alone.

She thinks she has more freedom, but it's an illusion.

I'm watching her. Following her from home to campus and back again. I've been doing it since the spring.

By the end of the first day, it was clear that this girl was going to drive me fucking crazy.

It doesn't help that she seems to have been designed in a lab to tempt me. Pouty lips, big brown eyes, petite with perky tits. She dyes her hair white blonde, and I constantly imagine threading my fingers through those silky strands, taking hold, and drawing her head back. Controlling her.

But that's not the job. I'm not supposed to get close. But the more I watch her, the more I want to.

She's constantly eating candy or cookies or cake, and it makes me want to sit her down and feed her properly.

She talks to flowers and trees. She hugs the trees, too. Most people would think she's weird, but she fascinates me. I've studied her like I'd study a dangerous opponent. In the fighting ring, I had mere seconds to read my opponent and find his weaknesses. The most dangerous opponent was one who was unpredictable. Not understanding someone's behavior would get me killed.

I don't understand this girl at all. She lives in her own little world. At first, I didn't think she understood how to behave, but now I think she does and just chooses to break the rules. She's half feral.

Right now, she's bouncing around campus carrying a big basket and wearing an outfit that I've only seen in porn. Why? What is she doing?

She's up to something.

At one point, she stops and looks around. I get a thrill knowing she's looking for me.

I want to get closer. I want her to notice me.

I've never wanted that before.

I watch her talk to some male students outside their dorm. They're leering at her, drooling over her tits and ass. I want to gouge out their eyes just for looking at her.

And for what? There's no reason for me to hurt them; they're not threatening her. But I want to kill them all the same.

She's just a job.

She disappears into the dorm, and I grind my teeth, wanting to follow her.

Instead, I force myself to stay put. I check my phone and see that my brother has texted.

**Jaeger: Movie night.**

This is his weekly invitation to watch a movie at his place. He and his woman love holiday movies, the cheesier the better.

I should hate watching those sorts of movies, but I go to watch them anyway. I want to like them. I want to under-stand them. What would it be like to be one of those cheerful people on the screen? To feel basic things like love and connection?

The hardest part is watching my brother's woman cuddle up to him. He looks at her like she's his world. He loves her enough to die for her, and she loves him right back.

I wonder sometimes how it would feel to love someone like that. But it's not to be. My heart's too scarred to feel much more than hate or the occasional surge of bloodlust. Even when I'm with a woman I've hired for the night, I feel nothing. It only reminds me that I'm numb to all decent human emotions and always will be.

Except now, I'm feeling something new. Something I've never felt before.

Kaiser: can't tonight

Jaeger: You still watching the girl?

I don't answer. There's no reason for me to be the only one watching her all this time. I can tag someone else in at any time.

But I don't want to. How can I explain that I want to be the only one to follow her? To watch her?

To prey upon her?

My obsession is growing. And that's dangerous. A good fighter can't become too fascinated with an opponent; that's how you make mistakes.

She comes out of the dorm, and I put my phone away.

She looks the same—her clothes aren't rumpled and her makeup isn't smeared.

It wasn't a hookup, although she does look satisfied. And her basket is empty.

She's walking up the path, straight toward me. I imagine stepping off the path and grabbing the back of her neck and forcing her to face me.

My hand starts tingling, the long, dead nerve endings waking up. It's been a long time since I've felt this much sensation on my skin. I lost the ability to feel anything long ago. In the fighting rings, it was an asset. I felt pain, but it was far away. Like my skin had become armor, and I could only register any brutal blow as heat or pressure.

It's been a long time since I've wanted to touch someone. I usually hate the way it feels—or doesn't feel. The lack of sensation reminds me that I'm a shell of a man.

Makes me feel half-dead.

But ever since I laid eyes on her, I've imagined touching her.

It's probably because I haven't fucked anyone since I started this job. I should just go to Camille's and hire a woman for the night. But I don't want to leave this girl's side.

Lately, every time I go to jack off, I imagine her face. My cock swells whenever I see her, and it's getting harder and harder to ignore. Makes me want things I can't have.

She passes me as I'm hidden in the shadows under a tree. She can't see me, but she pauses and looks around like she senses that someone's stalking her.

Satisfaction roars through me. I'm so close, I can smell her perfume. Or at least, I think that strong smell is her perfume. Smells like roses and there aren't any rose bushes around.

I'm strongly tempted to step out from behind the tree. Two steps and she'll notice me.

And then what?

Only my loyalty to my brothers keeps me from grabbing her right now and taking her somewhere we can be alone. Where I can touch her all over and figure out why she's gotten under my skin.

I follow her home, keeping a distance between us. There's nothing else I can do.

Then I spot an enemy, a shadow slipping along the sidewalk across from us.

It's a man in a baseball cap, talking on the phone. I've seen him before on campus but never this close to her home. He's like me in this rich neighborhood. He doesn't belong.

He watches her bounce up the sidewalk and disappear into her home, then finishes his call and leans on the brick wall opposite her house. Watching her, like I'm watching her. He raises his hand to light a cigarette, and the flare of light illuminates the pentacle tattoo on his hand. The symbol of the Vesuvio Mafia family.

Showtime.

I check my mask—a skull bandana that covers half of my face. I cross the street silently and jump him before he takes the second puff of his cigarette. I jab a hand into his throat, and he chokes and drops the phone, his hands rising to defend himself.

Too late. I punch him in the gut, making him double over with a gasp.

I propel him into the shadows so I can interrogate him. "Who sent you?"

He attacks without warning, fists swinging. I let him get a punch in just for laughs, his blow glancing off my biceps. I feel the shock of it, and I know it must hurt, but I can't feel it. I can't feel anything anymore. I hit him with a haymaker, and he goes down. The scent of his blood rises in the air.

The guy struggles to rise, but he's too stupid to know he's beat. He's a typical foot soldier, too dumb to tell me anything. I already know he was sent by the Vesuvios, the sworn enemies of the Poisoner. There's no reason for him to be watching my target unless he's up to no good. I take great satisfaction in slamming his head into the sidewalk until his body goes limp.

I pick up his phone and hit redial. It's a burner phone, so there aren't any saved numbers, but whoever I'm calling has a Metropolis area code.

"Joey?" a gruff voice answers.

"Joey can't come to the phone." He's too busy bleeding out at my feet.

"What? Who is this?"

"I have a message for Don Vesuvio." I don't think I'm

talking to the head honcho, but it might be one of his sons. "Tell him the Poisoner's daughter is off limits."

He cusses me out. "Says who?"

"Fraternitas."

He sucks in a breath, falling silent as dangerous men often do when I invoke the name of the brotherhood. The Vesuvios are a powerful family with a stronghold in this city, but no one fucks with Fraternitas.

Instead of arguing with me, he hangs up. Probably to call his bosses and tell them what happened. Letting everyone know that if Vesuvios wants the Poisoner's daughter, they'll have to go to war with Fraternitas. The fear will ripple through them, and they'll think twice about attacking my target.

She'll be safe another night.

The man at my feet comes awake. I lean down and break his neck, feeling a rush of disappointment that the fight is over so quickly. My blood is pumping hot through my veins. I want a worthy opponent, more fighting, more blood spilled.

This is all I'm good for. Killing and fighting used to be the only time I felt alive.

At least, until I saw her. I'm not sure why she makes me feel things. I don't understand it, don't like it, but I can't stay away. I want more.

I still smell roses. The floral scent is stronger even than the smell of blood and waste from a freshly dead body.

I pick up the body and stuff it in a trash can, which I then wheel down the street to the empty mansion where I'm squatting. I wheel the whole thing right into the basement, where I've stashed some tarps and a kiddie pool in case of this very situation. I'll wash any traces of blood off the sidewalk and call on my Fraternitas brothers to help me dispose of the body tonight.

But first, I want to check on her.

The lights are on in her bedroom, so I scale a wall, climb a tree, and settle in to watch her go about her bedtime routine. If she looked out the window, she'd notice me sitting in the tree, wearing my skull mask.

But she doesn't, and I don't know why it fills me with disappointment. I don't know why I want her to notice me.

Lately, she's stopped watching the terrible teen vampire show she likes and has been getting herself off every night. First, she grabs the tattered paperback she keeps next to her vibrator. After rereading her favorite pages, she touches herself until her hips are grinding in the air. She gasps like she can't get enough air and pushes her shirt up to fondle her own tits. Then her back arches, and she moans, long and low. The sexiest sound I've ever heard. She comes until she's limp in the bed.

The first time I watched her do it, I nearly fell out of the tree.

She reads the same book over and over again. I'm tempted to break in and read it myself. Study it to see if it will help me understand her.

No, I can't get close to her.

But that doesn't mean I'll let anyone else touch a hair on her head.

4

B *ella*

MONDAY, we have a day off from orientation, but I head to campus to meet Honey at the main library at noon. I still haven't told her about what I did to the lacrosse team, but she texted me an update late yesterday: "the UU lacrosse team all got sick and had to forfeit the summer championship! All of campus is talking about it. Did you hear about it?"

"No," I replied. "How tragic." I added a smiling demon face emoji to make it clear that I mean that sarcastically, but that's probably not enough for her to realize I'm behind the poisoning. I should probably tell her face-to-face.

I wonder how she'll take it. Not everyone can handle having a supervillain for a friend. Honey is a good-hearted person, I can tell. It's early days, but she's already an awesome friend. I don't want to scare her off. But eventually she'll hear me cackling triumphantly, and I'll have to tell her that I'm practicing my evil laugh.

Maybe she'll be cool with it. Maybe she'll help me practice!

But I have time to think about what I'm going to tell Honey. The bells have just tolled eleven, which means I have time for a little detour.

The poison garden here is famous. I'm familiar with poison plants; I have my own personal greenhouse both at Papa's townhouse in New Rome and at the house here. But I've always wanted to see the University's collection.

The garden is nestled out of the way, between two academic buildings. The black iron gate is decorated with two dragon-like serpents holding a cup in one hand and a sword in the other, and there's a pentacle etched onto each serpent's forehead. I'm learning about these symbols in orientation, and now I see them all over campus.

Unitas University loves to stick to a theme.

I also learned that the poison garden is open to everyone. I sidle up to the gates, and sure enough, they're closed but not locked. I bet no one even bothers to come here in the summer. The University is very private and doesn't allow tourist visits. Only faculty, students, and select guests are allowed.

Which means no one is around to admire these plants at their peak. Only me.

The back of my neck prickles with the now familiar sensation of being watched. I've been getting that sense more and more when I'm on campus.

But when I whirl around, no one's there. Huh.

Maybe my supervillain senses are being tripped because more students are coming back to campus. Some of them will be Vesuvios, my family's sworn enemies. I have plans for them, evil plans that go against Unitas University's founding principles.

UU was founded in order to foster peace among the four mafia families of Metropolis. We're learning a little about this in summer orientation, but Honey spilled the real tea about those four families or Houses, and which of their descendants will be attending classes in the fall. Campus is seen as neutral territory, which means no outright gang war. House rivalries, however, are encouraged.

But there's no murdering allowed. At least, it's frowned upon, so I'll need to be careful about my evil plans.

It's not like I want to kill Vesuvio freshies anyway. No, my endgame involves the big boys, the don and his sons. They're powerful and well protected, but nothing like a challenge, right?

First, I need to survive Mafia University. To do that, I'll need all the resources I can get.

Poison garden, here I come.

I push open the iron gate and enter the quiet space beyond. A sign greets me at the head of the path. "Welcome to the poison garden," the stylized script reads. "Enter at your own risk."

If they put this sign out front, people would probably be more curious. Instead, they hide it behind the entrance, so no one knows what's here.

I peer past the posted warning into the dark depths of the garden. There are patches of sunlight, but most of the plants grow in the deep shade cast by the yew and holly trees.

I like plants better than people. I wasn't kidding when I told Honey my best friend was a carnivorous plant. But I've never seen anything like this murder garden.

The heady scent of wet earth and bitter greens is intoxicating. I thought the scent of a greenhouse was my favorite, but this is better. All these greens out in the fresh air, wild. Nature's darkest secrets on display.

The path is lined with flowers that belong in a cottage garden. So pretty, so demure. All the more deadly because no one would suspect something so lovely could kill them.

If my mother were still alive, she'd want to paint them.

The yew trees are the tallest I've ever seen—beautiful evergreens with glossy needles and the most perfect bright red berries. A tea made from those dark green needles can send a man into a coma within a few hours. But researchers isolated a compound from the same tree's bark that's now used in chemotherapy treatments. This deadly tree saves lives.

Just another example of how plants hold all the answers.

I walk through the garden, admiring the beds of monkshood and daffodils. The air is cooler here, and the quiet is almost reverent. Or maybe that's how I feel because phytotoxicology is my religion and deadly plants are my gods. And they are powerful. It's easy to imagine the plant's victims buried under the groves.

This has just become my new favorite place.

I'm in love.

Some sun-loving plants like foxglove and deadly hemlock grow in a small patch of sunlight that manages to make it past the branch canopy. The foxglove has a long stem that's taller than me. I get close and study the pink buds with dark speckles. Such a pretty plant to be so deadly.

"Hello, my precious," I whisper.

Movement out of the corner of my eye makes me startle, and I whirl around.

"Who's there?"

This time I'm not imagining it. The biggest guy I've ever

seen steps out from behind a horse chestnut tree. He's over six feet tall and white with tanned skin and tattoos swirling down his arms and the back of his hands. But he moves so silently, I feel like I'm imagining him. He carries himself lightly, which tells me he's fast on his feet. He's nimble for someone so large.

He pauses by the tree, keeping his face in shadow.

Goosebumps break out over my skin. My breath comes faster.

I've had the sense that I'm being followed for the past few days, and suddenly here's this guy lurking in the poison garden.

My eyes adjust to the shadows, and I catch my breath. The man is wearing a black bandana covering the lower half of his face with some sort of design on it—the white imprint of a skull.

*Helloooo, Psycho Mask Daddy.* Did Christmas come early? And by Christmas, I mean Halloween.

"It's a little early to trick or treat," I say.

He shifts his stance but doesn't say anything. His arms are corded with hard muscle. He's all coiled raw power, and something in his eyes makes me think he wants to pounce.

"What are you doing here?" I blurt. I sound breathless, my heart speeding up, and that annoys me.

I refuse to be frightened by him. I'm not afraid of a big guy in a silly little mask. I'm more concerned about how wet I'm getting. Guess I have a mask fetish.

"Same as you." His voice rumbles in a way that makes me want to squirm. "I wanted to look at the flowers," he says, but he's not looking at them. He's staring at me intently. Studying me like he knows me.

He has beautiful blue eyes. Not that I care.

"What's with the mask?" I ask before I think better of it.

Maybe it's rude to ask. Maybe he has a medical condition that requires him to keep his face covered. "Actually, never mind. It's none of my business." Unitas is a mafia university, after all. Maybe it's common for people to disguise their identities. A fellow supervillain deserves my respect.

But now I want to know what he looks like. From what I can tell, he's older than the students, closer to thirty than twenty. Is he faculty? Maybe, but he's not in robes. He's dressed simply in jeans and a black T-shirt that clings to his broad shoulders, and his longish blond hair hangs around his face.

My cheeks heat. I don't know why he's staring at me, but I kind of like it.

Except, I know I shouldn't. It's distracting.

"Do you mind?" I wave to the exit. "I'm communing with the plants."

"Communing," he repeats.

"Yes."

"You talk to them?"

"Yes."

"Do they talk back?"

"Wouldn't you like to know." I want to turn away and ignore him, but I know never to turn my back on a threat. And, even though he's just standing there, this guy is a threat.

He does seem interested in the flowers, though, and points to the one I'm standing next to. "What's that called?"

"*Digitalis.* Common name, foxglove." I point to the unobtrusive sign on the ground next to the plant. The name is right there on the little sign, if this guy wasn't so busy studying me. "Eat any part of it and you'll become violently ill. But it's also used in heart medication. The dose makes the poison, you know."

He transfers his gaze to the flower, then back to me. How long is he going to stand here staring at me?

"There's a labyrinth across campus," I tell him. "It's famous. Why don't you go look at the flowers there?"

"This place is more interesting."

I snort, because he's right. "Anything is more interesting than a bunch of boxwoods. This is a poison garden," I say, since he doesn't seem to read signs. "Everything in here can kill you."

"Everything?" His eyes crinkle in a way that makes me think he's smiling under that mask. I can feel him sweep his gaze over me, and my insides quiver in response. I'm loving the attention... but I shouldn't.

"Yes," I tell him. I don't have to convince him. Maybe he'll eat something, pass out, and leave me alone. "Believe me or don't. But I'd be careful about touching anything. Like that—" I point to the vine creeping up the hemlock tree. He's planted his hand on the tree trunk mere inches away from it. "That's poison ivy."

He jerks his hand back and steps away from the tree. The sunlight blazes on his blond hair.

I'm tense like I'm going to run, but... I'd never outrun him. He'd catch me.

There's a liquid rush between my legs, and I gulp, hoping my reaction isn't obvious. My belly muscles have drawn up tight, and I can feel my pulse throbbing between my legs.

Why am I turned on by this guy who's lurking in a poison garden wearing a skull mask? I should be creeped out, but I'm staring at him like a moonstruck idiot and acting as if he's the hottest guy I've ever seen. Sure, his hair is pretty, but I've only seen half of his face.

I move closer to the tree trunk until I'm looking at him through a veil of poison leaves.

"That's a weed," he says.

"Not here. It belongs here." I reach out and stroke the reddish leaves. They're shiny with oily resin that causes a horrific, itchy rash.

The man leans away from me. "I thought you said it was poisonous?"

"It is," I say, "but I'm immune. I practically rolled in this a few times as a child. Most people get more allergic to it with exposure, but me?" I shrug. "It doesn't affect me anymore." I show him the oil on my fingers. "But don't touch me. Now I'm poisonous, too." I give him a wicked smile that's more of a warning.

He nods slowly. Maybe he can be taught.

And with that, I decide to ignore him. He makes no move to get closer. If he were going to attack me, he would've already. Maybe now he'll think twice before touching me.

I can feel him watching me as I move deeper into the garden. I feel the pull between us, like I want to keep talking to him, but I refuse to miss out on the reason for my visit to the garden. *Hecate, help me be strong!*

My mind is still on my audience when I find a patch of deadly nightshade to distract me. It's flowering, but the leaves look a bit wilted. I grab my UU-branded water bottle and dump the contents at its roots. The soil soaks it in. Yep, dehydrated, just as I suspected.

I resist the urge to look up at the man watching me, acting aloof like a boss! I crouch and press my fingers to the soil to see how much more water the nightshade might need.

Plants are so freaking durable, and yet they're fragile.

This subshrub will bow before a hurricane and survive, but get the equation of water/sunlight/nutrients wrong, and it will wither and die.

Kind of like humans. In some ways, humans are also so resilient. But if you possess the dark knowledge of poisons, it's laughably easy to kill them.

I smile to myself, thinking of the man watching me. It wouldn't take much nightshade to kill him.

"What else do you need, baby?" I murmur to the dark purple blooms. "More nitrogen? A bit more sunlight? You can tell me."

I'm startled by the creak of the iron gate at the garden entrance. I look around for the mystery masked man but don't see him. He must have left when I got distracted by the nightshade. I try not to feel disappointed.

A guy wearing a UU Lacrosse jersey walks through the gate, looks around, and then heads my way. It's Radley, captain of the lacrosse team. King of the tools.

"You." His eyes narrow at me. "I know what you did."

I rise, brushing dirt from my fingertips. "You'll have to be more specific. I've done a lot of things."

"You're the one who poisoned my team."

5

B *ella*

I cock my head and blink at the angry sports god. "Poison? Me?"

"I know it was you. Sailor recognized you."

Damn. I thought my disguise was good enough. The skirt was short, and I wore a push-up bra to show off my girls. I don't have epic cleavage like Honey, but it was enough to distract a bunch of horny guys.

But apparently not Sailor. She must have emerged from Radley's room long enough to spot me.

"You're the one who handed out those bullshit care packages," Radley says. "Admit it. I don't know how you did it, but you made them all sick."

I admit nothing. He has no proof. If he tested the contents of the gifts, he'd know the culprit was the electrolyte drink I bottled up specially for the team. I made a UU label for the bottle and everything. The drink contained a signature blend of herbs, including senna and a strain of bacteria cultured in my father's lab. It's like E. coli but faster.

The care package also contained extra salty snacks that would make them thirsty. I told them each item was carefully selected by their athletic advisor to provide the best possible nutrition need the night before the summer championship.

I lied.

"Oh no, that sounds terrible," I coo and make sympathetic noises, but he's not buying it, so I give up. "Did anyone die?" The dose wasn't deadly, but you never know when calculating these effects on different-sized guys.

A muscle clenches in his jaw. "Penn's in the hospital."

I might have put a little extra culture in Penn's bottle.

"Probably because he was already inebriated on Friday night. He really drinks too much. He should stop doing that or his liver will give out before he's thirty." Especially if he pisses me off anymore. And if he ever bothers Honey again, I won't hold back on the dosage. "You know, there are some herbs that might help him. I have some organic dandelion root—"

"Shut the fuck up." Radley's losing it. Red streaks his cheeks as he grinds his teeth. "You cost us the championship."

"Oh?" I twirl a lock of white-blonde hair around my finger. "Was that today?"

"Yesterday. No one from our team was well enough to play. I had to forfeit."

Poor Radley. He and Sailor were holed up in their room when I dropped the gift basket off. I had hoped he might miss it and be the only one on the field to accept defeat. I can imagine it now: the team captain up, bright and early, arriving on the green, waiting while one by one, his team texts him to say that they're too sick to show up, and Sailor coming to console him before he trudges to the opposing team captain to forfeit.

I told Honey that I don't get scared, I get angry. And when I get angry, I get even.

No one messes with my new best friend.

I smile at him, showing all my teeth. "Maybe you and your team should be nicer to people. For example, it's not nice to invite people to parties and then drug them. Karma is a real bitch."

"You're a bitch." Radley sets his shoulders and starts for me.

A giggle escapes me as I dart back out of reach. If he tries to grab me, I have several layers of defenses, but I'd rather not reveal them so soon.

Maybe I can lure him closer to the poison ivy and push him in.

YOLO!

"I'm going to fuck you up—"

"Touch her and die." The quiet order comes from nowhere, and I startle as Mr. Masked Man, aka Muscles, appears again on the side of the path. I was right, he moves quietly.

Radley stops short, stumbling over his feet. The way he blanches at the sight of the mask makes me think masked men aren't as common as I thought. He sizes the man up, which takes a while because the dude is oversized. "This doesn't concern you."

Muscles steps in front of me. "You will stay away from her."

Radley freezes. His eyes spit hate at me, but he doesn't move.

I stick out my tongue at him but pull it back in when Muscles turns to me. His voice is so deep and rumbly, it takes me a second to realize what he's asking.

"Do you want me to snap his neck?"

What?

His eyes are cold, serious. "Your choice. I can do it quickly."

My mouth falls open. Oh my goddess, is he talking about murdering someone? In the middle of the murder garden?

There's a tingle in my downstairs, and just like that, my panties are soaked. Again.

I'm panting a little, so it takes a second to collect myself.

"I can help clean up afterward. We just need a nice, clear plot," I say. "Like over there." I jerk my chin toward the grove of yew trees.

"You could," he says, like we're discussing our favorite brunch spots in Metropolis instead of where to hide a body.

"I could plant nightshade over it. Or lady slippers. They're endangered, and it's a crime to dig them up." I smile up at him, enjoying this moment of having a co-conspirator.

This whole time, we've been ignoring our potential victim, and Radley is turning redder by the minute. "Do you know who my father is?"

I roll my eyes. "Nope, and we don't care."

"Leave," Muscles orders.

Nostrils flaring, Radley gives me a look that says *this isn't over* and stomps away.

Aww, that was just getting fun. I wanted to see where it would lead.

Oh well. I grab my backpack from where I left it when I got here. Maybe Radley will be waiting for me when I exit the garden. Or maybe he'll wait until his friends are feeling better and get them to help him with their revenge on me. Either way, I'm looking forward to seeing what happens. I have a few more weapons up my sleeve.

But I am disappointed I won't get to see Muscles beat down a punk student. He's watching me closely again, and I let myself imagine crossing the space to him and pulling down the mask so I can stare at him as he's been staring at me.

After a moment, I shake off the fantasy because that's all it will ever be. But I've never felt so drawn to anyone in my life.

"Did you do it?" he asks. "Did you poison them?"

"Whoever did it must be a criminal mastermind. I wouldn't cross them." I flutter my lashes at him. The innocent act doesn't work on my father anymore, but I've noticed most men fall for it.

He doesn't fall for it. He looks even more suspicious of me. "You're trouble."

"I know. Isn't it great?"

Across campus, the chapel bells start ringing. It's noon. I've got to go.

I head out, tossing over my shoulder, "See ya never."

KAISER

THE MANIC PIXIE nightmare flips her hair in my direction as she flounces away. I shouldn't have let her see me. Even though I'm wearing a mask, I had no reason to show myself to her. I don't know why I did, other than I couldn't stop myself.

I thought getting close to her would help me understand her, but I only have more questions.

Is she not afraid of me? She's into me, I can tell, but then she tried to ignore me.

She's unhinged. And has some sort of immunity to poison ivy. *Now I'm poisonous, too.*

Her baby doll face probably fools a lot of guys into thinking she's sweet and innocent. Up close, it was too easy to get distracted by her perfectly plump lips. She has a way of pushing them out into a pout that makes me think of how she'd look sucking on my dick. All the blood has rushed to my groin. My jeans are so tight right now, it's painful.

What is going on with this chick? She definitely poisoned the lacrosse team. I knew she was up to something with that big basket and her little cheerleader outfit.

Now I know what.

It still doesn't make sense, but what about her does make sense? She's constantly doing the unexpected.

That's what makes her so fascinating.

I walk to the gate so I can make sure she gets across campus unscathed. Less than two weeks on campus and she's already made enemies.

I won't allow anyone to touch her. That right is mine.

I remember when Jaeger claimed his woman. How protective he was. No one was allowed to fuck with her, not even me.

I feel that way about Bella. The difference is, Jaeger is redeemable. I'm not.

There's too much blood on my hands.

I don't want to claim her, and I hate that I'm so into her. It makes no sense.

I tried to stay away, but I couldn't. I revealed myself to her, even though I knew I shouldn't. It will make my job harder. I didn't break my vow to Fraternitas, though, but I bent it.

I couldn't help it. My skin itches all over when I'm watching her, and it's making me insane.

I'm dying to get my hands on her. Touch her all over and see if I can feel anything more than numbness. I don't know why I'm so into her, but if I spend some time alone with her, I might be able to figure it out.

I pull off my mask, the rich scent of flowers almost overpowering. I'm smelling roses again, even though I don't see any around. I don't deserve to breathe such sweet air, but I gulp it down greedily.

I call St. James, who answers right away. "Any updates?"

"There are some new developments," I say. "She's getting into trouble. We need to move up the timeline."

"The Vesuvios?"

"No. Someone else." I tell him about Bella's run-in with the lacrosse captain and how I stepped in to help. "I stepped in to help her," I confess. "So now she's seen me." St. James doesn't seem too concerned about this, but guilt burns through me. Guilt and satisfaction that she was curious about me. She drank in the sight of me like I was a tall glass of water on a hot day. She tried to ignore me, but I could tell she felt the magnetic pull between us.

She wasn't afraid, either. Most people in the same situation would be freaked out, but she wasn't. She was annoyed, intrigued, and fascinated but not afraid. I don't know why, and I want to know.

I shouldn't want to know, but she's driving me fucking crazy!

"Did she poison the lacrosse team?" St. James asks.

"Yes," I say. I don't know how she did it, but I can guess the basket of treats had something to do with it.

"Is it possible her father was behind this?"

"He's the Poisoner, isn't he?" Bella's father, Benjiro Bosco, is the premier source of all poisons, both here in Metropolis and in New Rome. If you want to poison your enemies, he's your first call. "He might have helped, but she did most of the dirty work."

"The poisoned apple didn't fall from the tree." St. James sounds amused.

"We need to lock this down soon," I say. "She's already pissed off the lacrosse team. They're nobodies, but soon the mafia families will be on campus."

"Including the Vesuvios, and they're out for blood. I see the problem. They'll use the daughter to get to the Poisoner. Whoever controls the Poisoner, controls the game."

I keep silent. St. James knows the game better than anyone. He's played it successfully since he was barely older than a child.

"Is the Poisoner cooperating?" I ask.

"He will when I tell him we've kept his precious daughter alive. We're the only reason she's not already in the Vesuvio's clutches. Have they made any more moves to grab her?"

"Just that scout. I'll make sure no one gets close to her. The Vesuvios won't touch a hair on her head." My heart beats faster while I make that vow. I try to hide it, but my passion bleeds out through my voice.

St. James falls silent. He's noticed my obsession with her. He notices everything. "You've been remarkably diligent about this job, Kaiser. Damien and I appreciate it."

"You promised me a reward."

"I did, and you will have it. Anything you want, it's yours."

I watch Belladonna Bosco skip away from me, oblivious to the dangers around her. The palm of my right hand tingles, and I flex my fingers, imagining grabbing her ponytail.

"Her," I say. "I want her."

**6**

———

B<sup>ella</sup>

I KNEW I was being followed!

And now I know who it is. It wasn't a coincidence that I met Mr. Masked Man/ Muscles/Blondie in the poison garden on Monday. I'll bet anything it's him.

Who is he? What does he want?

If he's stalking me, why did he let me see him?

If he means me harm, why did he step in to protect me from Radley?

Maybe he wants to kill me himself. Maybe he's a Vesuvio... although I didn't see any pentacle tattoos on him. Maybe Dominus hired out? Hired a hit man to come after me?

That would be interesting. Oh, I have ways to defend myself. If he lays hands on me, he will regret it. But it's fun to fantasize about him actually overpowering me. Stripping away my armor and smashing through my careful defenses.

The fear excites me. Makes me hot.

I've never had such a sexy guy out to murder me. How would he do it? A knife? A gun? Or would he put his large hands around my neck and squeeze?

The threat of danger amplifies my arousal. The fear twists with lust, transforming it into something wicked and delicious. Something beautiful and deadly. Toxic.

My favorite!

As soon as I climb into bed at night, I slip my hand into my panties and find myself already slippery and wet. I don't even need to crack my favorite Viking romance novel —the one with a muscular, long-haired, blond guy on the cover.

There's a creak outside my window. I freeze before realizing it has to be the wind shaking the oak tree and making the branches scrape against the glass pane. There's no one there, of course. No reason for goosebumps to spread over me, imagining someone watching me.

Imagining him watching me. Stripping me bare with his gaze. I run a hand down my chest, between my breasts, and to my belly. I'm quivering, thinking of him.

I touch myself for a while, just picturing him. I didn't see his whole face, but what I did see captivated me. The dark ocean of his eyes, the blue broken by a white starburst around his pupils. His long hair, dirty blond with a little curl to it. The tip of one ear peeked out, and it was misshapen like it had been turned inside out. His tattoos were faded but beautifully sinister. One of them, a spiderweb, covered the back of his right hand.

I imagine that hand around my neck, trapping me, holding me down so I can't breathe...

And I come so hard, my head rings, and my ears echo with the sound of my moans.

What the fuck was that? I usually need a lot more stimulation to get off, but this time I didn't even take the time to grab my vibrator.

I lay with limbs splayed, unable to move. The wind rustles the leaves outside my window, and I feel it again—the sensation of being watched.

I'm alone in the big house. I like being alone, but lately, I've wondered if it's safe. Every creak of the hardwood floors makes me nervous.

I fall asleep, imagining the masked man standing over my bed, keeping guard.

$\sim$

FRIDAY MORNING, I head out early. I've dressed in a pink plaid skirt and a short white top that shows a strip of skin above my belly button. I even put my hair back into twin pigtail braids.

I look like prey. A cute, innocent schoolgirl, all alone.

I sense my stalker's presence as soon as I hit the end of the block and pull out my phone to use as a mirror, pretending to check my hair. I don't see a hair on Blondie's head.

But then—there, in the forest. Are those shadows dappling the truck of an oak tree or a man in a skull mask?

I whirl around but... no one's there. No man, masked or otherwise. The leaves of a nearby beech tree tremble, but that could just be the wind.

Or it could be him.

Either way, he's good. I like this game!

"Come out, come out, wherever you are." I blow a big

bubble of watermelon-flavored gum and let it pop in my face before licking it off my lips, using plenty of tongue. I'm trying to be sexy to lure him out, but I'm not sure if I'm nailing it.

I shrug and continue on. Today I'm going to eat breakfast at the infamous Three Diner instead of one of the Principessa bakeries.

Three Diner is close to campus, in a run-down area of Metropolis that's escaped gentrification. The shiny silver exterior hasn't changed in fifty years.

The place is packed when I walk in. A tattooed waitress in a pink uniform greets me with a grunt. "Only seats available are at the bar."

"Can I wait for a booth?"

"No."

I must take too long to decide because she turns her back on me. Rude waitstaff is another perk of the diner.

The door jingles behind me, and in walks a group of guys I recognize from orientation day with Honey. Lacrosse players. They look like they've recovered from their bout with food poisoning, but their energy is less cocky, more subdued.

They've suffered an L and everyone knows it.

One of them sees me, and recognition flares in his eyes. He nudges his buddies. One by one, they fall silent and turn to glare at me. They know I cost them the championship. Radley must have clued them in.

I smack my gum and give them a happy little wave. Their faces flush. Oooh, they're mad. Are they gonna do anything about it? Most guys are taught to never hit a girl. *Supervillain Rule #2: It's easy to beat an opponent who plays by the rules.*

If they do attack, it might be fun. Maybe I can turn it into a food fight, like on season three of *Vampire Varsity*. I've never been in one before. The waitress won't like it, but maybe she'll join in. Except she looks more the type to pull out a switchblade and start stabbing.

YOLO!

Before anything interesting happens, a shadow falls over me, and a hand clutches the back of my neck. It's large and warm and grips me firmly enough that I won't be able to quickly shake it off.

I go very still.

"She's with me," a deep voice rumbles above my head.

Goosebumps spread all over my body, like I'm outside facing an oncoming storm, and my heart trips.

I don't need to look up to know who it is. I can imagine that spiderweb tattoo on the back of my neck, and suddenly, my heartbeat is booming in my ears.

The lacrosse guys look up at him and blanch.

"There's a two-hour wait," the waitress rasps at them. "Come back later."

There are some muttered complaints, but they leave, slamming the door behind them. I feel disappointed. I was looking forward to Mr. Muscles beating them into a pulp.

"Hello again." I look up at my protector. And freeze.

He's not wearing a mask.

*Pretty,* I want to gasp. He's got a classically symmetrical face that's almost brutally good-looking. High forehead with that faint scar, blond brows, golden stubble covering his perfect jaw and chin. He's so pretty I can barely look at him!

*No, not pretty,* my instincts say. *Dangerous.* There's something predatory about those beautiful blue eyes. He's a hottie with a dangerous aura, and that only makes my heart flutter faster. My cheeks are warm, just being close to him.

I can't believe he's here, looming larger than life. He

takes up more than his fair share of space in the tight diner. And he's so tall he probably had to duck through the door.

I don't know how such a big guy snuck up on me, but he saved the day, again.

He's still touching me.

He's got me literally in his clutches. My body is primed after several nights fantasizing about him, so more than anything, I'm turned on.

What's going to happen now?

"What are you doing?" I ask.

He doesn't answer. He keeps his hand clamped on the back of my neck and guides me to a big booth in the far corner, by the window.

"Where are we going?"

"You're eating with me in case those guys come back."

Awww, he's still protecting me. "Why do you care?"

"Maybe I'm a nice guy."

I snort. "No, you're not." But, okay, I'll play. I wanted to sit in a booth, and he's apparently got the biggest one in the place, all to himself.

So I let him maneuver me but take the opportunity to sniff him. He smells nice. Like... meat. Barbecue. Smoke. Steak. Bacon. It's a comforting smell. We should bottle it and sell it. Papa's a perfumer by trade—at least, that's his official business. He mostly deals with botanical essences, but if he could distill this guy's scent, we'd make a mint.

Blondie settles me into the large circular booth and slides in after me, making me scoot deeper into the seat. There's plenty of space, but I kind of like how he's crowding me. Gives me tummy flutters. I wriggle my hips and press my thighs together to stuff down my excitement.

"How'd you score this booth if you're sitting all by yourself?"

"Dolores likes me."

The waitress strides by, slapping a menu down in front of me, and takes off without looking at us. I eye her retreating back. "Really?"

"No."

I go to grab the menu, and he slips it out of reach before I can get it.

"Hey, that's mine." I glare at him, but he's too busy reading the menu. "I want pancakes."

"No. You eat too much sugar."

WTF? How the heck does he know that?

Did he just admit to following me? I knew someone was tailing me on my tour of all the Panetteria Principessa locations.

"Okay, Dad," I mutter.

He lowers the menu long enough to shake his head at me. I wonder if he'd prefer I call him *Daddy*. I file that idea away for later.

"I'm hungry," I whine.

He raises his hand and catches Dolores's eye, and holds up two fingers, then five, then five again. She nods, disappears into the kitchen, and returns mere minutes later to lay out seven plates of food in front of us.

"Wow. She does like you." The tables around us are still waiting for their coffee.

He pushes a plate of bacon my way. "Eat up. You need protein."

I dig in. He's right, I probably should eat more than sugar-coated carbs for breakfast. I stuff my face and take the opportunity to study the man beside me. He's slow and methodical but somehow inhales an entire plateful within two minutes.

He's got his hair down around his shoulders, and I

realize why he looks familiar. He looks exactly like the guy on the cover of my favorite romance novel.

"Are you a professor?" I ask with my mouth full of bacon.

He pauses in the act of cutting his second steak. "Do I look like a fucking professor?"

I grin at him. Unitas professors seem to always be wearing scholarly robes. I don't know if it's required or they're just pretentious. Either way, I can't picture Blondie here behind a lectern, wielding chalk. I can picture him in a ring, throwing a chair at his opponent before putting them in a headlock. "Maybe you teach wrestling."

He gives me a look that says, *Try again.*

"MMA fighting?" I suggest. Mixed martial arts training would explain why he moves so gracefully.

He shrugs and keeps inhaling his steak and eggs. My guess must have been close.

Not much of a talker, this one. And I need to figure him out. My life might depend on it.

He threatened Radley easily, like it was no big deal, so I know those muscles aren't for show.

There's a faint scar on his forehead, disappearing into his hairline. He's dressed plainly in a white T-shirt, boots, and jeans. His tattoos look cool but don't give me any clues. He's not wearing any jewelry except a giant silver skull ring on his right hand. The design on the ring looks familiar, but I can't place it. Maybe he's in a biker gang?

Why would he be on campus? No one's allowed unless they're a student, professor, or a guest. He could be some-one's bodyguard, scoping out the place before the fall semester starts.

Then I have a thought, and my heart sinks. "Did my father hire you to follow me?" He's tried this before, hiring bodyguards. He worries about keeping me safe because of his line of work.

Normally, I wouldn't be fussed. I've had bodyguards before. When I'm sick of them, I just give them the slip. But the thought of this guy being hired to spend time with me takes all the fun out of things.

"No."

*Hmmm.* "So you're stalking me?"

He eats three sausages before answering my question with a question.

"Why do you say that?"

"I think you've been following me. Did one of Papa's enemies hire you?" *Like Dominus Vesuvio?* I don't want to drop the name, in case I need to play dumb about mafia stuff later on.

His right brow twitches. The movement is tiny, but I'm studying his face like I'm going to be quizzed on it later, so I notice. "What do you know about his enemies?"

"I know he has them." I'm not getting Vesuvio vibes from him, which might mean he's been assigned to protect me. "That's why he didn't let me go to high school. Things got hot, and I kept ditching my bodyguards, so he kept me home and made me do classes online. If you are my new body-guard, I want you to know, I'll behave." I don't want to jeop-ardize my newfound freedom.

"Are you capable of that?"

"Behaving?" I hold out my hand and tilt it back and forth. "Eh..."

The corner of his mouth quirks upward. He appreciates my honesty and rewards it. "I'm not your bodyguard."

"And yet you kept me safe. In the garden and now here." I'm about to ask why—not that he'd answer because this conversation is like interrogating a rock—when Dolores slams a plate in front of me.

"Short stack." She refills Blondie's mug with coffee, grabs three of his empty plates, and disappears.

I look up from the whipped cream-covered goodness with shining eyes. "You got me pancakes?"

"You ate your meat."

I sneak my fork across the table and stab a sausage off his plate. "Now I'm eating your meat."

A flicker of heat in his eyes. "Don't choke."

My entire body flushes. The air between us electrifies, and the hair on my bare arms rises. He's mere inches away. A couple of scoots and I could be right next to him. Or sitting on his lap. The thought makes my inner thigh muscles quiver.

What would he do if I leaned in and felt up the solid biceps in his arm?

Would he catch my hand before I could even touch him? Or would he let me?

I rate my chances of actually touching him at seven percent, with a one percent chance of him hauling me across his lap to punish me for the attempt.

I rock my hips on the seat, trying to scoot closer without him noticing. It doesn't work. He immediately clocks it with a flick of blue eyes, both daring me to do something and warning me away.

Hmm. There's now a seventy-eight percent chance he'll reject me, and I'm not ready for this conversation to be over. "Can I ask you a personal question?" He doesn't answer.

"Please," I whine.

He reaches out and swipes a bit of whipped cream off my lip. He holds my eyes as he licks it off.

All the oxygen in the room disappears. I can only blink at him, my body aquiver.

He barely touched me. And now there is an ocean between my legs.

"Ask."

"What happened to your ear?" I nod to his left ear. He tucks his hair back behind his right ear, and I see the right ear has the same rippled deformity.

"Cauliflower ear. Too much fighting without head protection." So he is a fighter. Good to know.

I open my mouth to ask another question, but my alarm goes off. I silence it and frown. "I'm supposed to meet my friend at the library." The reluctance is clear in my voice.

He dips his chin.

I sigh and reach into my backpack for my wallet. "Can I—"

His glare freezes me. You'd think I was reaching for a weapon.

"Okay, thank you for breakfast. And answering at least some of my questions." I scrunch my eyes at him. *I'm watching you, buster.*

He's not phased in the least. "Goodbye, Belladonna."

I'm halfway to the university before I realize I never told him my name.

7

———

# B *ella*

"So that's the story of my stalker," I tell Honey later. We're in our favorite corner of the cavernous university library, whispering. The library attendants are all wearing dark robes with a bright yellow stripe that makes them look like bumble bees. Every so often, one buzzes by and tells us to hush.

We're ignoring them so I can tell Honey all about my brunch date.

She's chewing her lip, looking distressed on my behalf. "What if he's dangerous?"

"Oh, he's definitely dangerous. But I can handle it." I have a few tricks up my sleeve. Literally, I'm carrying a vial of a botanical blend made from the extract of hemlock. It's less bitter, so it can be slipped into a cup of coffee. I could've poisoned Blondie at any point in our conversation.

But I haven't explained to Honey the extent of my *venefica* studies yet, so I just say, "So far he hasn't hurt me. The opposite, in fact. I thought he was hired to be my bodyguard, but he denied it." He already knows that I'm trouble. I haven't tried very hard to hide my supervillain tendencies for some reason. I wanted him to see it. To know me.

Usually, I do my evil deeds in secret, hiding them from everyone, including my father. But that moment in the poison garden, I wanted him to know. We were co-conspirators, and it felt wonderful. "Maybe it's not smart, but I want to see him again. Maybe he'll try to hurt me, but maybe not. Yolo!"

"Yolo?" Honey looks amused.

"Yeah. It means 'You only live once'."

"I know that. It's just... people don't really say that anymore."

"What do they say then?"

"Ummm, DIFTP. Do it for the plot."

I repeat what she said, but it doesn't roll off the tongue as well as YOLO. "The plot?"

"Like, in a book."

"Like a romance novel?" I love romance novels. I'm about to tell her about Thorbjorn, the muscular blond hero on the cover of *Viking Thunder*, when she asks, "What did his tattoos look like? Did he have any skulls on his hands?"

"Nope. But he did have a skull ring."

"Oh! He's Fraternitas." She looks a bit more relieved, but then her forehead crinkles, like she's puzzled.

"What's Fraternitas?" I ask. The word sounds familiar, but I can't place it.

"They rule New Rome. Unofficially."

"I'm from New Rome," I perk up. "I wonder if my father

does business with them." That would explain where I've heard of them.

"Um, they're not exactly legit." She still doesn't know my father's perfumery business is a front and that he does business with the criminal underworld all the time. "I actually —" She falls silent when someone approaches the polished wooden table and sits down across from us.

"Hey." The newcomer pulls her earbuds out of her ears. Her skin tone is a few shades paler than Honey's, and she's dressed severely, in a black skirt and sweater. Under the sweater, her white shirt is buttoned to the collar. Prim as a librarian, except she's our age and wearing smoky eye makeup that complements her long, glossy black hair.

Honey lights up. "Hey, Raine. Are you working a shift?"

"Just got off."

"I've been wanting to introduce you to my friend. Bella, this is Raine. She's studying library sciences here."

We exchange hellos.

"Bella's not staying on campus either," Honey says.

I nod to Raine. "My father doesn't think I can be trusted in the dorms."

"My stepbrother said the same thing," Raine rolls her eyes. "He just loves having me under his thumb."

"Maybe we can convince him to let you do a sleepover sometime," Honey says to her. "I could use the company."

"Or I just do it without asking permission. Anything to piss him off."

"You're invited too, Bella." Honey grabs her notes and starts stacking them. "We can do it before the semester starts."

A sleepover? I haven't done that since elementary school, and I've been longing to have one with grown-up friends. It'll be just like season six of *Vampire Varsity*, when they do a seance and summon the King of Hell the night before prom! "I'm in!"

Raine's phone starts ringing to the tune of *Funeral March*. She fumbles to silence it, baring her teeth in annoyance. "Got to go. My stepbrother's wondering where I am."

"Me too," Honey says. "I have a meeting with my advisor."

With a quick goodbye, Raine takes off. Honey and I pack up and follow. I didn't get a chance to ask Raine about her stepbrother or tell them both about my supervillain studies. I guess I can do it at the sleepover.

But before we part ways, Honey pulls me into an alcove under a brilliant stained glass window. Her face is bathed in blue as she looks around to make sure we're alone, then whispers, "Listen. I know Fraternitas. Before coming here, I worked at one of the clubs they owned. They even... well, let's just say I know a lot about them." She bites her lip. She's obviously not telling me everything, but this isn't the place and the time to grill her.

"Why would one of them be following me?"

"I don't know. I'll try to get more information for you. In the meantime, be careful. Your stalker got that ring because he killed someone." She pauses, waiting for her statement to land.

I nod, trying to suppress a smile. The fact that Blondie is a murderer only makes him more intriguing. I bet I know how he killed, too. I bet he put that spiderweb around his victim's throat and squeezed.

Honey looks worried again, so I pretend to take her warning seriously. "Got it."

"They have a code they follow. I've never heard of them harming an innocent. But they don't rule the city because they're nice guys. They're ruthless when they destroy their enemies. If one is stalking you, you might be in serious trouble. And if your stalker is who I think he is, you don't want to mess with him."

I'M STILL PONDERING Honey's words as I walk home.

I know my stalker is dangerous. My father is always worried his line of work will bleed into our personal lives. My mother died because of it. After that, Papa tried to shut me away from the world. He always wants to play it safe, but where's the fun in that?

I'm more fascinated by what Blondie might think of me than what he might do to me. I could call up my dad and ask him about Fraternitas, but I don't want him to freak out and pull me from school. I'll find another way to learn more about him. Contain the threat. Or tempt him to do something to me.

YOLO!

I like having a stalker. Especially one so pretty. I walk across campus, feeling a prickle on the back of my neck that tells me someone's watching. It gives me a little thrill.

Pane P's is closed, so I swing through a corner store and grab some donuts for dinner. I've got a long, lonely night of rewatching *Vampire Varsity* and reliving every moment of my brunch with Blondie.

But then I see my dad's Rolls is in the driveway and perk up. He's home, and that means some company until bedtime. He'll grill me about what I've been up to, and we'll have Thai or Chinese takeout for dinner.

My me time of fantasies of Blondie will have to wait. I skip up the driveway, never once guessing who lies in wait.

. . .

*Kaiser*

I stand in Bella's home with St. James and Damien, the leader of the Fraternitas. We're all in masks, mostly to protect Damien's identity. Outside the brotherhood, he's known only as The Devil.

We're in the Poisoner's office. Damien sits behind his desk, and Benjiro Bosco, the Poisoner himself, stands before him, like a supplicant.

"Once I sign this," he motions to the papers on the desk, "it's done? You will protect my daughter?"

"We will protect both of you," St. James says.

"You will keep her safe?"

"You have my word," I say. "She will belong to me. And no one touches what's mine."

The Poisoner's shoulders slump. He knows he's beaten. We've given him a good deal, and he knows it. I sense he's actually relieved. He can't defend his daughter against the Vesuvios, and he knows it.

St. James goes over the contract, and the Poisoner signs it. He has no choice.

I add my name. Just my first name because my last name is long forgotten. Damien and St. James sign as witnesses and add a wax seal.

I can't stop the feeling of triumph from spreading through me. Belladonna Bosco is officially mine.

"I need to tell her," the Poisoner says.

"She's on her way now."

I pick up the contract. Written proof that I now possess her.

She won't like it. She'll fight me, but the contract is signed. It's too late.

8

K *aiser*

WHEN BELLA WALKS IN, she stops short at the sight of her father surrounded by men in masks.

"Papa? What's going on?"

I'm in the back, keeping still to blend in with the shadows. From here, I can see every microexpression that flits over her face.

Her skin pales, but she doesn't scream. She takes in the sight of us in our masks with remarkable calm. First, she squints at St. James, then sweeps her gaze to Damien, who's sitting behind the desk.

The tingles in my palm spread up my arm. My fingers flex convulsively.

"We had some business to discuss with your father," Damien rasps. "And now you."

She blinks. "Me?" With her slight build and pale white-blonde hair, she looks innocent as a girl.

Looks are deceiving. She belongs in a devil mask of her own.

"It's okay, Bella," her father says, but he sounds like he's just been sentenced to death. Bella flinches.

"You're lying." Her shoulders hunch and her breath comes faster. She's recognized the stakes.

If I don't do something, she's going to act rashly, and I have no idea what she'll do. She's wild, unpredictable. I'm not worried about her hurting us, but if she tries something, I'll have to stop her, and I don't want to hurt her. Or for her to hurt herself, fighting me.

Two strides and I'm standing over her. I'm over a foot taller, so her head tilts back.

"Calm down." My voice is muffled in the mask. I lean down so she can look me in the eye.

It only takes her a second. "You," she gasps.

"Me." I can't hide the satisfaction in my voice. My hand aches, wanting to touch her, to claim her, but I make myself wait.

Her posture relaxes. "What are you doing here?" she demands. A bit breathless but more annoyed than frightened. She reaches out slowly, and her hand hovers in the space between us, pausing as if she's waiting for me to stop her.

Normally, I would. I don't let anyone touch me. But I don't stop her. I let her fingers brush my face and draw the mask down.

A sweet honey scent fills the air. Little Miss Psycho isn't afraid. She's aroused.

Or maybe both. Little shivers run over her body.

I want to scoop her up and carry her away. Out of this

office and away from her father and my brothers' prying eyes. I don't want Damien or St. James seeing her reaction to me. But they already have. St. James, in particular, sees everything and will turn a person's weakness against them. That's how we turned Fraternitas from a gang of street kids into a secret society that rules an entire city's underworld.

I don't want them looking at her. She's mine. The more I think about it, the more I like the idea. The thought of owning her has become so satisfying. She's the only one in the world who's ever gotten under my skin. When I saw the chance to own her, I took it. St. James came up with this whole arranged marriage contract. I should hate it, but I like the idea of owning someone fully.

She'll hate it, and I like that even more.

"I'm here to sign this." I show her the contract. "A marriage contract between me and you."

She looks dazed. She shakes her head a little, confused.

Her whole world is crumbling. Once she finds her footing, she'll fight me, and I can't wait.

I've already won.

I can't keep the triumph out of my voice when I explain, "The deal is done. You're going to be my wife."

She reacts immediately, jerking back. Instinctively, I grab her. I set a hand on the juncture between her neck and shoulder and grip her trapezius. The upper trap muscles hold tension.

I love the way she relaxes, responding to my touch. I squeeze the tight muscle, and she sighs, her mouth going lax.

Her skin is perfect. It looks so soft, I wish I could feel it, but even though they've been tingling lately, my fingers are still too calloused, too numb. Usually, I hate touching bare skin with my dead man's fingers, but with her? I can't get enough.

My cock is trying to beat a path out of my jeans. She's practically purring as I hold her by the scruff of her neck. My perfect little kitten.

I want to pet her all over.

She's not afraid of me, either, not really. Most women can sense the danger lurking inside me. Even the ones who are drawn to my good looks end up fearing me.

But Bella is different. She might be able to survive me.

A better man would feel sorry for what I'm going to inflict on her, but I feel only excitement.

I'm not capable of love. I lost that ability long ago.

But controlling someone completely? Now that I crave. I never thought I'd want a woman like this, but I want Belladonna Bosco. If only to punish her for making me feel things.

And now I'll have her. She'll be my bride and under my control. She won't be allowed to touch herself anymore, unless I give the command.

Last night while she slept, I broke into her bedroom and studied the dog-eared chapters of her favorite romance novel. I plan to buy my own copy and memorize the passages she reads the most.

We'll recreate each scene, one by one. She'll be my little toy to play with every night.

Her eyes will turn black as I stroke and tease her. She'll beg me, and I'll make her please me before I spread her legs and slam my dick home. I'll use her ponytails as hand grips. I'll make her drink my cum and spank her tight ass pink before licking the cum out of her.

And then I'll do it again.

And again.

She's watching me now, and I focus. I've spent so many nights fantasizing about her, but now my dreams are coming true. She raises a brow at me, silently questioning what I'm doing.

I massage her trap, loosening the muscle before I squeeze my fingers tighter. "Better?"

Her eyelids flutter, like she wants to surrender to me. But she fights it, her brow furrowing. I'm touching her in front of everyone, laying my claim, and she knows it. She wants to shake me off, but it feels too good, so she doesn't.

I'm starting to understand her. To know her intimately. With a little training, she'll be easy to control.

"I don't understand." She glances at her father, tensing a little again. She's just realized he's not stopping me from touching her. He's no longer her protector.

She looks back at me, and my chest swells. *That's right, little one. I'm the one who controls you now.*

"You're right, Bella. It's not okay, but it will be," her father says. He's a small man, petite like his daughter. She favors him, even though his skin is a shade darker than hers, and his hair is brown, while she's dyed her hair an unnatural blonde. "I know it's sudden, but this arrangement will benefit all of us."

"Yes, it will." Damien stands up. He fiddles with his cufflink, drawing everyone's attention to the glittering skull ring on his tattooed hand. Unlike my ring, the skull on his finger is wearing a crown. "It will profit us greatly, and it will keep you both alive. Come and sit, Miss Bosco."

Bella flinches when she hears her full name. She hunches a little, and I keep a firm grip on the back of her neck as I maneuver her in front of the desk. I have to leave her side to get a chair for her to sit in, but I return quickly.

She's scared and now wired with adrenaline. I want to soothe her but also let her know she can't escape.

She's a wild one, and my brothers are trusting me to keep her under my thumb. Literally, if necessary.

This whole situation is fucked. No one knows why, after a career of discretion, Benjiro Bosco threw caution to the wind and murdered one of the most powerful men in Metropolis. Benjiro covered his tracks, but St. James was suspicious and ordered an autopsy. The Poisoner is known for his proprietary blends, and the arsenic blend used to trigger a heart attack in Alfredo Vesuvio had never been used before. The regular autopsy didn't find it, but Atticus did.

We've partnered with the Poisoner before, but this reckless move left us stunned. St. James and Atticus dug deep into the history, and a pattern emerged. Over the past ten years, there have been several high-profile deaths that can be traced to the Poisoner. He's not as discreet as we thought.

The Vesuvios suspect him, but they don't have proof. When they find out, they'll do everything in their power to wipe him and the only person he cares about—his daughter —out.

I'm not going to let that happen. Today, we signed an official alliance with the Poisoner. The marriage will secure it. After I told St. James I wanted Belladonna for my own, he thought this up. It's perfect.

Except my future bride is on edge, her gaze flitting around the room like she's gearing up for an escape attempt.

I almost want her to run so that I can chase her.

I step between her and her father.

"You've been following me," she accuses.

"Yes. He has. We assigned Kaiser to keep an eye on you a few months ago," Damien says.

She blinks, as if she expected us to deny it.

"Kaiser?" she asks me. "That's your name?"

I nod.

"Last name?"

"Just Kaiser."

She frowns like she thinks I'm holding out on her. I'm not; Jaeger and I don't have a last name. Then she says, "Like a Kaiser roll."

The fuck?

"Kaiser roll." She does a little shimmy in her seat. Brat.

"Bella," her father warns.

"We've had our eye on your family for some time," Damien says. "We've had certain agreements with your father over the years. Now, he has broken them, and he owes us a debt."

"I stay out of my father's business," she says. "Are we in trouble?"

"Not if you do as you're told." St. James finally sees fit to speak. Bella startles, as if she's forgotten he was lurking there.

"Me?"

"We've updated the contract with your father, but it requires collateral."

"I've agreed to give Kaiser your hand in marriage," her father says.

Bella sits frozen. I rest a hand on the back of her neck. "Breathe." I can't have her passing out on me.

"Marriage," she repeats like she can't believe it. "But... I don't want to get married."

"It's necessary," I say. "For your protection. No one will lay a hand on you when you're my wife."

～

*BELLA*

*WIFE.*

My mind has gone completely blank. Someone is talking, but I can't hear them over the ringing in my ears.

I know it's common for the big mafia families to sell off their daughters and even sons in marriages to cement alliances, but I never thought it would happen to me.

"I don't want to marry anyone," I repeat. My brain is shorting out.

It doesn't help that every time I stare up at Kaiser's beautiful face, I lose my train of thought.

"I understand, Bella," my father says. "I know it's not what you wanted, but it's for the best. This will be good for everyone. Kaiser has assured me you can continue to go to school. You will both live here and..." He keeps talking, but I can't hear him.

This is nuts. Absolutely bananapants. I'm not going to think about what a marriage to my stalker will be like. I refuse!

I lean forward so I can stare at my father, trying to read between the lines.

Why the hell is he going along with this?

His gaze is intent on mine, his expression worried, almost pleading. I've never seen him like this. He rarely shows his emotions. He's usually so calm and in control, but now he seems resigned to our fate. Something about this situation has shaken him.

But we have so many ways to fight back! It would be better if I had my backpack; I carry a salve that looks like hand cream but can eat through metal. I came close to using it on Radley in the poison garden. But I'm not the only one armed; there are at least ten weapons within Papa's reach.

At any point, either of us can say a catchphrase that will rain a poison mist down on these guys. It wouldn't be pretty–Papa would have to run for an exit or shelter to keep from being badly burned, but he could do it.

I don't understand why he doesn't do it. It's a last-ditch effort, but...

I open my mouth and start the first half of the code sentence that will activate the system. "Shoshonna Bosco—"

"Belladonna. No," my father interrupts. His face flushes, like he's losing his temper. "Now is not the time." He's trying to communicate that this is important.

Maybe he has plans to use our defenses later?

"Invoking your mother's name will not change things," he says. Does he mean that he disabled the system?

Did he know this was coming? Why didn't he warn me?

I'm close to hyperventilating. Adrenaline dumps into my bloodstream, getting me ready to run.

Except I can't run. My new fiancé has his large, warm hand on the back of my neck, and he won't let me get away.

What did Honey say about Fraternitas? *They're ruthless when they destroy their enemies.*

And right now, Papa and I are their enemies. That's why he looks so worried. He knows they're formidable opponents, and they've found our weak spots. Papa will do anything to protect me. Same for me. Physically, we can't overpower these guys.

"The contract is complete," the man in the gray suit says. He takes the papers from Kaiser and spreads them out before me, showing the signature page. The wax seal. I hate how everyone's treating this like a business deal when it's my life.

I narrow my eyes at him. He's still standing in the light, so I can't see his face, and I know he did that on purpose. I can see that he's dressed like a CEO, too, ready for the boardroom. You could put him on stage at any shareholder meeting and no one would bat an eye.

But he's not the one behind the desk, the man in the devil's mask is. I get the sense that he's the leader, but I can't be sure. Ugh, I can't get a read on these guys, and I have to so I can fight them.

And then there's Kaiser, huge and touching me like he owns me.

I guess in the eyes of everyone here, he does.

"We will uphold our side of the bargain," Mr. Gray Suit says. "The marriage will bind us to you forever."

"And you to us," the man in the devil mask says.

I shake my head, silently refuting all of this. I need to focus on growing my supervillain skills so I can destroy the Vesuvios. I have things to do, people to kill.

This is a complication I don't need.

Kaiser's hand is still a heavy weight on my neck. I would shake him off, but it feels nice. An anchor in the storm that's currently wrecking my life.

Except... he is the storm.

"There will be protections in place for you," Papa says.

Against a fiancé who's over six feet tall and built like a tank? If he wanted to harm me, he could break me over his knee and not break a sweat. WTF, Dad?!

But I don't say that. I don't say anything. I'm still processing. I need to figure out how to get out of this.

Now Mr. Devil Mask is saying something about a new, stronger alliance.

*Blah blah blah.*

I can't believe this is happening. I refuse to believe this is happening. I have to figure out how to get me and my dad out of this.

Eventually, they wind things up. They're taking Papa back to New Rome while I'm to remain here with Kaiser.

"We'll talk again soon. When things settle down," Papa says. "It'll all be okay."

"Okay," I say, so this conversation will be over. Sending my father off with two masked men from Fraternitas seems like a bad idea, but I don't know how to stop it. My father seems resigned to his role of being a hostage and perfectly willing to sacrifice me, too.

What if Fraternitas doesn't let me see him again? Will he ever explain why he did this to me?

I watch him leave with his captors, still in a daze. I guess, if things go well, I'll see him again at the wedding.

What the hell just happened to my life?

"He'll be safe with them," Kaiser says. I must look worried, so I smooth my features out.

I can't believe I'm alone in my house with him. I can't even look at his big, dumb, gorgeous face right now. He's so hot. I don't want to be attracted to him, but my ovaries don't understand he's the enemy.

What am I going to do? I don't want to get married to the Un-Incredible Hulk.

I turn to him. "I don't care about that contract. We are not getting married."

**9**

———————

B *ella*

HE JUST GAZES AT ME. My stupid fiancé or whatever. He's not fazed at all.

"You will marry me. You don't have a choice."

"Is that what gets you hard?" I ask. "Forcing young women into marriage?"

"No. I don't want anyone else. I want you."

That gives me pause. "Because you want an alliance with my father. He's your prisoner."

"He's our ally. He will be treated with respect."

"But not me." I rub my arms, suddenly feeling like a prisoner in my own home. "They just left me here with you."

"You have nothing to fear from me," he says it so gently, I want to believe him.

But look at him. He's huge. Covered in tattoos. He's mafia muscle. I knew with one glance that he was dangerous. He's the sort of guy they send to shakedown the scary mofos, because he's the scariest one of all.

I wonder how many people he's killed?

"What if we do the ceremony, and then just live in different houses?"

"The marriage needs to be real."

I snort. "No, it doesn't. You're just making up random rules."

"We have a contract."

"Fine. We could just get married and then divorce."

"This marriage will be for life. Like the alliance. It ends with death—yours or mine."

Goosebumps break out over my skin. So it is a matter of life or death.

Preferably his.

"We're not consummating the marriage." But even as I say it, I lick my lips.

His gaze falls to my mouth.

"Oh, we'll be consummating it." His voice is rough, and my core clenches in response.

I've got to get out of here.

"I want some privacy. And some space. I can't think about this right now." I need to get away from him so I can make a plan.

"Stay in the house," he orders. Because apparently, he can order me around now.

"I'm going to the greenhouse. Is that acceptable, my liege?" I give him a mock curtsy.

His eyes heat. I'm being silly, but he's not playing a game.

"Yes, little bride," he says.

"I'm not your bride."

"Not yet. It's only a matter of time."

Nope, nope, nope. I rush to the door. I cannot deal.

"I'll know if you try to run, Belladonna," he calls after me. "Remember, I'm watching."

Full body shiver!

No, I will not be turned on! I don't like this anymore.

I escape to the greenhouse, my happy place. I turn on some opera music for the plants, pull on my favorite pair of gardening gloves, and putter around. Gardening usually makes everything better.

Except... it doesn't help right now. All I can think about is how I'm alone in this huge house... with him. Kaiser. A man I just met. A man I'm supposed to marry and remain married to until death do us part.

Fucking what?

He's been following me. For months! I thought I was so clever, confronting him in the poison garden and again in the diner. Now I feel uneasy. What does he already know about me? What has he seen?

Did he know this was coming?

He seems to be looking forward to the marriage. Fuck my life. That means I'll have to kill him.

But if I kill him, it probably won't be the end of it. Fraternitas has my father. Killing one of them won't do any good. They'd probably just assign someone else to marry me. And make me, or my father, pay a blood debt.

Maybe I can make it look like an accident.

That means not activating the poison gas in the sprinkler system. I need to figure out if my father disabled it, anyway.

The thought of my father makes my stomach hurt all over again. Why would Papa hand me over to a bunch of thugs? Do they have something over him?

I need answers.

My head is spinning. I turn off the Wagner because it's

too intense for me right now, so I stand in the silence and dig my hands in the soil, trying to focus on my chores. Usually, the greenhouse relaxes me, but all I can think about is Kaiser. How to kill him. How to outmaneuver him. How to control him.

"Breathe," he calls, and I almost drop the sapling I'm repotting.

He's snuck up on me. Of course, the bastard followed me. He moves too quietly. Like a panther. Sleek coiled muscle. Except he also looks like he's taken something to beef up those muscles. Nothing natural.

"Stop telling me what to do."

He looks me up and down. I'm still in the schoolgirl outfit. Does he think I'm cute? He's been handsy, and there's definitely a charge of attraction between us. But I seem to be more affected than him. He's older and more experienced, dammit.

I need a plan. But I can't think. I can only glower at my new fiancé.

"You're not welcome here."

He says nothing as he paces between the rows of plants, studying them. He has no idea what he's looking at.

In the shaded space under the racks, I've set up some woodchip beds for mushroom colonies. He takes particular interest in one bright orange cluster.

"Careful," I call. "Those are poisonous."

He backs away, and I roll my eyes. Am I really betrothed to a man who can't tell the difference between a false chanterelle and a real one?

I finish planting the manchineel sapling. "You're so beautiful," I croon to it. "You're doing so well. You're going to grow big and produce some lovely poison apples for me, yes, you are."

"Poison apples?" My intended is right behind me. I glare at him. I'm not ashamed to be caught talking to my plants, but I don't want him here, killing the vibe. If he insults my babies, I'll put poison ivy in his underwear.

Unfortunately, he's standing in a patch of sunlight, and his blond hair blazes like a crown. It's down around his shoulders, looking silky and a little curly from the humidity.

He looks like a work of art, dammit.

"This is the most poisonous tree in the world. Every part of it will kill you. If you try to kill it with fire, the smoke will destroy your eyes. Once it's grown, I'm going to see if I can use the fruit to make jam. For Winter Solstice." I give him a sappy smile. "Doesn't that sound nice?"

No reaction. He might as well be a statue. An obnoxiously well-sculpted statue.

Ugh. "Just assume everything in here will kill you," I tell him in a monotone voice. "It'll save time."

"Why would you even want to plant something so deadly?" He's moved closer to the sapling. I just told him it would kill him, and here he is, looking even more enthralled.

I understand the feeling.

I sidle sideways, keeping the tree between us. I study him through the spindly branches. "You're like everyone," I scoff. "You want the power these plants give you. You want to use them, but you don't respect them. You want control of the poison inside them, but deep down, you know you can never own them. At any point, they can be used against you. It drives you crazy." I brush my hand over the leaves, caressing them. Inviting him to do the same.

He doesn't make a move to touch the tree. Or me. He's too smart for that.

But I didn't really think that poisoning him would be that easy.

"You crave the danger. The high it gives you. And if you'd only take a moment and the trouble to appreciate the beauty in front of you…" I brush my lips over the leaves, then take a branch and lick the sap. My skin begins to burn, but it quickly fades to a pleasant tingle. "You could know the sweet taste of oblivion."

I lick the peppery afterburn off my lips. "Come and kiss me, lover." I flick my tongue at him. "It might hurt, but… it'll be worth it."

His eyes darken, a storm brewing over the ocean.

He's tempted to prove he's strong enough to master me. But he's still planning how to do it. He makes no move.

"What, are you scared? Too afraid to touch me?" I laugh in his face.

Still, he doesn't react. Most men his size would lose it if a woman taunted him like this. But he's still patiently waiting, watching, studying me. Interesting.

I turn away, determined to act indifferent even if my skin prickles under his stare. I grab a broom to clean up. "I'm not marrying you."

"You'll do as you're told."

"Why marriage?"

"It's how things are done. It's a clear sign of an alliance between Fraternitas and the Poisoner. Your father."

I flush a little under my clothes. He's only doing this out of obligation. I'm a pawn on the board, and he's the knight who's captured me. Nothing personal, it's all part of the game.

I guess a part of me hoped he wanted me. A sad, pathetic part that I need to cull, if I'm going to become as powerful as I want to be.

Kaiser doesn't want me for me. I'm a job he's been

assigned to complete. I should've nipped my crush in the bud.

"Everyone will look at our union and assume my father is under Fraternitas control. Why else would he give up his beloved heir?" I think out loud, proving that I understand the stakes. "And in a way, he is under your control. Because if he betrays you, you will hurt me. I'm a hostage." I'm not asking if this is true; I already know it.

"You understand. It's nothing personal."

"Okay, Curly."

He doesn't react to my nickname.

I can't get a rise out of him, and now I know why. He doesn't think of me as a real player.

I don't have to prune the hopeful part of me. My girlish crush is already withering on the vine.

"You really don't have a last name?"

"Nope."

"Everyone has a last name. What was your family called?"

"Fraternitas is my family."

Ugh, spare me from mafia men and their stupid gang loyalty.

I finish sweeping up and lean the broom against one of the racks. Outside the greenhouse, the sun is sinking. The day is getting dark, and the light slanting across the racks of plants is a rich gold.

I crouch down and pull out a rack of mushrooms, setting it on the floor between us.

"There's one thing you and your overgrown frat bros didn't think about."

"And what's that?"

I fuss over the mushrooms, waiting until he's moved closer. I'll teach him he's not welcome here.

His shadow slants over me, and I smile up at him. "I won't be so easy to control." I rise and stomp on the mushrooms, releasing a cloud of spores into the air.

KAISER

BROWN-GRAY DUST BLOOMS between me and Bella. I throw up a hand, shielding my face. My future wife just told me everything in here is poisonous, and even though she's not trustworthy, I'm not about to risk my life to test if she's telling the truth.

Sure enough, my throat muscles squeeze and I choke on air. I'm having some sort of reaction to the spores. My eyes feel gritty, and I squeeze them shut, backing up and turning away.

Only to spin back around when I hear the sound of the greenhouse door opening and banging shut.

My bride is running away.

I have two choices. Let her escape, or hunt her down and bring her to heel.

And I'll have to run through the mushroom cloud to do it.

No pain, no gain. I've beaten worse odds against opponents much bigger than the sexy little psycho in a schoolgirl skirt and cute blonde braids.

I charge forward, knocking into a rack of plants. I open my eyes long enough to catch the rack and set it carefully back in place. Don't want to destroy anything.

It's not the plant's fault that their gardener is both my dream girl and my nightmare.

The mushroom dust coats me. The past few weeks, I've been feeling things more and more, and the dust is uncomfortable enough to register. When I focus, I can feel the desperation to scrub it from my skin, but it's nothing I can't power through, and I have years of practice in powering through. I race to the door and out into the fresh air.

Outside, dusk has fallen, but there's enough light to showcase the vast acreage of the backyard in all its glory. Papa Bosco must have spent a fortune on this place. It's more of a park out here, the long green lawn bordered by forest. You'd think we were in the middle of nowhere, versus in a city.

I can hear Bella cackling in the distance. She's paused on the edge of the woods, unable to resist hovering to see if I'll chase her.

Her curiosity will be her downfall. I almost feel sorry for her that she's never faced a true opponent.

When I catch her, she'll learn.

I stride into the open field so she'll see me. The sunlight blazes on my hair. Even at a distance, I can tell her expression goes from glee to shock, and then to horror.

I break into a run, charging like a bull toward her.

She's frozen, staring at me long enough that I can see her eyes light with wild excitement.

Then she whirls and disappears into the trees.

*BELLA*

He's hot on my heels.

Getting closer.

I run, careening through the thick underbrush, and weave through poison ivy-covered pine trees. It would be a shame if Kaiser crashed into one.

I can't stop the laughter bubbling out of my throat. I sound crazy. Maybe I am.

But this is the most fun I've ever had.

The sight of him, racing across the field toward me, sent a thrill through my nethers.

Am I scared or horny? Or an awesome, fizzy combination of both? Sc-orny!

I'm one hundred percent sc-orny for him.

It's partially my fault. I primed the wrong neural pathways by picturing his face when I orgasmed.

I knew fantasizing about being murdered by him was a bad idea!

Now I hide behind an old oak, pressing into the poison ivy. My pulse pounds in my throat.

I hear a twig snap as he stomps after me. I wait, but he doesn't appear.

He's gone quiet.

Is he coming? Holding my breath, I peek out from my hiding place, feeling like the sacrificial blonde in a horror movie.

And there he is, staring back at me. "Boo."

"YOLO!" I scream with delight and sprint in the opposite direction, straight into a bramble patch, but I'm small enough to duck and wriggle through a foxhole.

Kaiser tries to follow and bellows when the thorns tear his skin.

I drop to my belly and crawl the rest of the way. The back of our land ends with an overgrown orchard. Beyond that, there's a long-forgotten graveyard bathed in evening light.

I've explored back here already. I looked up the history of the land, and apparently, it's University property. I need to tell Honey; her advisor has her doing a huge project about the history of Unitas.

If Kaiser doesn't kill me first.

My little obstacle course hasn't deterred him at all. And instead of losing his temper, he's even calmer and controlled. Makes me wonder what it would be like to let him catch me.

NO! BAD BELLA! Do not let him win!

He survived the gauntlet of the forest, and now he's pushing through a patch of hogweed.

Bad call. That stuff will cause second-degree burns if he's not careful.

I'll be sure to tell him... Once I'm safely out of reach.

## 10

Kaiser

WHEN I EMERGE from the woods, I look like I've gone three rounds with a blackberry bush... and lost. Because that's exactly what happened. I've got leaves in my hair, mushroom spores in my nostrils, and scratches all over my arms from the briars. I can't feel them, but I know the scratches are bright red.

Now I'm mad enough to charge through a patch of overgrown flowers. The Poisoner must be feeding them a crazy amount of compost because the stalks are as tall as me. I rip through them, no longer caring if I wreck a nice flower bed. These things have huge white flowers but look like weeds.

I've reached the final strip of lawn. It's broken up by a few neat rows of trees with fruit growing on some of them. Tiny green apples. Bright red cherries. Yellowing pears.

I stroll through a ditch of rotting peaches and face a worn stone wall enclosing a graveyard.

There's no sign of Bella, but I sense she's close. It's something in the air—the echo of her giggle, a whiff of her sugary scent.

I plant a hand on the wall and scale it easily.

Some people would be squeamish about trespassing on sacred ground. But I'm not. My soul was lost long ago.

I stalk between fallen gravestones and moss-covered statues, hunting my prey. She's quiet for once. I move silently, waiting to catch more of her scent. I thought she just smelled like roses, but I was wrong. Her scent is sweet like flowers and those sugared donuts she inhales by the dozen. But when I get closer, there's a tart edge, like lemon. It makes my mouth water.

I can't wait to strip her down, scrub her off, and taste her. She doesn't realize it, but that little chase through the garden of horrors only makes me want her more. Now I have an excuse to punish her. What's more, I think she can take it. She's stronger than she looks.

Most people are frightened by me. I get the sense that Bella's thrilled by the fear. Like a kid going to a horror movie or a haunted house and enjoying the jump scare. It's all a game to her, and she seems excited by it.

Works for me. I've never met a woman who can handle my intensity. The women at Camille's avoid me. They prefer Jaeger. That's why, when I hire one, I only use them for one night, and never again. One and done, no repeats. Camille finds me a woman who can handle the rough stuff and gives them strict orders never to speak to me again. Of course, after I use them, none of the women want to. Which is fine, I never wanted more.

But with Bella, I want more. So it's a good thing that she

doesn't seem to be repelled by the predator in me, that she seems fascinated by it.

"Yoohoo," she calls from somewhere over my head. I look first to the towering oak, but she hasn't climbed up there. She's up on the roof of a big crypt, perched on the edge beside a stone statue shaped like a little dragon. The forest did a number on her, too. There are smudges of dirt on her face, green stains on her pink plaid outfit, and her hair is a mess, falling out of its neat braids.

I get a pulse of heat in my gut, seeing her ruined a little. It's not as destroyed as she will be tonight, when I have her subdued at my feet.

"You're going to pay for this."

She kicks her feet, unbothered by my threat. "You have to catch me first."

I growl and start forward, only to realize I'm dragging a piece of greenery. It's one of those giant stalks topped with a lacy white flower, stuck to my jeans. I rip it off and toss it away.

She tilts her head. "I hate to tell you this, but that's giant hogweed. It's phototoxic. I'd go wash that sap off if I were you. And avoid the sun tomorrow. For like two days."

Shit. I swipe at my arm where the stalk smeared its goo on me. My palm is sticky with it, and my skin feels prickly. It feels worse than the mushroom dust, but the sensation might be in my head. Although my nerve endings seem to be coming back online these days, it'd be bad timing to have my pain receptors heal right when my future bride makes me run a gauntlet of poison plants.

Fucking poison plant jizz. I had no idea something green could be so toxic.

I circle the crypt slowly. I can climb it or just jump and

grab her leg. It's dangling low enough for me to reach. But I don't want to hurt her.

Physically, it would be so easy to overpower her. But I don't want to conquer her with brute force. I want to lure her in. She's unlike any other opponent I've ever had, and I'm giddy with the thought of mastering her. I'm even willing to lose a few rounds, as long as when the final bell rings, she's kneeling at my feet, gazing up at me like I'm her world.

I return to face her. She's been sitting quietly this whole time, braiding some of the green vines she's gathered into a crown.

She's up to something.

"You're not afraid of me," I say. There's a wild gleam in her eye. She's not cowed, and I like that. She's willing to stand up to me. I've faced grown men in the ring who were more afraid of me than she is.

This is a good sign. Maybe she'll be strong enough to withstand my intensity. I want her to last a long time as my toy. She's already held my interest longer than any previous fucks.

"You have blackberry stains on your shirt. And a flower in your hair. It makes it hard to take you seriously."

I reach up and she's right. I free the white blossom and throw it on the ground. I look back up just in time to see her throw the viney crown at me. I catch it, then channel my rage and rip it apart while holding eye contact with her.

She giggles. She looks even more deranged like this. Like a little doll someone took out of a glass case and played with too hard.

My dick swells. St. James promised me a reward, and I told him I wanted her. She's going to be my little doll, my little plaything. I'm going to take care of her, keep her safe.

And in return, I get to be the one who plays with her too hard.

Our marriage will just be another level of ownership over her. And she knows it. That's why she ran.

But... she's not running now. No, she's waiting for me to make my next move.

She's curious. A bored little kitten who's desperate for attention. I'll only have to dangle a bit of string in front of her, and she'll lunge for it.

I've read her file. I know her father pulled her out of school when she was only ten and has been homeschooled ever since. She's been sheltered, shut away far too long with only plants to talk to. No friends, which means... no boyfriends or girlfriends. No holding hands, no kisses. No third base.

I've never bothered with virgins before. She'll be my first. And I get to be the one to break her in.

First, I have to earn my reward. Keep her in line. Once I do that, she's all mine.

The sun's about to set. It's time.

"What's the matter, Curly? Are you giving up?"

"My name is Kaiser."

"What's that? Mo? Larry?"

I shake my head, and she grins.

I say nothing, letting the moment stretch. After a minute, her knee begins to jiggle.

"Why are you taking so long?" she whines. Bored little brat.

"I'm wondering how I will punish you."

"Punish me?" Her mouth falls open. She's not mad at the idea. She's panting.

"Mmmm." I keep my voice low. "Should I tie you up? Feed you your meals by hand?"

I pause, but she's silent, transfixed.

"There's a special massage oil my brothers swear by. It has something in it, something that makes it hurt. An herb. Cinnamon?"

"That's a spice. Cayenne?"

"That's it. I'll rub it on your ass and wait until it begins to burn. Then I'll tip you over my lap and spank you."

Her breath shudders out of her.

"Or maybe we'll work up to that. I don't want to take you too deep, too fast."

She looks disappointed.

"Or do I? I could put pure peppermint oil on your nipples and play with some ice. I could punish you for hours. Take breaks to tease you to the edge. I'd have to gag you."

She licks her lips slowly.

"Yeah, you'd like that, wouldn't you? That's the trouble. You'll like all this too much. And if you like it, then it's not punishment."

"You'll hurt me."

"You'll like it. That's right, baby girl. I know what you like. I've been watching for some time. Keeping you safe. Protecting you." I lower my voice, making it hypnotic. And it's working. "I'm doing you a favor. There are men after your father, bad men. They'd like nothing more than to catch you and do to you what he did to one of them. But I won't allow that. I'm not going to let anyone touch a hair on your pretty little head. You're going to be my wife. No one will mess with you ever again because I don't let anyone touch what's mine." I'll fuck anyone up who tries something. She will be safe from everyone. Everyone but me.

"Are you done?" She rolls her eyes and mutters something about monologuing. "Did you think it would be that easy? That I would be that gullible?"

"It's the smart move for you and your father. Fraternitas is a powerful ally."

"I can take care of myself."

"The Vesuvio family is dangerous. They're known for their brutality." I could tell her stories, but I'd rather spare her the details. "You'll never see them coming."

"I saw you coming."

"Not until I allowed it."

She wrinkles her nose, not liking that. "You made sure I saw you."

"Yes. Make no mistake, Belladonna. You belong to me. My bride. My wife. Legally. Illegally. Every way I can own you, you will be mine."

Her cheeks are blazing pink. Her scent is stronger than before. She's responding to me.

She wants me. She wants this. Us.

But after a second, her face hardens and she leans forward. "Fuck. That." I smile to myself. If this were easy, it wouldn't be half as fun.

"If you knew I was stalking you, why didn't you do something about it? I know you're capable of... retaliation."

She smirks, loving that I noticed her competence as a fighter.

"I wanted to know why you were following me. You were a threat. What would you do with a threat?"

"Watch it. Get close. Then eliminate it."

"Yes." She looks thrilled that I know the answer. "Keep your friends close and your enemies..."

"Good girl." I let the words vibrate from the back of my throat. Maximum growl.

She shivers all over. If her mouth hangs open much longer, she'll be drooling.

I have her right where I want her.

"Let's play a game, little bride to be. You run, I chase. If you get back to the house before dusk, you win."

Her eyebrow twitches. She's stifling an eager "yes." She cocks her head like a raven who's spied something shiny. "Why should I play?"

"Because if you win, you get a reward."

She narrows her eyes. She's wary but curious. I'm betting on her boredom here. "What reward?"

*Got you.* "You'll find out. Unless you lose."

She frowns. "I need a head start. Ten seconds."

"Five. Ten is enough to gather some of those weeds and poison me."

"I could do it in five," she huffs. "But fine. Close your eyes?"

I'm going to regret this. But no pain, no gain. I feel it, the energy crackling between us, the promise of what could be between us when all that fighting turns to chemistry. Right now, it's all push and pull. I want to know what she's going to try next.

And she wants a reward. She's spent too many nights alone, frigging her clit raw. She's ready for something more.

And after what she said about not consummating the marriage, I'm not waiting. Her initiation into what I want from her in the bedroom starts tonight.

"Better run, Bella." I turn my back and start counting down. "Five."

There's a scrambling sound as she slides down from the roof. I wince when I hear a few loose pieces of stone tumble to the ground. But she makes no sound, so maybe she's all right.

"Four." I pull out the gloves I stuffed into my back pocket. I found them lying beside some empty pots when she was setting up her little mushroom trap. I should've worn them before I tore out the hogweed. I won't make that mistake again.

"Three." The graveyard is quiet except for the crickets creaking. Insects make a lot of racket. The sound rises and falls in waves.

"Two." I open my eyes. She's not running to the house. She's still here in the graveyard. Hiding.

"One." I take a few heavy steps toward the wall, making sure to crunch the dried grass underfoot. Make her think I've left.

Then I loop around the back of the crypt.

There. In the green vines. She's still a statue. Quiet.

Does she think I'm stupid? Or does she want to be caught?

What else is she planning?

I hesitate. I could grab her, but... I'm not sure if she's set a trap.

I sidle up beside her. She's looking the other way. She doesn't hear me coming. She doesn't know I'm beside her. She looks so happy, thinking she's one-upped me. I take a moment to savor this moment of victory.

Then I clamp a gloved hand over her throat.

Her shriek is stifled by my flexing fingers. I've got her now. I hold her in place with one arm, letting her fate sink in.

"You should've run."

"Back to the house? That's where you want me. I wasn't going to fall for that." She licks her lips. There's still a sheen to her lips from the tree she made out with earlier. The one that grows poison apples.

She warned me about the hogweed sap. I bet the stuff on her lips is poisonous, too.

But shouldn't it be poisoning her?

"You're coming home with me, little bride." She's not my bride, not yet, but she will be. She doesn't like it, wants to deny it, so I'll keep reminding her.

With my hand around her neck, I draw her forward only to push her back against the stone. The movement is slow and gentle, but the manhandling shows her that she's at my mercy. "I'm going to teach you some manners." I place my thumb on her lips.

Her eyes widen when she realizes I'm wearing gloves. I can touch her any way I like as long as I don't let my skin touch hers. Not until I've washed the poisons off her.

"I won," I tell her. "Fair and square. That means I get the reward. But if you're good, I'll let you share it with me."

"What's the reward?"

"You'll see. You'll need to be a good girl for me." I shake her a little. "At least until morning."

She considers this. I could choke her out right here and now, but she somehow thinks she has options. The upper hand. She's delusional.

"One night," she agrees.

It's true what they say. Curiosity did kill the kitten. Tonight I'm going to devour her.

But first, I'm going to play with my food.

**11**

---

B*ella*

As Kaiser carries me back to the house, I have to consider if I've made a mistake. Maybe I am gullible.

But this is so much better than rereading *Viking Thunder* for the eleventy-hundreth time. Or binge-watching seasons one through three of *Vampire Varsity*.

I can poison him tomorrow. Right now, I want to know what he has planned for me. I want to know more about him. I didn't win this round, but I'll take the L in exchange for intel behind enemy lines. Lose the battle to win the war, right?

Or maybe I'm just telling myself that. The chase left me exhilarated. Excitement always makes me reckless. I ride the feeling like a runaway train and make bad choices.

But... making good choices is so boring. I love that crazy, fluttery feeling I get when I'm being reckless. The crazy fluttery feeling I get whenever I'm around him. I love it! I want more.

Bad choices for the win!

He's got me over his shoulder, draped like a mink stole. My braids are now a lost cause, and my face is turning red from being upside down, but I have an excellent view of his butt.

I poke it to see if it's really as round and firm as it looks.

Slap! His hand claps down on my rear, and I stiffen. "What was that for?"

"Behave."

"You behave." His gloved hand didn't spank me hard enough for it to hurt, but my finger throbs like it's broken. His glutes are like granite. I tell him this, and he grunts.

A smarter person would stop sassing the man who might kill them, but what's the fun in that?

I'm giddy like I'm in the grips of a sugar rush and cannot be held responsible for my actions.

He swings by the front door, picks up a black duffel, and carries me upstairs to my ensuite bathroom. He flips me upright and sets me carefully on the sink counter. "Stay."

I stick my tongue out at his back. The second he moves away, I'll run again.

"What are you doing?" He's removed the gloves he borrowed from my greenhouse and set his black duffel back beside the sink. "What's in the bag?"

He's set it out of reach. Now he's rummaging around under my bathroom counter. "Do you need a tampon? I only have a Diva Cup. I'm on birth control that stops my period."

"I know," he says. That gives me pause.

"Did you look at my medical records?" That's unsettling. I don't want him knowing so much about me, but I am flattered he did his homework. I'll need to find a way to use the information he knows against him.

He emerges with a new bar of soap. He unwraps it and sets it in the shower, then starts to strip.

Just like that, I can't move. He starts with his shirt, whipping it off and revealing all the glorious muscles rippling under his tattoos. His skin has a golden tint to it, like he works outside. Maybe when he's my husband, I can get him to mow my lawn shirtless.

*New kink unlocked.*

Next, he puts his hands on his belt. I press my legs together and whimper.

He glances at me.

"Don't mind me," I say, waving a hand. He's been doing a good job of ignoring me so far, but there's a glint in his eye that tells me he knows exactly what he's doing.

I can't even be mad! I'm only human, and his body puts Thorbjorn's to shame. And Thorbjorn is a fictional character!

If I had the body of a demigod, I'd use it as an unfair advantage, too.

He pulls down his jeans, revealing tree trunk-like thighs, and the gods are smiling at me, because he's wearing black briefs.

I get a brief glimpse of the outline of his dick before he turns away. My insides cramp, anticipating that log jammed up inside of me. He doesn't have to choke me to death. He can just impale me with that thing, and I'll die happy.

While I zoned out in a lust coma, he stepped into the shower and started washing. He's not going to remove his underwear?

Then I notice his back. Among the tattoos is a huge scar in the shape of a skull. The design looks a lot like the skull ring he wears. Probably some Fraternitas thing, marking their members with a skull brand. The sight of it unsettles me a little. I can't imagine how much it hurt.

He's scrubbing with the new bar of soap, his face stoic. It's got to hurt, but he's acting like it doesn't. He's got scratches all over him from the blackberry briars, but the real issue is going to be the hogweed sap.

"I have some good soap for removing plant toxins," I say. "Downstairs."

He jerks his head, flinging his wet hair out of his face. He looks like he's in a shampoo commercial if the shampoo company wanted to get all the viewers pregnant.

He ignores my offer to get the soap. He probably doesn't trust anything I'd give him. That's fair.

"Phototoxic?" he asks, and it takes me a second to figure out he's referring to our conversation about hogweed.

"Yeah... it'll blister in the sunlight." I peer at his skin, and it already looks a little red. He's definitely getting a rash. "Just wash really well and then make a paste with baking soda and water and apply it to any part of your skin that the plant touched. I can help."

He doesn't shout, "No." His dead-eyed stare says it all.

"Just trying to help," I mumble.

He goes back to washing, giving me more fodder for my spank bank. He even washes around the big silver skull ring he wears.

"Does that ring mean you killed someone?"

He glances at me, and I shrug. "Someone told me that about Fraternitas. You all get rings after you kill someone."

"Yes."

Another bolt of lust slices through me. "Just one?"

He shakes his head, and I have to grip the edge of the counter to keep from falling off.

"More than one? How many? Ten?" I feel like Delilah in *Viking Thunder* when the hero hits her with his sex lightning. Electrified to the point of weakness. "What's your body count?"

He squints, looking like he can't believe I'm getting excited.

"You've killed so many people." I don't realize I have my hand between my legs until he steps out of the shower and comes to stand before me. My head tips back to take in his wary expression. I'm so turned on, I'm making more bad decisions, but I can't stop myself. "That's so hot."

Water's pouring off of him, soaking my living moss bath mat. Meanwhile, I'm leaving a wet spot on the marble countertop. I move my fingers slightly, brushing my sex. If I make my movements small, maybe he won't notice.

He reaches past me to his duffel bag and pulls out a pair of black latex gloves. The sort a professional thief might wear.

Or an assassin.

I should get ready to fight for my life, but I'm mesmerized. This is just like my fantasy...

He grabs my hand and pins it in the small of my back, making me arch toward him. One more inch and he'll be close enough for my nipples to brush against his bare chest.

His hair is even more curly when it's wet. I want to touch it, but I don't dare move.

"What are you going to do now—"

He shoves two gloved fingers into my mouth. The force tips my head back.

The gloves are slick and leave a rubbery taste on my tongue. I'm gonna die.

But Kaiser's shirtless in front of me, and I can't look away.

"Oh, Bella." He looks me over like I'm a plant he just rescued from a commercial nursery, one that has promise but desperately needs pruning. "Belladonna. Beautiful woman."

He's looked up my name!

"Or... poisonous plant."

I waggle my eyebrows at him. *Why not both?*

His sigh gusts against my cheek. "You need to be good for me. But you don't know how. That's okay, baby. That's why they gave you to me. I'm going to train you."

What?

He pushes his fingers a little deeper, inching toward my throat. I panic, struggling, and grab his wrist with my free hand. It might as well be a fly that landed on his arm for all it deters him.

"Relax, baby girl. Breath through your nose." His coaxing tone reminds me to inhale. I follow his instructions, and my panic subsides.

Holy Hecate, I'm so fucking wet.

"This is how it's going to go. You're going to listen and obey, and I will teach you to be good for me. Nod if you understand."

He doesn't let me nod. He moves his fingers, moving my head for me. Ugh, why is this so hot?

"You're going to watch your mouth for the rest of the night. If I ask you a question, you can respond. But otherwise, you're on voice restriction. You get one fuck up. I'll spank you for it, but you can still earn a reward. But if you do it again—" He pauses before he finishes the threat. "I'll leave you alone for the rest of the night. And I'll be taking your vibrator and romance novel with me."

No! My expression must communicate my distress because he chuckles.

"That's right. No more playtime. Unless... you obey."

He pulses his fingers, gagging me before pulling back and resting his fingers on my tongue."So what's it going to be?"

He waits. I think about it. I could bite him. But nipping his fingers won't get me the upper hand.

So I lick his fingers, and he leans in and gives me what I want. What I'm willing to die for.

"Good girl."

**12**

———

# B *ella*

HE WASHES ME FIRST. Draws a bath, adds a ton of my favorite honeysuckle bubble bath. My breath catches when he returns to my side and whips off my shirt, but he's quick, his movements impersonal as he undresses me. He uses a knife to cut off my bra and undies, but I don't notice it until they've fallen in pieces to the floor. My heart speeds up, but he gives me a break, going to check the water temperature before carrying me over and setting me in the bath.

I sink into the water, staring up at him. He's naked and huge, leaning over the tub. His muscles are distracting, but not enough to make me forget the sinister black gloves. If this were a horror movie, he'd be about to drown me.

But he only takes a washcloth and gently cleans my face. He focuses on my lips, frowning like he's trying to solve a puzzle. He's trying to figure out how I was able to lick the poison sap from the manchineel tree, but that's my secret. It makes me smile, which makes him frown more.

Then he runs the washcloth down my neck and over my collarbone. My body tightens and I gasp, remembering that I'm naked. Then it's his turn to smirk.

He's got me right where he wants me. He's rubbing me all over, and I know what he's doing. He's trying to lull me into a sense of complacency. The thing is... It's working. I'm mesmerized by the flex of his muscles, his dark tattoos. I dreamed of the chance to study his ink up close, and now it's here, and I'm hypnotized. He smells like my own lemon sugar body scrub, a familiar scent, which relaxes me further.

He maneuvers me around so he can wash my front, my back. He's intent, like he's tending to a prized orchid.

I keep waiting for him to do something sexy. He barely brushed the washcloth over my breasts or between my legs. But all this scrubbing and gentle stroking is working me up more than watching him strip. Slow burn style.

I start squirming. His gloved hand comes around my neck. "Be still." He squeezes a little, reminding me of when he had his fingers in my mouth. "If you need help with the voice restriction, I can gag you. You'll have to thank me for it, without using your words."

I blink. What does that mean? I'm curious, but I don't want to try a gag. My throat is a bit raw. Maybe next time.

If there is a next time.

He sets me against the side of the tub so my back is supported and spends a long time picking leaves out of my hair. Then he washes it properly, massaging shampoo into my scalp until I'm limp in the water. I'm half asleep when he uses my homemade chamomile rinse. He applies a purple mask to my mids and ends and leaves me to relax.

It's not until he's back that I realize he washed my hair

perfectly. He even towel-dries my hair before applying leave-in conditioner and a touch of oil on the ends.

How did he know?

He's been watching me. Closely. And he's right... I never knew. Not until he let me see him.

Does he have cameras in here? What else has he seen?

I felt so safe in all my secrets, but he might know them all. And then I'll have nothing. No defenses. All my scheming won't save me... or my father.

My skin prickles with the cold. He wraps me with a towel warmed by the heated rack, but the cold sinks deeper, to my bones. The sugar rush is over, and reality is setting in. Reality and regret.

I thought I could outsmart him, but now I'm here, naked in front of him, obeying his commands, when not a few hours ago, he and his thug friends were shaking down my father in his own office.

He's playing me. I like it, but I can't forget what this is. I can't forget he threatened me and my father, then had the audacity to claim he was protecting me.

I will make him live to regret it.

I will keep pretending to be the fragile flower the world thinks I am. It won't fool him at first, but eventually he will lower his guard. I'll be his perfect bride if that's what it takes. I will study him as he's studied me. I will poison him from the inside out.

Kaiser and his friends will pay for messing with the Bosco family. My victory over them will be the talk of two cities, and destroying them will cement my status forever.

I will be the one who brought down Fraternitas. The ultimate supervillain.

But first, I have to survive the night.

*Kaiser*

HER FOREHEAD IS WRINKLED when I dry her off and lead her to bed. She let down her guard and now she's regretting it.

She doesn't need to be on guard. I'll protect her from everyone who would hurt her.

But there's no protecting her from me.

We walk into the bedroom. She stalls halfway to her king-sized bed, where I laid out some of my tools while she soaked in the bath. A ring gag. A box containing three sets of nipple clamps. Some rope and a suede flogger. Nothing too intense, but it probably looks scary to a novice submissive.

I stroke her hair from her face. I blow-dried it a little bit, the way she does after a shower. I followed her hair care routine to a T, and her hair looks like it always does, like it'd be soft and silky to the touch.

Her eyes roam over me. I took the time to dry off and change into loose black pants but left my chest and feet bare. She likes the look of my muscles. I have the urge to flex and show off, which I resist.

Her expression balks when she notices I'm still wearing the black gloves. Even though I washed her, I haven't removed them. I want to touch her, but I'm not going to, not until I understand what's going on with her. She said she was immune to poison ivy, but she also licked the poison apple tree in front of me, so her immunity may extend to other plants.

My arm is numb where I had to scrub off the sap. I know it hurts, but, like always, I have to concentrate to feel the ache. This came in handy when I was a young man in the fighting rings. Back then, I thought I was just learning to handle pain, but it went too far. It's like I turned off the part of my brain that connects to my skin. The pain is there, but it doesn't register. It feels far away.

I need to remember the lesson of the hogweed. The rash isn't bad—I've lived through much worse—but it's a good reminder that Bella is more than she seems to be. I'm dying to touch her all over, but I need to be careful.

Even though she looks very nervous right now. She bites her plump lower lip, and I have to bite back a growl. My dick is hard enough to pound nails, but I'm not going to pounce on her. Not yet. I have to go slowly, or I'll lose control.

Some day I'll be able to spank her hard, pull her hair, and bite hard enough to bruise and break the skin. She'll wear my marks under her clothes.

But first I'll have to break her in.

I have all the time in the world. No one will take her from me.

She's new to all this, but if I do it right, she'll crave the sensations I give her. I will master her until she submits to me fully.

"You don't have to fight me, little one. I'm going to give you everything you want," I murmur, using my thumb to smooth out her forehead. "What are you thinking? You can tell me."

"I want to know what you're going to do."

"Why? So you can fight me? You don't always need to be one step ahead. There's great power in surrendering."

She rolls her eyes. "Says the man who would never surrender."

"You want to dom me?"

"Would you let me do that?"

"How would you do it? Talk me through it."

She licks her lips, and my cock jumps in my pants.

"I'd tie you up?" She frowns when she hears the question in her voice. "To the headboard. And take off your pants. I want to see it." Her eyes dart to my crotch.

My dick pulses. I've never fucked a woman raw. I've always sheathed up. My skin is so numb, so it was never a huge loss of sensation. I still feel the pressure, the build-up, the release.

I never longed for skin-to-skin contact, but I'm dying to sink into my soon-to-be-bride's hot, wet pussy. Something tells me I'll feel it with her. All the more reason to be extra careful. The predator in me is ready to be unleashed.

"Do you think you deserve to see it? I was going to make you earn it."

"What were you going to make me do?"

"That depends on how good you are. I don't trust you to touch me yet, so I was going to tie you up. Stroke you all over. You were good in the bath for me, so I won't use the special oil on your clit. Just your bottom. But first... I want to play with your pretty nipples. See how sensitive they are."

"Do you like them?"

Is this what she's worried about? "They're everything I've dreamed of."

She looks excited, then a shadow passes over her face. "You've been watching me. You... were assigned to me."

"To watch you come and go. Not to study your every move. Not to break into your room and read your copy of *Viking Thunder.*"

"You know about *Viking Thunder*?"

"The book with a blond like me on the cover. The one you read over and over? Yes, I know about it."

She blinks and shakes her head a little. "So you watched me at night."

My voice is thick when I admit, "Yes. And I saw everything."

"That time in the garden... when Radley came at me. Were you protecting me?"

"Absolutely."

When I lock onto something or someone, I get obsessive. And jealous. It's the closest emotion to love I can feel.

She shivers. "You wouldn't have let him hurt me."

"I would've killed him before he touched you. From now on, you're off limits to everyone. No one else goes near you, little bride."

"You won't let Fraternitas hurt me?"

"They won't touch you." My brothers will respect my claim. She's my reward. "You're mine."

"Even if my father disobeys?"

"He won't. Not while I have you."

"And that's why you wanted me. To control me."

"More than that." But I do grab her hair and draw back her head. "I only watched you a few days before I knew... I wanted to own you."

"And what will you do to me?"

"Give me one night to show you, little bride. One night. I'll even make you come. Or..." I release her hair. "I can read you a bedtime story, tuck you in, and let you sleep." My dick throbs. If I could feel it, I bet I'd be in agony, needing to fuck her *now*.

*Go slowly.*

She's biting her lip. "You could hurt me."

"You're mine now. I don't break my toys." Anymore. Hurting her, killing her, would be a breach of contract, so I'm going to have to practice restraint. She's unlike any other toy I've ever had. I won't just own her for a night. She'll be mine for a lifetime, so I need to take care not to push her too far, too soon. "Do you have a safeword?" Asking for a safe-word is what a good dom would do. I might even honor it.

She nods. "Kumquat."

Do not smile. Do not. This is serious. "Kumquat. Got it. What are your limits?"

She hesitates. Opens her mouth, closes it. I can hear her neurons whirring as she tries to figure everything out.

"It's okay, baby." I make my voice soft. "We can try some stuff and figure it out as we go." Meaning, I'll play with her the way I like and see if she can take it like a good girl.

"No kissing on the mouth." She raises her chin. "If we kiss, the oxytocin will make us fall in love."

I shake my head. "Not going to happen."

"You're not going to kiss me? Or fall in love?"

"I won't kiss you until you want it."

"I won't want it."

"You will. But if you do... don't fall in love with me."

"Don't kiss me then," she shoots back and tilts her head. "Maybe you'll be the one who falls in love."

"You don't have to worry about that with me." Love requires a soul. I lost mine long ago.

There's nothing left of me but base desires. Food, shelter, sex. Life, liberty, and property. I take care of my own.

That's why I don't want a lover or a partner. I want a wife in the most medieval sense of the world.

A possession. A trophy. A toy.

But all this talk about kissing makes my cock weep.

"Come to bed, little bride."

She shivers and nods, and I cup her small face and stroke my thumbs up her cheeks. The black latex slips over her pretty skin. The sight is jarring. Usually, I wear these gloves when I don't want to leave DNA evidence on my victims, but I'm not here to choke her to death. I want her to live a long, blissful life as my pet.

"You're still afraid to touch me." She sounds mournful, but it's like a glove thrown between us.

Challenge accepted.

I hold her gaze as I peel off the gloves. My fingers ache with sensation. My sense of touch is coming back. I've never wanted to touch my toys before. But with her, I don't just want it.

*I need it.*

If my hand shakes a little as I reach for her, it's only from the force of holding myself back from leaping on her, ravaging her.

I bury my fingers in her hair and rub her scalp. The dyed strands slip over my fingers. I can't feel the sensation, not really. I can't feel things like other people do, not anymore. But I know the strands are soft. Her eyes half close like they did in the bath, and she's practically purring.

I maneuver her to the bed and sit her down, then lay her out. She's mine to touch, mine to torment. I set my hands on her shoulders, and they look large and rough compared to her small frame. All that unblemished skin, ready for my marks.

Tonight I'll be gentle. I want to examine my prize. Her sweet little breasts with dark nipples. The small bumps of bone in her delicate spine. The soft, wet place between her legs.

"Do you think I'm pretty?" Her brown eyes search mine. Her scent rises between us, and I'm licking my lips, ready to suck the lemon icing flavor off her skin.

"Yes, little bride. I think you're perfect."

**13**

---

# B *ella*

I'VE SPENT SO many nights in this bed, alone, fantasizing about a giant man who would touch me all over.

And now it's happening! He leans over me, covering my naked form with his shadow. The reality is scarier than the fantasy. I have no control over him. He's invaded my bedroom, and he's touching me like he has a right to.

Which, by his mafia man rules, he does.

I don't even want to fight. I want to lie here and take it.

Yolo!

Up close, I'm reminded of how big he is. My bedroom feels smaller with him in it. He dominates the space.

But proximity is a two-edged sword because the closer he is to me, the more I learn about him. His strengths. His weaknesses. This is all homework for destroying Fraternitas. Big, beautiful homework.

He's got scars all over him: under the tattoos, cleverly disguised by the swirls of ink. Also, his chest is perfectly smooth. No signs of razor rash, either. It's like he has no chest hair.

I didn't notice these details in the bathroom. I was too preoccupied with lust... and wondering if he was going to choke me out and drown me.

The fear gives my excitement such a delicious edge.

He runs his hands down my front, focused on my skin. My nipples pucker, and he explores them, lifting my slight breasts. I'm not super curvy and have always wished I was. But he doesn't seem to care.

*You're perfect.*

I let my head loll back on the pillow with a deep sigh. His shape blurs. His scent sharpens. There's a growing tension deep in my belly, and I want him to stroke my clit the way I like, but I'm also afraid. He's teased me so long that when it comes, my orgasm might break me.

I can't take it anymore. I reach for him, and he catches my wrist. His grip is gentle, but it's obvious he's strong enough to break my arm. All that coiled power lies in wait. "No touching."

He doesn't want me touching him? Is it a control thing? It must be a control thing.

At least he took off the gloves. He's touching me again like he did in my father's office, firm strokes meant to calm me. It's working. Maybe marriage to him wouldn't be so bad... No, stop that thought. *Bad Bella.*

"You're thinking too much," he murmurs and touches his fingers to my forehead again.

He's right.

He grips my chin, turning my head this way and that. I

let him. I can't physically fight him, so I might as well want to relax and enjoy my fantasy.

"Good girl." He rubs my shoulders, rewarding me. Then his hands brush the sides of my breasts, moving down over my belly to the valley between my thighs.

A soft stroke above my clit makes me jolt.

Too much. It's what I wanted, and it's too much.

"Kaiser."

"Hush now."

I hum deep in my throat. I don't care if I've become compliant. I'll do anything as long as he keeps touching me.

"You're going to be so good for me." He has two fingers on my swollen sex now, and he's barely stroking me. "Whenever I want, you'll open your legs..." I open them now. *Touch me!*

"Just like that. So sweet. But only for me."

*Yes.*

He inhales deeply. "Sweet like strawberries. I wonder, will you taste as sweet?" His fingers glide closer to my clit.

I whimper and try to close my legs, but he doesn't let me. He's between them, pinning my knees gently apart. Fuck. Oh fuck, he's right there.

"Lie still for me. Unless you want me to tie you up." He pauses for my answer, but I can't. I don't know what to do. The thought of him tying me up is too much. His hand covers my belly, holding me still, while the other plays around my clit. His touch is light, but his fingers are calloused. He rubs one petal of my sex between his fingers, then the other. The rough side of his thumb has me rising off the bed.

He presses me back down. "Stay." This is ridiculous. He doesn't need to tie me up; he can hold me down with one hand.

I shake my head at him, pleading. The pressure is over-whelming.

"Have you ever had anything inside you? In here?" His fingers nudge at my entrance. I suck in a breath and nod. "And what about your ass? No? That's okay, little virgin. I'll make it good for you." His voice caresses me.

His fingers slide into me, and my hips buck against his hand. The angle is perfect. My clit rubs against the heel of his hand. Two fingers, then three... stretching me. Just enough...

He pulls his fingers out. They're wet. My cheeks are on fire.

Why did he stop?

"You come when I say so."

*Shut up and fuck me!* I half-bare my teeth at him.

"Bella..."

*Uh, fine.* I nod. He puts his fingers back and works me up again. I try to watch him finger fuck me, but the heat and pressure are too much. My heels dig into the bed as I move against his hand.

"That's it, take what you need."

"Are you close?"

I nod, panting.

"You may come." He seems confident my body will obey his command, and that arrogance is what does it. I slip over, shuddering, and writhe when he slips his fingers back inside me. New sensations light up my body as I squeeze around them.

Fuck, I can feel him inside me, and it feels good.

The aftershocks fade, and I'm melting into the bed. He's still got his fingers inside me, studying me like he's memo-rizing my responses. Which should be worrying, but in this moment, it's super hot.

Usually, I don't like too much internal stimulation, but this is nice. In fact, my cunt feels empty, aching. I want more.

"Good girl," he says, and it triggers another pulse of pleasure in my groin.

"You're being so good for me," he murmurs and pushes his fingers deeper inside me. "One day you're going to take all of me here. You'll have to stretch to take me, though. It'll hurt and you're going to love it."

I'm panting, working up to orgasm again just from his voice. He's touching me so intimately; no one's ever been this close to me. It's scary and exhilarating.

"You said you'd punish me." Back in the graveyard. I glance down at the foot of the bed, where he's placed a skein of rope and a polished wooden box that might hold all sorts of torture implements.

"I don't need those things to punish you. I don't need anything to dominate you." He holds my eyes as he licks my taste from his fingers. And then when he pushes them against my lips, I open my mouth and do the same.

"I want you to cum for me again. And I'm going to sleep beside you, all night. If you try anything, you will regret it. But if you keep being good..." He strokes my folds lightly, and I sigh as my pleasure rises.

In no time, he has me panting again. He tells me about the things at the foot of the bed—the rope, the gag, the nipple clamps. "They'll pinch like this," he says and closes a thumb and forefinger around my left nipple. The pain sends a pulse of desire between my legs.

My mouth falls open. I can't believe I'm responding like this. Then he flips me over to my front and smacks my ass. I shriek into the pillow, but he follows it up with a deep massage. "So perfect for me." His thumbs run up the length of my spine. Goddess help me, I'm putty in his hands.

He makes me cum again with one hand shoved between me and the bed and the other clamped on the back of my neck, pushing my face into the pillow. I can't decide whether I like this way better than the first.

By the time he grinds the base of his palm into my clit, grounding me, I'm boneless in the bed. He turns me back over and arranges me on the pillow, and I'm too limp to move.

"You earned this." He stands up and shoves his boxers down. His dick springs free. That bulge was not lying. He's big and long, and it hurts just to look at.

"You can't touch it. Not yet. But that's it, lick your lips for me."

He's still ordering me around. It should be annoying, but every command makes my body pulse with need.

He brushes his fingers against my sex and uses the moisture to wet his dick. It's so hot, I'm trembling. I watch him fist himself, jerking off. The muscles in his arm and chest ripple and flex. I can't look away.

Finally, he plants one knee on the bed and lets his cum spurt onto me. I gasp, but it's too late. He's already sprayed onto my belly, a few drops glazing the shallow between my breasts.

I can't believe he came on me. I touch the pearly substance. It's still warm from his body but rapidly cooling.

He puts his hand on my belly and rubs it in. The look on his face is reverent. "There. Now we can go to sleep."

**14**

———

# K *aiser*

"Good morning!"

I wake with a jolt. Bella leans over me, a big grin on her face.

I slept in. I never sleep this long. My body feels heavy, sluggish, like I slept too deeply. That's not like me. My twin brother says I sleep like a wolf, in ten-minute naps between long stretches of being alert. I learned to sleep this way on the streets—it saved my life more than once—and the habit stuck.

Strange that I'd let down my guard so much with the Poisoner's daughter. She's not to be trusted. But my body felt otherwise.

Not only did I sleep, but I also spent the whole night in bed with her. I've never spent the night with a woman. I don't share my bed with anyone. Ever. A woman is a warm hole I'll use for a few hours, then never speak to again. I don't allow them to touch me, and I don't cuddle. I'd rather be stabbed in my sleep.

But with Bella, it's different.

It was a first for her, too. At first, she was restless, and it was obvious she's used to having the big bed all to herself. Every time she rolled over, her arm would fly out and her hand would smack me in the face. I tucked her into my side, holding her until she settled. I expected to hate being skin to skin, but instead, it felt right. I didn't even feel the urge to push her away after a while. No, I pulled her closer, wanting more. Finally, I gave in and dragged her on top of me.

Her weight felt good. Too good. So I slept hard.

I haven't slept so well since I was a small child. Or maybe ever. Jaeger and I didn't feel safe in our home long before we ran away.

It's dangerous to sleep so deeply. Bad things happen when you're dead to the world, vulnerable. My heart is racing now, responding to the threat.

I need to get up fast. I'm supposed to be keeping tabs on my little bride, and who knows what sort of mayhem she can get up to in the quiet hours of the morning.

"I made you coffee." She holds out a blue mug.

The coffee smells amazing, but there's an oily sheen on the surface. Probably poison. She serves this to me while my arm is bright red from the rash that weed gave me last night. It probably hurts like a burn. Just because I can't feel anything but numbness doesn't mean I've forgotten what she did.

And now she's trying to do it again. I glare at her. How stupid does she think I am?

She chuckles and wriggles her shoulders. "YOLO." She sips from the mug.

Is she really drinking poison? I watch her for signs of distress, but she only wrinkles her nose. "Needs sugar. I have some honey downstairs, but I noticed you took it black in the diner. A good spouse should know how you take your coffee."

Now alarm bells are flashing in my head. This would be a picture of domestic bliss—a loving wife brings her husband coffee in the morning so he can start his day—except I'm almost positive there's poison in the cup. A typical marriage doesn't have two spouses plotting against each other, and make no mistake, we are both plotting against each other. I intend to have absolute control over her. I don't know what she's plotting, but it's probably my death. Or a way to hamstring me. She wants to test me, like she did last night. She's looking for weakness so she can free herself and her father from Fraternitas.

I will never let her go.

Last night was everything I ever dreamed of. My own little virgin, obeying all my commands. I didn't even need to restrain her. She was so good for me, I'm hard just thinking about it. She talked a big game, but when I touched her, she melted. And she seems fascinated by my body.

Maybe it's wrong to use her innocent curiosity against her, but it's just the sort of depraved thing a man like me would do.

As inexperienced as she is in the bedroom, she's that much more knowledgeable about poisonous plants. I guess she would be fascinated by them, given what her father does.

She seems to have no qualms about using what she knows against me. My arm feels tight and hot from the rash.

And now she's offering me a poisoned cup of coffee. "Are

you sure you don't want it?" she asks, an innocent look on her face and tilt to her head.

I take the mug from her and sniff it. Smells like normal coffee. No trace of almonds, which can mean cyanide, or garlic, which would mean arsenic.

Bella blinks at me, acting clueless. I need to read up on my poisons if I'm going to survive being married to her.

I set the mug on the bedside table. I'm not going to drink it, but I need to keep it away from Bella. She's perky like she's already had a pot of caffeine.

"So, I was thinking." She sits on the edge of the bed next to me, swinging her legs, like we're a normal married couple chatting about our day. "My friends and I want to do a sleepover. It'd be good for me to have some companionship. What are the chances I can go without you hovering over me?"

Slim to none. But I can bug the room and listen in to any plans she might be making to escape.

"Let's make another deal," I say. "Be good for me the rest of the week, and you can go to your friends on Friday night."

"Deal." If she's annoyed at having to ask permission, she doesn't show it. She keeps chatting about her schedule while I get dressed in the jeans and a T-shirt I pull out of my duffel bag.

I go to her closet and choose an outfit I want to see her in. A white dress with yellow flowers.

I lay it on the bed next to her.

"What's this?" she asks.

"Put it on."

"But I'm already dressed." She's in black and pink hot pants and a matching top. If she thinks I'm going to let her out of the house looking like a wet dream, she's gonna learn fast.

"All right." She shrugs and bounces off to the bathroom to change. When she emerges, the sight of her makes my muscles tighten. My dick, which was already hard, presses more firmly against the zipper of my jeans. I can feel that discomfort. Fuck, she still looks like a wet dream. My wet dream. She's let her hair down, and it brushes her collarbone.

"Do you like it?" She sways back and forth, letting the light fabric swirl around her knees. She looks ready for Sunday school.

I want to fist that hair and drag her to her knees. Jack off over her face, make her suck me with those pouty lips. Come all over her. Defile her, so everyone who sees her knows she's owned.

She smiles like she knows what I'm thinking. That I'm close to losing control.

This is how she owns me. And I won't allow that.

I need to put her on a leash. I've never been into collars, not like St. James and some of his acquaintances at that sex club he owns. I can see the appeal of having a sub in bondage, but I don't just want to control her body. I want more.

Total ownership over her mind and soul.

I'm incapable of being loved—my fucktoys only ever felt awe mixed with fear, and then relief when the night was over—but I intend to train Bella and prime her body to always respond to me. Soon I'll be able to get her off with just a touch. She'll love the sensations I give her, even if she can't love me.

Or she might resent the control I have over her. The things I do to her. She'll hate me for making her like them.

But she'll crave them. And because I'll be the only one who touches her, she'll crave me.

It won't be love, but it'll be close enough. She'll be loyal and devoted to me, even though she'll resent it. I can take the hate, as long as she accepts my control.

"Let's go. We need food, and then you need to get to class. After that, I'm going to pick you up and we're going on an errand."

"An errand?" She perks up. "For Fraternitas?"

I don't answer because it's none of her business. I control her schedule, not the other way around.

"Are you murdering someone?" she asks.

"No."

"Would you tell me if you were?"

"No."

She wriggles in that way she does when she's excited. "If you are going to murder someone, can I help?"

I give her a look that says *I have a ball gag, and I'm not afraid to use it.*

She giggles.

It's going to be a long day.

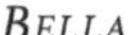

*BELLA*

MY FIANCÉ TAKES me to breakfast at the diner, where we sit in the same booth. He makes me eat a veggie omelet before rewarding me with pancakes. He eats the equivalent of half a cow and drinks a pot of coffee. I notice he didn't dare taste the coffee I gave him earlier. That's fine. Poisoning him that way would've been too easy.

What are the chances I can use baked goods? Or honey? I can't wait to find out.

He drops me off at class. I was hoping to catch up with Honey, but she arrived late. I texted her about sleepover plans, and she confirmed, so I'll have a chance to tell her everything then. At the end of class, Honey gets called up to the front to talk to the professor. I wait for her, but Kaiser's hovering in the classroom door. He's breaking the rules by roaming free on the campus. Either that or he got special permission.

I want to linger to see if I can chat with Honey, but she's still talking with the professor, so I catch her eye, give her a wave, and head over to Kaiser. When Honey notices who I'm with, she visibly startles and pales. I give her a thumbs up and indicate that I'm going to call her later. She nods, biting her lip.

Not exactly how I wanted to tell her about Kaiser, but at least she knows now. I'm hoping she'll have more info about Fraternitas for me at our sleepover.

Kaiser puts his hand on the small of my back and escorts me all the way to his Jeep. He's also brought me lunch: a portobello mushroom sandwich from Pane P's and a peach iced tea.

"We have a few errands in New Rome," he explains as he pulls away from the curb.

"Like what?"

"Like marriage counseling."

I nearly spit my iced tea out. "Marriage counseling? Why do we have to do that?"

"Because I fucking said so." Kaiser shifts gears and speeds up to merge onto the highway.

"It's not a real marriage," I argue, but I'm distracted when his bicep flexes and his shirt sleeve moves, revealing a nasty-looking burn.

"Ooh, you got a rash. Does it hurt?"

He doesn't answer. Which is fine. I was going to offer to kiss it better, but if he's going to be rude...

"It looks painful. Next time you'll think twice before playing in my secret garden."

"It looked like a bunch of flowers."

"Just because it's pretty doesn't mean it isn't dangerous. People think natural means healthy. I can name twenty ordinary household plants that will kill you."

"Like belladonna?"

"I'm probably the only person you'll meet who grows belladonna. Which is a shame. It's a lovely plant. It just happens to have dark purple berries that can cause you to go mad."

Kaiser doesn't say anything. I take a little nap and wake up when he parks the car. I stare up at the neo-Gothic building. The sign reads *St. Xavier's Cathedral.*

"A church? We're going to a church?"

"Father Francis is waiting." He opens my door, pulls me out of the car and guides me in with his hand on my back.

I half expect him to burst into flames when he enters the church, but he walks in like he owns the place.

I can't believe he's making me do premarital counseling for an arranged marriage.

A priest is indeed waiting for us. He's around forty and looks like someone's kindly uncle. Kaiser shakes his hand and introduces him as Father Francis.

"Good morning, Belladonna," the priest says. He has a short beard and deep smile lines around his blue eyes. A disarming face, but something about how he studies me unsettles me.

"Call me Bella."

"Shall we?" He sweeps out a hand and leads us to his office, which smells like old books with a faint whiff of incense. Bookshelves cover the walls from floor to ceiling. The leather-bound volumes have faded text on the spines. It reminds me of the oldest parts of the main library at UU.

Father Francis settles into a plush armchair that looks older than me. The burgundy velvet is worn down on the arms.

Kaiser maneuvers me to a couch facing the priest. I sit at one end, but Kaiser sits in the middle, and his weight tips me toward him. Then he puts his right arm around me and pulls me close so my thigh is flush against his. And as if it's not enough that we're practically welded together, he reaches across with his left hand to grab my right wrist. There are wrestling holds with less contact than this.

Suddenly, I'm hot all over. I try to tilt away from him, but then I'm just snuggling into his arm. I cross my legs, but it only makes me aware of how wet I am, just from him manhandling me. Meanwhile, he looks unbothered. It's so unfair.

Father Francis smiles at us. "I'm so glad we could meet together today."

"This is a farce. You know that, right?"

Kaiser's arm squeezes me gently, but I ignore the warning. "He knows."

"I do." Father Francis tilts his head. "I helped oversee the negotiations."

My heart speeds up. I feel like I'm about to explode. How did a priest get caught up in all this? He must have some ties to Fraternitas. Now it makes sense why Kaiser brought me here.

"Then you know this marriage is fake. My father signed a contract." My face is flushed with anger. I haven't forgotten that my father signed the contract on my behalf. "No one even asked me."

"Is that important to you? Do you want Kaiser to ask you? Get down on one knee?"

Is he serious? He has to be mocking me, except he seems genuinely interested in my answer.

"I don't want to get married at all."

Father Francis nods like this is normal. "I understand that the situation isn't what you'd choose. But people marry for many different reasons. Security, stability, heirs, love—"

"Lust," I throw out and wish I hadn't said anything. I don't want to be in lust with Kaiser. Although if I confess to this priest all the things Kaiser did to me last night, will that get him in trouble? How much authority does Father Francis have over Kaiser?

As soon as the thought comes, I dismiss it. The priest probably only has as much authority over Kaiser as Kaiser allows. But maybe I can learn more about what's going on.

"Marriage is sacred. I'm here to help you find common ground. See what values you share. Even though this is an arranged union, there are ways you can come to terms with a partnership. Meet each other's needs."

Right now, I need to kill someone. And then maybe have an orgasm.

It doesn't help to know that Kaiser would be great at meeting both of those needs.

"Bella, what do you want out of this partnership?"

"Respect," I say before I think about it. Damn it, I should've said "Freedom."

I don't know why I'm even answering. Maybe I just want to see where this conversation leads. But I can't discount the fact that the priest has years of experience eliciting deep secrets from people, and right now, he's using that power on me.

"Communion," Kaiser says before the priest can ask.

"Do you think you can come to respect Bella?"

I lean into his arm, the one with the rash on it. He sucks in a breath and says, "Yes."

"And Bella, do you think you can give Kaiser what he needs?"

"Isn't communion your area of expertise?" That's what they call their fake cannibal ceremony, right? Holy Communion.

Father Francis grins. "I don't think that's the sort of connection Kaiser wants with you."

"I don't know, sometimes I think he wants to eat me."

Father Francis continues as if I didn't say anything. "To commune with someone is to share a deep intimacy. Closeness. Connection. All humans crave it. But it requires a level of trust. Do you trust each other?"

"Nope."

Kaiser shakes his head.

"But you do desire him."

"I plead the fifth."

"She does," Kaiser says.

I elbow him in the ribs and immediately regret it. "Ow." It feels like I banged my funny bone on a doorjamb.

Kaiser helps me rub it better. His big hand massages my skin, and it feels good, as it always does when he touches me.

When I look up, Father Francis regards us with a satisfied expression. "Well, that's a start."

Just when I think this can't get any worse, Kaiser straightens, becoming alert. I catch a glimpse of someone walking past the half-closed door.

"I need to speak to Atticus."

"Go ahead," Father Francis says. "It'll give me a chance to get to know Bella better."

Fuck.

Kaiser rises, and I instantly miss his heat. I don't want to be left alone with the priest and his scary questions.

But I can't beg Kaiser not to leave.

"I'll be right back." He pauses in the door to point his finger at me. "Be good."

"I'm not converting to Catholicism. So don't even try," I say to Father Francis. "I avoid all religions made up by a man in a desert."

If he's insulted by the way I dismissed most belief systems, he doesn't show it. "You don't need to share my faith for me to share my wisdom. Do you have any questions for me?"

So many. "What can you tell me about Kaiser?"

"He's loyal. He'd do anything for his brothers. Even before that, he was willing to sacrifice himself for his twin."

"He has a twin?"

"A twin brother. Both of them have been part of Fraternitas from almost the beginning."

I want to ask him more about Fraternitas, but I need to be more subtle about it.

And I want to learn more about Kaiser.

"What's his last name?"

"He's never told it to me."

"Does he have any other family?"

"Fraternitas is his family."

That's exactly what Kaiser told me. Word for word, which is kind of creepy. I've heard how gangs recruit young men by preying on their need for a family. If Fraternitas did that, then it isn't just a bunch of loosely associated criminals; it's a brotherhood. The members aren't just willing to kill for power and profit. They're willing to die for each other.

If that's true, then they're more dangerous than I ever imagined. "When did he join?"

"He was almost one of its founding members. I don't know what he's told you about his past, but when I met him and his twin, they were living on the street and had been for years. Since they were very young."

"How young?"

"You'd have to ask Kaiser if he remembers when he left his childhood home. I met him when he was eight."

I suck in a breath. My childhood was no picnic. After my mother was murdered, my father retreated into his shell. He protected and cared for me, but he kept his distance emotionally. And the nature of his business meant we kept to ourselves. We didn't get close to people or make friends in case they would betray us.

Still, I always had a warm, safe place to live and plenty to eat. Papa was able to buy me whatever I wanted.

I can't imagine what it would be like to be an eight-year-old growing up without a roof over his head. Without a fridge full of food or an adult who could pay a heating bill.

My gut twists.

"I had a ministry providing food to anyone who needed a free meal. A few, like Kaiser and his brother, would come, and once they trusted me, they brought more and more children. That's how I started what would become the school." He picks up a brochure with a picture of the cathedral on it. The text reads 'Hieronymous' School for the Lost.'

"It started with me teaching runaways after I fed them. Then I expanded the hours and raised money to build the dorms. There wasn't much, but I had to do something. At first, the children slept on padded mats on the floor."

My stomach churns, and my throat feels tight. I remember last night, how Kaiser tucked me into his side. At some point, he pulled me on top of him. When I woke up this morning, he was wearing me like a weighted blanket. I got the sense that he was able to sleep anywhere, anytime, in any condition. "Kaiser did that?"

"He would never stay the night. The older children were like that. They'd bring the young ones in and encourage them to stay, but they preferred street sleeping. I tried to meet them where they were." He gives me a brief smile. He seems lost in memory. It may be an act to lead me on, but I sense real emotion in his voice when he talks about his ministry. At least part of this is genuine.

"He did allow me to teach him to read."

"And then he joined the gang. Or helped start it."

"He joined after it started. There were a few years when he and his twin were... separated from us."

What? "What does that mean?"

"That's Kaiser's story to tell. But I hope you will ask him."

My thoughts are swirling. Father Francis has given me some answers, but I only have more questions.

I want to know everything about Kaiser. I tell myself this is so I can destroy him anytime I wish, but really, it's because I want to know him.

"Ask him. I'm sure he will tell you, Bella."

I shake my head, remembering the scars on his back, the ones he covered with tattoos. "He won't."

"You won't know until you ask." But I do.

Kaiser lied when he said he wanted communion. He doesn't want connection; he wants control. He won't let me touch him, even when he wants it. Instead, he makes the rules. He touches me, pretending we're close while manipulating my every move. Intimacy that's as fake as an arranged marriage.

"It's not like we're really getting married."

"The marriage will be real."

"If my father wants an alliance so much, he should marry Kaiser." As soon as I say it, I want to take it back. I want Kaiser all to myself. For now.

"That won't be enough to seal the alliance. Your father doesn't value his life. He values yours."

"Whatever."

Father Francis folds his hands together, his expression turning serious. "Do you know what they call your father? The Poisoner. Several months ago, Alfredo Vesuvio ordered delivery from his favorite restaurant. By the next morning, he was dead. At first, the doctors thought he'd had a heart attack. But the head of the Vesuvio family learned later that a second autopsy showed traces of arsenic. Your father poisoned his food."

"No, he didn't," I blurt, before I remember I'm supposed to be mining the priest for information, not volunteering it. "He wouldn't do something like that."

"Evidence suggests he did. No one else blends poisons like your father. His techniques are so far advanced, we don't even know the extent of what he can compound. And we're his allies."

I want to snort. The Boscos and Fraternitas are not allies.

Wait. Father Francis said, "We."

"Are you part of Fraternitas?"

He holds up his hand. There's no ring. "Not officially."

"Unofficially?" I'm betting on a priest not lying to me in his own church.

That's against the rules, right?

He gives me that subtle smile, the one that's starting to unsettle me. "It was my idea."

**15**

---

I'm quiet when Kaiser drives us away from the church. He came back soon after Father Francis admitted his involvement in the brotherhood. I figured the priest couldn't be trusted, but now I know.

It's all information.

"I'll see you at the engagement party," Father Francis says.

"What engagement party?"

His eyes crinkle with a condescending smile. "Yours."

Right. I'm a little distracted, chewing over everything I've learned about Kaiser and my situation.

I can't believe what he told me about the Vesuvio guy. My father wouldn't poison someone directly. It's not his style. He sells poisons to people. If he had poisoned someone, no one would ever find out. So, I know he didn't do it.

The real thing that bothers me is that I have no idea why my own father reduced me to a bargaining chip. I know why Fraternitas wanted me—I'm leverage to get my father to do their bidding—but I don't understand why my father would so willingly hand me over. Isn't he even going to try to fight?

I look up and recognize the street names. We're in a section of the city close to my father's lab. He hasn't made any move to contact me, but I'm tired of waiting.

I check my door, but it's locked. Kaiser isn't taking chances that I'll throw myself from a moving car.

And I'm supposed to be pretending I'll be a good little wife. Get more intel.

Let his guard drop. Making him chase me through the city will set me back.

"Can we stop and see Papa?" I hold my breath, hoping he'll say yes. So far, pretending to defer to Kaiser has still allowed me to get my way. Mostly. I'm filing everything I learn about him away so I can figure out how to manipulate him.

Kaiser says nothing, but he takes a right at the light. A few minutes later, he's in front of LilyRose, our business's flagship store.

"Go ahead," he says. I don't hesitate. I exit the car and rush into the store.

The first half is an atrium-like space, clean and airy, with a pale wood floor. I hurry past the stands that showcase glass vials of perfume and signs inviting customers to book a consultation so our staff can help them customize a signature blend. The store is mostly empty of customers, but Katya, the manager, sees me and comes over.

"Bella. How are you?"

"Hey, Katya. I was just in the area and thought I'd drop in to see Papa."

Her eyebrows draw together. "I see. He told us he'd be working off-site for a few days. Are you able to reach him on his cell?"

"Oh yeah," I wave a hand. "I just forgot. I'm busy with school these days."

Her face brightens as she asks me about school. We chit chat and then I excuse myself to grab something from the store room.

Deeper in the store, the ceiling drops and the colors darken. The place is less zen and more like a luxurious den with thick Turkish rugs leading to private meeting spaces. I hear murmuring behind one door. Some employees must be in a consult. Probably Solange and Jon.

As I walk, I try my father's cell, but it goes to voicemail. He must be working from home. Or maybe he took a trip out to one of our farms. Which is rare but not unheard of.

What I don't like is that he didn't tell me. He turned me over to Kaiser, told me I was going to marry him, and then left town?

Or maybe Fraternitas has him locked down. All the more reason to figure out how to free him and fight back.

I quicken my steps. I'm not heading for the storeroom but my father's private lab.

Once I pass the employee's spaces and the deep stockroom, the scent of roses and lily of the valley hits me. The sweet floral perfume was my mother's signature scent. The place smells so much like her, I can imagine her rounding the corner in one of her floral kimonos. It makes my heart ache, but I welcome the pain.

I miss her.

I always wondered if Papa was aware that he was keeping Mom's memory alive in his workplace. I don't know why he surrounds himself with the scent of her when he can barely say her name. He doesn't even wear his wedding ring anymore. Sometimes it's like he doesn't want to remember she even existed, and if I'm honest, that hurts as much as my grief.

But it's old pain. I have bigger problems to deal with right now.

I enter my father's office. It looks business-y but has a door that leads to an open workspace. Most people would assume my father compiles his perfumes up here in the workspace or the smaller lab. Only a few people know the truth—Papa's main lab is in the basement, several floors below the main floor, along with his secret greenhouses.

On the far wall are a set of paintings. On the left, a watercolor of a lily and a rose. On the right, a peace lily surrounded by lavender. And in the middle, a belladonna plant growing between the trunks of two trees. They're all signed *Shoshonna B*, and my mother painted them.

I touch the frame of the left painting and hesitate. If I press a certain pattern, a hidden door will open and lead me to my father's secret lab. He might be down there, hidden from Fraternitas. Or he might be avoiding all his secret labs so as not to lead Fraternitas to them.

A phone rings in my father's office, shattering the silence and making me jump. I wait for it to stop ringing, but as soon as it does, it starts again. It's an old-fashioned phone, with a cord and a ring that could wake the dead.

I head back into his office and pick it up. It's my father's private line, coming from our house.

"Hello?"

"Belladonna."

"Papa." My shoulders relax, hearing his voice. I can imagine him here at his workspace, wearing his microscope goggles, the kind my mother used to tease him about. She'd pick me up, mischief sparkling in her brown eyes. *"What do you think about having a Papa who looks like a bug?"*

"You're in my office."

I glance up, looking for cameras. I don't see them, but they must be here. I never thought about it.

"You're looking well."

"Thank you." I fiddle with the skirt Kaiser wanted me to wear. My outfit is more preppy than usual, but I guess I look good. Normal. "It's good to hear your voice."

"Did you need something?"

"Yes. I need you to tell me what's really going on. "

A pause. He's hesitating, which makes me wonder if someone's listening in. "Now is not the time."

"Papa, please. We need to talk."

"I know. We will, soon. When we're truly alone."

So he does think Fraternitas is monitoring this conversation. They've bugged his phone line or his office. Or both.

Drat.

"I don't even know when I'm allowed to see you."

"I'll be at the engagement party."

"What is this engagement party?" I ask before I remember Father Francis mentioned it to me, too. "When is it?"

"Early August. Fraternitas is making the arrangements."

"And the wedding?"

"It depends on a few things, but it will happen. Probably before the end of the year."

Ugh. My first real semester starts at the end of August. I never thought I'd be attending university as a married woman.

Kill me now.

"You can't be serious about this," I sigh into the mouthpiece. "This is all so sudden and... I don't understand."

"You don't have to understand. I am your father and the head of this house. One day you will inherit all of this, but until then, you will obey me."

My breath comes faster. "Papa, please talk to me."

"There's nothing to talk about." He's doing what he always does, withdrawing from me. It only makes me frantic, and when I finally lose it and start crying or raging, he tells me I'm too emotional.

I bite my lip to keep from lashing out at him. I can do this. I can remain calm. Give him a taste of his own medicine.

"I am your daughter, and you're asking me to enter shark-infested waters." It's more like he's throwing me in, but I refuse to believe I don't have a choice. "I deserve to know what's going on."

"I know you don't want this marriage, but it's for the best. There's a lot at play—"

"They think you poisoned some mob guy," I blurt. I don't care if we're bugged and Fraternitas overhears this part. I want them to know the truth. "I know you didn't. We just have to prove—"

"Not now, Belladonna." His voice is harsh. I flinch like I've been struck. "The deal is done. The marriage is happening."

I shake my head. He must see it on the cameras because he says, "I negotiated for you to be able to attend school and have access to your greenhouse. It's not the prison sentence—"

"It is!" I'm losing it. My emotions are like a storm, too big for me to control.

Energy surges through me. I want to grab things and smash them.

"Bella, enough." Papa is quiet in the face of my temper tantrums. It's so unfair. I hate acting childish around him.

Even when I was a child, my feelings were sometimes like a tsunami crashing over me. My father never knew what to do. My mother was the only one who would hold me until the storm died away. Once she was gone, my father shut down even more.

Whenever I threw a tantrum, he simply turned away.

"You will marry Kaiser. He will be good for you. He will protect you."

"I don't need—"

He cuts me off. "You want more independence, but that comes with responsibility. And you're too reckless. You would wreck your own life, and I will not have that."

"I won't."

"You will. You already have. Poisoning the entire lacrosse team? Making enemies your first week on campus and for what?"

My lower lip trembles the way it used to when I was little and Papa lectured me. He wants an answer. "They were mean to my friend," I say in a small voice. I even sound childish.

"Is she powerful? Does she have assets that would make her a good ally?"

"No. I don't know," I whisper.

"So you did all of this with no strategy? You never think of the consequences." I can hear his disgust. "I have tried to teach you, but you refuse to learn patience. Planning. You need to grow up."

My eyes burn with unshed tears. I refuse to cry or scream at him. I won't give him the satisfaction.

"Fraternitas can look after you. You're their responsibility now. The sooner you give in to your fate, the better."

Before I can argue, he hangs up.

KAISER

. . .

I sit in the car, watching people come and go past the parfumerie. A meter man rolls by and pauses. I'm illegally parked, but he doesn't tag my vehicle and just moves on.

Bella's been inside for a few minutes. My fingers are tingling again, that pins and needles sensation, the kind I get from sitting too still for too long. My dead limbs, waking up.

I want to go after her. Grab her by the scruff of her neck, like a little wayward kitten. Most fucktoys I can't wait to be rid of, but her? I want her close. At all times.

For fuck's sake, I slept with her on top of me. I still can't believe it.

She must have drugged me. I don't know how, but why else would I sleep like she slipped me a sleeping pill?

She's driving me crazy again. I can figure out most opponents after studying them for a few seconds. Her? I've watched her for weeks and still don't understand her.

I need to figure her out, fast, or she'll be the death of me.

Right now she'll be talking with her father. We have his office and home rigged with cameras. We haven't told him this, but we believe he knows. Still, it'll be interesting to hear what Bella says to him. She might be naive enough to think her father has more control over his domain. She'll be less guarded.

I need all the insight into her mind I can get. And speaking of insight...

I pull out my phone and dial Father Francis. He greets me, and I ask, "What did she say?"

"She asked about you, actually. She's curious about you."

"Trying to find my weakness."

"I believe so, yes. A fascinating young woman. You have

your hands full with her. She was very well behaved, but I can tell her brain was working overtime. She's not yet resigned to her fate."

I don't answer. I'm watching the LilyRose storefront closely. I should be relieved that Bella is her father's problem for a few minutes, but I just want to go after her.

"I told her some details of your childhood. She has more questions, and I encouraged her to ask you."

My body gets tight, my muscles ready to spring into action.

Father Francis interprets my silence correctly. "You don't have to share if you're not comfortable—"

"No. She can ask." As much as I hate talking about my past, I want her to know. But I have to be careful. Back then, I was at my weakest. And I don't want to reveal my weakness to her.

"I meant what I said earlier. About trust. It's the foundation for any intimacy. If you share some of your secrets with her, it would be a show of good faith. A sign you are willing to trust her."

Which will allow me to lure her in closer.

"All right."

After the call ends, I think about it. I don't have to tell her everything. Just enough details to make her feel like I'm opening up. If she feels sorry for me, it'll be easier to convince her to soothe my pain. A trap and my sob story will be the bait.

Except I don't want to lie to her. The thought sets my teeth on edge. I want her to look at me with those soft brown eyes, which are way more expressive than eyes have a right to be. I want her to really trust me, and not just because I manipulated her.

But because she wants to.

I glance at the store. Bella's been inside for a while now. I don't like having her out of my sight. She's my responsibility now. Is her father giving her all sorts of new ways to poison me?

I tap on my phone, texting one of my Fraternitas brothers, Argos. He's a tech genius and in charge of security. St. James will have made sure we have eyes on the Boscos.

Argus texts me back a link. I click on it, and my screen fills with a live feed. Bella stands in an office, holding a black landline phone to her ear. Her face is frozen in a mask that tells me she's furious but trying not to cry.

I don't know what's going on, but I know this: I'm going to kill whoever put that look on my little bride's face.

**16**

B<sup>ella</sup>

I STAND with the phone to my ear until someone knocks at the door, breaking the spell.

It's Kaiser.

As always, his presence alters the space. The room seems to shrink around him. The balance of power shifts until the lion's share rests on him. He's in my father's territory, but there's no denying he's the most dangerous person here.

He sweeps his gaze around the room, scanning for enemies. Once he gets to my face, he doesn't say anything, but the muscles in his shoulders and chest slightly swell. He's tense, ready for a fight. He turns his glacial gaze on the phone I'm still holding, like a sniper settling his target in his sights.

*You will marry Kaiser,* my father said. *He will be good for you. He will protect you.*

He's here to protect me now.

"Who's that?" he growls.

"My father." I replace the handset on its cradle.

"Are you okay?"

"Yes," I lie. "Everything's fine. We can go now."

I hold my head high and walk out of LilyRose, the store named after my mother, with Kaiser shadowing me.

I wish my mom were here. She would defend me. She'd take my side.

If only my father were more like my mom.

I miss her so bad. The sight of her in her floral robes, the scent of rosewater clinging to her skin. She had glossy black hair that hung down her back in loose curls, and she was warm and soft and always ready with a hug.

I could really, really use a hug. Instead, I have to get back into my fiancé's car and go through with a bunch of bullshit. Alone.

In the car, I don't dare look at Kaiser. I'm still raw. My eyes ache from the strain of trying not to cry.

The silence stretches.

"We should go," I say. "You're illegally parked."

He takes my wrist and turns it over, frowning. My left palm hurts from where I've been digging my nails into it. He rubs a thumb over the marks, soothing them away.

Despite myself, I sigh. I lean back in my seat, letting the tension seep out of me.

"Thank you for coming to get me."

He raises my hand, and something brushes against my palm, so light, it might not have happened. A kiss.

My eyes are closed. I didn't see it. I can pretend it didn't happen.

After a moment, he sets my hand down on his knee. I

can feel his muscles flex as he turns the car on and begins to drive.

I intend to pretend to sleep all the way back to Metropolis, but after a few minutes, Kaiser parks the car.

I open my eyes. We're downtown, tucked in a forgotten corner of a strip mall. Most of the storefronts are closed or run down, including the one we're parked in front of. There's no sign that says it's open, but someone propped the door ajar with a giant hardback book. The windows are full of stacks of old paperbacks.

"What's this?"

Kaiser shrugs. "Thought you'd like it."

I'm speechless. He took me to a used bookstore. This doesn't seem the sort of place Kaiser would know about.

"This is where I bought *Viking Thunder*. It was hard to find."

"It's a pretty old book. I have my mother's copy." What he says dawns on me. "You bought your own copy?" He nods.

"Why?"

He doesn't answer, just gets out of the car. He opens my door, and I pop out, eager to pepper him with questions. "Did you read it?"

He sets his hand at the small of my back and steers me to the bookstore.

"Did you like it? You did, didn't you? But you'll never admit it." He stops then and turns to me. "I liked it. I read it because you like it." What? I can't believe this.

We enter the bookstore. The scent of dusty old books hits me, and I inhale deeply. The smell reminds me of my mother's library. Even the piles of paperbacks... She kept stacks like that beside her bed.

"Get anything you want," Kaiser tells me. "My treat."

"You might regret that."

He shrugs. "Challenge accepted."

I smirk to myself. There are two places I should never be turned loose: a plant nursery or a bookstore.

There's no sign of the bookstore owner, only a fat orange tabby cat lounging in a rocking chair. He lets me pet him, kneading his big paws into the plaid blanket he's using as a bed.

I dive deeper down the rows of towering shelves. To my surprise, Kaiser follows. He even seems to browse, picking up books and reading the jackets before reshelving them. I study him through the stacks.

He's acting like my dream man. He realized I was upset and did what he could to cheer me up. It's so obvious he's doing this so that I will like him. I refuse to like him.

He's my captor.

I can't think about my conversation with my father yet. His criticism was so hurtful, I can't examine it too closely yet. But I do wonder if he made himself the bad guy so I would run into Kaiser's arms.

And it worked. I can feel the shift. I'd rather be here with him than with my father.

Kaiser's in the religion section, looking up at a huge Bible. I get close and nudge him.

"Have you read it?" I ask.

"Sections." He moves on, and it's my turn to follow. "Father Francis assigned passages for us to copy out. To practice our handwriting."

I blink. That sounds intense. "He said he taught you."

Kaiser nods.

"He told me you lived on the streets but would go to the church for meals."

"Yes." He pulls a book off the shelf. He's brought me to the romance section.

He's distracting me, and it's working. I find an old copy of *Wolf and the Dove* and hand it to Kaiser. "You should read this."

I unearth a copy of *Silver Devil* so old it doesn't even have a cover. I hide it before Kaiser sees it. The hero in that book is depraved. I don't want him to get any ideas.

I fill my arms with Beverly Jenkins' Destiny series. Then I get to the sci-fi/fantasy section and find a hidden treasure trove of Mercedes Lackey and Anne McCaffrey. Kaiser has to help me hold the stacks.

"My mom loved these books," I tell him. "She kept tons of copies of them in our lake house. Anna, our housekeeper, told me my mother called them her manuals for life."

Kaiser raises a brow.

I frown, trying to make sense of what my mother might have meant. "I think she meant relationships. Some people aren't good with emotions." Like my father, I think but don't say. "Their partners need emotional catharsis and support. A couple coming together to live happily ever after is the dream. The fantasy." I look longingly at a beautiful hardback edition of Robin McKinley's *Sunshine*. Without asking me, Kaiser adds it to his stack.

"Studies show that reading fiction makes you more empathetic," he says. "Mental rehearsal."

"What do you know about mental rehearsal?"

"From fighting. Training for the ring." Once again, he's surprised me.

"We need more men to read romance novels," I say. "Too bad the patriarchy calls them trash and looks down on people who read them."

"The patriarchy likes it when people fight."

"What?" I think about it. "When people talk things out and don't fight, there's no need for a strong man."

"The strongest men make peace."

He dips his head and leads me to the checkout counter. "Not if the leaders keep them fighting. The ones in charge want to stay in charge. They do this by creating fear. That's how you control a strong man: make him afraid. Of everything."

"Then more women should be in charge. And non-binary people." I wrinkle my nose at him, daring him to disagree.

The bookstore clerk finds us like that. He's a young man, handsome if you like pale, skinny dudes who look like they're on a grad school stipend diet. His eyes are beautiful, though. Soulful. I bet he writes his own poetry.

And I have an idea. An awful idea. A wonderfully awful idea.

~

*Kaiser*

I KNOW Bella's up to something when she flashes me a warning smile. Then she turns and gives the clerk her full attention.

"Hi! I'd like to get these." She flutters her eyelashes at him.

He looks surprised but returns her smile. "There are some good finds."

"Thanks." She tosses her hair over one shoulder. It's painfully obvious she's learned to flirt by watching that stupid vampire show. It would be pathetic, except she's mesmerizing. The clerk leans in, asking her about books she's read.

I touch Bella's back, and she ignores me, her full focus on the guy.

She's doing this to piss me off.

And it's working. I don't feel much, but the one thing I can feel is rage. I've kept it close, used it to fuel me. It rises now, speeding my heart. Blood pounds through my veins.

I glare at the guy. I could snap his spine with one hand.

My future wife and this bookstore dweeb reach for the same book, and their hands nearly touch. I've had it.

"Enough," I say, inserting my arm between them and handing the clerk my credit card. "We need to get going."

"What's the hurry?" Bella pouts.

I lean down and whisper in her ear. "I have plans for you."

"Ooh, like what?" Her attention's on me now, where it should be.

"Like re-enacting page 269 of *Viking Thunder*."

Her forehead creases as she tries to remember that scene. I've got her curious, but I want more. I want her to look at me with the same interest she showed him. I want her to flirt with me.

The clerk finishes ringing me up, and I grab the paper bag full of books and take her arm to propel her out of the fucking store. Taking her here was a mistake—except I don't regret it. I wanted to cheer her up, and now she has a smile on her face. I never care about people's feelings, but I care about hers.

I want her to be happy.

This isn't good.

She can never find out this instinct of mine, or she'll use it against me. And I need to fight those instincts. If I give her a long leash, she'll use it to get into trouble.

I'll have to set her straight. Immediately.

I wait until we're both in the car and speeding away before I put my hand on her knee.

"Let's get one thing straight, Bella. You do not let another man touch you."

She smirks. "If I do, what will you do about it?"

I wait until we're stopped at a red light to turn to her. "Break every bone in his body. Then slit his throat and fuck you in his blood."

She blinks rapidly. *That's right, little bride. There's a hand on the leash.*

Her chest rises and falls. She's so quiet, I wonder if I've gone too far. But then a sweet, musky scent floods the car. She's turned on.

*Fuck me.* The blood roars in my ears.

I put the car in gear and lay on the gas. I need to get her home, now. My cock is throbbing in time with my heartbeat.

If she says anything else, I'll pull over and spank her ass pink. My palm itches, so some thuddy impact will feel good.

She keeps quiet, though. Every so often, I glance over and find she's watching me, her lips parted.

Fuck, I need to stop staring at her mouth. She told me kissing was a hard limit, but now all I can think about is taking her lips. Claiming her. Winding my hand in her hair, pulling her head back, and dominating her mouth with mine. I want to kiss her so much her lips will be perpetually puffy and sore. I wouldn't feel much. My lips would feel weird, numb on hers. But I'd kiss her hard enough to feel something.

I'd touch her pussy at the same time and make her come whenever my lips touched hers. Train her to crave my kiss.

We get to the house, and I park. She twists in her seat, reaching for the books.

"Leave them," I order. "Go to your room and wait for me. On your knees in the middle of the bed, facing the door."

I wait for her sass, but she just gives an unsteady nod. She wants this.

After a moment, she opens her door and slides out. I would be a gentleman and open her door, but I don't trust myself to move. I need to get myself under control first so I don't lose it and break her. And I think she knows it.

"Bella," I call after her. She pauses.

"You will wait for me naked."

She gives me an unsteady nod and slips up the steps and inside her house.

*BELLA*

I'M SHAKING as I hurry up to my room. I poked the bear only to realize the cage holding him is made of paper. And now he's about to come raging toward me.

I'm so freaking excited. I can't wait to see what happens next. Will he punish me? Use the flogger and rope? Is this the training he keeps threatening me with?

I race through the house and burst into my room. He's coming and I want to be ready for him.

I go to the bathroom first to freshen up. My cheeks are flushed, and my eyes are black. I look scary and horny.

On my sink is a new box of samples from one of our bottling companies. They use our botanical blends to make scented lotions. The box was delivered this morning. I picked it up with the morning paper, but I haven't had a chance to open it. I was too distracted by an article about a warehouse fire down by the docks. A building owned by the Saint family. There are no suspects, but I bet it was the Vesuvios. They're always up to no good.

I've noticed some thugs with pentacles tattooed on their cheeks hanging around Three Diner, but I always pretend I don't see them. Kaiser seemed very aware of them, but I'm still playing innocent. I'm not ready to take on the Vesuvio Family.

I have to deal with my intended first.

That's where this box comes in. I rip it open and dig through the samples until I find the perfect one. I want to bathe my skin in a signature scent. One that will always make Kaiser think of me.

Among the pretty samples is a white packet of something that doesn't belong. Hmmm. "How did you get in here?" I hold it up to the light, imagining all the things I could do with it. I don't have time now, but when I do, I could add it to some lotion... later.

For now, I smear a silky cream on my skin, one that smells like lemon and sugar.

By the time Kaiser comes upstairs, I'm waiting in the bed like he asked.

The stairs creak under his weight, and I know he made some noise on purpose to let me know he's coming. I suppress a giggle.

He opens the door and sees me lounging back against the cushions, my copy of *Viking Thunder* in my hand, and I'm still wearing my clothes.

"I told you to kneel."

"Oops." I give him an innocent look. "I forgot." I wish I could ignore him and pretend to find page 269 in my book, but I can't tear my eyes away from him. I'd sooner look away from a crouching panther.

"You love being a brat."

"YOLO."

He prowls around the bed. My heart beats faster at the intention I read in his eyes. First, he plucks the book out of my hands.

"Did you really buy your own copy?" I ask.

He nods. "I broke into your bedroom and marked down your favorite scenes."

What?

He lets the book fall open and shows me the page number—269.

I read a few sentences and remember the scene. "When he dicks her down six times? I asked my online friend Mina, and she said that it's impossible. No man can do it."

He sets the book on my bedside table, holding my eye the entire time. "Challenge accepted."

## 17

B *ella*

HE TAKES my ankle and pulls me down so I'm lying flat on the bed. I squeak.

Inside, I'm screaming in delight. HERE WE GOOOOOOO!

I expect him to rip off my clothes—that's why I didn't strip like he told me to—but he simply rests his hand on my front. Not on my breasts, but higher, at my collarbone. His hand spans almost from shoulder to shoulder, and I relax.

He slides his hand up, collaring my neck with a thumb and forefinger. He pauses there, and I shiver. It's crazy to be so intimate with someone like this. To have them so close to you. Knowing soon they'll be inside you. A thousand books don't do it justice.

He looks thoughtful, too, as if he's deciding what to do with me. I would tell him to hurry up, but... I'm already in trouble. I need to know what I'm in for. All the submissive blogs tell you not to "write checks your ass can't cash."

Kaiser sets his thumb at my mouth and rubs my lower lip. He's staring at my mouth. Does he want to kiss me?

I stare up at him, an ache building between my legs. I feel a pull to him, a yearning, like I'm one half of a magnet drawn to him. I need to move to him, and I won't rest until we fit together.

He's still toying with my mouth. I keep expecting him to thrust his fingers between my lips, silencing me, but he seems fascinated by the shape of my lips. Their softness. He's lost in thought, mesmerized.

I told him no kissing. Now all I can think of is how I'll feel when he breaks that rule.

When he pulls me up by the back of my neck, I feel relief. I love how he manhandles me and tells me what to do. I don't have to think anymore. I don't have to think about the harsh way my father spoke to me. How he'll always judge me.

How awful that makes me feel.

When Kaiser tilts my head and runs his lips down the side of my neck, I'm Delilah, swooning in her lover's arms. I'm as beautiful as a Valkyrie or Luna, the werewolf queen. Tonight I want to lose myself. Be someone desirable and strong, untouched by my raging feelings. Someone worthy of love and attention.

He grips the back of my neck, holding me like a naughty kitten. His hand massages the tense muscles, and it feels amazing. He knows just how to touch me. How does he always know?

He kisses from shoulder to ear, sucking on my skin hard enough to leave a mark. He didn't shave this morning, and the golden bristles on his jaw chafe me in the most delicious way. I'm trembling now, my nipples aching where they press against the bodice of this dress. Emotions move through me, a tidal wave ready to sweep me away. Scary and wonderful. I've always felt things too strongly, but with Kaiser holding me tight, I'll be safe. I can feel everything, and he'll hold me together—or pick up the pieces if I shatter.

His teeth graze my shoulder, and I cry out. He hums deep in his throat, a rumbling growl, and I shudder.

"This is what happens when you tease me," he murmurs against my skin.

"You need to be ready to face the consequences."

*You never think of the consequences—* I banish my father's voice.

"Okay, Daddy," I say, to test it.

Instantly, Kaiser jerks his head up. "No," he says.

My neck feels cold without his mouth on it. "No? You don't like that?"

"No." He's serious. "Don't call me that. I'm not your dad."

"You know I don't mean actual father, right?"

His nostrils flare, and he shakes his head. This is a boundary.

I remember what Father Francis told me today. Kaiser has baggage, some childhood trauma. Maybe something happened to him when he was a kid or to someone he knew. The thought makes my stomach cramp. I swallow against the bile filling the back of my throat.

He's still holding me. He hasn't fully pulled away.

"Okay," I tell him softly, really meaning it so he knows I won't cross that boundary again. He's safe with me. "I'll never say it again."

He nods, an upward kick of his jaw, but I feel it like a heartfelt thank you.

After a moment, he returns to kissing me. He drags his

lips over the wing of my collarbone, and I gasp. My breasts tingle, knowing he's so close to putting his mouth on them. This is my reward for respecting him, and I love it.

It's too much, but I love it. I want him to kiss me forever. It's probably releasing oxytocin and therefore dangerous, but I don't care.

I reach up and push a lock of hair out of his face. Just to touch him. Just to make sure he's real. He doesn't seem to notice I'm touching him.

"Kaiser," I whisper.

A shudder rocks his body. His gaze snaps to mine, predatory. There's nothing human in there. He draws back out of reach and fists his hand in my hair, hard enough to make it sting. I cry out, and it seems to excite him.

"Mine."

He grabs the lapels of my cute little dress and rips it down the front. *Yes!* My limbs jerk as he shreds it further, pulling the pieces of fabric off of me. Then he maneuvers me so I'm lying on my back with my legs off the bed. His hands caress my body. He touches me like he owns me, and in this moment, he does.

"This is what happens when you disobey me," he says.

A frisson of fear runs through me. What is he going to do?

He moves so he's leaning over me, sets his hands on the tops of my thighs, and massages the muscles there. He digs his thumbs into the tender crease. Not enough to hurt, but enough to make me sigh with the tension he's wringing out of my body.

Then he puts his hand on my belly, pulling the skin taut, and licks between my legs.

I try to shoot up off the bed, but he won't let me. He slings my legs over his shoulders, lifting my bottom so I'm helpless to move. I can only watch him fasten his mouth on me. His tongue starts probing right away, tasting me deeply. It's so fucked up, how he's eating me like I taste delicious. His stubble scrapes against my tender skin, but the burn rolls into blissful sensations, making the pleasure more complex. His hand squeezes my bottom, and I stare into his ocean eyes.

Suddenly, I'm laughing. "This is my punishment?"

His eyes narrow. His finger presses between my bottom cheeks. Oh gods, there are nerve endings there I've never felt. It's so wrong. Lighting shoots through me. His tongue lashes my clit.

He pulls away.

"No!"

"You're right." He wipes his mouth and licks the wetness from the back of his hand. "You're enjoying this too much." Oh fuck me.

He leaves the bed to grab supplies from his black bag. The duffel bag of doom.

"I thought we were going to do page 269."

"Later. I need to train you first." He holds up a black matte toy. "Train you to take me."

My whimper must sound frightened because he sits down beside me and pets my thigh. "Easy. I'll make it good for you."

A few minutes later, he has my hands bound in front of me with hot pink rope. He wound rope around my shoulders, too, in a sort of harness that frames my breasts. But that's not as alarming as having my hands tied. I feel so helpless. It makes my heart speed faster.

He lays me back and I test the ropes. There's no give. They're snug.

There's no getting away now.

When I squirm, he swats my thigh. I suck in a breath. It didn't really hurt, just stung me. Surprised me. But I felt a responding pulse in my pussy.

He notices my reaction and slowly moves his hand to check between my legs. *No, no, no.* His eyes flicker when he feels how wet I am.

"Interesting. You liked that."

"No—"

"Shhh." He sets two fingers to my mouth. "No talking now. Thump your fists down three times if you want to safeword." He pushes a ball gag into my mouth and buckles it behind my head. I'm tied up and can't fight him or yell at him.

"I wonder if you'd like a little more." He pinches my nipples, opens the wooden box, and holds up a wicked-looking piece of metal. "Nipple clamps. Let's see how well you take them."

Oh no. Now he's made it into a challenge, and I want to take them for him.

Until he lets one bite my nipple. I jerk a little, grunting behind the gag.

"Really? These are the easiest ones." His voice is so gentle, it's its own form of torture.

He's being mean to me while pretending to be nice to me?

"Meanie," I try to say, but it's muffled by the gag.

He clamps my other nipple.

"Breathe."

I pant through the sting. Okay, it's not so bad. The sting fades, and now my nipples are held as snug as my torso. It's nice.

He prepares a dildo shaped toy, slathering it with lube. Then he nudges the flared head of the toy at my entrance.

Not pressing in yet but testing the boundary.

I tense up.

"Relax. I know you're tight. You've never had anyone play with you here?"

I shake my head. The few teenage boys I met when I was in high school seemed so immature. So disappointing. I tried, but I never felt attracted to them. If I had bothered to fool around, I would've hooked up with a girl.

But I preferred to lie in bed and fantasize about Viking werewolves.

"It's okay, little virgin. I'll be gentle."

The toy vibrates against my clit. He lets it buzz around my opening, awakening the nerve endings there. It feels so good. "You like that?"

I nod.

"Good girl." He's praising me for answering him, and I could come from that alone. He doesn't really punish me. He finds what I like and does it, then asks me to obey and praises me when I do. He's good at this training thing.

It makes me worry about what he has planned for me.

But I'm not worried enough to keep from rocking against the vibrator.

"Should I let you come? Do you think you've earned it?" I use my eyes to plead with him.

"Can you take this? Just a little?" He turns off the vibration and presses the toy into me a centimeter at a time. It slips inside me, stretching me a little, but it's a nice stretch.

"That's it. You take it so well. You're going to take me like this. Soon. Would you like that?"

I nod frantically. He turns the vibration back on. Low at first but building. I shift my hips, feel it rub my inner walls. The toy is hard and slick. Bigger than his fingers. More solid.

Then he adds a finger. It stretches me, adding to the

sensation. I like how warm and real it is, but my eyes are wide, and I'm inhaling hard to deal with the pressure. "Too much? It's okay, little bride. We'll get there."

He rubs my clit, and I want him to turn the vibrator up. Instead, he moves the vibrator down from my pussy, letting it buzz over my skin all the way down towards my rear. It feels weirdly good, but I clench up.

He hums and moves the vibrator back up, while positioning himself so his head is between my legs.

"So sweet." And he starts to eat me out with the vibrator dancing over my clit. His tongue fucks my hole, lashing at the inner walls. I feel him staring at me, but I can't look at him. It's too intense. I'm going to come— He pulls away.

And now I understand why this is punishment. My cunt throbs, screaming for release. I let out a sob behind the gag.

"I don't think you've earned it yet. You didn't do what I said. This is punishment for me, too." He pets my pussy, mesmerized. "I love the way you taste." He leans in again, nipping at my inner thighs. I yelp behind the gag. That hurt! Did he draw blood?

"Look at that. Look at how wet you're getting."

And I moan because he's right. I can feel my channel growing slick, preparing for him.

He makes a growl sound deep in his throat. The next thing I know, pain rocks through me.

He bit me. He actually did it.

My muscles seize. My orgasm is so sudden, huge and overwhelming, the only thing tethering me to earth is the feeling of wet teethmarks on my inner thigh.

Fuck, that hurt. My cry explodes in my throat, stopped up from the gag.

"Did you come, baby?" he asks. He grips my pussy,

squeezing my clit so pain wracks me, followed immediately by a rush of pleasure so intense it sizzles my nerve endings.

"You drive me fucking crazy." He looks at me like he wants to hurt me.

*Yes,* I beg him with my eyes. *Please punish me.*

"You're not supposed to come until I say. We'll have to work on that." He looks absolutely evil.

I nod, my eyes wide.

"You're going to pay for that one." The threat is quiet. Intense. My heart races, and I tense my muscles like I'm going to run. He fixes me with a glare, and I freeze.

"Don't even think about moving."

I look from him to the door and back again. *Come on, Bella, move!* Except if I run, he'll chase me. Catch me. Do terrible things to me...

He puts his hand around my throat. "Calm down."

I blink at him. My pulse slows. He flicks one of my clamped nipples, and I wince but keep my eyes on him.

"That's it. I'm in control. Now stay."

He stands and strips off his shirt, then his jeans, rewarding me.

But when he returns to my side, my heart flutters. He's so much bigger than me. Physically, it doesn't take much to dominate me, and he's a trained fighter who's studied how to destroy people.

"You gonna be good for me?"

I think about it, then shake my head.

His lips quirk. "At least you're honest." He unbuckles the gag. "Ask me to punish you."

What?

I lick my lips.

He seizes a handful of my hair. "Do it."

"Please... punish me." Pleasure pulses in my core when I say it, and I gasp.

He tugs my hair. "Since you asked so nicely..."

He lifts me by the harness, setting me on my feet long enough for him to sit on the bed. He keeps hold of me, though, so my weight barely touches the ground before he's guiding me over his lap. He's careful to position me so my clamped nipples don't brush his thighs. Which I appreciate, but moving jostles the clamps anyway, making me aware of them.

When I'm in position, my tied hands hang down in front of me. My feet touch the floor until he shifts so I'm fully suspended on his lap. Face down, ass up. Classic spanking position.

This was a bad idea.

He rubs my bottom and squeezes the tops of my thighs. It's happening.

He touches my pussy, and I suck in a breath. My clit pulses with need. One touch and I'll go over.

"You're so wet," his voice is filled with wonder. "Your body is getting ready for me." He rubs me with the faintest touches. I kick my feet. If he's not going to make me come, I want him to get on with it.

"No, no. You're not in charge." He keeps touching me until I want to scream. Then he moves his fingers between my ass cheeks and spreads the wetness around my bottom hole.

"Oh no."

"Oh, yes." He's rubbing around my bottom, stimulating the nerve endings there. *Kumquat.* My safeword is on the tip of my tongue.

But I don't say it. He's not even hurting me. It feels good. I just don't want it to.

He chuckles. I don't think I've ever heard him laugh. It's almost worth it to let him finger my asshole to hear it.

I tense my ass cheeks.

"All right, if you're so eager." He smacks his hand down on my bottom, and I'm almost disappointed that it doesn't really hurt. His hand falls with barely any force. He might as well be patting me.

Finally, he smacks me harder, but it's deliberate. His palm thuds down, and I feel a jolt in my pussy. It's nice.

He pauses and strokes between my legs again. I squirm because I want to come. The heat from his palm spreads over my bottom, and I wonder if he could spank me to orgasm.

A crack rings out. He smacked my ass harder. I feel the force before I feel any pain. It's not the worst I've felt, but the surprise, the dominance, and the echoing sting take my breath away.

He's kept a hand between my legs, still playing with my folds. "You're so wet. You love this. You love that I'm in control."

I huff. There's a sick edge to this pleasure. He's stronger and I'm surrendering, but I'm ashamed. It's awful and wonderful at the same time.

He spanks me again, hard enough to jar me forward, making the nipple clamps swing.

"Fuck," I whisper. His hand slaps down a few more times, and it hurts, but he keeps stroking me. The pain makes the pleasure sharper. More intense.

I'm losing it. I'm not in control. I strain to get my feet to the floor, but he holds me up, off balance, suspended over him.

A few more slaps and my ass is hot. He's still touching me. I'm going to come like this. From the resounding thud and the answering response in my core. My mouth opens with a cry—

He pulls me up and sets me on his leg so I'm straddling it. The ridge of his muscle hits my clit. I see stars.

"Rub yourself on me. That's it."

I try to rock on him, but I can't. My feet don't touch the floor.

He bounces his knee, and I cry out. My breasts are small, but the force is enough to make them bounce, and I feel the nipple clamps all over again.

I feel like I'm on a cliff, teetering on the brink of orgasm, and this force is pushing me closer to the edge. I'm fighting it, but I'm losing my grip.

I prop myself up with my bound hands and roll my hips.

"Yes, that's it." His blue eyes darken. He bounces his leg again, and tears spark in my eyes.

He slaps my right breast, and the shock of it almost sends me over. "Do it, beautiful. Ride me." He slaps my left breast, jolting the nipple clamp.

"This is your punishment." He bares his teeth, pulling my hair as he slaps my breasts. "For teasing me. Tempting me. Trying to poison me. You deserve this." Another sharp smack. "Say it."

"I deserve to be punished." The words feel like daggers ripping into me. And the pleasure rising feels just as savage.

He grips my neck, glaring at me like he wants to kill me. "You wanted to come so badly, do it. Do it."

"No—" I'm panting, because I'm afraid of my orgasm. "It's too soon—"

"It's not too soon if I want it. Because I'm in charge, little bride. So do it. Do it now." He bounces his knee. My pussy slams into his hard muscle, and it shoves me off the cliff. I come, thrashing. I'm out of control, and I hate it. I fought until the end, and it was no use. The pleasure obliterates me.

He watches me come, a hungry look on his face. Like he's drinking in my reactions. Feeling the pleasure through me.

And suddenly, it's too much. The intensity, his intention. His hand on my back, gently stroking me. Bringing me down, grounding me.

I shut my eyes, shut him out, but I don't want him to look at me. I turn my head, unable to hold back the swell of emotion. My jaw tightens, and then my muscles aren't under my control. I'm shaking, and tears are leaking down my face.

**18**

———————

B*ella*

"I'M SORRY," I sniffle. Kaiser's quick to move, releasing the ropes that bind my arms behind me. As soon as my hands are free, I swipe at my face, feeling frantic.

What guy wants to watch their sex partner fall apart?

I try to clench my teeth, get myself back together, but the water is rising. The more I fight it, the more it pulls me under.

"Shit." Ugh, I'm a mess. I don't want this. I try to climb off him, but he stops me.

"It's okay." Kaiser's soft breath hits my face. His hand comes to the back of my neck, squeezing in that way he does. Grounding me.

It's too much compassion.

I twist, turning away as much as I can while sitting on him. My sex and nipples ache, but that's not why I'm crying.

I shake my head so my hair covers my face. The locks soak up the salt water.

"Shhh, don't hide from me." He strokes the wet strands away from my face. "I want your tears."

It's so surprising, I open my eyes to his stormy eyes inches from mine.

"It's okay," he says again, kneading my tense muscles. "This is a release."

"It's too much," I whisper.

"No." He grips the back of my neck and presses his fore-head against mine. "I want it all."

I gasp. The sobs are coming, surging. Hecate, help me, I can't breathe.

I'm caught in the wave, drowning. Dragged along, ground against the ocean floor.

He presses me against him, holding me as I cry until I heave. He's not leaving, he's getting closer, I realize when my thoughts surface again. He's not afraid.

I go back under. Emotion grips my throat until I can't breathe. I shake against him but not for long.

And then it's gone as if it's never been. Leaving me with the wreckage.

Kaiser is still here, petting me.

I feel empty.

"Better?" he asks.

I lick my lips. The tsunami came. It surged through me and left me gasping in the wreckage, but now it's gone. I feel empty. It's a welcome feeling.

"Yeah. Sorry."

"Don't be sorry." He's still rubbing my neck and shoul-ders. Squeezing hard the way I like. It feels good, a sensation to fill the space the sadness left.

"I don't usually cry like that."

"Maybe you should."

I shake my head. I don't like to cry. I cried a lot after my mom died and my dad explained she wasn't coming back. I had intense, stormy tantrums, screaming for her, and my dad didn't know how to handle them. He'd shut down, and my tears only sent him away. I remember him closing the door, shutting me in my room alone. I screamed "Mama" until I passed out on the floor.

Eventually, he hired a stern nanny who told me I needed to be good. I learned that Mama wasn't coming and needed to keep the tears to myself.

Kaiser is still stroking my hair. I can't look him in the eye.

"I'm a lot to take," I say.

"I can take it." He means it, I know this. He's not running out of the room. He didn't let me run away, either. Maybe he really does want it all. "Your father upset you."

I press my lips together. My father can't get through a family dinner without expressing his disapproval of me. I've gotten better at keeping my cool, letting his words roll off me, but today...

He's leaving me alone. Locking me in this marriage. Now that I think of it, he's probably been counting down the days until I was eighteen to do this. Marry me off, make me someone else's problem.

"He doesn't want to talk to me."

"I'm sure that's not true."

"You don't know him like I do." If I could turn myself into a doll—pretty, pliant, quiet, and obedient—my father would be thrilled. I'd finally get his approval.

"He's too hard on you." Kaiser frowns.

It's nice that he cares.

"He has high standards."

"He should be proud of you."

"You should tell him that," I tease, smiling at the ridiculous thought of Kaiser storming into my father's office to dress him down. The mafia man defending me to my own father.

"I will."

Oh no. His muscles tense under me, like he's about to hunt him down right now. He's serious. "No, don't. Don't say anything, please," I beg, horrified that he would actually do it. "Promise me." I lift my hands to his face, but he grabs my wrist, stopping me from touching him. He moves so fast, I didn't see his hands. I freeze.

He doesn't like to be touched. I knew this.

But he relaxes and brings my fingers closer until they brush over his jaw. His lips. I shouldn't like it, but I do. I stretch my fingers, touching as much as I can, greedy to feel the shape of his perfect cheekbones, the prickle of his stubble on my fingertips.

For a second, I forget what I was saying. Then I remember that I need to keep him away from my father.

"He says I have to get married to you," I say. "That's what we argued about." Reminding him that he and I are on opposite sides of that argument.

"He should still be kinder to you."

"You can't confront him just for hurting my feelings." That won't end well. "Don't hurt my father. Promise me."

But he can't promise. Because if Fraternitas gives him the order, then my father is dead. And probably so am I, for that matter.

Kaiser isn't a comfort. He's a sword hanging over us. Nothing more. And here I am, crying on his shoulder. Some supervillain I'm turning out to be.

It's all part of my master plan, I tell myself. I wanted to get him to let his guard down.

But I don't feel very clever or powerful. I feel weak and miserable.

"I'm cold," I say, even though I'm just numb. I rub my arms to sell it, but when he studies me with those too-wise eyes, I don't think I'm really hiding anything.

*KAISER*

WHEN BELLA STARTED CRYING, I wanted to destroy things. I knew she was overstimulated, that the tears leaking down her cheeks were a release.

But I still wanted to hurt someone for doing this to her. Her father.

She looks at me with real fear that I might storm out of here and shake him down. Because of course she's afraid of that. I'm the bad guy.

And I'm the reason she's crying. The scene was intense. I lost control of the predator in me and wanted to punish her for the way she drives me to obsess over her. For the way my skin has been tingling nonstop in her presence.

Bella is my responsibility now. She's not in control; I am. I need to take care of her because she thinks she has no limits. I need to set the boundaries that she won't.

Usually, I love the sight of a fucktoy's tears, but not these. My cock is hard because I'm with her, but I have no desire to fuck her right now. Pain slices through me. It feels like someone slashed me with a knife, but it hurts much worse. I know it's all in my head, but it doesn't help.

I want to stab myself for hurting her. It's a strange feeling, all my violence turning inward. How can someone so small have such power over me?

"Let's go to bed," I say, and she sighs, curling into me. She's still in the harness, but she doesn't seem to notice it.

I find her wrists and rub the red marks there. I'm a piece of shit. I kiss each fingertip. "You did well tonight. You're good, so good for me."

She huffs like she doesn't believe me.

"You are. It's my fault it got too intense. I pushed too hard and got carried away."

"You didn't—"

"I did. But you did so good for me."

"Really?" She sounds so lost, it's breaking my heart. I rub her back.

"Really. And it's okay to cry. It's a release."

She sniffles. I ease her up and unwind the rope harness. I massage her marked skin for a moment and lie back so I can pull her over me. She sighs, settling her weight on me. I can't feel anything, my skin is still weirdly numb like I'm wearing a layer of armor or latex, but the weight of her body is perfection. I love how she curls into me, pressing her face into my chest. It's as close to heaven as I'll ever be.

My dick is poking into her, but I ignore it. This isn't about me. It's about her. I run a hand up her back, finding the rope patterns and rubbing to smooth them out.

"It was intense," she admits.

I stroke her hair, encouraging her to talk. Sometimes I mute her so she gets out of her own head. But right now she needs to process.

It was intense. Too intense. I need to remember she's still new to all this. But she's so eager to learn.

"You had a long day." Our first full day together. The first of many.

She wipes her eyes one last time and finally meets my

gaze. Her eyes are red, but she looks so innocent, and I want to kiss her mouth.

I brush back her hair instead. The platinum color illuminates her face. She doesn't dye her eyebrows, and the contrast between them and the white blonde at her hairline is stunning. It calls attention to her dark eyes.

So much emotion. So much expression. I can read her moods; they're fast and changeable. Intense like storms.

And never boring. I could study her forever and not get tired of it.

She lets her head drop, going limp against me. I love moments like this, when she's calm in that way she gets when she comes. I feel like a hero, even though I know I'm the monster in her story.

"Father Francis told me you have questions about me." Open up, earn her trust.

Her lip quirks in a half-frown. She's learning that the priest didn't keep her confidence and that he's loyal to Fraternitas.

"He said you grew up on the streets. With your twin brother."

I nod.

"Is that why you trained as a fighter? To escape?"

"I didn't want to be a fighter. Fighting was the only way to survive. And I ended up being good at it. I had to be."

"When did you start?"

Memories swirl in my mind. Leviathans in the deep. "Thirteen."

"No way," she gasps. "That's so young."

I don't say anything; I'm lost in shadowy memories. Running away with my brother, living on the streets. Finding the underground tunnels where it was warm enough for us to survive the winter. Father Francis feeding us, teaching us. After a few years of that, Jaeger wanted to move into the dorm, but I refused. I was the reason we were hanging around the street fights long enough for Maestro to notice us. I wanted to find a way off the streets without Father Francis' help. I didn't trust him.

It was almost our downfall.

"Hey," she says, her hand hovering close to my face, ready to touch me to bring me back. "You survived."

Barely, but I don't tell her that. I'm not ready to share that much with her.

I stroke the side of her neck. It's red from where my stubble scraped her, the bristles harsh on her skin. I should be sorry that I rubbed her raw.

I'm not sorry. I want to leave my mark on her. But I am sorry that she's so upset. That I'm the brute she has to marry.

But maybe I can be good for her. Be what she needs. Today, her father was cruel to her. Argos sent me a recording of their call that I listened to after I sent Bella to the bedroom. He didn't say anything I haven't thought of myself, but the way he said it... I could kill the Poisoner for the way he spoke to her.

But killing my future father-in-law is not the solution. Killing is all I'm good at, but for her, I can be better.

She needs care and protection. Someone in her corner. A champion.

I want to be that for her. A rock in the storm. A fortress.

A husband who doesn't let anyone fuck with his wife.

I shift her to the side so she's lying in the crook of my arm.

She yawns, her eyes fluttering. "I'm so tired."

"Sleep." I tug the blanket free so I can cover her with it.

She hums and looks down at my crotch. "What about

you?" She's wondering whether I need to come. My cock strains painfully under her attention.

I ignore it and brush a kiss on her brow. I imagine taking her hand, guiding it to touch my cock. I wouldn't feel much from her touch, but the pressure would still feel amazing. A few strokes and I'd come all over both of us.

I file the fantasy away for later. I don't let anyone touch me. Bella's different, yes, but I still can't let her touch me. She's dangerous enough as it is.

I'll wait until she's passed out and jack off in the bathroom. Possibly a couple of times. I'll have to, or I'll be awake all night. "I'm fine. Go to sleep."

I lie next to her a long time after her eyes close, just watching her sleep.

**19**

———

B *ella*

Friday, as promised, Kaiser drops me off on campus. "Be good," he orders.

"Of course!" I trill and give a reassuring smile. He narrows his eyes at me. He knows I can't be trusted.

Our relationship has moved into new territory, but the fundamentals are still the same. Great orgasms can't make me forget that he's in control. He's a threat to my freedom and my father, and one day, I will destroy him and everything he loves.

I can feel him watching me as I bounce away. And I like the attention. It's flattering and comforting. Fuck me, I love it.

I think I'll miss it when it's gone.

It's good I'm getting a break from him tonight. I need to

remember my priorities. Kaiser is a stepping stone on my way to becoming a supervillain. If I were Lucrezia Borgia, I would've already sprinkled cantarella on his steak.

The bell starts tolling the hour as I make my way toward Honey's dorm.

For some reason, she's not on the main quad with the regular students. Or on "Blood Quad," the one reserved for the members of the Houses—usually direct descendants of the founding mafia families. No, they stuck her all the way back on campus. I follow a winding path past the labyrinth and through the fields until I reach a grand set of iron gates decorated with statues of griffins. Once I'm within the walls, I walk down a dark road lined with trees and iron streetlamps that look like something out of another time.

What the fuck is this place?

I keep walking and finally come to my destination.

"Holy Hecate." I stare up at the gloomy mansion. It's huge and striking with red brick and black trim. And it looks abandoned. The front lawn is a tattered mess of brambles, and there's an empty fountain and a creepy statue half-covered in ivy. Trees and overgrown bushes crowd the sides of the structure, and more vines cover half the building, like the forest is trying to pull the castle-like place back into itself.

Even the air feels oppressive. It reminds me of the grave-yard behind my orchard—even the statues and dragon-like gargoyles match.

The door opens, and Honey comes out to the stoop, waving to me. I walk slowly toward her, feeling reluctant to approach. The porch is covered with cobwebs. We could host a haunted house here for Halloween and not even need to decorate.

"What's up with this place? Are we in an episode of *Vampire Varsity* right now?"

She giggles. "I know, right? The witch's coven meets at midnight." She waves a dramatic hand toward the turret. She's wearing a green velvet robe that pools past her bare feet, and her hair is tousled. I've never seen her in anything but preppy clothes, looking perfectly put together. She looks younger.

"What are you wearing?"

"Do you like it?" She poses.

"It looks like a costume for a play."

"Raine said the same thing. Shakespeare or something. C'mon, there's a whole wardrobe like this. We can play dress up."

"Yes! I can make flower crowns." I drag my suitcase up the creaky wooden steps.

"What did you bring? You're only staying one night."

"I know. I brought supplies. Is Raine already here?"

"Yeah, she got done with her shift at the library early."

"Welcome to my humble home." She sweeps her arms out, and I catch my breath. In the golden light, framed by the heavy wooden door, Honey looks like a vision. A pagan priestess. A medieval queen.

"Wait, you have to tell me what this place is." The door creaks as she opens it. There's grimy stained glass on either side of the door depicting vines and roses. I spot some familiar imagery: a pentacle, cup, sword, and serpent are hidden in the center of the roses, and a bull, knight, and fire-breathing dragon-snake are rampaging over the door.

"I don't know. It's a mystery."

"There are gargoyles on the roof." They look like ivy-covered lumps, but I bet they're griffins to match the gates. "And a turret."

"You want to see the tower? There's an amazing view of the labyrinth."

"Hecate help us," I murmur and drag my suitcase over the warped wooden floorboards.

Honey gives me a mini tour. As old houses go, it has good bones, but it definitely needs renovation. The front foyer and grand staircase are gorgeous and pretty clean, but we pass whole rooms full of ghostly-looking furniture draped in white sheets. Every room has high ceilings and elaborate molding. Giant paintings cover the walls, half covered in dusty drop cloths. Dark and forbidding landscapes in elaborate gilt frames. Portraits of people long dead, the faces glaring down at us.

It's the creepiest fucking thing I've ever seen. Honey seems to know her way around, though. I keep stepping in spots that make the floor creak and groan, but she avoids every one.

"Wait, I thought this was a dorm," I say.

"It is. This is on original university property. I checked the records."

"But you're the only one here?"

"Yep. Lucky me." She shrugs in a way that makes me think she doesn't feel lucky.

I can't imagine living in this giant house all alone. It sounds like something out of a horror movie. "How do you sleep at night?"

She just sighs.

We come to a drawing room with a huge fireplace. Honey's placed tons of candles behind the grate, and the effect is almost cozy. The scent of cedar and lemony furniture polish covers up the musty old-house smell. An ancient mirror hangs over the mantle, tarnished in a way that wigs me right out.

"Is this place haunted?" I ask.

"Definitely yes." Raine pops her head up from behind the couch. She's made herself a nest of blankets on the ancient Turkish-style rug. We exchange greetings.

"We should probably do sleepovers here more often," Raine says to Honey. "Keep you company."

I glance up at the creepy mirror. The smudges make me feel like shadowy figures are lurking in the back of the room. I'm about to whisper, "YOLO," when a bit of movement in the mirror makes me jump.

"What is it?"

"Nothing." Because there is nothing there. "I thought I saw a spider." But it was probably a ghost.

"Oh gods." Raine starts twitching.

"It's okay, it was nothing." I try to soothe her.

"Yeah, the spiders are practically my roommates," Honey says. We stare at her in horror. "I mean, I won't let them get you. Um, I'm glad you guys are here?" She smiles weakly.

Hecate, help us.

I wheel my suitcase over to Raine and start unpacking. "I've got snacks." I toss bags of candy on the big leather Chesterfield.

"What's this?" Honey points to a black box with gilt detailing.

"Beauty samples. Lotion, moisturizer, perfumes," I list off as I pull the bottles out of the box.

"Ooooh!" Honey's eyes light up. I knew she'd love this. Both she and Raine love makeup products. They promised to help teach me how to do a smoky eye.

"*Aqua Tofana*?" Raine asks, holding up a green glass vial. "Wasn't that a poison women used to kill their abusive husbands?"

I grin. "Just my idea of a little joke. I love that you got the reference." Raine is really well-read.

"I want to hear the story," Honey says.

Raine tells her about Giulia Tofana, the early 17th-century poisoner who sold a mixture of arsenic and belladonna to her clients.

"She was a supervillain," I say. "I want to be like her when I grow up."

"She wasn't a villain," Raine says. "She helped women escape their abusive husbands. There was no divorce in Italy. The systems were unjust, and she just balanced the scales."

"Yeah, some men are just asking to be poisoned." I think of the Vesuvio brothers.

"So wait, did you create these?" Honey asks, sifting her hand through the samples.

"Most of them. A few are just random extras the company must have added by accident. Like this." I pluck out a small white packet that I noticed when I first opened the box. It's actually a sample of oxytocin-based fertilizer. Papa and I have been experimenting with using oxytocin to stimulate plant growth. "Don't know how that got in here. But everything else is fair game. Help yourself."

They pick through the box. It's early in the night, but I figure it's as good a time as any to share my life update.

"So, I have news. I'm getting married."

"What?" Honey and Raine say in unison.

"Yeah. It's a long story." I hold up the box mix I brought. "Can I tell it to you while we make brownies?"

"Yes!" Honey jumps up and leads us to the kitchen. It's a long, low-ceilinged room with a stone floor and pistachio colored appliances.

"Do you want normal brownies or fun brownies?" I ask.

Raine narrows her eyes. "What does that mean?"

"My father owns lots and lots of farms. And greenhouses. We grow all sorts of plants."

"Oh," Honey says.

"So... weed." Raine shrugs. "I'm down."

I pull out my container of special butter. "YOLO."

**20**

---

S *leepover 5:49 pm*

THE BROWNIES ARE in the oven, and Honey is making popcorn on the stove.

"So you're seriously getting married," she says, shaking her head like she can't believe it.

"My father says I have to do it. He's in trouble. Everyone thinks he poisoned some mafia don. It's a whole thing." I wave my hand.

"Who do they think he poisoned?" Raine asks.

"His name is something cheesy... Alfredo." I snap my fingers.

"Alfredo Vesuvio?" Honey glances at Raine. "Son of Dominus Vesuvio?"

"Yeah, that's him."

Honey keeps looking at Raine, biting her lip.

"I need chocolate," Raine mutters.

Honey takes the popcorn off the stove, marches to the pantry, and returns with a basket full of candy bars.

"What?" I'm missing something. "What is it?"

"Raine's from the Vesuvio family," Honey tells me.

"Wait, really?" I lean in so fast I almost knock the candy basket off the island. *Cool, Bella, be cool.* But I can't keep the interest out of my voice when I ask, "You're a Vesuvio?"

Raine groans. "I'm not. I mean, I am, but not really. Veronica—that's my mom—was a rebel and pretty much an outcast. Dominus is her uncle."

"Dominus?" Tingles run down my arms when I hear his name.

"He's the head of the Vesuvio family. Big, bad mafia don," Honey explains as if I don't know who he already is. I don't say anything. As far as everyone's concerned, I need to be a clueless schoolgirl and a pawn in the game between my father, Fraternitas, and the Vesuvios.

"He's the worst," Raine confirms. "My mom tried to escape the family when she was younger. Ran off, had me. She got lucky; Dominus never recognized her as part of the family. Then her luck ran out."

I make sympathetic noises, my mind whirling. "What happened?"

"Dominus sent some men to get Veronica and bring her back into the fold so he could marry her off to secure an alliance."

"Your mom had an arranged marriage?"

"Yeah. Dominus made an alliance with the Saint family and made her marry my stepfather, Calix Saint. And then shit went sideways... It's actually kind of a cluster right now. But long story short, I'm not really a Vesuvio anymore. I'm considered a Saint now." She sighs and lifts the silver chain she's wearing around her neck. It has a small charm in the shape of a cup or chalice, decorated with blue stones. Silver and blue, the colors of the Saint family.

We're learning about this in our orientation classes. The Saints were one of the four families that helped found the university. I'm wracking my brain, trying to remember more about them, when Honey says to Raine, "So you could live on Blood Quad."

"No, thank you. My stepbrother won't allow it. Even if he did, I wouldn't want to." Raine shudders. "I don't want anything to do with the Houses." She's still fiddling with the cup charm on the end of her necklace. Both Honey and I stay quiet. We all know that, as the daughter of two different Houses, Raine is already involved as much as anyone can be.

"Remind me who the families are again?" I say. "And which House is which? I just remember the bull and snakes or whatever."

"The Bulls, the Swords, the Saints, and the Serpents," Honey rattles off. "Those are the Houses. The Bulls are led by Dominus Vesuvio and the Vesuvio family. The head of the Swords is Royal Regis. Then there are the Saints led by..." She hesitates and looks at Raine.

"It's in transition," Raine says. "TBD."

"And the Serpents are led by the Serpente family," Honey says.

"Right, right, that one's easy," I say. The four families have their crests and insignias all over campus. Stained glass, tapestries, statues, and artwork depicting bulls, swords, chalices, and snakes—anywhere they can stick a symbol. "What about you, Raine? Are you in danger of being married off?

"Nah, my stepbrother would never allow that to happen. That's one good thing. He's protective." Her face turns dark as it always does when she mentions her stepbrother. "Let's talk about something else."

I want to ask more about the Vesuvios, but I don't want to be too obvious about it. Besides, Raine isn't in their House anymore, and it doesn't sound like she was close to any of them before. Once the fall semester starts and more students are on campus, I'll be able to get more intel on the Bulls.

I'm still a supervillain-in-training, and besides, I have to deal with Fraternitas first.

"Wanna see my future husband?" I pull out my copy of *Viking Thunder*.

"Tada!"

Honey and Raine stare at the cover.

"Oh, wow," Honey says.

"So... he's a cover model?" Raine asks. "For romance novels?"

"No, he wouldn't let me take a picture, so this is the next best thing. He looks like this, just with more tattoos. And less bulky, more... buff. Hard." I realize I've zoned out imagining Kaiser's abs, and stop before I begin drooling. "I mean, so many muscles. It's... gross."

"Yeah, so gross," Raine deadpans.

"Shut up."

She smirks. "Congratulations."

"Thanks. It still sucks. I'm trying to get out of it, but..." I shrug. "We'll see."

"What's his name?" Honey asks. She's got that thoughtful look on her face, again, like she's worried about me.

"Kaiser."

She sighs, like she already knew. "He's the scary twin."

"Wait, he's a twin?" Raine grabs my book and takes another look.

"Yup. You want to meet him?" I tease. "We can have a double wedding."

"My stepbrother would lose his shit," she says with an evil smile.

"Jaeger's taken, actually," Honey says.

"That's fine," Raine says with a wave of her hand. "I've got enough scary ass men in my life."

"So, Kaiser's the scary twin?" I ask.

"Everyone in Fraternitas is brutal in their own way. But some of them can be nice. Sort of." Honey explains to Raine that she worked at a club run by Fraternitas.

"Did you ever date any of them when you were there?" I ask.

"They don't date," Honey says. "They stake their claim." I suppress a shiver, imagining Kaiser claiming me. "And no, they never were interested in me."

"Did you want them to be?" I ask. I'm not judging, just curious, but she flushes, which gives me my answer.

"I had a boyfriend at the time anyway," Honey says, "so it doesn't matter. We're not talking about this. My life isn't as interesting as yours."

"Agree to disagree. Next sleepover, we're diving into your guys' lives. But tonight, I need all the help with Fraternitas I can get." I tell them about my bullshit marriage counseling session with the "hot priest," as Honey calls him. "I asked Kaiser when he started fighting, and he said thirteen."

"That can't be right," Raine whispers.

"I think it is," Honey says. "They were super young. I heard that they were in the underground fighting rings.

They were champions. Rumor is they killed their own trainer." She shakes her head. "But I don't know."

I frown. I'm greedy for more information about Kaiser,
but I don't think anyone has the full story except him. "Do
you know if he still fights?"

"Not that I know of, but that's how Fraternitas started. In
the underground gambling and fighting rings. They ran the
books and also made money from their own bets on the
side. St. James was the mastermind behind it. He's a genius."

"How old were they?"

"Just kids. Teenagers. But now they have their hands in
everything. They used to use the tunnels under New Rome
to run guns. Then they took over the city. Assassinated the
dons, slaughtered the soldiers. There were whole gangs
wiped off the streets."

I suppress a little wriggle. My friends won't appreciate
that I'm perving on my soon-to-be husband while hearing
about how he and his friends went on a murder spree
through the city.

"They have a place under the city where they go. They
call it the Abyss. They take their victims down there to
torture them and then dispose of their remains. They own
the underground. It's the source of their power from when
they were street kids, running free under the city."

"How do you know so much about this?" Raine asks.

"When I worked for them, I heard things. I kept my head
down and my mouth shut. Wherever I am, I try to blend in.
It's safer that way." Honey gives us a warning look. "None of
this can leave this room."

"What happens at sleepover, stays at sleepover," I vow,
and Raine nods.

"They were always gentlemen to me," Honey says. "Lucy
runs the club, and they respect her. She wears a ring, so she's

their equal. After shifts, she would send us home with an escort. Mine would drive me home and drop me off right at my door. He never tried anything." She looks almost disappointed. "Not once. But maybe it was just me."

She's doing that thing again where she's down on herself. I think maybe an ex-boyfriend was one of those shitty people who tear people down to feel strong. The thing is, he's gone, but she still believes his lies. And apparently, none of the Fraternitas members ever took an interest in her, which I don't believe, but what matters is that she's making up stories of rejection and using them to beat herself up.

"Honey," I say. "Listen to me carefully. You are the hottest person I've ever seen. If you were my type, I would fuck you in a heartbeat."

"I think that's a compliment," Raine says dryly.

"Thank you." Honey's blushing again, which only makes her look more beautiful.

"Damn it. You want to know the worst thing about this arranged marriage? Kaiser is exactly my type." I hold up *Viking Thunder*. "I'm such a cliche."

"We can't change who we're attracted to," Raine says glumly. "Even if we wish we could."

"Maybe you'll like being married to him," Honey suggests with a wistful smile. She's so sweet, of course, she'd wish for a happy ending for me.

"Whatever. I'll think about it tomorrow. Right now, I have brownies and butter popcorn. I feel no pain." I grab the brownie pan and make a selection.

"Should you be taking more edibles?" Raine asks.

"YOLO!" I cram the brownie into my mouth. "It doesn't usually affect me, but let's do makeup before it hits."

We decamp to Honey's glorious bathroom, where Honey sets me up on the counter and starts brushing stuff all over my face. I'm wired. Honey keeps having to ask me to hold still. I want to hear more about Kaiser.

"Did you ever talk to him?" I ask while she frowns at my face, holding up different makeup palettes to compare shades.

"I never got near him, but he always seemed like he was in a bad mood. Or when he was a little more chill, I always got the sense it was because he just murdered someone."

I can't help it. I let out a giggle. "That's him."

Raine calls from inside the clawfoot tub where she's lying, eating popcorn. "Have you already...?"

"Done it?" I ask.

Honey laughs. "I swear, Bella, you say things people haven't said in twenty years."

"What should I say?"

"Made the beast with two backs," Raine suggests.

"Okay, Shakespeare." Honey's getting more giggly. The weed's hitting.

"Yeah," I say. "Now who's dropping references that are two hundred years old?"

"More like four hundred years. But it's classic," Raine throws popcorn at both of us.

"So you do like him," Honey says.

"I like it when he touches me."

"Awww," Honey says as Raine hoots.

"I think I like it too much." I frown at my reflection. "When I'm with him, I kind of lose my mind."

"I'm not seeing a problem here," Raine says.

"I get it." Honey brushes blush onto my cheeks. "You want to be smart."

"Yeah. He makes me dumb."

"YOLO," Raine says and tosses popcorn in the air to try

and catch it in her mouth. It rains down on her, falling in her hair and bouncing off her face. "Oops."

"Does he like you back?" Honey asks. "Do you know if he's going to claim you?"

"Claim me?"

"Fraternitas has all sorts of rituals, and one of them is claiming an *elita*. Elita means 'chosen one.' It's different from a marriage. For them, it's more intense."

"Kaiser hasn't said anything about that." My chest is tight. Will he claim me? Do I want him to? I feel disappointed that he hasn't even mentioned it.

"I don't know the exact details, but I do know when they claim a chosen one, it's them claiming ownership and vowing to protect you with their life. It's like their vow to Fraternitas. It's all about loyalty." She tells us about a few *elitas* she knew from the club. "Kaiser's brother claimed my friend Elodie last fall. They have some sort of ceremony that's secret, for Fraternitas only, but maybe once you're married, she'll tell you about it."

"Okay." This is overwhelming. I want to know more, but I'm also worried about what I'll discover.

"You can also get Kaiser to take you to Pandemonium," Honey says. "It's a wild party at Club Empire, the sex club they run in New Rome. If there's a claiming ceremony, it'll be on that night. Then you can ask him about it."

"Sex club?" Raine sits up, sending popcorn flying every which way. "I want to go."

"Maybe we can all go," I say. "I'll get Kaiser to take me and see if you can come as guests."

"We might have to sneak in," Honey says. She glances at Raine.

"Three, two, one," I count down and we all shout, "YOLO!"

. . .

*SLEEPOVER 8:12 pm*

WE WATCH the sunset from the tower, dressed in costumes we found in a closet.

"It's so beautiful." Honey eats a handful of popcorn and sniffles. She's got on vivid mermaid makeup that actually looks amazing, except now it's a little smeared. "I'm crying because I'm so happy." She giggles through her tears.

"Amateur," Raine smiles. She's only gotten more mellow. "Hey, is that a graveyard?" She's looking out back into the forest.

I'm looking the opposite way, toward the official university campus. Across the field in front of Honey's house-dorm lies the labyrinth, and from this vantage point, I can see the pentacle design hidden at its center. Beyond the boxwood hedges rises the dome of the conservatory and the stone buildings on the quads.

"I'm the king of the world!" I scream, pumping my fists into the air. I'm wearing a bear robe, the kind that has the head still attached. Both Honey and Raine declared it creepy, but I don't care.

"Are you even high?" Raine asks me.

"No. I'm just like this."

"I'm so glad I know you," Honey coos, laying her head on my shoulder. I tell her I love her, and we cuddle until the bear head flops on her and she freaks out.

*SLEEPOVER 11:29 pm*

. . .

"Do the thing!" I shout. We're back in the drawing room.

"I don't want to do the thing," Raine says.

"You're so good at it!" Honey encourages. She's stretched out on the couch, playing with the curls on her terrible wig.

"I'm not good at it," Raise protests while lying on the bear rug I found.

"Do it, do it," I chant. "Do it for the plot!"

She grimaces. "Fine." She juts out her chin, lowers her voice and mimics an old-school Italian gangster. "Just when you think you're out, they pull you back in."

"Yes!" Honey screams.

"More elderberry wine?" I hold up the bottle we found in the dusty cellars.

"More wine!"

I fill their mugs. A little slops on the ancient rug, but it's okay. The rug is red and brown and hides a multitude of sins. Any stain becomes part of the pattern. "I've been thinking," I say. "Do you want to form an alliance?"

"What?"

"We should join forces, have each other's backs."

"You're so pretty," Raine murmurs to the bear head.

"I'm in," Honey says. "We need to stick together."

"Fine."

"Excellent. What shall we call ourselves?"

"The Villains," I say.

"The Villainesses," Honey corrects. "Raine, what do you think?"

It takes a moment to explain things to Raine, but once she gets it, she holds up a finger. "I know. I know. How about The Villaini? Gender neutral term."

"That is actually brilliant." I raise a toast to her.

"I don't know, guys," Honey says. She's added glitter to her mermaid look, and now it's everywhere. "I don't think

I'm cut out to be a villainess." She turns to Raine. "You're smart." She points to me. "You're named after a poison."

"And she's obviously psychotic," Raine puts in.

"Thank you." I give a little bow.

"What can I do? I'm only good with hair and makeup."

"That's not true—" Raine starts to protest.

First rule of friendship: support your friend.

I lean in and get Honey's attention. "Did you know there are bees that feed exclusively on the pollen of a type of rhododendron? The honey they make is poisonous."

"I read about this," Raine says. "There was a thing with the Roman soldiers…"

"They ate the honey and it incapacitated the army," I fill it. "For weeks."

"Yes! Murder honey!" Raine pumps her fist into the air.

"Murder honey! Yeah!" I cheer with her.

"So?" Honey says.

"So, Supervillain Rule #1: Your best offense is a good disguise. You're sweet and gentle, Honey. No one would suspect you of anything. Just saying."

She ponders this.

Raine speaks up. "Did you know, in medieval France, some women would poison their husbands all the time? No, really. They'd poison them in the morning." She points her finger and stares at it like she's zoned out and lost her train of thought. She's feeling the weed.

"And?" I prompt.

"And give them the antidote when they came home. Kept them faithful."

"Now that's what I'm talking about." I fist-bump her.

"I almost feel sorry for Kaiser," Honey says.

"Don't. He can handle himself."

"But he doesn't have to." Raine hugs the bear's head. "Because now he has you to handle him."

"Good job, and that's right," I say, because she worked hard on that delivery, and dirty jokes should be encouraged. "I can definitely handle him. A little poison goes a long way."

"Do it for the plot," Honey says.

**21**

---

# B ella

AT DAWN, my eyes ping open.

There's a chill in the air, and I'm grateful for the big black blanket I have covering me. All the white candles in the fireplace are out, burned down.

Raine's on the floor, still snuggling with the bear's head. Honey's asleep in the big armchair. I took the couch, and the springs weren't so great on my back. No wonder I'm awake.

Then again, no matter how late I fall asleep, I tend to wake up early. I love the quiet hours before the sun rises.

I get up and wrap myself in the blanket, which turns out to be a robe of some sort. I put it on and sneak out of the drawing room, tiptoing over the creaky floorboards and down the hall toward the grand staircase in the front of the house. I find a window and look out over the fields. This early, with the light glinting on the dew on the long grasses, reminds me of mornings at our family farm. My mother liked to stay up late reading or painting, and then sleep in. My father and I liked to rise early. "You keep farmer's hours," Mom always said. Those were the happy days before we lost her.

I sink my hands into the big black robe that Raine found last night.

It's actually an executioner's hood.

I feel something in my pocket. She must have put the bottle of Aqua Tofana in there before she took it off.

I hold it up to the light.

Fun fact: Belladonna is almost tasteless. Even slightly sweet. You can poison someone slowly, and they'd never know it. Like the unsuspecting husbands who lived in Rome during the Italian Renaissance.

I know exactly what I'm going to do with Kaiser. I won't kill him—no, that'd be too easy.

He thinks that might makes right. Those are his rules. *Supervillain Rule #2: It's easy to beat an opponent who plays by the rules.* He's confident in his height and his weight and his physical strength, but physical strength is only part of it.

He thinks that he can overpower me, but there are many forms of power.

Even when you are smaller, you can still win.

I'm going to seduce him. All the dressing up last night gave me an idea. The best offense is a good disguise. I've been pretending to be a good girl, and it's working. He's opening up. I'm going to turn it up to eleven. He thinks he's training me, but I'll be training him.

He'll think he's in control, but I'll make him obsessed with me. I want him to lose his mind. Once he's feral for me,

I'll have the upper hand. He will be in my thrall and do anything for me.

I will make Fraternitas regret this marriage.

But by then, it'll be too late. They'll have lost Kaiser's loyalty.

I'll be his poison. He will be addicted to me.

After brunch with my friends, I head to the spot where Kaiser told me he'd be waiting to pick me up. There's no sign of his Jeep, but there's a matte black Lykan parked in Kaiser's usual spot. I'm admiring the car when the driver gets out and faces me.

He's a big blond guy who looks exactly like Kaiser, except he isn't.

"Hello, Bella. I'm Jaeger. Kaiser sent me to pick you up."

"I'm not supposed to talk to strangers or get in the car with them."

"I'm not a stranger. I'm going to be your brother-in-law."

He holds up his phone and plays me a video of Kaiser telling me that this is his brother, Jaeger, and I'm to obey him as I would Kaiser. The video ends with the two of them side by side, glowering at the camera.

"I guess you pass the test." He is an identical twin. They even have a few matching tattoos, although I can spot differences. "What's your name again? Bagel?"

"Jaeger."

He opens the passenger door for me, and I slide into the seat, feeling grouchy that Kaiser didn't bother to pick me up himself so I could start on my nefarious plan. And then I'm grouchy that I'm grouchy. I should be relieved that I don't have to see him so soon.

Now I'm grouchy that I'm grouchy about being grouchy. I can't help my emotions. Raine and I were just talking about this. I need to chillax. I have a plan. I just need to focus.

Jaeger puts the car in gear and pulls away from the curb. If I don't look directly at him, I can imagine it's Kaiser in the car. But there are a few uncanny differences.

"Where's Kaiser anyway?"

"On a job."

"For Fraternitas?" No answer.

"Is he murdering anyone?"

Jaeger grins. "He told me you'd ask me that."

He smiles too much. Kaiser doesn't smile that much, so when he does, it's earned. This guy is a clown compared to him. I don't like it.

But I should use this time wisely. I want to ask him about his *elita*, but I got that intel from Honey, and I'll need a legitimate way to have that information to protect her as a source. "Do you live around here?"

"New Rome."

"With Kaiser?"

"In the same building."

"Anything you can tell me about Kaiser? His likes, dislikes? Preferences?"

"Kaiser doesn't like anyone or anything."

That's not true. But I don't say that. "Good talk."

Another grin. "He was assigned to guard you in the spring. He was told there would be a reward for keeping you alive."

"What reward?"

"You."

"Whoever took the job got to have me?" I don't know if I'm flattered or incensed. *Flat-censed.*

Jaeger shrugs. "If they wanted you. And Kaiser wanted you. He chose you."

All of a sudden, I'm not grouchy anymore. "Really?" He nods.

Kaiser wanted me? He chose me? It feels too huge to contemplate.

Jaeger says Kaiser doesn't like anyone, but he does like me. I know it. He lets me sleep on top of him and everything.

What would it be like to really be his? To have him care about me more than anything else? I can't allow myself to even imagine it.

In the end, it doesn't change anything. He's still the enemy. Him choosing me doesn't mean anything more than that I fit a set of his preferences. I should be happy. If I'm his type, it'll be that easier to trick him.

But I don't feel happy. I'm quiet the whole ride, ignoring Jaeger's unsettling smile.

When we get home, I make myself scarce. I have a lot of work to do to enact my plan, and I need to take advantage of the fact that Kaiser isn't here to discover what I'm doing. My greenhouse has a sink and a small lab. With *Gianni Schicchi* blasting on the surround sound, I pull out the extra packet of fertilizer the bottling company sent me and get to work.

Night has fallen when Jaeger finds me.

"I'm going to leave now, so you need to come inside the house." I could argue that the greenhouse is attached and therefore part of the house, but he's glaring at the glass walls as if he doesn't trust them. "There's a guard watching the house. Kaiser will be here before midnight."

I frown. "Why so late?"

"He's hurt."

"Hurt? Who hurt him?"

Jaeger raises a brow. "You care?"

"Of course I care. He's going to be my husband." I'm the only one allowed to hurt him.

"You want to know his weaknesses." He gives me a suspicious look, and I suppress a smile.

"I want to help him. Isn't that what a good wife is supposed to do?"

Jaeger isn't buying it. "Go upstairs and get ready for bed. I'm locking down the house."

"Aye, aye, captain." I salute him and turn away to hide my smirk. I might regret hurting Kaiser, but I can't wait to deal Fraternitas a death blow.

This is going to be fun.

*KAISER*

WHEN I GET HOME, I can tell that something has shifted. My senses tingle, alerting me as soon as I open the bedroom door. I pay attention to my instincts. Time after time, they've kept me alive. Right now, they tell me I'm walking into danger.

And there she is, my little bride.

Kneeling on the bed.

"Hello, husband," she says in a throaty voice. "I've been waiting for you to come home."

Candles are burning all around the room, releasing a thick, musky scent. I can feel them dulling my senses as soon as I breathe in the smoky air.

In the candlelight, Bella glows.

It's a trap, and she's the bait.

But what lovely bait she is.

"You dressed up for me." She's in a gold bra and the tiniest pair of shorts I've ever seen.

"Do you like it?"

"Yes." I get close to examine her. She's done something to her face to highlight her eyes. I heard the audio recording of the sleepover, so I know she and her friends did their makeup, but I didn't know what it looked like.

She looks like an Egyptian queen, with dark paint around her eyes, and there's a sprinkle of glitter on her cheeks, like a spattering of gold stars. Her skin seems to shimmer, but maybe that's a trick of the light.

She's put her hair into ponytails. Sexy little fuck toy.

*No, not fuck toy. Future wife.*

She bites her lip, looking up at me. "I heard you got hurt."

I have a shallow slice over my ribs. I can't even feel it, but St. James insisted I get it flushed out and bandaged properly.

"Who told you that?"

"Jaeger."

I feel an insane surge of jealousy. There's no reason for me to want to feel rage toward my brother for being with her all afternoon. I was the one who asked him to guard her. But my emotions surge so hot, I feel dizzy.

"I'm fine." I put one knee on the bed, getting closer to her. Her eyes roam over me greedily, then focus on my sleeve.

"You're bleeding."

There's a red smear on my right bicep. "It's not my blood." She sucks in a breath, and her eyes go black.

Her scent fills the air. Lemon sugar with a musky edge.

I strip off my shirt and use it to wipe the blood off. Now she's panting. Is she afraid or turned on?

I put my hand around her neck, turning her head this way and that. Her pulse flutters against my palm. "Are you my prize?"

"Do you want me to be?"

"Yes." I release her throat and take hold of a ponytail, drawing her head back.

"Then yes."

I drag her head to the side and fasten my mouth on her neck, sucking hard enough to leave a red mark.

She gasps. "Kaiser!"

She tastes amazing. A little salty, a lot sweet. I swirl my tongue over her skin, licking and sucking. I want to open my mouth and swallow her whole. "I want to destroy you and put you back together again."

"Yes," she whispers.

"You waited on your knees for me."

"Yes."

"You want me. You want this."

"Yes."

"Be careful what you wish for." I tear her bra to shreds and drag my mouth over her perfect little breasts. I can't get enough of her taste.

I pull her down onto the bed, my mouth still fastened to her nipples. Her flavor is like a drug. It's woodsy and wild, Earth and salt with an edge of lemon tartness. I want to devour her. I set my teeth on her nipple, biting her a little. She jumps, and I hold her down.

"No escape."

Her breath comes faster. I bite her again, and she whimpers.

"Too much?"

"Give it to me. I can take it."

"You're wrong, little one. But I'm not a good man. I've got you now, and there's no escape."

I flip her over and lick up the back of her spine, planting

kisses on her delicate shoulder blades. She loves it when I suck on the back of her neck. She turns to liquid.

I pull her up against me and half in my lap so I can reach around and cup her sex. I slide my palm against her wet folds. Rub her lightly until she's used to my touch, then apply more pressure. Slowly. Minute by minute, until I'm scrubbing her clit and she's grinding against me. I angle her hips to rub the side of her clit against the ridge of my calloused palm.

I could stay like this, right here, my teeth nipping her shoulder, my dick rubbing against her until the pleasure overwhelms the pain.

I could have my fingers in her and make her come and be satisfied.

But my mouth waters. I need to taste her again.

She is my reward.

She's what I fought for.

My prize.

I lay her out like a buffet before me and tie her down so she's spread-eagled, with enough give in the ropes for me to move her around. For the final touch, I grab the gag and buckle it around her head.

She stares up at me, fear and lust mixing in her eyes. I have her right where I want her.

I start with her feet, licking between the toes until she's squirming. Ticklish.

I lick the bottoms of her feet. She's all sweet and clean for me.

I kiss her ankles and lick a line from her ankle bone to her knee. I spend a long time kissing behind her knees before licking up her legs to where her pussy weeps for me.

I lay down, my face in her sex. Finally, I'm home. I'm going to live here for a long time.

My dick presses into the bed, and I roll my hips, rubbing myself against it as I lick her.

Her first orgasm comes quickly as she squirts on my tongue.

"Again." I thrust my fingers inside her, feeling her muscles clamp down.

I tend to her pussy for a long time. Until she's screaming. Until she shakes her head, whimpering behind the gag.

Tears run down her face. She doesn't want another orgasm.

"I know," I croon. "I know." I'm so cruel to her. I rise over her, leaning down to taste her tears. They're so sweet and delicious. I lick her face and rub against her jaw, always making sure to avoid her lips and feeling the kick of disappointment when I remember she doesn't want me to kiss her.

"Do you want a break?"

She nods, black tracks of mascara mixing with the tears streaming down her beautiful face. Her makeup is destroyed, and I love the sight. I love knowing I wrecked her. It makes me feral.

I untie her and rub her little wrists and ankles, then I drag her up by her hair. "Up on your knees, little one. That's it." I stand by the bed, while she kneels on it in front of me. I've positioned her at the perfect height for what comes next.

I haven't allowed her to touch me yet. But it's all I can think about lately.

I've always sheathed up with my partners. My skin didn't feel much sensation, anyway.

But I don't want anything between me and her. It's the first time I've wanted anything like that, and I'm shaking with the need to feel her.

But I still need to be in control.

"Hands behind your back. Do you want to learn to please me?" She nods again. Only then do I unbuckle the gag.

"Good girl." I rub away the marks around her little mouth. "Do exactly what I say. I'm going to help you make it good for me."

## 22

B *ella*

"Good girl," Kaiser croons over and over. "Good girl."

My mouth is full, my head tipped back to accommodate the toy that fills it.

"Breath through your nose." His hand is around my neck, lightly stroking. "That's it. You can take it."

I relax my jaw and let him press the dildo in deeper. My eyes are wide and fixed on him. The approval I see in his gaze is everything.

"So pretty. So sweet for me. And only me. Because you like what I give you, don't you?" His hand roams down my front, playing with my nipples until my abs clench. I whimper, and he eases the toy out. I take a break, releasing my arms and rolling my shoulders before getting into position again. He waits for me to nod before pressing the toy past my lips again. I keep my arms boxed behind my back the way he instructed. He's still clothed, and I'm naked before him, and it makes this servile position sweeter.

I let my tongue swirl around the toy.

"Fuck me," he mutters. He massages my neck, a sign that he wants to challenge me. I suck in a breath and tip my head back further so the dildo can slide all the way to my throat. The toy is hard and inflexible. I don't really like it, but I want to please him. Earn his praise.

"That's it, you're taking it so deep. I'm going to teach you to choke me down."

I don't know how long we've been like this, me on my knees and him fucking my face with the toy. He's training me to take his cock.

My eyes water a little. The toy hits my gag reflex, and I tense up, trying not to choke. It doesn't work. My shoulders hunch up, and I gurgle, but he's already sliding the toy out. He rests his hand on my back as I gasp for air. "Shhh, baby, it's okay."

"Did I do it? Did I do good?" I pant.

"You did so good," he reassures me. "I'm going to keep training you until you're the best."

I nod. That makes me feel better. He's taking responsibility. I'm not the one in control.

My gaze darts to the huge bulge in his pants. "Did I earn it?"

"Lie down on the bed, facing up." He uses my hair to guide me, and fuck if it doesn't make me wetter. "Tip your head back here." I end up with my head half off the bed, tilted so my mouth and throat are in a straight line.

"Yes," he growls. He pulls down his boxers and palms his cock. It's already huge and hard, jutting out as if seeking my mouth. I tense up again. He's so much bigger than the toy.

"You're so fucking hot." He's jacking himself over me. I

get a close-up of his dick and the hot sight of him pleasuring himself, but I want more. I open my mouth wide, inviting him to give me a taste.

He hesitates, letting his cock bob over my mouth. His breath comes in a rush.

"You want this? Just a little then." He lets the head of his cock dip low enough that I can touch it with my outstretched tongue. I get the barest taste before he steps back. A shiver seems to go through him.

He's never allowed me to touch his cock before. This is the first time, and he seems to be overwhelmed.

Suddenly, I want to make it good for him. I lick my lips, making a show of savoring the salty sweetness. "Mmmm."

He curses and comes back to me, as I knew he would. "You like that? Here's more." He gives me his cock again. "That's it, lick me." He's still in control, moving his cock around, smearing pre-cum on my tongue. I obey him and am rewarded with a breathy groan.

His whole body shakes, and I marvel at the power I have over him. He leans over me, bending so he's at the right height to slide the head of his cock into my mouth. I purse my lips around it, holding it, sucking hard. He's hard and hot and thick, swelling further to fill my mouth. Bliss.

"One day I'll slide right in here." He cups my throat, and my heartbeat leaps as it always does when he threatens to choke me. I swirl my tongue around him faster. "Oh yes, that's so good. You're so good to me, baby." He feeds me a little more of his length and slides in and out. I can tell he's being careful. His body is bowed over me, every muscle taut. He reaches down and mauls my breasts, gripping them, squeezing and plucking the nipples. Then he grips my pussy. My clit is raw from all the licking, so I squirm, but he holds me tight. Then he smacks me down there, and I shout as stars burst behind my eyes. He does it again and again until my orgasm cracks through me. He grips me again, squeezing the shit out of my lower lips. It hurts but sends me flying higher.

"Oh fuck," he snarls. "Fuck me." He glides his hand up and down his cock faster and faster. Finally, he explodes, letting his cum rain down over my chest. He did this last time; it's his favorite.

"Fuck me." His tone turns reverent as he slides his hand through his release, coating my chest with it. He rubs it in like it's lotion.

He keeps petting me for a while. He even rubs a balm on my poor, overstimulated sex.

"What's in that?" I ask and he shows me the container. It smells faintly floral, like rosewater. The main ingredients are probably lanolin, paraffin, and a petroleum derivative but also some herbs.

"My brother Atticus makes it. He works his subs pretty hard."

I've heard that name before. "Atticus is in Fraternitas?"

"Yes. And a member of Club Empire. It's a sex club St. James owns."

"Sex club?"

"Yes." He fixes the bed and lies down, pulling me on top of him. He doesn't allow me free rein to touch him, but he seems to love this. He sighs deeply as my weight settles on him.

Honey told me a bit about Club Empire. I want to ask all the questions. "Are you a member of the sex club?"

"Yes."

"Can we go?"

He just smiles. I pout at him, and he chuckles. "Of course. Why do you think I'm training you?"

"Hmm. So you're going to train me to be good for you, then you'll take me to the sex club to show me off."

"Yes."

I should be happy. I am happy. This is what I wanted: more chances to gather intel about Fraternitas.

But why does my stomach twist, knowing he's training me because he thinks of me as a pet, not an equal? It's not like I actually want to lose myself in being his sub. Why do I want to pretend it's real?

"Who is St. James?" I ask.

"Another one of my brothers. You met him and the Devil that day we came to sign the contract with your father."

"He's in charge."

"The Devil's in charge. St. James is the power behind the throne."

I file this away. There's so much I don't know and so much I need to know.

Kaiser strokes my forehead, smoothing out the lines there. He smirks like he knows my brain is working overtime, but otherwise, he has a contented look on his face. I smile to myself, knowing I did that. I put that look on his face.

"I met Jaeger today."

"I know. You'd like his woman, Elodie. She's in college, too. Taking classes at NRU."

"Really? Can I meet her?"

"Soon."

Yay! "Are you and your brother close?"

"Yes. Growing up, we had to be. He had my back and I had his."

"And now? He said you live near each other."

"I have a place in the same building as his and Elodie's penthouse, yes. But my place is here. With you."

I blink at that. His voice is serious, like he's making a promise. I lean back so I can study his face. He might just be talking about where he lives, but I hear a deeper meaning. Has his loyalty shifted?

No, it's too soon. He's talking about his home. His priorities. But it's a start.

I'll take it.

He runs a finger down my cheek. "I ruined your makeup."

"That's okay. I wanted you to." My skin is taut under the mess he made of my cheeks, the smeared mascara drying with my tears. "Why do you think I wore it?"

"My sweet bride," he sounds like he's falling asleep. I smile to myself.

The poison is working.

"Goodnight, husband," I test it out.

He doesn't respond. He's out.

In a moment, I'll put my head down and rest. For now, I want to study the way the golden candlelight outlines his perfect face.

**23**

———

# K *aiser*

BELLA'S UP TO SOMETHING. She's pliant and eager, as if resigned to her fate.

I don't trust it. But I can't keep my hands off her.

It's not just sexual. Every time we're in the same room, I have my hands on her. My hand at the small of her back, guiding her. On the back of her neck, massaging the tight muscles until she relaxes.

In the morning, I brush her hair and dress her like she's my little doll. In the afternoon, after her classes, we watch a terrible vampire show together while I rub her feet. After an episode or two, I lie down and set her on top of me, so she can grind her pussy on me. Even fully clothed, she can come like that, with me goading her.

"I want it inside me," she whines.

"Not yet, little bride." I pinch her nipples, enjoying her pout.

"You're going to make me wait until marriage?" She sounds aghast.

"Maybe," I say, to torture her. "Maybe I'm old-fashioned."

She snorts.

"Maybe I don't want to hurt you." But I do hurt her, pinching her nipples to make her rock faster.

Before we're married, I intend to make her come in every room of this house.

Fuck her on every rug. Prop her legs over the arms of every chair and eat her out.

Press her face into each window while I rail her from behind.

But I'm taking it easy. Going slowly. Putting her through her paces.

"You're kind of gentle with me," she says one night after a long scene. "You don't really hurt me."

I stroke her silky hair. "You don't need pain."

"You don't like inflicting pain. You think it makes you a bad person. A lot of doms think that." She's so solemn as she tells me about the articles on dom drop she's been reading. "You don't have to hold back, Kaiser. You can punish me." She reaches up, tentatively, to touch my hair. I allow it for a few seconds before capturing her hand and pressing a kiss to the palm.

"I don't want to punish you. I want you to purr for me." I knead the back of her neck until her eyes half close. I spent most of my life in the rings punishing people. Hurting them. I want something different with her. "I like it when you relax and go limp on me."

"Is that why you wear me like a weighted blanket every night?"

I trail my fingers down her spine and cup her bottom. I could tell her that I've never liked it when people touched me, but I crave the feel of her draped over me. I could tell her that she's the only one I've wanted this way.

But I don't. I don't dare allow her that power over me.

She has power over me all the same.

"There are other ways to punish you." I edge my fingers toward her pussy.

She jerks her hips away, but I hold her fast. "No," she whines, dropping her forehead on my chest as she whines. "Too many."

"But I need another taste," I whisper in her ear. I'm already hard again under her. I don't want to come, I just want to kiss her pretty pussy while my balls ache. "Please."

"Oh no..."

But she doesn't have a choice. I pull her up so she's sitting on my face and hold her there no matter how much she squirms. She's beautiful like this, her lithe body above me, her nipples like ripe berries. Her hair is falling around her face, her eyes are wild, and her sex is dripping nectar into my mouth.

She sighs, but after a minute, she's pressing herself into my mouth. I fuck her with my tongue as she grips my hair, grinding desperately against me.

I'm training her to crave me. Every night, I send her to the bedroom to prepare for me. I give her instructions. She's to shower, shave, and wait for me naked, kneeling on the bed.

She never obeys. She always pushes it. One night, she'll be in a schoolgirl outfit. Next, a hot pink push-up bra and thong that matches the ropes I wind around her.

My dick swells as soon as I walk in the room and smell the candles she's always burning. My mouth waters as soon as I get a hit of her scent. I can't remember what it was like to not want anyone to touch my dick. I want her hands and mouth on me all the time, and she's all too willing to oblige.

She always wears a full face of makeup, so much so that it's almost clownish. I make it my personal mission to destroy it. My favorite is when she brushes glitter on her cheeks. I make her lick me until there's glitter all over my fucking balls. It's obscene what I do to her.

But she loves it. She loves to act like a brat, but she craves being my little slut.

"This is how you kneel for me," I instruct her during a session with a crop.

"And this is how you crawl for me." She crawls so prettily, I reward her with a warming oil on her pussy. And then she sasses me, so I punish her with peppermint oil.

I keep imagining her in my collar. My skin tingles, imagining me laying her down and finally fucking her.

I fantasize about claiming her. Dragging her down to the Abyss, saying our vows, and sealing them with blood. Marriage vows are nothing compared to that claiming ritual.

What would it be like for her to truly be mine?

"I'm taking you to Club Empire," I finally tell her.

Her eyes light up.

"All of my brothers will be there. Them and their chosen ones. The *elitas*." I know her friend told her about the *elitas*. I know she's fascinated. That might be why she's played the part of being my perfect toy—to learn more about the ritual.

And she's good. She's almost got me fooled into forgetting she wants to destroy me.

If I'm not careful, I'll let her under my skin, more than she already is.

BELLA

TONIGHT'S THE NIGHT. Kaiser binds me with a rope that creates an elaborate harness around my torso. He's taking me to Pandemonium.

"You will be on your best behavior. Or we'll come straight home."

"And you'll punish me?"

"I'll read you a book and put you to bed. In a chastity belt." It's a good threat, and he knows it. He's smirking as he makes the final knots in the harness.

I love this sort of rope work, the feeling of being held snug. I love that he took the time to learn how to do it. I can't get out of it on my own, but he seems to know just where to tug to have it all unravel.

I'm wet by the time he stands and tests the knots. I stare up at him, desperate. He runs his thumb over my lower lip, studying me like he wants to kiss me. He won't. He respects the rules.

Sometimes, I wish he'd break them. Give in to desire.

Give in to me.

But he doesn't. That's not what we have. We're locked together but still enemies. Ours is a careful game, based on the threat of mutual assured destruction. I need to get close enough to poison him without him finding out.

That's all.

He dresses me in a loose white skirt and top that's almost modest, until I check the mirror and realize the fabric is so light, the hot pink rope he's bound me in shows through.

Once we're parked outside the club, he adds the final

touches. First is a sleek, hot pink mask that does little more than frame my eyes. He dons his own mask—the skull bandana he was wearing the first time I saw him.

The sight of it makes me quiver. He's dressed the same, too, in jeans and a black shirt.

The last thing he does is fasten a white ribbon around my neck. I hold still. It feels important. He gazes at it like it means something.

I go to touch it, and he catches my wrist. "Behave." He holds up a pink ball gag and then pockets it. I get the warning; he'll gag me if I'm disobedient.

I'm too distracted to sass back. He's parked his Jeep a block away, but I can see the long line of people waiting to get into the club from here. He guides me down the sidewalk with his hand clamped on the back of my neck, and I'm glad of it. We pass a few burly men in skull masks, and he nods to them in greeting. They nod back. I can feel their eyes on me, studying the ribbon around my throat, and I'm even more grateful for Kaiser's claiming touch. I'm supposed to be a badass, but I've never been to a club before, and it's all a little overwhelming. Wearing the outfit he dressed me in—the see-through fabric, the way air drafts up my skirt, reminding me that I'm not wearing underwear—makes me feel small. Submissive.

But I like it.

We bypass the people waiting in line behind a velvet rope and go inside. I stop in my tracks, staring at the sights. Outside, people were in long coats, even though it's still summer and pretty humid. Inside, right in the lobby, they've shed the shielding garments and strut around, showing off outfits even more revealing than mine. There are bustiers and babydoll nightgowns, sequin lingerie and stilettos. The club attendants are in neon latex catsuits. A domme walks by, leading three submissives, wearing cock cages and nothing else, on a leash.

I've never seen so many dicks in my life. Or nipples. Or butt plugs! A cute submissive in a baby doll dress that barely covers her privates walks by and gives me a smile. When she turns away, I see the sparkly pink jewel winking between her ass cheeks, and my first thought is that it would match my harness.

YOLO!

I would stay stalled out in the door for a long time, but Kaiser propels me forward. "Eyes on me, little bride. Or do I need to blindfold you?"

I stare up at him, letting him maneuver me around. I want to look around, but obeying him this way makes me hot.

We enter a bar area where he orders a drink. He sets me on a stool and lets me taste the liquor, which burns my tongue. He's standing close, blocking my view of the room. I plead with him with my gaze, and he relents with a smirk.

"You can look around now."

I do, and stifle a gasp. The room is full of people in creepy devil masks. Mostly men, though I do spot a petite woman with beautiful full sleeve tattoos on her arms. She's in a wheelchair, holding a stein of frothy beer. On her finger is a skull ring with dark red jewels in the eye sockets.

Across the room, there's a big man with a willowy woman sitting on his lap. He has a skull ring with blue jewels in the eye sockets, and she has a silver collar with a matching blue jewel around her neck.

Kaiser sees who I'm staring at. "An *elita*," he tells me. His hand is on my thigh, stroking under my skirt. I'm already aching to come, and his touch makes it unbearable.

I look around for someone else in a white ribbon, but I

don't see one. I do see two more women and one man in silver collars. And there's a trio of submissives with black ribbons around their neck. Two are masc-presenting and one is more femme. They're with a bare-chested man who's lounging on a couch by the door.

One of them holds his drink until he's ready for it. The other two are cuddled close to him, staring up at him in adoration.

"That's Atticus," Kaiser tells me and raises his drink in a salute.

At some unseen signal, the room begins to clear out.

Kaiser offers me more liquor, and I shake my head with a grimace. His drink was yucky. He tosses it back and strokes my hair back from my face.

"Things are about to start. Do you need to go to the bathroom?"

I nod. He leads me to the bathrooms and leans down to ask, "Do you need me to undo the harness?"

I hesitate. I like how it's chafing me. "I'll figure it out."

"No getting yourself off," he warns. The fires in my belly burn hotter.

"Hurry back." Kaiser folds his arms across his chest, looking like a bouncer blocking the door.

I'm washing my hands at the sink when I hear someone calling my name.

"Pssst, Bella." I turn to see a woman in an angel costume beckoning me into the handicap stall. After a second, I realize it's Honey in elaborate gold makeup.

"Hey," I say. "You guys made it."

"Shhh." She pulls me into the stall. A figure in a cheesy red devil outfit is next to her. When I look closely, it's Raine.

"I got an invitation," Honey says, "but Raine's not supposed to be here."

Raine shrugs. "I ran away."

"YOLO," I grin. "I'd better get back out there. Kaiser's waiting for me."

"You're wearing a white ribbon," Honey observes.

"Yeah, Kaiser put it on me. Do you know what the colors mean?"

"Black means you're an initiate. A metal collar means you're claimed. White means you're innocent, but he's marking you as off limits. It warns everyone else off."

I touch the white ribbon around my throat. It's not black, but it's a start. "He says he wants to claim me."

"Congratulations," Honey whispers. "Unless—"

"No, it's good," I say and accept their murmured congratulations. Outside the door, someone turns the music up, and the walls start pulsing with the heavy bass.

"Showtime. We'll see you out there," Honey says.

Before I exit the stall, I turn back. "What to make things really interesting?" I pull out a small pink bottle that I hid in my ponytail. It looks like cherry lip gloss but that's a disguise. "Take a drop or two of this. Not more than that—it's strong."

Honey hesitates. "Is that molly?"

"It's not unlike molly." I hold it out to Raine, who has a devilish gleam in her eyes. "Do it for the plot."

She takes it. "Yo-fucking-Lo."

**24**

———

K *aiser*

BELLA'S GRINNING when she comes out of the bathroom, which makes me suspicious. I take hold of her, pulling her close. I touch her lips because I have to. Touching her is a compulsion I can no longer resist. "Why are you smiling?"

"I'm just happy to be here."

Liar. She's taken down her ponytail, and she looks so innocent with her hair soft around her face. I need to be on my guard to keep her out of trouble.

I lead her down the hall to the large ballroom where the main event is already underway. Two Fraternitas members guard the door. They recognize me and wave me on. We enter a rounded hallway that feels like a tunnel. The music is already so loud, it shakes the walls and seems to press on us from all sides.

Bella hunches her shoulders, and I pull out earplugs. I

thought she might need these. She lets me put them in and relaxes. I run a hand down her back to soothe her.

"Welcome to Pandemonium," I say and pull back the velvet curtains to reveal a rave.

The room is vast and filled with people. The center is one giant dance floor, and colorful lasers slice through the air, turning the wild movements of the dancers into a stop-motion music video.

I find an open spot and pull Bella close, protecting her from the people on the edges of the moshpit. She's quiet, taking everything in.

Above our heads are several open stories with narrow railed walkways so people can reach the floors of private rooms. Some of the doors are lit already, glowing red, blue, pink, yellow, or green.

"Can we dance?"

I nod and lead her further into the fray. I guard her back while she raises her arms and sways to the music. I can't see it, but I know every movement makes the ropes slide over her sex. Soon she'll be begging for release.

She ends up dancing with a woman dressed like an angel in a costume complete with feathered wings. I stay on the periphery, shoving people away when they get too close. Protecting her, always.

The dance floor is full of half-naked people writhing together, but I only have eyes for her. My captive. My fiancée.

My future wife.

Her hair is a bright halo. She looks like an angel herself, but she dances like she's possessed. She's glowing; she might as well be spotlit.

It's a joy to watch her. She's so wild and free. And I remember, it's her first time in a club. First time on a dance floor. Her father never let her out. And now she's here with me.

She's mine. And everyone knows it. Because all my brothers are here, standing in the shadows. Bella probably doesn't notice all of them, but I do. The lights reflect off their skull masks. They're watching, and whenever one of them looks my way, they also notice the white ribbon around Bella's throat. She's not ready for a collaring ceremony, not yet, but tonight I'm openly staking my claim.

I used to want to hide her away. Keep her hidden from everyone. But now I want the world to see her. To stand in awe of her beauty. To worship her as she deserves.

I watch her dance, the lights bathing her in red, green, blue, purple, yellow, and back to red.

Wicked thoughts flit across her face, chased by ecstasy. She's so expressive. All that emotion, innocence, and deviousness in one perfect package.

She's beautiful like the sky. Like a flame.

And I want her. I wanted to own her, but now I want more. I want her to want me. I want her to be happy... with me.

She deserves so much better than me. In a few years, she'll be able to snap her fingers and have anyone she wants kneeling at her feet.

It hurts to think about. It hurts to watch her, knowing she's shackled to me for life and will never be free. That, deep down, she'll always see me as her captor.

Her enemy.

Every once in a while, she gives me a calculating look, and I know she's plotting against me. I want her to let her guard down and keep it down. To trust that I won't destroy her.

But who am I fooling? All I do is destroy.

But in the noise and chaos, I allow myself to imagine us having more. What it would be like if she were really mine. If she looked at me with softness and longing, not just when she's in lust but all the time. What would that be like? To give her all her firsts and watch her enjoy them. To be her husband, not just in name, but in truth.

I've spent my whole life fighting. I don't want to fight anymore. I just want to be with her.

It's impossible, but I still want it. Even though it hurts like my insides are getting shredded. It kills me, this wanting something I'll never have, but if there's anything I'm good at, it's taking the pain.

The music swells, the beat drops, and suddenly, Bella is in front of me, gazing up at me with longing.

It's only lust, but I'll take it. I'll take whatever I can get. I gather her hair back, noting the sweat on her brow. She's hot and horny from dancing. The room is getting steamy from all the bodies in here, and many of the dancers have gone from grinding on each other to actively fucking. It smells like sex.

I cup Bella's pussy over her skirt. I can feel her heat through the fabric. "You wet for me, little bride?" Her eyes go black.

I grip the collar of her shirt and rip it down the front. She helps me shed the pieces. The harness pushes her breasts up and leaves her nipple free for me to torment. I'm the only one who gets to see them, so I pull out the nipple clamps I have in my pocket, waiting for this moment. I tease her nipples and clamp them. She hisses in pain and curls into me. My cock throbs, and I grit my teeth to get my lust under control. If we don't get upstairs soon, I'm going to take her right here on the floor.

*No, go slow. Make it good for her.*

I swing her up into my arms and walk us out of the main room, up a staircase to the private rooms. Several of them are taken, their doors opaque or backlit in a way that allows anyone to see the activities inside. I reserved one for us near the middle, where we can look down on the dance floor. I switch on the light, adjusting it until we're bathed in a light pink glow. I choose a setting that makes sure the door is lit in a way that lets people know someone's in here, but won't let them see inside. I'm not giving the voyeurs a show. Not yet.

I set Bella down. She hums to herself, laying a hand on my chest and petting me through my shirt. I grit my teeth again. I want her touch, but my nerve endings are coming awake after a long time dormant. The slightest brush of her hand is overwhelming. At the same time, the sensitivity reminds me that I've spent my adult life being numb to both pain and pleasure. Does that mean I'm doomed to forever feel dead inside? I hate that.

Bella deserves better.

I snatch her hand and press a kiss to the inside of her wrist. I can feel her pulse thudding there. I lick and suck on it, noting how she gasps, how her lips part.

I can do this. I can make her feel good. Give her the intensity she craves, a rollercoaster ride that both keeps her safe and leaves her gasping for more.

I reach down and rip off her skirt. I back her up into the room until I find a low platform that will put her at the right height to suck me off. "On your knees."

She goes down and immediately boxes her arms behind her back. She looks up at me, patiently waiting.

"Good girl." I grab a handful of her hair. I'm too impatient to strip. I press her head to my crotch, using her face to rub my cock. It's rough and degrading, but it's what I need.

And she seems to like it. She sticks out her tongue to lick at the front of my jeans until I can't take it anymore.

I take out my cock and let her have a taste. Lightning shoots up the backs of my legs at the touch of her tongue. It's too much. Her wet heat on my sensitive glans is good but also makes me go numb, like my nerve endings are over-stimulated. It feels like my skin got too close to dry ice or a flame.

I grit my teeth and bear it, and it gets easier. Her eyes are dreamy, and the way she works to bob her head, sucking hard to earn my cum? I'm a lucky man.

I gather her hair up so I can watch her try to swallow me down. All the blood flows to my cock. Her tongue swirls around me, and my knees go weak. I have to fight the urge to thrust deeper and bang on the back of her throat.

She can take me. Not all of me, but we'll get there.

She'll take me in her pussy tonight. It's time.

The sight of her on her knees, naked with her ass split by the hot pink rope, almost sends me over. I lean down and pull on the lower half of the harness until she moans. The tugging increases pressure on her clit. There's got to be a puddle under her by now.

It also makes her throw herself forward, swallowing as much of my dick as possible. *Fuck me.*

I pull her off and set my thumb on her lips. "You did so good for me, baby. But I'm not coming in your mouth, not tonight." I slide my fingers around her throat and draw her up slowly, letting her get her feet under her and stand so I don't choke her out. Her pulse hammers at my palm.

I move her backward until her knees hit the couch and she goes down. The couch is one of those loungers that's as big as a bed.

I inspect her sweet pussy. Her poor skin is chafed red

from the rope, so I undo the lower half of the harness and cup her, feeling her wetness pool on my palm.

"I'm going to take you here," I say, stroking around her entrance. "Would you like that?"

She gives me a frantic nod. The nipple clamps swing. I smile.

"You see that door? One day, I'll fuck you against it. I'll turn up the lights so everyone can see everything but our faces. They'll watch you take my cock like a good girl. Then I'll cover your face with my cum and make you wear it out of here so everyone will know you're my little slut. Would you like that?"

"Yes, yes," she squeaks. She's soaking my fingers.

I pull off my clothes and lie back, positioning her over me. My cock stands up, ready to be sheathed inside her. "You're in control. You decide how deep you want to go."

She looks uncertain. Should I tell her it's the first time for me, too? I've never fucked anyone raw. She'll be my first. My only.

I cup her ass. "I've got you, baby."

Slowly, she moves herself down. She only has the tip of me inside her before she stops, tensing.

"It's okay. Take your time," I say, even though I'm dying. I'm barely inside her, and I can feel her wetness, her heat, the sweet kiss of her inner muscles. I'm still numb, but I sense the sensations. They're distant, like they're behind a curtain, but they're there. Both pleasure and pain.

It's heaven and hell, but it's her, so it's better than anything I imagined. I wanted to be close to her. I wanted to know her, and now she's here and on top of me, and I'm inside of her. Just knowing that makes it so good, it's unbearable. I could nut right now. There's a tingling sensation in my spine, in my balls. I brace against it.

Her clamped nipples are right in front of me but too far for me to reach with my mouth. I free a hand and unclamp them one by one.

She cries out, her inner muscles clenching on me as she slides further onto my dick. *Fuck me.* The pressure is perfection. I'm going to die from this. I'll go willingly. *Just please don't let me cum before she does.*

I focus on her face, her frantic expression. Forget everything new I'm feeling, I need to make this good for her. Her hands brace on my abs. Her legs are shaking. "It's so much."

"You can take it."

She whimpers, but her muscles ease, letting me in. Her eyes flutter closed.

"Eyes on me."

She obeys. She looks at me like I'm her god.

I cup the side of her face and drink in that look. She won't let me kiss her, but I can have this. "Are you ready for me to move?"

She looks concerned but rocks a little, experimenting. Then nods.

"Easy." I work my hips, showing her how to ride me in an easy, rolling motion. I'm still holding her up, and she's not fully seated on me, not yet. I can't give her all of my dick, not yet. I have to hold some back.

I hold her tight and increase the speed of my thrusts.

"Look at me," I order. "We'll come together."

"I can't—"

"I got you." I steady her with one hand and find her clit with the other. The bliss breaks over her face.

And suddenly, I feel nothing but pleasure. Usually, I can't feel anything but pressure, but I can feel this. She's so expressive, but now I'm with her, drowning in the ecstasy in her eyes. She feels everything so strongly, and somehow, I can feel it through her.

It wrecks me. It's everything, but it's too much. "Fuck," I growl and punch my hips into her harder, careful to pull back before I give her too much. One day, I'll fuck her and give her every last inch. She wants the intensity, but she's a damn virgin. I can't break her, I won't. I don't leash my violence for anybody but her.

She breaks apart, moaning, and I let myself go, cursing and letting my cum spurt into her. She fucking wrecked me, and I was barely inside her.

"Good, baby. You did so good."

I pull her shuddering body over me. The skin of my naked chest is numb, but underneath the layer of muted sensation, tingles spread like tiny needles pricking my skin.

It hurts, but that's okay. I'll take the pain if I can have her like this.

I MUST HAVE FALLEN ASLEEP, because when I wake up, someone is screaming.

They're not nearby but close.

My head's pounding. Pain radiates out from behind my eyes. Headache. Like I've had too much to drink.

My skin is still tingling, like more nerve endings are coming alive. It hurts so bad. I grit my teeth. I've hurt worse.

I'm lying on the couch and Bella's on top of me, fast asleep. The room is stuffy and too warm.

And somebody's screaming. I need to check it out.

I shift Bella off of me and make sure she's comfortable before I grab my clothes and dress to open the door. The rave is still going on, but there are fewer people on the dance floor. More doors are lit up on the wall opposite me.

"I can see god," someone screams. A few of the party people are literally trying to climb the walls. Everywhere I look, people are laughing. High-pitched hysterical laughter.

But something's wrong.

I glance back at Bella, who's sleeping, completely out. Then I grab my skull bandana and exit the room, making sure the door locks from the inside.

Something's up. My brothers might need help.

I find Atticus at the bottom of the stairs in a pair of boxers with fuzzy slippers on his feet.

"What's happening?"

"They've gone completely crazy," he sounds calm. We look out over the dancers. There's a two-drink limit at Club Empire on most nights. Tonight is special, but the bartenders know to cut people off before they get drunk.

"Drugs?" I ask.

"That's my guess."

A shout rings out and then another. At the far end of the room, the velvet curtains shake, and then a steady stream of men in suits bursts onto the dance floor. They're all armed. Several are holding machine guns.

The fuck? I go to take a step, and Atticus stops me. "Wait, so far no one's shooting."

He's right, but I don't like it. They came into our house, armed. Who the fuck are these guys? They're in dark blue body armor with some sort of silver insignia on their sleeves.

They advance across the floor, grabbing dancers, pulling off their masks, and then shoving the confused people away. Even in their altered state of mind, the dancers realize they're in danger and start to flee.

"They're looking for someone," Atticus observes.

I see St. James enter the ballroom, a group of Fraternitas by his side. "Come on," I say. We both fall into step behind him. He's in his typical gray suit, no mask, and he's pissed.

Our group meets the group of armed men in the middle of the dance floor. I step forward, making myself a target. One of them tries to rip off my mask, and I grab his wrist and pull him toward me so I can punch him in the face. He drops, and I take his gun before it hits the floor.

Suddenly, all the guns are trained on me.

"Stop," a deep voice commands from behind the gunmen. "Don't shoot." Which is a hell of a thing to say when you bring an armed guard with you.

"What is the meaning of this?" St. James snaps.

The guards part, and a tall, dark-haired man steps out, murder written on his face. "I'm here for Raine."

**25**

---

K *aiser*

"LET ME GET THIS STRAIGHT," St. James says. He's gathered all the members of Fraternitas who aren't on crowd control into a private room. He's speaking in Latin, which is what we do when we might be overheard. His voice is calm, but we all hear the murderous intent. "A pair of college students broke in and not only infiltrated our security but were on something? MDMA mixed with something else, some sort of herb—"

"My preliminary tests tell me the psychoactive compounds are from a plant called magic mint. Latin name *salvia divinorum*," Atticus interjects. "It's used in religious ceremonies. Like ayahuasca."

"That explains the hallucinations," Asmodeus says. "But how did they drug the entire club?"

"Someone spiked the punch," Atticus says. St. James's jaw clenches.

I stand. "It's my fault. The Poisoner's daughter has to be behind this. I thought I had her under control." While I was thinking about how I'd make love to her, she was plotting how to create chaos.

"A failure on all fronts then," St. James says. "We've identified the original culprits. That one is a known guest," He points through the one-way glass to a young woman in an observation room—one of Bella's friends, Honey. She's looking defeated in her angel costume, the wings drooping. "She's been under our protection for years, but she doesn't know it. She had an invite. That wasn't the problem. The problem is that she brought a guest named Raine. Raine used a fake ID, but she belongs to the Saints. Her step-brother is Ransom Saint, and he thought she'd been kidnapped. That's why he stormed the gates."

Asmodeus whistles. "What a cluster."

St. James glowers at Honey. "Indeed."

"What will we do with her?" Atticus asks.

"Cut her loose. But no more invitations to the club. She's officially banned from all Fraternitas property." St. James gives the rest of us our orders and turns to me. "Lock her down," he orders. "The engagement party is in two weeks, and the Vesuvios have agreed to attend and talk in terms of a truce. It needs to go smoothly."

I nod. But when I go to leave, Atticus blocks my way. He peers into my eyes like a doctor would at a routine check-up. "Unilateral mydriasis," he murmurs. "And subconjunctival hemorrhage. How's your head?"

"It's killing me," I admit. I wait while he studies me. I'm used to him doing this after fights, to make sure I don't have a concussion. I owe my life to him. He's healed me up more than once.

"Your fiancée is poisoning you."

"I know," I grit out. "I can't figure out how she's doing it." I refuse to eat or drink anything she offers me.

"Can't or don't want to?"

I grunt.

"Recreational drugs are a poison," Atticus muses. "One that the victim craves. Get me samples of anything you suspect, and I'll test them for you."

"Will do."

He nods and steps back. "Good luck, man." He shakes his head, smirking.

I head back up to Bella.

She's still stretched out on the couch, sleeping like a baby. She looks so peaceful, but she's responsible for all the drama tonight. People could've been killed. Some were hurt —a few guards and club attendants when the Saints broke in. It's a miracle that no one died.

So much mayhem, and she's oblivious.

She's in big trouble.

I thought I could get her under control.

I'm not one to admit defeat, but she's chaos. Like weeds in the garden or an untamed jungle. You try to beat the wildness back, but nature always wins.

I don't want to tame the wildness. I don't want to break her to my will. I want her to be chaos. I want her to be free.

For the first time in my life, I've met my match. Because I would rather die than hurt her.

She wants to fight me? Fine. I'm always the last one standing.

But, for the first time, I want to lose.

*BELLA*

THE DAYS after Pandemonium are quiet. Kaiser watches me closely. He finally gave in and fucked me. I'm sore but feeling good.

He doesn't fuck me again, but he does touch me nonstop when we're together. My plan is working. The poison is setting in.

I'm feeling like a real supervillain when it's time for me to go to class. Summer orientation is kind of boring right now. They're talking about sorting us into different Houses. *Blah blah blah, mafia alliances, blah blah.* I'm up to my ears in mafia alliances already. I can't focus on the Vesuvios and figuring out who framed my father until I've dealt with Fraternitas, so I'm only half listening as I look for Honey. She's not always able to sit with me; the professor pulls her up to help him with special projects. Today she's in the back, though. When I crane my neck and catch her eye, she gives me a grimace and looks away.

That's my first sign that something's wrong. But I don't think much of it because I can be clueless about these sorts of things.

After class, I wait for her in our usual spot in the library. Typically, Raine finds me here, but there's no sign of her.

Finally, Honey comes in, drops her bag, and slumps down. She doesn't look happy to be here. What's going on?

"Are you okay?" I ask.

"I'm fine," she says in a clipped way that tells me she's really not. "I've been banned from Club Empire. For life. As well as all Fraternitas properties."

"What? Why?"

"Why? Because of all the shit that went down at Pandemonium, that's why."

"What happened?" I'm missing something. "Is Raine okay?"

Her face softens. "Raine's in trouble. Her stepbrother thought she'd been kidnapped. He broke into the club with a bunch of armed men and demanded she be returned to him."

"No way."

"Way. Now she's on lockdown. I don't even know if she'll be allowed to return to school."

"I can't believe that happened." I wrack my brain, trying to figure out how I missed all the action. Oh yeah, I was getting dicked down for the first time in my life. "I was... out of it. With Kaiser."

"It happened after you both went upstairs. It was a cluster. And it would've been fine, but everyone was out of it by then. We shouldn't have taken the lip gloss."

The lip gloss? Oh, right, the drugs I gave them.

"We both took it, and it was fine. But I think Raine kept sharing it. At one point, she poured some into a punch bowl she found..."

"Oh, no. I didn't realize that would happen. I thought it would be fun for us."

"It's done," she says wearily. "It's not your fault; we're the ones who took it with us. It just sucks." She looks down at her notebooks. "You know, I'm kind of out of it today. I think I'm going to study in my room." She stands, and I rise with her.

"Wait, you're really banned? Is there anything I can do?"

"No." She packs up without looking at me.

I feel panicky. Is my friend breaking up with me? "I'm so sorry—"

"It's fine. We're fine, Bella. I just... need some space. I need to figure some stuff out."

*It's not you, it's me.* I remember characters saying this on *Vampire Varsity* when they broke up with someone. This feels similar, but pointing that out won't help.

"I'm sorry," I whisper again to Honey's retreating back. She's been more stressed now that we're about to start school, so I don't take it too personally. But what I did didn't help.

Not everyone's immune to drugs like I am. I need to remember that.

I hope Raine's okay. I send her a quick text. "Thinking of you. Hope you're okay."

I know her stepbrother monitors her cell phone, so when the dots appear like she's texting back, I don't expect much.

"Hanging in there," she texts, along with an emoji of a rain cloud and a smiling sun.

I want to apologize for the part I played in getting her in trouble, but I don't want to say something incriminating. So I add a heart and let her know I'm here if she needs me.

It feels lonely, sitting at the big library table by myself. But I'm fine. I'm used to being alone. If I lose my friendships, it'll suck, but I'll survive. And I believe Honey; she might just need some time.

I tell myself the churning in my stomach is indigestion and open my textbook to study. We're learning about how the mafia families sorted themselves into Houses. It's stupid college games, but everyone acts like it's important, so I'm trying to care. The Bulls undergo trials to test their strength. The Swords do puzzles and tests that require strategy and logic. The Saints require devotion, and the Serpents prefer deviousness.

At some point, I'm supposed to decide which House I want to try out for. When I first came to college, I was thinking I'd eventually infiltrate the Vesuvios from within, but I'm not sure if I can pull that off.

I want to stay with my friends, but Raine is already a Saint. I don't know which House Honey will go for. She's smart and loyal. She could be a Sword or a Saint.

I'm probably a Serpent. I feel like a snake.

I close *Time for a Truce: The History of Unitas University*. I can't focus on this stuff. I've got too much on my mind.

Pandemonium was a cluster, and I missed it. Does Kaiser know what I did?

He hasn't said anything about it. Maybe he doesn't know.

Will he find out? And if he does, what will he do to me?

A few more days pass without him mentioning Club Empire, and I think I've gotten away with it. Kaiser and I have settled into a routine: I wake up and get some gardening in while he sleeps in, he takes me to orientation and picks me up, and we eat dinner together like an old married couple.

Something's changed, though. It feels clichéd to say it, but he looks at me differently now that he's taken my virginity.

I don't feel different. Not like Luna, the werewolf queen, when she has a one-night stand with an evil vampire. Or Delilah, who fucks Thorbjorn on the Moon Altar to unlock her Valkeryie powers. Virginity is a social construct.

But something is different. I can't be sure, but... he looks at me like I'm his equal.

Friday night, we're eating in the dining room, and I've done everything I can to make it a nice candlelit affair.

White linen tablecloth and my mother's fine china. I even picked some lovely red flowers and placed them in a beautiful vase for a centerpiece.

Kaiser doesn't cook, and he refuses to eat anything I make him—which is smart—so we ordered Thai and then I plated it under Kaiser's watchful eye. He wouldn't even let me add a garnish. Again, he's being smart. He doesn't know the difference between cow parsley and hemlock, so it's good he's suspicious of anything green I bring into the house.

His caution hasn't kept me from poisoning him slowly and upping the dose more and more every day. Not through his food, though. He'll never guess how.

I smirk to myself as I finish my pad thai.

"This is nice," I say, and I mean it. It feels very chill. Very old married couple.

"I have something to show you," he says, and brings out his phone. "We need to talk about Club Empire. I'm going to show you some footage from Pandemonium."

Oh no. Here it is.

I am curious, though. I know it wrecked my friends' social lives, but I am a teensy tiny bit excited to see what actually happened.

He plays the video, fast-forwarding through the footage. You can tell the minute the drugs take hold. People stop fucking and start laughing. A few of them get on all fours, crawling and pouncing like they're pretending to be cats. They keep trying to catch the lasers.

He slows the speed and gives me volume. "I can see god," someone screams to the soundtrack of hysterical laughter.

"Oh wow." I try to keep the delight out of my voice but can't. "Guess that's why they call it Pandemonium."

He puts down the phone. "Do you know how this happened?"

"If I had to guess, someone gave out some drugs to people. Like MDMA or something."

"Something with *Salvia divinorum*? That's right, someone put it in the punch. Atticus had it tested."

Oooh, busted.

I shrug. "Sounds like a good time."

He leans in, grips the back of my neck and pulls me close. "I know you did it."

All the breath whooshes out of me.

This is it! He knows. And now I know he knows. And he knows I know that he knows. And... wait, I'm confused.

BUT OH MY GOD THIS IS SO EXCITING!

"You're in big trouble," he growls, and I suppress a squirm. He's big and angry and not fucking around. He's a beast I'm training, but he's not fully tamed yet. "You've been a bad, bad girl."

I'm panting a little. "What are you going to do about it?"

"Go upstairs and prepare for me."

My stomach swoops in the way it always does when he says that. I'm instantly wet. Just as he's trained *me* to be.

Every step I take toward my bedroom only makes me ache more.

I reach my bedroom and smile. Showtime. Here we go...

I light the candles and inhale their strong scent. By the time Kaiser comes upstairs, their incense will permeate the air.

I strip naked and rinse off. When I'm done with my shower, I go through my ritual of oiling my body for him. It's my own recipe. I even labeled it as a love potion—my idea of a joke. The label is funny, but the contents are serious. And they're working.

Kaiser is obsessed with me. He's angry with me right now, but he would never hurt me. He wants me too much.

We're locked in a struggle. It's a race: will he bend me to his will? Or will I trap him first?

Who will win? Who will figure it out first and gain the upper hand?

What else has he figured out?

By the time I'm done preparing, I'm quivering with horniness. I'm naked like he asked, but I also put on a sexy robe that I want to wear. It's silky with a sash.

I settle into bed and draw it around me, imagining how he'll remove it later.

Will he unwrap me like a present? Or rip it off?

Either way, I'll love it.

I'm excited, but now that I'm in bed, my head feels heavy. The bed feels so soft and comfortable, so I stretch out and relax. I don't need a nap, but it would be good to conserve my energy.

I'll just close my eyes for a minute...

When I come to, I feel like I've been asleep for hours. The room is hazy with smoke. Thick with incense. The musk coats my face and tongue.

I sit up. How long have I been out? I can't believe I fell asleep on the most exciting night of my life.

"Bella," Kaiser murmurs. He's somewhere in the room, but I can't see him.

His voice is muffled, almost distorted. The drug must be hitting him hard.

"Kaiser?" I scoot off the bed and stand. And then I see him. He's on the floor by the foot of the bed. He must have fallen a few steps into the room. I can only see his jean-clad legs, sticking out from beyond the bed.

The smoke must have been too much for him. He is down for the count.

So much for our hot night together. *Oh well.*

I sigh. "I knew it was a risk, drugging you like this," I say aloud. I rise, wrapping the robe more firmly around myself and heading to one of the standing candelabras. "It's so hard to get the dosage right." I lick my fingers and snuff out some of the candles, one by one. "But how am I supposed to poison you? You won't drink or eat anything I make. I offered you the mad honey, but you wouldn't touch that either. You've been so careful." I glance back at him. He hasn't moved. I can't see his upper torso, but his legs are in the same spot.

Poor guy.

"I had to find a different way, and obviously, I went too far. Too bad. I was so looking forward to teasing you tonight." I fiddle with my sash. "I wore this for you to rip off. I keep hoping the drugs will lower your inhibitions. You're so careful with me. I figured I could alter your state of mind so you wouldn't hold back." I bite my lip, wondering if I've shared too much. But no, he's out of it.

"I know you know I'm poisoning you. You knew in the beginning. You guessed some of my strategy when you washed me off in the shower. You're pretty smart, for someone so pretty. You're a worthy adversary, you really are." I come around the bed to where he's splayed face down on the floor. "Too bad you didn't figure it out in time to stop it..."

His hand shoots out and grabs my ankle. I scream. He says in a distorted voice, "Except I figured it out a week ago."

## 26

B*ella*

KAISER ISN'T DRUGGED at all. Not only that, but he got me monologuing.

Supervillain Rule # 3: Never monologue!

I jerk back, but he's holding me tight. He raises his head, and I see he's wearing some sort of dark mask over his face and strapped to his head.

What?

His breath comes heavy through the mask he's wearing. It looks like a gas mask, which means none of the candle smoke got through.

What happens now?

He tugs, and I fall to the rug. He rises up, towering over me. A monster in a black mask. He looks a little like a bug. An alien bug—a sexy one I want to fuck.

Great, now I have a new kink.

"Are you going to hurt me?" I ask, breathless. He totally has the upper hand.

It's so fucking hot.

"I'm going to make you pay." He reaches for me. I freak out. I scuttle back away from him, breathing hard. My robe gapes open, flashing him. It gets caught under me, but it makes him pause, looking down on me.

I flip over to all fours and start crawling. He likes it when I crawl. I like it too, but now I'm doing it to distract him. I can feel the robe billowing out behind me.

I'm almost to the door when I scramble to my feet.

"Stop," he orders in his sexy Darth Vader Bug voice. I feel him grab for me, but all he gets is a handful of fabric. I slip out of the robe and run naked out of the room.


*KAISER*


MY BRIDE RUNS FROM ME, into the dark house. Her pale skin flashes ahead of me in the gloom.

She wants me to chase her. I'll always give her what she wants.

"Come out, come out, little one." My voice is distorted because of the mask. The straps hold it tight to my face, but at least I don't have another headache from the fucking candles.

I spent a week getting her to let her guard down. I needed to outwit her. It's the only way she'll respect me.

"I can smell you, little bride."

There's an excited whimper from around the corner by the stairs.

Bingo.

I stomp forward, letting her know I'm coming. Drawing it out. I'm the monster in her story, right? She loves this game we play. She also likes it to feel real. I can do that for her.

Happy wife, happy life.

I shove a table with a vase on it out of my way. The vase falls, and I catch it before it hits the floor. If it breaks, it might shatter, and she could step on it with her bare feet. Can't have that.

"I'm going to make you sorry, baby girl. But you'll like it. You always do." I pause and listen closely. I hear her breathing quicken.

I let my feet fall heavy on the floorboards, turning into the lumbering oaf she thinks I am. I need all the surprises I can get with this girl. But it'll only work once. She's too quick and catches on too easily. I see her eyes shining in the corner. She thinks that I can't see her, but the moonlight is falling in such a way, it's like she's lit up. Excitement ripples through her. She loves this.

She loves the challenge. The thrill of facing a worthy opponent.

I'm going to prove to her that I am husband material. Make her obsessed with me like I'm obsessed with her.

I'm her first, and I'll be her last. Her only.

I will have her for my wife or die trying.

And death is an option. Who knows what other traps my bride has set for me?

"You said that I've been holding back. Maybe I'll give you a taste of the cane. It has a wicked bite."

She lets out a squeak. She can't hide her emotions, and I love that about her.

"I could punish you for days. Years. We have a lifetime together, remember?"

I can practically hear the pitter-patter of her heartbeat.

I jump out from behind the corner. "Got you."

She shrieks, as I knew she would, and darts for the stairs. I follow her, letting her get ahead of me. I don't want her going too fast in case she trips and falls.

Once we're downstairs, I'm not holding back. I chase her through the living room and into the dining room. She pushes a chair in my path, and I narrowly avoid it.

I curse, and she giggles like a maniac, speeding away.

There's a creak in the kitchen, then a crashing of silverware. The pantry door's swinging, but she wouldn't be so silly as to go in there and get trapped. No, she's faking me out. She's squatting in the shadows by the cabinet, hoping I'll pass her hiding place without spotting her.

I walk past her, pretending to do just that.

I pause out of sight, near the door to the greenhouse. That's where she'll head. Her territory. I've got to catch her before then. If she gets her hands on more poison, I give myself only thirty minutes to live.

I can't let her win this round.

I've beaten every other opponent I've ever faced, but I fell prey to her. I underestimated her, but I will not make the same mistake again.

She is the deadliest opponent I have ever faced. And she might be the death of me.

I can hardly wait to see how this ends.

∾

*BELLA*

.   .   .

I CROUCH in the corner of the kitchen, holding my breath. My house has become haunted by a gas-mask-wearing monster. He just lumbered past me.

Should I grab a knife? No, that would be stupid. He's a fighter for a living. I need to keep this benign, in case he catches me.

He's gone.

If I run, I can get to the door to my greenhouse. I count down in my head. Three, two, one—I spring forward, making a break for it—

A shadow falls on me. "Got you." Kaiser slams into me, wrapping his arms around my middle, lifting me right off my feet. I shriek, kicking.

"Behave," he orders, and I freeze automatically. His voice is so creepy.

He tosses me up into his arms, carrying me like a bride back up the stairs. I stare at the creepy gas mask.

What happens if I lift it off?

Before I can touch him, his muscles flex in warning. He growls, "Now you're in for it."

I squeal, half in horror, half delight.

We're back in the bedroom, where he throws me on the bed. I bounce, but before I can get my limbs under control and scramble away, he's on me. I can sense the anger emanating from him, but he's perfectly controlled as he pushes me down. He shoves my legs apart and lays on top of me, his full weight crushing me into the bed. And oh my goddess, it feels so good.

"Are you going to behave for me?" he asks.

I can barely wheeze from under his weight. "No."

More growling. He lifts off me and flips me over, gripping my neck to shove my face into the pillow. I struggle and he lets me up enough so I can turn my head and breath, but then he spanks my ass hard enough for tears to spring into my eyes.

Finally—finally!—he's being rough with me. He's been treating me like his possession but handling me with such care. And now he's finally let himself off the chain.

It also helps that he's not drugged tonight. His senses aren't dulled. His movements aren't slowed. He's not feeling the heavy fatigue. He's possessing all his faculties, and he is going to unleash every single one of them on me. I cannot wait!

He spreads my legs and checks between them. Fuck, he's wearing the murder gloves again. And I'm so wet, his fingers glide right in.

"You little slut. You love this, don't you?" He spanks me again, and I yelp. Then he thrusts his fingers deep. It pinches. The pain sizzles through my core, turning into something else. He finger fucks me like he hates me, and I love it. I want more.

He twists his fingers inside me, his thumb finding my clit and rubbing it.

"Oh fuck," I squeak, and he reaches around to hook the fingers of his free hand into my mouth. The black latex slides over my tongue. He adjusts the angle so he can hit the back of my throat. I gag. My throat closes around his fingers as my pussy does the same. Oh fuck—

"You're going to come for me like this."

I groan around his fingers. And then I do, like he's got my clit on a chain and he tugs me into oblivion. I fall apart, held together only by his fingers in my pussy and my throat.

And then his fingers are pulled out, and I'm gasping for air. He's moving, propping me into position on my hands and knees. And then he's inside me. It hurts at first—more than I remember from Pandemonium. The stretch makes me whimper.

"Oh fuck," I mumble. "Oh fuck me."

"You want this?" He rams himself home. "You got it."

He punches his cock into me, thrusting me toward the headboard. I cry out, tears leaking from my eyes. It hurts, but I'm so happy. Electricity is shooting through my body, and my limbs jerk, no longer my own. I'm so wet, my thighs are drenched. I'm soaking the bed.

He rocks me forward, and when I come again, falling limp to the bed, he pulls me up and plows his cock into me from down below. I look down to where I'm sitting on him and watch his dick saw in and out of my pussy. *Hecate, help me.*

"Oh fuck." One orgasm rolls into another. And another. My eyes roll back into my head.

"That's four," he grunts. "We're going for six, remember?"

What? Oh, right. Page 269. "Six for me or for you?"

"You first."

"No, no, no–"

He sets his gloved hand around my neck and squeezes. "Yes."

## 27

B *ella*

I MUST HAVE ORGASMED SO HARD I passed out. When I come to, he's wiping me down with a warm washcloth. He's removed the gloves and the gas mask. He pats the washcloth over my pussy, checking for tears.

"Ow." My inner muscles are sore.

"Page 269," he says smugly.

Now I know what people mean when they say "he understands the assignment." Kaiser understood the assignment. He could teach the course. He graduated magna *cum* laude. Emphasis on the *cum*.

There are small bruises on my skin where he gripped me, and I touch them in wonder.

"You okay?" He hovers over me, looking concerned. There are red marks on his face from the gas mask straps.

"I'm awesome." I touch myself, checking for blood. "I thought I tore."

"No blood."

"Next time."

He hums, swiping the washcloth over me.

I reach for him, and he stills when I touch his wrist. He doesn't like me touching him, I've noticed that, but he's letting me do it now. "I'm serious. I want it. I want you to make me bleed."

His face is as stern as ever, but he has a smile in his eyes. "All in good time, sweetheart."

Sweetheart?

"We have time. Remember? You're going to be my wife." I'm stunned, still caught up on the soft way he said *sweetheart*.

"We're going to have years together. Years of me learning every part of your body."

He touches my lips, and I realize my mouth is hanging open. What he's saying is too much to imagine.

"Really?"

"Really."

I can't believe it. The picture he's painting is... very attractive. Dinner and then a chase through the house.

It can be like this.

"Would you like that?" He leaves the question hanging while he returns the washcloth to the bathroom.

I'm still braindead, but a *yes* is on the tip of my tongue.

Then I notice he's taken all the candelabras out of the room. The air still has a slight skunky flavor, but it's a lot fresher in here.

"Did you figure out how I was drugging you?" I ask.

He gives me a flat look. "The candles."

"What about them? I love candles. Lots of people have a candle obsession."

"Especially when they smell like hashish."

I knew I went too hard on the opioid compounds in the most recent batch.

"You even decorated the table with poppy flowers," he says.

I giggle. "You noticed."

"And you put on the episode of *Vampire Varsity* where the chess club gets high and gets possessed by the spirit of a succubus."

"Season five, episode twenty-one. It's a good one."

He shakes his head. "You left so many clues."

"It's only fair. Supervillain code of honor. Make sure a worthy adversary has a chance to beat you." I twist one of his curls around my finger.

"You think you're a supervillain?"

I deepen my voice. "You're in my clutches now, Mr. Blond," I say in a fake British accent.

"No. You're in mine."

*Kaiser*

I LIE BACK and pull her into my arms. I never thought I'd enjoy cuddling with a woman all night, but I want a lifetime of this. The fire that ignited after I took her virginity still burns under my skin, but I welcome it. Every time I touch her, I feel a little bit more.

She's still playing with my hair. "You said you figured it out a week ago. Why did you wait so long?"

I cup her cheek. "To lull you into a sense of complacency."

She grins. She loves that. "To get my guard down."

"Yes. And study your every move." I grip a handful of her hair in my fist. "Because I want to know you. I want to know everything about you and what's going on in that brain of yours. You act like you've had the upper hand all this time, and I needed to know why." I release her hair and put my hand around her neck.

She blinks. Her body softens, but her forehead furrows. She looks like she just realized something, something awful. "You figured it out. It was the candles."

"I'm sure you have more tricks up your sleeve." I pull her forward until her forehead presses against mine. "I will learn all your secrets, little bride. I'm going to turn you inside out. I'm not a good person." I squeeze my fingers until her pulse flutters and her eyes half close. "I would own you if I could, but I don't think I can."

Her sigh shakes her small frame. I release her and study her beautiful face. She's wide-eyed, looking shaken.

She reaches for me, hesitates. I tense, bracing myself. It's an instinct to stop someone from touching me. But her touch? I long for it.

Her fingers hover over my lips. A threat. Everything I ever wanted.

"Kiss me," she whispers.

At first, I'm not sure if I heard her right. "Are you sure?" I need to know if she means it. "Aren't you afraid we'll fall in love?"

Her gaze falters. "I'm not worried about that anymore." She looks unhappy. I'm missing something. "I mean it, Kaiser." It's the first time she's said my name. "Kiss me. I want—"

I stop her words with my lips. I can't wait any longer. I want to hear what she wants, but I want to kiss her more.

Her lips are soft and sweet. I can feel them. I can taste her. She's so sweet. So deadly. The perfect poison. If I die tonight, I'll die a happy man.

Our breath mingles. Her tongue slips out, touching mine. I groan and fist her hair, forcing her closer. She melts against me. Her weight is delicious, calming the raging fire in my skin.

"You're so fucking beautiful," I say.

"So are you." But she sounds a bit sad.

"The minute I saw you, I wanted you. It was wrong, but I didn't care. You were made for me—"

I tug her hair, and her breath catches. I'm rock hard again, even though I just came. I could break Thorbjorn's record.

"I'm not a good man. I knew if I asked, they would give you to me. And you're everything I want." I want to chase away the pout she has on her pretty face.

"I'm a lot to take." She angles her head so it's half in shadow. "I'm not a good girl."

"No, you're not." I tug her hair so her face is fully in the light. She still looks troubled. "You're like me. Do you know how many men I've killed?" Her gaze sharpens on me. She was curious about this when we first met.

"I don't even know anymore. Does that scare you?"

"No," she says with a smile. "It turns me on." She hides her mouth with her hand. "I sound deranged."

"No, it's okay. Give it to me. Give it all to me." Because something is still bothering her, and the need to figure it out is crawling under my skin.

"I want to ask some questions."

"Ask." Because at this point, I'll give her anything. I just want to be close to her. Breathe her air. Study her wicked little face. I can't stop touching her, and even though my skin is more sensitive than ever, I want her to touch me.

"You told me you had to fight. You *had* to. Did you kill them all for Fraternitas?"

"No, there were years that I was fighting in the underground for a man known as Maestro."

"I heard you killed your trainer."

"He wasn't our trainer. He was our slaver." Her eyes search my face.

"He's the one who made us fight. The one who figured out how to heal us so we could fight again." I flex my fingers. The compounds he gave me numbed the pain but probably fucked up my nerve endings. That and the stuff he did to me at night, when I was helpless in a cage.

I shake my head to get off the path of those dark memories. "No one thought we would win. No one."

"You and your brother?"

"Yes. Watching Jaeger fight was the worst. Knowing that at any moment, he could die. I would have done anything to save him from the ring. We trained together, taught each other everything we knew. We had to. And we met Atticus there. He learned how to heal people fast. How to dose us with stuff to make our muscles grow. He has a lab too, you know."

"Lab Daddy." She licks her lips. "He's hot."

"Yes. Watch it." I tighten my grip on her hair again. "You're mine, little bride, and I don't share. I want you all to myself."

Her gaze drops from mine for a moment. The predator in me can sense something is wrong, but I don't know what.

"What is it, Bella?"

She shakes her head, sighing. Her tone is solemn when she says, "You have me."

My heart surges in my chest. I want it to be true, but I don't know if I can believe her. She sounds so reluctant. "You're really not afraid of me. Even though I'm a killer."

"Death is inevitable."

"I thought you'd be this sweet innocent virgin. Too innocent for me."

She gives me a wicked grin that doesn't quite reach her eyes. "Who says I'm not?"

"No. I know better now."

Her gaze drops to study my tattoos on my chest and shoulders. I feel uneasy, knowing she's seeing the scars under the tattoos. Her fingers flex like she wants to touch them.

"You were made to fight. Is that why you don't like to be touched?"

I guess it was inevitable that she noticed that. I ache, wanting her touch, but fearing it. Just under the surface, my nerve endings are on fire. "Yes."

"It's okay," she whispers, pulling back her hands. "You're safe with me."

## 28

B*ella*

I DID A BAD THING.

I remember when Kaiser told me he would never fall in love.

Now he's gazing at me like I'm his whole world.

My plan worked. The poison I used bound him to me. Not the candles—the lotion I've been slathering my skin with. It's specially compounded to make him love me.

It should make me gleeful, knowing that I've got him under my spell.

It doesn't. It makes me feel like shit. My stomach churns. I'm trying to hide it, but Kaiser is perceptive. He knows something is wrong. That I'm not happy.

It's all a lie. His attention, his tenderness, is all because I made him feel this way.

He's obsessed with me, just like I wanted him to be. But

not because he actually likes me. The connection he feels with me is manufactured. It's fake.

I thought I'd enjoy having the upper hand, but now that I have it, I hate it. It was better when he was really fighting me. At least then I knew what we had between us was real.

I tamed the beast, but it's horrible. Like declawing a lion.

Why did I do this? I don't want Kaiser to be like this. I want him to be... him. I want him surly and dangerous. Whatever he really feels for me—lust, distrust, even hate—I want it. I want it all. I'm greedy for him, the real him.

Because he was perfect in his own awful way. Evil and bad with a kill count greater than mine. Of all the people on Earth, he would be the one to accept my supervillain tendencies. To encourage them. If I hadn't used the love potion, we could've had something real.

Now I'll never know. We'll never have a true connection, communion. He's taken all my firsts, and I can't even really be with him. Not while I'm still poisoning him.

How the mighty have fallen. He doesn't know his obsession with me isn't real; it's manufactured by me. But I don't want to be his captor or the villain in his story.

I want to be with him.

I wish we could have that.

But we can't. It doesn't matter if I can't have Kaiser's love. From the beginning, we've been locked in a struggle to fight for the upper hand. Now that I have it, I can't throw it away. Not until I free myself and my father from this bogus alliance. I still need to figure out how to do that. I'm not just up against Kaiser, but the whole brotherhood. And then I need to figure out who framed my dad for Alfredo's death and deal with the Vesuvios.

There's no room for Kaiser in my life.

I wish it could be different. But it can't. Kaiser made his

choices. I made mine. We'll always be enemies. Even though my body is sated by the orgasms he's given me and we'll sleep tonight in the same bed, we're not on the same side.

"What's wrong, Bella?" Kaiser asks.

He sounds so earnest, my heart aches. It's on the tip of my tongue just to tell him.

Even if I wanted it to be different, what are my options? If I tell Kaiser what I've done, it won't go well. Sure, he shook off my drugging him with the candles, but this is different. It's so much worse. I've toyed with his emotions—him, a big, strong man who prides himself on winning every fight.

If I confess all my secrets, he'll kill me. Not immediately. He'd confer with Fraternitas, and they'd figure out how to get my drug out of his system. I don't know about mafia contracts, but what I've done is probably grounds to break the alliance. They'd send men to kill my father, and Kaiser would probably take his revenge on me. His loyalty to his brothers comes first.

Nothing's changed. It doesn't matter how sweetly he speaks to me, how softly he strokes my hair. I'm still his enemy, and he is mine.

He says he wants to figure me out, but I can't let him. He can never know me the way he wants to.

What we have will always be fake. It hurts so much, like my own poison is burning me up from the inside. Worse, I can't let the hurt show. I have to act like everything's normal, like Kaiser's love is real. My life, my father's life, depends on it.

"Nothing," I say, forcing a shadow of a smile to my face. "Nothing's wrong." I pretend to be tired and hide my face in the pillow. I'm so devastated, I can't even cry.

This is the price of being a supervillain, and I have to pay it. For my pride's sake. For my dad's sake.

I never thought I'd share a bed, a home, a life with someone who loved me and still feel so alone.

THE NEXT FEW days are agony. I wish I could talk this out with my gal pals, but Raine is still locked up in her stepbrother's castle.

Honey is willing to sit beside me in orientation class again, but she doesn't have time to hang out afterward anymore.

Which is why, when Kaiser picks me up at university and says, "Your father wants to see you," I'm relieved.

He drives me to New Rome. My happy feelings last until he drops me off at the door of our home. When I walk in, I feel like I'm in the wrong place. There are no plants, no decorations. None of Mom's paintings are on the wall.

Did Papa remove them all as soon as I moved out to go to school? I was the one watering all the plants, but I figured he would take over when I left. The walls look bare, and the breakfast nook feels empty without the giant money tree dominating the space. It used to feel like a jungle or a garden; now it feels like a tomb.

I'm glad I don't live here anymore.

I take the elevator to the lower levels and find my father in his secret lab.

"Papa." It's a relief to see him. He looks thinner, his skin a little sallow, but so familiar my heart aches. He's even wearing his microscope goggles that help him work but make him look ridiculous. He invented them when my mother was still alive, and she always teased him about them.

These days, no one teases him. He and I don't have that sort of relationship.

Right now, I feel the urge to run into his arms, but he's not a hugger. I rein in that urge—I'm always reining myself in around Papa—and linger in the door.

"Bella." He looks up from his work, removes his goggles, and looks me over, his expression relieved. So he does care about me. "You're looking well."

*And you look like you've been working too hard,* I want to say. I want to ask him if he's eating enough and scold him about his long hours. My mom would've. But I bite my tongue.

"You wanted to see me." My arms hang awkwardly at my side. I don't know what to do with my hands, so I fold them in front of me. "Is everything okay?"

"I merely wanted to check on you. I'm told you caused quite a stir at one of Fraternitas's places of business."

He called me here to chew me out for Pandemonium. I know it was a ruckus, but what happened to having a little fun?

I shrug. "It was a joke. I've already apologized." To my friends. Not to Fraternitas. If they want this alliance, they'll have to deal.

He sighs. "I told them I'd address your behavior."

"Why? Are they going to break the engagement?" My heart speeds up. Last time we spoke by phone, I was frothing at the mouth to get out of this wedding. Now? I still want out, but I feel some reluctance. If the contract ends, will Kaiser leave? Do I want him to?

"No." My father frowns.

"Right." I relax, ignoring how relieved I feel, knowing that I'm still shackled to Kaiser. "Then everyone needs to chillax. I'm not a child."

"And yet you insist on acting like one."

"I wouldn't if I were treated like an adult who gets to choose who she wants to marry." *Just because you like Kaiser, doesn't mean you want to marry anyone,* I scold myself. I don't want Fraternitas to have the upper hand. It's a matter of principle.

"We've been over this." He picks up his goggles and polishes them with a cloth. I stare at his bare ring finger. He used to wear a wedding ring, but not since Mom died. It bothers me, but I've never said anything about it.

"We have not. I'm still waiting for an explanation." I fold my arms over my chest, holding my breath. It's hard to stand up to my father like this.

He shakes his head slightly. "Not here." He glances up toward the corner of the ceiling, and I look, but I don't see anything. But I get it. He's warning me about cameras.

Even if this place is bugged and we're being watched, there are many ways he can communicate with me. All these weeks, waiting, and he couldn't just slip me a note?

"Papa, you sold me into marriage. I deserve to understand why." If I understand the politics at play in this alliance, maybe I can craft a new, better solution. "This is all a mistake." My voice rings out in the quiet lab. "I tried to tell them you didn't kill Alfredo Vesuvio but—"

"Belladonna," he snaps, then softens his voice. "It's done." He closes his eyes as if he's very tired. "I admitted that I sold the poison to Livia."

"What?"

"Livia Vesuvio. Alfredo's wife. Fraternitas knows she came to me, here, after hours, and I sold her the compound she could use to kill her husband."

My mouth is open, but I don't know what to say. I swallow. "That's not—"

"It's the truth. It happened. And now I am paying for it. We both have to live with the consequences."

I shake my head. That's not what happened, and he knows it. "I—"

"Do you know what happened to her? Livia? After Alfredo died, his father ordered an autopsy. Dominus is the head of the Vesuvio crime family. He has three children, all boys, but Alfredo was the oldest and his favorite. His heir. When the autopsy revealed traces of poison, Dominus was out for blood." He pauses to let me figure out where this is going.

*Out for blood... Livia.* "No," I whisper.

"Yes." He braces his hands on the counter, his expression bleak. "He killed her. Well, he handed her over to his other sons. I will spare you the details of everything they did to her before they dumped her body in an alleyway behind their house. They claim they have no idea who murdered her, but everyone knows they did it. The police have closed the investigation. Livia's body is unclaimed. It will go to a pauper's grave as a message to everyone who would mess with the family.

"Not only that, but Alfredo and Livia's three children are missing. No one knows what happened to them. Dominus might have killed them. Or disinherited them and turned them over to his enemies to be tortured as they see fit. Or he's imprisoned them for his own purposes. His own grandchildren."

Hecate, help me. I press my hands to my heart and stomach, trying to keep my horror in.

He leans on the counter like it's the only thing keeping him upright. "I can tell you more tales of their brutality, but I believe you understand the stakes."

I get what he's telling me. Once the Vesuvios discover

who sold Livia the poison, they will hunt us down until we're dead.

This is why Papa caved to Fraternitas.

"Fraternitas found out I was involved, and now I owe them a debt," he says quietly. "They will protect us, and in return, we do what they say."

No. It can't be this way. There has to be another solution. "We can fight back—"

"No, we can't."

I'm back in my father's office, surrounded by Frateritas members in skull masks, feeling helpless, and I hate it. "You didn't even ask me," I whisper. "You didn't give me a choice."

"You don't get to choose. Those weren't the terms—"

"You could've made them the terms—"

"Kaiser chose you. You belong to him now."

That gives me pause. I like that Kaiser chose me. Still… "I don't belong to anyone."

"You do now."

"I'm not an object you can trade away." He shakes his head, and desperation flares through me. This is why it rankles me so much; he couldn't wait to give me away. "I thought you loved me. You're my father—"

"I am your father, so you will do this to honor me. To honor your family."

"Honor?" I grit my teeth so I don't curse him out. Fuck his honor. Fuck everything.

My father's face darkens. He has a temper, too, but unlike me, he channels it into a weapon. "You no longer have the luxury of being naive." His voice is cold, like he's talking to an employee who stole from him. "I've sheltered you too much. You don't live in the real world. The Vesuvio family is dangerous. They're one of the four families that rule Metropolis. They have an army. We have a reputation, a few employees and a bunch of plants. If we fight them alone, we will lose.

"I've sheltered you as long as I can, but I can't shield you from this. It's too big. We need allies who can have our back. Fraternitas will be those allies. If you were capable of strategy, you would understand this is the best move. The only move."

"It's not a move. It's my life!"

He flicks his fingers, like he's washing his hands of me. "Emotional," he mutters, almost too low for me to hear. "Like a woman."

*Shut up, shut up,* I want to scream. There's a bitter taste in my mouth, and my jaw is locked like I'm going to throw up.

But I won't. I refuse to get emotional.

My eyes burn, but I wait until I'm sure tears won't fall, then loosen my jaw and fire my best shot. "If my mom were alive, she would never allow this."

My father's face turns to stone. The light from his eyes fades, as it always does when I mention my mother. "If your mother were alive, she would agree with me."

"No, she wouldn't." My body aches like he's punched me in the gut. "How dare you? How dare you say that?"

"You want the truth, Bella? Then listen to me. One day, I will die."

My muscles freeze. There's a voice in my head screaming *no, no, no, don't go. Don't leave me.* I'm five years old again, reaching for a mother or father who will never come.

"When that day comes, it is my final wish that you remain in an alliance with Fraternitas. Do not let your mother's sacrifice go to waste."

I knew it. I knew he blamed me for her death. "You never loved me, did you?"

"I do this because I love you."

"No, you never loved me, and you never loved her," I rave. "I know you didn't. You never avenged her!" He wants me to be a mastermind like him. Uncaring. Unfeeling. Willing to do anything for power.

But he's the one who refused to avenge my mother's murder. For a decade. As soon as I found out, I did something about it. I may be reckless, but I'm not a coward.

My father's face is purple. He could be having an aneurysm right now. I've done the equivalent of stabbing him in the heart.

I don't care. He deserves the pain. He took my mother's paintings down from the walls. He's done everything to erase her from his life, and I will never forgive him for it. "That's why you never speak of her. You can't even say her name. You failed her."

He stares at me. *That's right, Papa, I can wound you, too.* But it doesn't feel like winning. It feels like we're both pulling each other down to drown in the mud.

After a long moment, he gets himself under control. My father is gone. The robot that's commandeered his body since Shoshonna Bosco was murdered is here. "If you would grow up, you would understand. There are things more important than vengeance. I had a child to protect."

My face splits into a bitter smile. "Good news, Benjiro. You don't protect me anymore."

**29**

---

B*ella*

I STORM out of my father's lab. Kaiser's waiting there. He probably followed our shouting down the stairs. "Is everything okay?" he asks.

"Fine," I say in a flat voice.

My father followed me out. I turn my back on him as if he doesn't matter.

"I'll see you at the engagement party," he says.

"Don't fucking bother," I toss over my shoulder and walk out. Fuck him.

Fuck everything.

I thought talking to my father would help, but it never does. My father stands there like a rock and lets my rage wash over him, and in the end, he's not moved.

I hate it so much.

I hate him. He's my only family, and I love him, but I hate how he is. I hate that I want him to be proud of me.

Well, he made it clear today that he'll never be proud of me.

If that's true, then I have nothing to lose.

It's time to fully enter my supervillain era.

By the time I get to the car, all my emotion is spent, and I feel like curling into a ball under an oak tree and hibernating until the leaves cover me. I could do it, too. Kaiser would protect me.

He's the one who watches over me, not my father. What I said was true. Everything my father told me was probably true, too. We've laid out the brutal facts between us, and nothing is solved.

I'm so tired.

"What happened?" Kaiser asks.

I don't answer. I don't look at him. He might as well be a chauffeur.

"Do you want to go to the bookstore?" He's offering an olive branch. He's being so sweet, and of course, he is. I drugged him to want to take care of me. "Or to Pane P's? You wanted to try those new muffin things."

"Cruffins." I try to force a smile, but it doesn't work. "Just take me home."

My father's voice plays over and over in my head.

*You don't live in the real world.*

*If you were capable of strategy...*

*I will spare you the details of everything they did to her...*

Kaiser is merging onto the highway toward Metropolis when I sit up. "Wait. Take me to the city morgue."

He frowns. "Why?"

"There's something I have to do." My breath comes faster, remembering what my father said. *Livia's body is unclaimed. It will go to a pauper's grave as a message to everyone who would mess with the family.*

I fucked up. I want to make it right. But then I realize this is nuts. What am I going to do, walk in and claim a body? I'm no relation to Livia.

I need to start thinking things through.

I slump in my seat. "Never mind."

Kaiser hesitates. He's doing all the right things and trying to make me feel better. All because I made him love me.

I don't deserve him. I should tell him everything now and let him put me out of my misery.

But no. The pain I'm feeling—that's what I deserve.

I deserve all this misery, and more.

At DUSK, Kaiser finds me in the greenhouse.

"I made some calls," he says. "Pulled some strings. Here," He sets a plain white urn on the work table.

I stare at it, not understanding until he says, "Livia Vesuvio's ashes. St. James called in a favor at the Metropolis morgue."

"You were listening," I say.

"Yes."

I close my eyes, feeling very tired. "Cameras?"

"Yes."

I nod. My father was right to be circumspect.

I wait until the moon rises and head out the back door of the greenhouse.

Kaiser follows me at a distance, into the forest and the orchard beyond. I don't try to lead him into a trap. I avoid all poisonous things. I'm poisonous enough, just by myself.

I don't want to spread the ashes; it doesn't feel right. One day, her children will be found, and they'll want them.

Where do I put her?

The wind picks up, rustling the leaves of the hazel tree above me. It's a big tree—bigger than any hazel tree I've ever seen—with a hollow at the base of its largest branches. Someone's hammered toe holds up the trunk.

I climb up and place the urn there. I wrapped it in a plastic bag to keep it safe from the elements or a curious squirrel. Livia will be safe up there.

When I climb back down, I lean against the tree. I feel Kaiser's presence; he's close, but he's in stalker mode. Giving me space.

He's here for me, but I have to do this alone.

*You never think of the consequences,* my father told me. And he's right. I didn't think of what would happen when Livia sought me out and begged me to sell her a poison to end her abusive husband's life.

I couldn't have predicted this. Would I have done it if I'd known what would happen?

I don't know, but I think so. Because sometimes doing something right leads to bad things happening.

"I'm sorry," I tell her. "I'm so sorry."

And then I'm sobbing and can't stop. For all the mothers who do their best to stand up to evil men but die anyway. For their children who will grow up without their love.

For my own mother and my childhood self.

*You need to grow up,* my father said.

He's right.

Kaiser picks me up and carries me back to our bedroom. He handles me like a child, washing my face and putting me to bed, but I don't fall asleep.

It's midnight when I sit up. Kaiser is sleeping deeply when I slip out of bed. He frowns but doesn't stir.

I head back down to my greenhouse. To the small dark room beside it, where I keep the most potent poisons. Some I use to kill weeds. Some I use to kill pests.

Some I've used to kill men, but no one knows about that.

What I have with Kaiser is new. Fragile. A fresh green sprout breaking from the soil. So easy to rip out. So easy to kill.

He's told me we can have a life together.

But I refuse to be a pawn in this game.

They can make me marry him, but they can't make me be anything but a wife in name only.

Whatever we have between us cannot grow, so it's best to pull it out by the roots while it's small. Before it's taken hold.

I would mourn what we could've had, but the time for tears is over.

I need to grow up.

I open one jar filled with a thick white liquid. It's a balm made of different compounds distilled from tansy, larkspur, and hellebore and causes blistering, pain, and nausea. I spread it over my skin.

Pain bursts through me, searing every nerve. My mouth opens in a scream.

I can't cry out; it'll wake Kaiser. I shake with the force of holding the sound in.

It feels like dying. It feels like everything I am is burning away.

And it feels like absolution.

I open another jar and another. I dig out all the poisons and smear them on my skin. I open the vials and gulp the tinctures down.

It hurts, but it's necessary.

I know the mistake I made with the Vesuvios. I thought I wasn't strong enough to take them on. I thought I needed to wait, to hone my abilities at Mafia University and build resources.

But I'm Belladonna Bosco. Poison runs in my veins.

I should've made sure I killed them all. Dominus, the don, and all of his sons, his capos, not just Alfredo. Instead, I waited, and Livia and her children paid the price. Her death, and possibly theirs, is on my head.

Everyone underestimates me. Fraternitas. My father. Even Kaiser. But not after this.

I will make the Vesuvios pay. It'll mean the end of the alliance, but everyone will know what I've done. Kaiser will hate me forever, but I deserve that.

Those are the consequences of my actions, and I accept them.

But I refuse to be weak. I'll prove to everyone once and for all who I am: a supervillain.

I fight through the pain raging through my body, gripping the side of the work table until I can stand without shaking. I continue to coat myself in the poisons.

It's time for the Endgame.

*KAISER*

BELLA'S not beside me when I wake up in the morning. It's not unusual, but something feels off. The house is too quiet, and the empty space next to me feels wrong. I trust my instincts.

I call her name, and when she doesn't answer, I head down to the greenhouse.

I'm still cursing myself for taking her to her father. I should've known when he asked to see her that he was going to be an asshole and upset her again. When I listened to the conversation replay, I got why she's so upset. She pleaded with him for an explanation, a sign that he cared about her, and instead of listening and reassuring her, he just turned cold.

I'm tempted to order her never to see him again. She'd hate me for it, but it might be for the best.

Except, I don't want to give her orders anymore. I don't want to force her to do anything anymore. I don't want to lock her in a cage.

But I never want to see that lost look on her face again. In the car, she was a shadow of herself. That's why, as soon as she went to the greenhouse, I got on the phone with St. James to negotiate the release of Livia Vesuvio's remains. He argued with me, saying it wasn't smart to get involved in the Vesuvio's business like this. He's spent weeks trying to get them to agree to a truce.

Claiming Livia's ashes will piss them off, but it was the right thing to do. St. James didn't like it, but he has a soft spot for this sort of thing, and in the end, he caved and made it happen.

I thought laying the ashes to rest would help her, but Bella cried herself to sleep.

She may still be upset. I need to find her.

I open the door to the greenhouse. The thick scent of greens and flowers hangs in the humid air. "Bella?" I call. I don't see her anywhere. She's not standing at any work table or bending over the plants.

Did she run? My heart rate speeds up, ready to run after her. But Argos would've alerted me if she left the premises.

I'm about to pull out my phone and check the cameras around the perimeter when I notice her lying on the daybed under the windows. She lies there, fast asleep, bathed in the morning light. She's wearing her favorite hot pink gardening gloves. She must have been up early to garden and decided to take a nap.

I move to her side, quietly so she doesn't wake. She looks so peaceful like this, if a little pale. I crouch by her.

"Bella. Bella, wake up."

No response. That's when I notice her breathing is shallow.

I touch her forehead. Her skin is clammy. Her sweat coats my fingers. I take her hand, lift it, and let go to test her reflexes. It falls limp at her side. She doesn't flinch at all. She's completely out.

Dread rises in my throat, choking me, and alarm bells screech in my mind. I try to wake her again, but she doesn't respond.

I check her pulse. She still has one, but she looks like she's on death's door.

## 30

K*aiser*

Bella is unconscious and won't wake up. I've tried everything and now I'm panicking. There's a roaring sound in my head, and the predator in me looks around for a threat, but there's none in the sunny greenhouse.

My fingertips are red from where they touched Bella. I touch her again, using my opposite hand to wipe away more sweat, and after a few minutes, my skin starts to burn.

I have to think. She has to have been poisoned, right? I look around to see what Bella might have been working on, but there are no plants at her favorite workbench. It could be anything in this place.

The predator in me wants to smash every pot and kill everything with fire, but I need to be smart.

I call everyone I can think of. I even call the number for the Poisoner, but the line seems to be dead. I throw my phone across the room, where it lands in one of the mushroom trays. At least it didn't shatter.

I need to get a hold of myself. I want to destroy everything. Instead, I go stand over Bella, watching for signs of her waking up. What else can I do? Jaeger roars up in his Lykan. He brought Atticus with him.

"Be careful not to touch her," I say, showing them my hands.

Atticus frowns but wastes no time checking Bella over. "She's in a coma. No sign of why. Heart rate is normal. Vitals, all normal. Temperature slightly elevated, but not enough to be concerned."

"It has to be poison," I say. "Can't you give her medicine?"

"Not until I know what poisoned her. Inducing vomiting might cause more harm than good. When my team gets here, we'll do bloodwork and run some tests. Did you contact the Poisoner?"

"I couldn't get through."

Atticus has me move Bella back to her bedroom, which is better suited for a sickroom. He sends Jaeger to call St. James and connect with Bella's father. Then he turns to me. "Let me see your hands."

I show them to him. The red has faded. The burning sensation is distant, like a sunburn.

"It looks like you touched a toxic plant."

"I didn't. I just touched her."

"Could she have smeared something toxic on her skin? Like she was working with a plant and wiped her forehead, transferring it to her skin?"

"That's probably it," I tell him about how she touches poison ivy and other toxic plants. "She says she's immune."

"Hmmm." Atticus takes a skin sample and offers me a salve and a bandage, which I refuse. I want all his attention focused on Bella.

Atticus's assistants arrive. I recognize them as his

submissives from Club Empire. They must all have medical training. They surround Bella, drawing blood, setting up an IV. They have all sorts of portable medical equipment. St. James makes sure Atticus has an unlimited budget for this sort of thing. Their ambulance-like van is like a lab on wheels.

Fraternitas members don't go to hospitals. Hospital staff can be bribed, and Atticus is more skilled than any regular doctor. If anyone can save her, it's him.

I watch from the doorway, feeling helpless. Bella looks so small. So lifeless. Jaeger hovers at my shoulder. He doesn't touch me; he knows I can't stand it. But he stays close enough to make me feel like I'm not alone. An assistant approaches Atticus and whispers in his ear. Atticus frowns. "What is it?" I ask.

"Her liver enzymes are slightly elevated," Atticus says.

"What does that mean?" Jaeger asks.

"All signs are pointing to her being poisoned. I don't think it's just from wiping something toxic on her forehead, though. Could she have eaten something, drunk something poisonous?"

I flex my hands. I wish I could put my hands around an enemy's neck and squeeze. "This whole house is filled with poisons. She's the Poisoner's daughter." For fuck sake, she's still poisoning me somehow. There's no way I'd be sleeping so deeply every night if she weren't.

And I'm letting her do it because I want her. I want everything from her. I'll drink her poison down and ask for more.

"All right. We test everything. I can't create an antidote unless I know what did this." Atticus gives his assistants instructions to take samples from all the plants downstairs. "Be careful and collect anything else that might be poisonous. Solvents, cleaning solutions, room sprays, balms, lotions—"

"Candles," I add to the list.

Atticus's team leaves to search the house. Two head to the bathroom and start pulling bottles off the shower shelf.

"If it's here, we'll find it," Atticus says.

"She handles poisonous plants all the time," I say. "She knows the risks."

"Maybe she was careless. You said she was distraught last night, right?" I close my eyes and nod.

"It could've been an accident. Or... would she poison herself?" I start to shake my head but stop. Why would Bella knowingly ingest poison? "Maybe she did, thinking she was immune."

"Is there anyone who would want to incapacitate her? An enemy?"

The only enemies are the Vesuvios, and they prefer brute force to anything subtle like poisons. But there is someone with a knowledge of poisons she visited only yesterday. Someone who might want to drug her, to make sure she's obedient to his will.

Benjiro Bosco. The Poisoner.

I'm out the door before Jaeger can shout for me to wait.

I drive at breakneck speed back to New Rome. Jaeger follows me in his car, but I use every maneuver I can to outpace him. By the time I pull up to the Bosco residence, he's too far behind to stop me.

This place is a fortress, with bars over the window and layers of security, but there's a side door that isn't secure. I kick it in and sprint through the house, bursting into her father's lab. "What did you do to her?"

The Poisoner looks up at me, surprised. "What do you mean?" I stalk toward him, every muscle taut and ready to fight. "Bella's sick. Poisoned. She's in a coma." I loom over him. "Did you do it? Did you poison her?"

"I would never do anything to harm my daughter."

"You did something. Or... you upset her... and she did something." I grab him by the throat. He's petite, like his daughter. It would take nothing to crush his throat like a soda can.

"Take your hands off me," he says. His gaze is steely, but he sounds calm. There are shouts from the rooms upstairs. My brother has come, and he has reinforcements. They thunder down the stairs. Jaeger appears at the door with Asmodeus at his back.

"Kaiser, no," Jaeger calls. "You can't kill him."

"Can't I?" I squeeze until fear flickers in my future father-in-law's eyes. The predator in me is roaring, dying to taste his blood.

"Atticus says we need him alive," Jaeger says. "If she dies, you can kill him, alright?"

I release the Poisoner before he turns beet red. He bends over, heaving, and Jaeger and Asmodeus insert themselves between me and him. The Poisoner rubs his neck where I started to choke him. He swallows a few times and rasps, "What are her symptoms?"

"Here." Jaeger holds up a phone. On the other end of the line, Atticus rattles off a bunch of information, including Bella's vital signs. "Her temperature is also elevated. One hundred and one and rising. Her body is fighting something."

The Poisoner signs and straightens his shirt. He doesn't seem too concerned about his daughter. Fucking father of the year. "It sounds like poison. But she likely did it to herself."

"What?" Why would she poison herself?

"What do we do?" Atticus is asking.

"Nothing. This will probably pass," the Poisoner says.

I'm still too stunned to speak. Why would Bella do this? She was broken up over Livia's death, but I never thought it would come to this.

I think back over last night. Bella cried over Livia's ashes. A woman she never knew but mourned like she was mourning her own mother. It was almost like she blamed herself for Livia's death.

Is this her way of punishing herself?

I rub a hand over my face. Jaeger touches my shoulder briefly, bringing me back.

Atticus is asking the Poisoner to explain.

The Poisoner sighs and takes a seat on a nearby stool. "Since she was little, she's always been fascinated with poisons. She was exposed to many of them at a young age. When she was three, she crawled through a dog door and into the woods. She was lost for half an hour. We searched everywhere and found her playing in a patch of poison ivy. Her mother was horrified, but we monitored Bella, and she never had symptoms.

"When she was four, she figured out how to unlock the door to the greenhouse. She found a bucket of yew berries and ate as many as she could. Her skin turned red, and she fell into a fever, but after a long night, she woke up and was fine. Her body seems to process things differently."

"Why wasn't this in her medical records?" Atticus asks.

"Her mother had medical training. She called in a few favors, but we never took Bella to a hospital. We didn't dare leave the safety of our home in case our enemies were lying in wait."

"How many times did this happen?" I ask.

"Only once more." He swallows as if he's bracing himself

against what he's about to say next. "The day her mother died, Bella was trapped for seven hours in a room with highly poisonous plants. She was unconscious with a fever for three days, but then she recovered fully. That was the last time it happened."

"So you think she'll be fine? If we do nothing?" Atticus asks.

"Keep her hydrated. Monitor her vitals." The Poisoner shrugs. "Her mother kept journals—there might be something in them that will shed light on what Bella has done."

*What Bella has done.* I don't like how he talks about her. I clench my hands into fists. It would be so satisfying to punch him. Drive my fists into his face over and over, until his skull caves—

But I can't. It won't help Bella. It will hurt her.

Atticus says he wants to see the journals.

"I'll dig them out of storage," the Poisoner says. "And I can come and run some tests if you like—"

"No." I move closer to him. Jaeger and Asmodeus block my way, and I ignore them. "She doesn't want to see you." *I don't want her to see you.* The Poisoner nods, his expression resigned. "Let me know if I can help."

"You've done enough," I say. The way he speaks to her, I should cut out his tongue. The only thing stopping me is knowing Bella won't like it. But she can't stop me from threatening him.

I point at the Poisoner. "If she dies, I'll kill you. Come near her and I'll kill you. She's not yours to protect anymore."

I wait for him to shout at me or insist that Bella belongs to him, but he just nods.

I leave the room before the predator in me pounces, and

I have to come up with a way to convince Bella that she's better off with him dead.

Jaeger catches up with me on the stairs. He lopes along by my side. "What do you want to do?"

"I'm going home," I say.

"I'll drive."

There are a few Fraternitas members standing around my car who straighten when I storm out of the house. They're there to keep me from going on a rampage.

And suddenly, that's all I want to do. I can't kill the Poisoner, but I need to spill blood. My skin feels itchy, all over like it's too tight.

I want to throw my head back and roar.

I round on my brother.

"Did you call them?" I ask.

"You can't kill your father-in-law," Jaeger says, annoyingly calm. It's the last straw. I charge him. He waits until the last second to duck me. But I know his moves better than he does. I taught them to him. I kick his shin. He goes down but hammers a blow to my knee. I stagger, barely managing to stay upright.

He comes up and pops me in the face. Blood trickles in my eyes. It hurts, but it's a good, clean pain. It cuts through the itchy feeling. It feels right.

I charge my brother again, roaring. I slam a haymaker into his jaw and two more into his gut before I realize he's not trying to hit me back. He just takes the blows and straightens, his hands loose at his sides. I punch him in the face, but my heart isn't in it.

This isn't a fair fight. The predator snarls, wanting more, but I'm back in control.

I can't kill my brother. I face him, chest heaving. We're

mirror images of each other. Identical. Even the black eye he just gave me matches the one I gave him.

The rest of my Fraternitas brothers have formed a loose circle around us. We're on a public street in the middle of a nice neighborhood, putting on a free show.

I wipe the blood off my face. Jaeger resets his jaw.

I go to offer him my hand, and the men around us tense.

"It's okay," Jaeger says at the same time I say, "We're good."

We clasp hands. My knuckles throb from hitting him, but the pulsing pressure feels good.

"Your car or mine?" I ask.

"Mine."

I get into Jaeger's car without another word. A few minutes later, we're roaring down the highway.

I feel him watching me, but he doesn't say anything. He lets the silence hang between us. Leaving me to wrestle with the questions I don't want to answer.

Did Bella try to kill herself? To escape me?

When we get back to the Metropolis house, Atticus takes one look at us and sighs. I'm no longer bleeding, but my black eye speaks for itself, and half of Jaeger's face is swollen.

"How is she?" I say.

"Better than you. But no change." Atticus doesn't tell me that fighting is a waste of time and energy. He doesn't have to. I know it in my bones.

I return to watching over Bella. I wish I were a better man, but I'm not. I wish I could deserve her.

But I never will.

## 31

K *aiser*

DAY AND NIGHT pass with no change in Bella. I move an armchair close so I can sit by her bed. Atticus sends all but his most trusted nurses away. They check her vitals every hour on the hour.

The Poisoner made good on his promise and gave Atticus Shoshonna Bosco's journals. Atticus and I pore over them and found the ones that have notes about Bella's health episodes. He made copies of the most helpful passages for himself. The rest of the journals I stacked beside Bella and me. I find the happiest entries and read them aloud.

There's an entry about Benjiro taking the family to the city to see the cherry blossoms. According to the diary, Bella preferred to chase the ducks. The journal entries end in springtime, thirteen years ago. That's when Shoshonna died.

I don't want the story to end that way, so I close the journal and say, "She loved you."

I never knew my mother. I'd like to think she was a kind woman; she probably wasn't. But when I was reading the journals, I could feel the love like a motherly presence. Like someone who loved me deeply was standing by my side.

My brother calls, asking for an update.

Bella lies still as a corpse. I've learned to put my hand on her chest to make sure she's breathing. "Still the same."

"Elodie sends her love. She wants to know if there's anything we can do."

"I'll let you know."

"All right." A pause, like he's thinking. "She's more than a job, isn't she." It's not a question.

"Yes." She's more than a job. More than an alliance.

She is everything.

"She doesn't want me," I tell him. "I'm the brute she has to marry."

"Eh, you can't be sure about that."

I snort. I am a brute, and he knows it.

"Bitches love brutes."

"Excuse me," a feminine voice says. It's his woman, Elodie, scolding him for calling her a bitch and himself a brute.

Jaeger and I both listen to her rant until she runs out of steam. "Okay, Bunny," he tells her. "Got to go," he says to me, sounding happy. "You want my advice?"

Not really, but I'd kill to have what Jaeger has with Elodie, and he knows it. So I don't hang up.

"Don't be too hard on yourself. Tell her what she means to you. And, brother?"

"Yes?"

"Buy her a ring."

In the middle of the second night, Bella cries out. "Mama," she whimpers, twisting and jerking. "Mama!"

I hit the button to call the nurse attendant and turn on a low light. Bella's cheeks are bright pink—evidence of the fever.

I hover my hand over her forehead, afraid to touch her in case I make it worse. "Shh, baby. It's okay."

She calls out in terror. "Don't leave me. Don't leave me alone." The nurse hasn't come. I stride to the door and bellow, "A little help? She's awake." I want to drag the attendant out of bed, but I don't want to leave Bella's side.

She's thrashing, throwing off the covers. I race back and strip them away from her. I can't stop myself from pulling her small body into my arms. She moans, fighting harder.

"Baby, please." I hold her tighter, feeling helpless. If only there were someone I could kill for her. Someone I could fight.

But there's no one. She did this to herself, under my watch. I was supposed to take care of her, and I failed.

"Mama, I'm scared," she cries like a child. "Come back. Don't leave me."

"I won't, baby. I'm here." I press my lips to her hairline. My skin tingles like I've been burned. "I won't leave you."

The nurse finally comes in, looking half awake.

"Where have you been?" I snarl. I make him take her vitals while I hold her. I refuse to let her go. *I won't leave you, baby. Never.*

A few hours later, I wake with a start. I'm in the chair. I must have fallen asleep. I have the strangest sense that someone brushed my forehead. But it can't be Bella, who's asleep. And no one else is here.

But I feel that sense that someone is standing beside me. Someone lovely. I feel a presence. A motherly presence.

Maybe it's Shoshonna. Maybe it's Livia, haunting us until we find her children and give them her ashes.

Whoever it is, I press my hands together and bow my head. Father Francis tried to teach us about his God, and he would smile if he could see me now, praying to an unseen presence.

"Please," I whisper. "Please."

When I lift my head, I feel a sense of peace. I could be imagining it, but the room smells like flowers. Roses or something stronger. Something sweet.

*BELLA*

THE SCENT of roses wakes me. It smells like roses and lily of the valley. My mother's signature scent.

The room is too hot, the air pressing in. There's a slow beeping sound that's driving me crazy. My skin feels tight, and my mouth is too dry.

I open my eyes. I'm in my bed. Kaiser's beside me, asleep with *Viking Thunder* propped open on his chest. Like he was reading and fell asleep. I lick my lips. I need water.

Moving makes me dizzy, and there's a dull pain in my right arm. I glance down and see something stuck in the crook of my elbow, taped there. A needle that leads to a tube that leads to an IV.

*What the—?*

I pull the tube, and the IV stand shakes.

Kaiser's eyes pop open. "Bella?"

I grit my teeth and dig my nails under the tape on my elbow. It hurts as it peels away.

"Bella. You're awake."

"Get this off me," I croak.

He grabs a bottle of water, breaks the seal, and holds it to my lips. I drink a few mouthfuls until he makes me take a break.

I lick my lips again. It tastes like someone's put cherry Chapstick on them. "How long have I been out?"

He looks around blearily for a clock. "Fifty-two hours."

Hecate, help me. That's a long time. I knew I'd have a temporary reaction to all the poisons I took, but this is a little dramatic. I overdid it.

My father would say *I told you so*. Kaiser looks like he lived through a war. He helps me drink more water, and I feel better. I scoot until I can sit up, then get back to peeling off the tape until I can rip out the IV. He reaches for me, and I flinch. I don't want him touching me. I can still feel the poisons swirling under my skin. They're not killing me anymore. I've assimilated to them. They're a part of me but still deadly.

He hesitates with his hand hovering just out of reach. "Do you feel okay?"

"I'm fine." I look up and see a stranger walking through the door. "Who's this?"

"Your nurse," Kaiser says.

"I'm Tommy," the stranger says, grabbing a stethoscope and approaching. "I'll just check your vitals."

Kaiser seems fine with this, so I lie back and let the nurse do his thing.

"Temperature's normal," the nurse sounds surprised. "I'll inform Atticus."

Kaiser tells me Atticus has been overseeing my care. I nod absently. I notice a stack of old notebooks on the bedside table. They look familiar. I wait until the nurse leaves to ask Kaiser, "What are those?"

"Your mother's journals." He stands beside the bed, looking worried.

"Oh." I reach out and stroke the closest one. It has a pretty cover, blooming peonies on a green background.

I remember Kaiser's voice rising and falling close by. I was in the dark and couldn't see, but I could hear him. "You read them to me."

"Yes. I thought it would help. Your father found them for us."

I raise my head. "Did he visit me?"

Kaiser looks like I've punched him in the gut. "No."

I sigh. I guess I can't be disappointed.

"Bella." Kaiser sits on the bed. "He wanted to. It's my fault he didn't come."

"What?"

"I told him I would kill him if he tried to see you." His face holds no expression, but I know him well enough to know he feels guilty. He's torn up about this. "I thought he had done something to you."

"No. He wouldn't." I pick at the bedspread. I like that Kaiser defended me to my father. "When my father poisons someone, no one ever finds out."

"Bella, why did you do this?"

"I was testing something." I quote one of my favorite movies. "*I've built up a tolerance to deadly iocane powder.*"

Kaiser doesn't smile. He looks like someone died. "I thought..." He shakes his head. "I thought you were dying."

"No. I'll be fine."

"Fuck," he breathes out and drops into the armchair next to the bed.

"It's okay. I'll be okay."

He rubs his face. He's got a few days' worth of golden stubble covering his jaw. "Your father told us this happened before. He didn't seem concerned. The last time you were sick like this was when your mother died."

I think back over the years. I would've been five. *Darkness tight on my skin. Burning heat.* The memories are blurred, but they're there. "I remember."

"I shouldn't have threatened your father. He cares about you. "

"Not enough to—" I cut myself off, but Kaiser knows what I was going to say. *Not enough to stop this arranged marriage.*

He stares at me, looking haggard. I want to put out my hand and comfort him.

But I don't. We can't touch anymore. It's for the best.

"It doesn't matter," I say. "He couldn't have done anything."

"He was so worried. We all were."

"Don't worry," I say. "It'll never happen again."

KAISER

Bella's awake, but she's not herself.

Atticus comes and looks her over, pronouncing her out of the woods. He prescribes lots of liquids and rest.

I order every type of soup I can think of. I call in more favors until I reach Royal Regis, the head of the mafia family. Royal's wife, Leah, owns Pane P's. I offer him a favor in exchange for a special delivery of Bella's favorite baked goods.

It doesn't work. Even the cruffins—a disgusting mix of muffins, croissants, and cream—don't tempt her.

She stays in bed, drinking plain broth and tea. Color returns to her cheeks, but she still acts listless.

I put on her favorite season of *Vampire Varsity* and tell her that I think Luna shouldn't have ended up with Dargon, the evil twin. She usually argues passionately about that.

She says nothing.

And she doesn't let me touch her. At all. She's careful to make sure our skin doesn't touch, even by accident. I never realized how much I touched her until I couldn't touch her anymore. She's shut down, and normally I'd rub her shoulders and neck to get her back online.

She's still recovering, I remind myself. She's not herself.

But it feels like more than that. It feels like the old Bella died. She's gone forever.

I've never seen her act so cold, so remote. Almost robotic. A lot like her father. The emotion is gone, buried deep. She doesn't laugh, doesn't cry. The only time I see a flicker of anything is when I show her the journals.

"You can keep the journals," I say. "Your mother would've wanted you to have them."

She nods, running her hands over them.

"Do you want to read them?"

"No." She stacks them up and puts them to the side.

I take a deep breath. "Your father would like to come visit. Do you want that?"

"No." She lays her head on the pillow and stares at the ceiling. I know she's recovering, but it feels like she's shutting me out. "Keep him away."

"He would want to see you."

"His life is better without me in it."

I begin to protest, but she says, "No, it's true." She sounds tired. "He blamed me for her death. And he's right to. I'm the reason she was murdered."

**32**

K aiser

I can't believe what I'm hearing. I try to remember what I know about Shoshonna Bosco's death. It was in the files St. James gave me when I started the job.

"It was a turf war," I say. "Someone wanted your father to work for them. He told them no, and they refused to take no for an answer. They had men on you. Following you."

Bella stares into the distance, not really seeing anything. I don't know if she's even listening.

I try again. "You were five. It wasn't your fault. It couldn't have been." I move my hand closer, and she flinches away from my touch, coming awake again.

"It was my fault we were out in the first place. I wanted to go see the ducks. Mama said no, but I threw a fit and she took me to the park. That's when they found us. The bad men. We left as soon as she noticed them, but it was too late. They followed us. She didn't think she could make it home, so she went to the closest place she could hide. One of our nurseries. It had a warehouse where Papa grew the most poisonous plants. That's where she hid me..."

I stare at her, feeling a growing sense of dread. I want to stop her, to tell her it's okay. But I want to listen. I want to know her. I want to know everything.

"I remember..." she says and trails off. She's far away, gone back in time. A little girl, clinging to her mother.

"What do you remember?"

"She must have been terrified. But she didn't show it. She told me it was a game. We were going to play a game. I was to hide and be very quiet. No matter what. Until Papa found me. She left me there. She told me she loved me and to be good for her and hide. And she left.

"I didn't find out what happened until later. She drew them away from the room, and they killed her right in the warehouse. I heard voices—men I didn't know—but they didn't come into the room marked as dangerous. They left her body for my father to find."

"They didn't find you." I know that much. I also know they spent hours torturing Shoshonna before leaving her body for her husband to find. "I was so quiet," Bella whispers. "I was good for her. I waited for hours hidden in the plants. The grow lights turned off. I fell asleep... My father found me. I was barely conscious. He carried me out of the warehouse. I remember the cool air on my face."

Bella's father must have carried her right past her mother's body. "And then we were hiding. I was in a coma for days. Then I woke up and cried for Mama, and my father told me she was dead."

I flinch. Bella was just a child.

"That's why he hates me."

"He doesn't—"

"It's okay, Kaiser." As much as I love the sound of my

name on her lips, I wish she'd use a dumb nickname. "He does. I've accepted it."

"You can't blame yourself." She's carrying a heavy burden, and I don't know how to fix it. "Tell me what to do. Anything, I'll do it." Maybe she'll name her mother's killers. St. James couldn't find out who was behind the hit. He told me he thought the Poisoner might know, but no one else ever found out.

"There's nothing you can do." She shrugs. "It was a long time ago."

"The things that happen long ago still matter. They shape us." I flex my hands. The tattoos over the scars. "I know this."

She's watching. She's right next to me, swathed in a blanket, but she feels so far away. What can I do?

Father Francis would tell me to open up to her.

Telling her about my past will feel like I'm carving out my heart, but if it makes Bella feel better, I'll butcher myself right now.

"For a long time, I thought Jaeger hated me."

She blinks. "What?"

"My brother. My twin."

"I know who Jaeger is. Why did you think that?"

"Because I tried to kill him." She gives me a questioning look, and I continue. "It happened when we were in the fighting rings. We were champions. Crowd favorites. Maestro sometimes allowed us weapons or gave our opponents a weapon and us nothing. We'd have to use our wits."

"That's not fair," she says. "It sounds like you were gladiators."

"Yes. One day, Maestro pitted us against each other. I learned later he billed the fight as a final match between twin brothers." My voice sounds flat, like I'm talking about last night's baseball game. "He gave me a knife, and Jaeger got nothing."

Bella sucks in a breath but says nothing.

"I think he thought that I had been in more fights, so I was more popular."

"You said you didn't want Jaeger to fight."

"I didn't. I would get into trouble, so Maestro would put me in the ring more often."

"Did that work?"

I shrug. "It did." But then, after the fight, I would be punished. I'm not ready to talk about that yet. "Jaeger was good, but I was better. Maestro wanted me to kill him. So I did. Except I pulled back at the last second. While he was bleeding out, I walked up to Maestro to claim my victory, and then I stabbed him through the eye."

"Good. I'm glad he's dead." She looks so fierce, I want to smile. My bloodthirsty bride. "Then what happened?"

"I got us out of there. The crowd was on my side, you see. I knew they would respect their champion. Atticus saved Jaeger."

"Atticus—"

"He was there. He was apprenticing with the man who always patched us up, and Atticus had learned to bind our wounds. Stop the bleeding. He and his mentor developed ways to heal us faster, make us strong." I make a fist and flex my bicep. I've put on weight since those lean fighting days. Maestro never fed us enough. Now my muscles are bulkier, but I'm still strong. The veins cord on my arms when I flex.

Bella shifts in her seat. Her fingers twitch, like she wants to touch me. But she doesn't move.

She won't touch me anymore.

I miss it. I'd give anything for her to touch me again.

"After that, we went back to Father Francis. Met up with St. James and Damien and joined Fraternitas."

"Damien?"

"The Devil. Don't tell anyone."

"Don't worry, I'll wait until you forget you've told me, then use it against you." She sounds like she's joking, but I know she's not.

"Bella," I turn to her.

"So he forgave you? Jaeger?"

I remember the point of my whole story. "Yes. I thought he was angry with me, but he never mentioned it. Then last Christmas, we talked, and he said he understood why I did it. I did it to save him. To save us both. He said there was nothing to forgive." I'll never forget the weight that rolled off me that day. It allowed me to start living again.

I also had to apologize for the way I treated his woman, but that's another story.

I should apologize for beating him outside the Poisoner's house earlier. And to Elodie, for doing my best to fuck up her man's face.

Maybe next Christmas.

"I don't know if it's a good idea for you to talk to your father. But one day, you might ask him what he thinks of you. I think you'll be surprised."

She sighs. "I know what he thinks of me. That I'm a spoiled brat who does what she wants and doesn't think of the consequences."

My blood heats, hearing her talk about herself that way. "No." I don't know what to say, how to put into words everything that she is. How I see her. Her lovely face, laughing, teasing, and sly. The way she radiates. She outshines the sun. "You're—"

She holds up a hand. "It's true. My father is right."

"He's not." I search for the words to explain why, but they won't come. My lips and tongue won't move. "He's wrong," I finally say. "He can't talk to you that way. Tell me to kill him, and I will. I'll kill anyone who hurts you."

She gives me a sad smile. "I know."

*Talk to me,* I want to beg her. *Tell me who to fight, and I'll fight them. I'll do anything for you. Anything.*

I did what Father Francis said and opened up to her for nothing. It's no use. To her, I'll always be the enemy. The man who wanted to own her.

She doesn't need me to protect her from her father. I'm the biggest threat to her. Her light and her freedom, everything that makes her who she is. What can I do to prove that I'm not her enemy? How can I show her that she owns me?

I don't know if it's the right time, but I pull out the gift I got her. "I want you to have this," I say. There's so much bursting on the tip of my tongue, but I can't say it. I'm not good with words.

So I open the black velvet box and show her the sparkling set of rings inside. "Oh," she says, with a hint of interest.

"Do you like it?" Jaeger's woman helped me pick it out. It's not just one ring, but three that nest together. Diamonds and emeralds in a leaf pattern that reminds me of her plants.

"It's beautiful," she says but makes no move to take it. My heart sinks. She's rejecting it. She's rejecting me.

Then she jokes, "Are you asking me to marry you? A little late for that?"

My heart is pounding. "I thought it might be nice."

Her gaze softens. Pity. My skin crawls. I don't want her pity.

"I do like it." She touches one of the emeralds. "When is the engagement party?"

"Saturday. We've arranged to host it on neutral territory. The home of Senator Blumkist. The Vesuvios will be there."

She freezes. Her head is bowed, and I can't see her face. "The Vesuvios?"

"The senator is in the pocket of both Fraternitas and the Vesuvio family. He'll oversee the terms of a truce."

"All right. I'll wear the ring then."

I put the jewelry box away. There's a boulder in my throat. She doesn't want to wear the ring until we have to fake it to the world.

*You don't have to do this if you don't want to. I'll call off the engagement.* It's on the tip of my tongue to say it. But if I can't have her love, I'll take her any way I can get her. I'm a coward. I'm afraid she'll leave me.

Because why would she stay?

*BELLA*

Kaiser is disappointed. He tries to hide it, but I can tell.

He reaches for me, and I lean back, out of the way. I can't let him touch me. The poison's in me, on me, lying in wait.

He wants me to open up to him. To be his good little bride. I can't be that anymore. I can't be a good girl, or daughter, or wife. Not even to pretend. What we had is gone. It had to die for me to be reborn.

But I want to touch him. My hands ache with longing. If only I could brush my fingers down his face, soothe him like he soothes me.

He leans in to kiss me, and I turn my face away. "Not now. I'm not feeling well."

"Okay," he says. "I understand." Now I can hear the hurt in his voice. I lured him in, made him crave me, and now I'm withdrawing his favorite drug. "I'll be better soon," I say.

"Take all the time you need."

He's being sweet.

It doesn't matter, I tell myself. I can't be with him. He'll never belong to me. Besides, how could we even be together? He's my enemy. What do I expect him to do? Renounce his membership to the gang that raised him? The gang that he thinks of as his family? All those psychos and skull masks, they're his brothers and sisters. They'd do anything for him, and he'd do the same for them. I don't know much, but I know enough to know that family is everything. I can barely have a conversation with my father, and I'm still ready to take on all of Fraternitas simply because they threatened him.

Even if Kaiser was willing to leave Fraternitas, what would we do? Run away? Live on a farm? I imagine Kaiser as a farm boy, tilling the fields. Like my father did when my mother was alive.

Even in my imagination, the picture is weird.

So I let the fantasy die, like everything else. I imagine a cold, winter field. All life is hidden under the soil. I imagine it until I feel frozen.

Is this how my father feels? Is this how he keeps from letting his emotions show?

THE NIGHT of the engagement party arrives all too soon. I wear an elegant gown that's so dark green it looks black. The designer dress and my full face of makeup feel like armor. On the drive over, I'm lost in my thoughts. I wonder what happens when I enact my plan of vengeance. If I do what I'm about to do, many people will die. That's what I want, right? The Vesuvios and Fraternitas locked in a bitter struggle.

Except... I don't want Kaiser to die. I have to make sure that he stays safe. I should be one hundred percent focused on what I'm about to do, but I can't be. I'm worried about Kaiser. I need him to be okay. I don't want anyone to touch a single hair on his pretty blond head.

I care about him. He means something to me, and I want to protect him. How can I do that and still be a supervillain?

"Bella," Kaiser's calling my name. "We're here." I realize we're parked outside the senator's house.

I take a deep breath. Showtime.

"Where did you go?" he asks me softly.

"I'm here." I try to put on a smile, but it slips away.

"No, you're not." He almost sounds sad. "You went somewhere. I wish you'd come back. Come back to me."

*Don't leave me,* I hear my childhood self scream. I slam the door shut on the memory.

"I'm here. I'm fine."

He looks at me like he knows I'm lying.

I can't look at him too long. The sadness on his beautiful face... it weakens me. I wish I could reassure him. Make him feel better.

"You don't have to fight me, Bella," he says, but I do. I do.

"I'm not fighting," I lie. "I'm going to marry you. That's what everyone wants."

"I want you to be happy."

There's nothing to say to that, so I pull down the mirror and reapply my lipstick. "How do I look?"

"Beautiful. You always look beautiful."

"Do you have the ring?" I keep my voice brisk.

He pulls out the black velvet box, then hesitates.

"You don't have to do this," he says.

I stare at him. Is he serious?

We're parked outside a grand mansion in the most expensive part of Metropolis. We're about to shake hands with a senator and his crowd, and then announce to everyone the date of our wedding.

"I thought tonight was important," I say. "You're going to meet later with the Vesuvios and plan a truce." He told me St. James spent weeks trying to get the Vesuvios to sit down and plan a ceasefire between Fraternitas and them. They finally agreed to send a few representatives to the engagement party. Tonight.

"Yes." But he looks troubled.

"Let's get on with it then." I'm ready for this part to be over. For all the bullshit to be wrapped up until I come face to face with the Vesuvios.

I hold my hand out for the ring. I'm wearing opera gloves. My skin feels slick underneath them.

Kaiser sees the gloves and hesitates.

"I'll wear it over the gloves," I say, and pluck the ring out of the box and slide it onto my pinky finger, where it fits even over the glove. "See? It fits. Unless you wanted to present me with it in there. Down on one knee, the works." I frown, wondering if the theatrics will be better.

"Whatever you want," Kaiser says. He sounds so serious, like he's making a vow.

"This is fine, I guess. Good idea, getting me this thing. It'll really sell the marriage." *Which will never be real,* I add silently. I don't look at him. I can't. I need to get out of this car, but Kaiser's not moving, so I open the car door. He catches my arm, gripping me over the glove. All the air rushes out of my lungs. He's been so careful with me the past few days. I've missed his control, his touch.

"Bella." Each syllable comes out like he's wrestling with it. "Tell me what you want."

"I want to go inside and get this over with."

"Then tell me what you're afraid of. I'll take care of it."

I shake my head. What can I say? *I'm afraid of looking at you. I'm afraid you'll figure out what I'm about to do and stop me.*

*I'm afraid I'm falling for you. That I'll be too weak to go through with my plan.* There are so many women I need to avenge. I can't let one pretty man stand in my way. "I'm not afraid of anything. Not anymore."

The senator greets us at the door.

"A pleasure," I say and offer my hand. He makes a big show of kissing it. I feel his lips over the glove. Kaiser moves closer.

"Careful." I smile and thread my arm with Kaiser. "My fiancé gets jealous."

"I was so sorry to hear your father couldn't make it."

This is news to me. But it'll make things easier. "He sends his regards," I lie.

"He sent me an eighteen-year-old Bordeaux. Shall we open it later?" He winks at me, laying it on thick, and I play right along.

"Oh, we must," I say and join him in a fake laugh. The senator takes me around and introduces me to a million people. Kaiser hovers, stone-faced at my side, while I shake hands and talk and flirt. I use all my charm. I can hear myself talking, and I know I don't sound like myself. But I'm not pretending I'm in an episode of *Vampire Varsity*. No, that'd be childish.

I'm not a child anymore.

This party is full of beautiful people. They glitter

together like a chandelier made of glass sharp enough to cut. At least Fraternitas is honest about being violent. These people would smile in my face and stab me in the back.

That's okay. If they were truly my enemies, I could poison their wine before they even got close.

After cocktails on the lawn, we sit down to dinner. There's a violin quartet playing softly beside us, and every scrape of the strings sets my teeth on edge. After dinner, a few couples take to the dance floor. Kaiser takes me on a tour of the house, and we end up on a balcony overlooking the drunken crowd.

"I thought you said the Vesuvios would be here," I say to Kaiser.

"They sent a few capos." He points out a few burly men in badly fitted suits.

"That's it?" I was hoping there'd be someone from the head family. Dominus or his two remaining sons, Francesco and Salvatore. I want to meet them. Shake their hands.

"Sal and Frankie Vesuvio were supposed to be here. The senator told us they'd be coming. We begin truce talks at midnight. But you won't be there." I half expected this, but it's still disappointing.

"Afraid I'll poison someone?"

"Yes."

"Then why'd you let me come?"

## 33

K *aiser*

I FROWN. "It's our engagement party."

"You don't think I'm a threat." She runs a finger around the rim of her wineglass. "That's why my father isn't here. You think he's a threat to the Vesuvios?"

"The Vesuvios told us they wouldn't come if he were here."

"Ah. But I'm just the daughter. No one's afraid of me."

*I am. I'm afraid of what you've become.* "This truce is important. It will keep you safe."

"Hmmm. There's no such thing as safe. Everyone dies, Kaiser. You know that. You've killed enough."

I stiffen. It's not the reminder of my past that hurts. It's the careless way she tosses it out, like she doesn't care if it hurts me. "You're pushing me away. Bella, I'm not your enemy."

"Of course not. You're my future husband." Her voice is flat. No emotion. It's like she's numbed herself to everything. All her beautiful, wild emotions, she snuffed them out. It's like seeing a garden destroyed.

*Don't do this,* I want to plead with her on my knees. *Don't become like me.* I know what it's like to be numb to everything. To watch the world around you like it's a movie filled with happy people and wonder what it would be like to feel things again. *You are meant to burn bright. My light burned out long ago. I might as well be in the grave but not you. Never you. You are so full of life.*

*I don't want this darkness for you.*

I open my mouth, but the words stick in my throat.

She turns away. "Take me back inside. I need to powder my nose."

I escort her to a small bathroom and hold her glass of wine. As soon as she disappears, I pour a vial of sleeping potion into the wine and swirl it until it dissolves.

Then I wait, feeling like the walls are closing in around me. This mansion is huge, but the hallways are narrow and covered with awful paintings. A big wooden clock ticks down the seconds. It's almost midnight.

The senator is coming up the stairs, heading for his study, where we'll meet the Vesuvios.

Bella exits the bathroom just as he passes.

"Senator, I just have to thank you for a lovely party." She sounds like someone else. A stranger.

"The pleasure was mine," the senator says.

She moves closer to him, offering her hand. That's when I notice... she's no longer wearing gloves, and the ring I gave her sparkles on her ring finger. "Wait—" I say, but she's already shaking his hand. I move closer, and the senator makes space for me. "And here's your jealous fiancé. I remember."

"Senator," I say. I glare at him until he releases Bella's hand. I can't kill him. St. James will have my head.

"This way," I tell Bella. I'm to take her to a private room and give her a sleeping draught that Atticus prepared.

There's so much riding on this meeting. We can't mess this up. But as I have the feeling that I already have.

My cell buzzes with a text. St. James and Damien have arrived. They're waiting in the study with the Senator.

I walk Bella into the room. A library with a low couch.

"It's time. The Vesuvios will be here soon. I need you to drink this." I hold up a glass of wine. We agreed that we'd drug her tonight because she's a wild card. And the way she's acting now? I'm missing something. I need to figure out what it is before it's too late.

She takes the glass and swirls the wine, studying it like she knows what's in it.

I feel like Judas. Except Judas betrayed his love with a kiss, and I can't even kiss her.

She drains the wine in one long gulp.

I want to tell her I'm sorry, but I can't get the words out. Everything's changed between us, and I don't know how to fix it.

In five minutes, she's out. I hesitate before arranging her on the couch and covering her with a blanket.

When I walk out of the room, Jaeger is waiting. He's wearing a white tux. I study his black eye.

"I'm sorry."

"It's nothing," he returns easily. He never lets anything bother him for long. "I'll keep her safe."

I head to the study where the senator is holding court. He's behind his desk, showing off a bottle of wine to the

Vesuvio capos. I join St. James and Damien beside the window.

"Did Atticus test that?" I ask St. James, looking at the bottle of wine.

"We did one better," St. James says. "We swapped it out with our own."

"Save some for Sal. He loves this shit," one of the capos says.

"They better get here soon," the senator jokes.

"They're coming," the capo says. "Frankie just texted me."

The wait is killing me.

Out in the hall, the clock chimes midnight.

It's now or never.

I face my Fraternitas brothers. "I need to speak with you."

St. James and Damien glance at each other as if to say, 'Now?'

"I want to call off the engagement."

"Now?" St. James shakes his head, like he doesn't believe what he's hearing. "It's done."

Damien frowns, studying me. "You don't want her anymore?"

"I want her." I struggle to explain. "I don't want to force Bella to marry me." I look apologetically at St. James, who did all this work to give me what I want on a silver platter when I asked him for Bella a few weeks ago.

"The marriage will convince the Vesuvios we're in lock-step with the Poisoner," St. James says. "You mess with the Boscos, you mess with us."

"I understand, and I still want to protect her."

"Without the marriage?" Damien has a shadow of a smile on his face. "You want to claim her."

"I want her to claim me."

"It's too late." St. James waves a hand at the window. Outside, several black cars have pulled into the mansion's circular driveway. The rest of the Vesuvios are here.

"There has to be a way," I say, feeling desperate. "Some sort of contract. I'll do anything—"

"A toast to the truce," the senator says and raises his glass, but a tremor goes through his hand.

He opens his mouth again, then chokes.

The capos stop talking and stare.

The senator drops the glass. It shatters on the floor while he clutches at his collar. Slowly, he falls, hitting his desk on the way down to the floor. St. James and Damien cross the room with me on their heels. St. James checks the senator's pulse, while Damien rips open the senator's shirt, sending buttons flying and starts chest compressions.

But the senator's face is purple. The capos back away. With muttered curses, they run out of the room.

The worst has happened. Someone poisoned the senator. But, how? *Bella.*

I race down the hall, back to the library.

Jaeger is there, leaning against the door. He sees my face and opens the door for me. "She's safe," he says, letting me pass.

But I don't breathe until I see her lying there, looking peaceful.

Still asleep.

BELLA

I wake up in a dark room. My mouth feels grimy, like I need to brush my teeth. The last thing I remember was falling asleep on the love seat in the senator's house. Now I'm in my bed. Alone. "Kaiser?"

"I'm here." His voice comes from my left. He's sitting in the armchair beside the bed, where he's been sleeping lately.

I sit up, still in my ball gown. He took off my shoes but didn't tuck me in. He just set me on the bed. "What time is it?" It feels late.

"Three a.m."

Still the middle of the night. I touch my hair. It's still in the fancy updo I styled to match the dress. My gloves are gone, though. I took those off. "What happened?" What I mean is, *what happened after you drugged my wine?*

"You know what happened." Kaiser clicks on the light. I wince, holding up a hand to block it until my eyes adjust.

Kaiser looks at me like I'm a stranger. Like I'm the enemy.

I feel a deep sadness, mixed with relief. It'll be easier if Kaiser's the villain. "We were at the party. I fell asleep."

"I drugged you."

"I know." I could taste the additive when I drank it down. It made me a little drowsy, but it was nothing I couldn't fight. I decided I wouldn't fight it, though. I lay down and let sleep take me.

"I don't know how you did it, but I know you did," Kaiser says.

"What are you talking about?" I feel a stab of glee. Like I used to feel. I stuff it down.

He stands and steps toward me. His shadow falls over my face. "It's you," he says. "You're the Poisoner."

**34**

———

B*ella*
"You figured it out." I shouldn't feel so good about it, but I do. The way Kaiser's looking at me, with fascination tinged with fear, is so satisfying. "How?"

"The senator died at midnight. Minutes after you shook his hand. You poisoned him. How?"

I lift my hand and inspect my palm. "A little of this, a little of that." Kaiser moves so he's blocking the light. His hair blazes gold, but I can't see his expression. My heart beats faster recognizing the power move. The predator in the dark.

"He's not the first. You've done this before. How many?"

"I thought you'd never ask." I scoot to the edge of the bed. "The first was when I was eight. Papa finally let me go to a sleepover, and I was so excited. That night, my friend told me her stepfather was mean to her mother. That he hit her. She showed me bruises where he'd hit her, too. I wanted to tell Papa, but she begged me not to. Her stepfather was a judge. No one could touch him. But the next time I went to her house for a sleepover, I was prepared."

"You poisoned him."

"It was easy. A little monkshood sprinkled on his cake, and he was done for."

"No one suspected?"

"He had a weak heart. He was overworked. My friend was relieved. No one suspected a thing. But then I did it again. My friend introduced me to another girl in my school who said her father was hurting her. That he sometimes came into her room at night. She told a teacher, but her father was powerful and had just been elected mayor. So we planned another sleepover. I used a slower-acting method that time. I made it last a few weeks. I was learning.

"See, my father, he doesn't kill people. He prefers more subtle methods. A stroke that leaves you paralyzed. A sickness that lingers. A long, slow decline until your heart stops. Something that looks natural."

"But you killed them."

"I did what needed to be done. A weak man can still hurt his daughter."

Kaiser blows out a breath. "The judge, the mayor elect." He counts on his fingers. "Who else?"

"One more. The principal of my elementary school was touching students. He told them not to tell anyone, that they'd be punished if they did. So I punished him. I used bloodroot to rot his skin and a compound from narcissus to torture him. And finally, I used belladonna to kill him. It was slow and painful. Everything that he deserved." I clench my hands into fists. I'm not sorry. I'll never be. No one can make me regret what I've done.

If I could do it all over, I wouldn't change a thing.

"He was the third. Then you stopped."

"Papa found out and pulled me out of school. Hired tutors and bodyguards. He locked me down as long as he could. But when I turned eighteen, he knew he couldn't control me anymore."

"That's why he made the alliance with us."

"Yes. You were meant to be my bodyguard. A man who could finally control me. But you can't, can you? You won't do anything to me." Because the poison I gave him didn't kill him. It bonded him to me.

Kaiser shifts closer. My heart skips a beat. He's still dangerous. "This is why you weren't afraid of me. You've been poisoning people since you were a child. You're lethal and no one knows."

"The best offense is a good disguise."

"I knew you were dangerous."

"Mmm, you did, didn't you? Your instincts were right. You came so close to beating me, Kaiser. I had to come up with new ways to poison people because of you." I want to tell him about the lotions I developed. The way I coated my skin to absorb the contents into my body. How I went into the bathroom, took off my gloves, and coated my palm with poisonous balm before I shook the senator's hand.

I want him to know everything about me. I still feel that pull between us. He'll hear about all the people I've killed, and he won't judge. How can he? His body count is so much higher than mine.

For now.

"Tell me about Livia."

I suck in a breath. "She found me in the diner. It was my first time there, and I was so excited. I'd heard so many things about it. A waitress with red hair told me there was someone to see me. Then Livia sat down. I asked her if I should know her, and she said no. Then she told me she was the wife of the man who killed my mother."

"No one knows who was behind that hit."

"She did. Alfredo bragged to her about it. He and his brothers would laugh about what they did to my mother while she begged them to stop."

"So you helped her poison her husband."

"She wanted a way out. I gave her one. I didn't know they would kill her. I should've guessed, though. She was so sad."

"She knew."

My heart aches, remembering Livia's face. I looked up a picture of her after; she looked so different. A poised, very pretty woman with perfect hair and designer clothes. When she came to the diner to meet me, she wore no makeup, no jewels. Her hair was down, half covering her face. Her true self, but she wore it like a disguise. "She probably did know they would find her out. I told her to do it slowly, but... she wanted to get it over with. It's my fault. She died, and it's my fault." Will I ever be able to forgive myself for Livia's death? For my mother's?

"That's why you killed the senator."

"No. He was just a warning. First shot fired."

"It worked. Spooked the Vesuvios. They refuse to deal now."

"Good. I don't want to deal with them. You know that after I spoke to Livia, I went to my father? I told him I found out who killed Mama. He said he knew. He'd known all along. And he didn't do anything. For years."

"He was being smart. Going to war with the Vesuvios was a suicide mission. He wanted to keep you safe."

"Life isn't safe. It doesn't matter what you do. You can tiptoe around, or you can leave your mark. Either way you die." I think of my mother and Livia. Then I think of my father and Kaiser. Who lives, who dies. I have never felt more like his enemy. It's me against him.

"I'm not going out without a fight. Evil men walk around

like they own the place. Like they own us. And we're just supposed to take it? Well, I'm not going to take it anymore."


*KAISER*

I faced down men all the time in the ring. Bigger and badder men who wanted to stab me and rip out my entrails. I faced them and never felt afraid.

But I'm afraid of Belladonna Bosco. Her wicked mind, her deadly skills. The fear curls in my belly and at the base of my spine, like the respect you pay to a black adder. "What are you going to do?"

"What should've been done in the first place. I'm going to kill them. I'm going to kill them all."

I don't know what to say. *Let me help, I want to help. Or let me do it for you. Let me fight for you. Let it be me.*

I don't have the right to say any of that to her. Because I am the man who would use my power over her. I am everything she hates. Everything she is right to rebel against.

The only way to fix it is to go back in time and destroy everything I am, everything I've fought for, and everyone I fought alongside. I can't do that. I'm not strong enough.

But it turns out I don't have to say anything because in the painful seconds that follow, the lights in the room go out, plunging us into darkness. I tap my phone to check the cameras on the perimeter, but they're out. "Something's wrong," I say.

Bella starts laughing. A high-pitched, hyena-like sound. Chills race over my entire body.

Before I can ask why she's laughing, a call comes through.

It's Argos. "You okay?"

"We're in a blackout." I head to the lights and flip the switch. Nothing.

"I see that. Security system's offline."

"Sentries?" We posted guards around the perimeter. Not Fraternitas, but former Tier One operatives from a security firm we contract with. Sounds of gunfire crackle outside.

"Shots fired," I shout. I race to Bella. I've got to get her somewhere safe. She's wearing a ballgown, so I dip and toss her over my shoulder.

"Kaiser, wait—" She thumps on my back, but I ignore her and hustle out of the room and down the stairs.

"I've got Bella. We're headed to the saferoom."

"Backup's en route. Stay on the line."

"Copy." I enter the safe room and hit the code to secure it. Only after the steel locks set with a muffled click do I set Bella down.

"We're under attack," I tell her.

She backs away, straightening her gown. "I can tell. They didn't take long, did they?"

"You think it's the Vesuvios."

"I know it." Her smile is pure evil.

Chills run up and down my arms. My heart speeds up, knowing I'm in close contact with a deadly predator. "You planned it this way."

"I did," she giggles. She's giddy. "I wanted them to come for me."

Panic flares through me. I can't let her face the Vesuvios alone. They only understand brute force.

Fortunately, I'm an expert in brute force.

I turn to the screen on the wall. It looks like Argos has gotten the security system back online. On screen, shadowy figures approach the house. "You need to stay here in the safe room."

"Excuse me?" She looks outraged.

"I need you to stay safe. I can't focus on fighting if I'm worried about you."

"But—"

"You can obey me, or I can tie you up. Those are your options."

"Fine," she mutters, seething. Her dark eyes glitter with dangerous light. "But it's not fair. This is my fight. I'm going to kill them all."

"Not if I kill them first."

**35**

———

K *aiser*

IN THE UNDERGROUND FIGHTING RINGS, anything goes. Above ground, in legit fights, there's a referee to make sure there's no foul play. No hitting the groin. No gouging out eyes.

In the underworld, no one cares if a fighter lives or dies.

I learned to keep moving. To be fast. To figure out my opponent quickly. No one bet on Jaeger and me in the beginning. But that was okay; Maestro rigged the fights. He had a few of his more seasoned fighters train us, and I learned every move I could so Jaeger and I could survive.

When I first started fighting, I was the underdog. By the end, I was the reigning champ.

The Vesuvios have forgotten that. They've come for my woman. It'll be the last thing they ever do.

Finally, I get to kill someone.

I wait until the machine guns go silent. There are a few

isolated shots here and there. The Vesuvios are executing our security guards one by one. That's our first layer of defenses gone.

The first wave of the Vesuvio army hits the door. There's a heavy thudding sound, too loud and rhythmic to be a fist. They've brought a fucking battering ram.

I race through the house, grabbing supplies, setting up a few distractions. Then I head back to the front of the house to greet them because that's what a good host does. I wait for them at the top of the stairs, out of their line of sight.

They march in wearing goggles and body armor. Pretty good tech for mafia thugs. And they're well trained—they clear the room expertly before filing in.

"Clear." The leader radios the boss. "We're in."

"Get the girl."

"Copy. She'll be in the safe room," the leader says to his men. "Let's go." I've set up a few bottles of wine in the hall, so I hear when they knock a few of them over.

"Hit the lights."

I already told Argos to kill the lights for good. There's a pause during which I'm sure they all turn on their night vision goggles.

Below me, a few men are standing in the foyer. I toss a flashbang grenade down and cover my eyes. Light flashes, blazing bright between my fingers. A few men scream as the light stabs their eyes.

I take a running leap, vault over the stair railing, and land on an unlucky soldier. I roll and slam my fist into the closest bystander. He sags, and I send his body flying into two more of his buddies. I keep it moving. Chop a jugular. Kick out a knee.

Somebody recovers enough to fire at me, but I'm moving

too fast. I take out as many of them as I can and haul one up to use as a body shield to head down the hall.

Gunfire greets me. I toss my human shield one way and dive the other. I get clear of the line of fire, then reach into my pocket and hit a button that triggers a few small devices I've fixed around the house. Random alarms start blaring to cover up the sound of the bombs beeping. The gunmen get distracted by all the new noise. Then the tiny bombs explode. They're not that dangerous, but the explosion ignites the gasoline I splashed around.

Fire blazes. The flames tear down the trail I've left for it and turn a few rugs into an inferno. One gunman wheels past me, screaming, his whole body on fire. Smoke fills the air. The safe room has a special air supply and oxygen masks, so Bella will be okay. I pull out my skull bandana and cover my face, then turn on another fun device Argos invented. I still need to deal with the rest of the gunmen.

There's a clicking sound and cursing as the guns nearest me start to jam. Got to love modern technology. The jammer isn't perfect—a few bullets do fire—but it stalls things long enough for me to run at one of the shooters. I grab his gun and use it to pull him forward into my fist. He goes down.

I use his gun like a club to beat another one's face in. Three more abandon their guns and attack me. I take the first hit. That's the secret of fighting. Everyone has a plan until they get punched in the face. But I let them hit me. I see how they move, how they react.

And what did Bella say? You have to give your opponent a chance. So I do. I give them one. One tries Krav Maga, another Muay Thai, the third a blend of Judo and Jiu-Jitsu. Their kicks and punches thud into my deadened skin. Then it's all over for them.

They all go down hard. They're mercenaries, fighting for

cash and glory. I'm fighting for my woman. Failure isn't an option.

I will pile the bodies of her enemies at her feet.

A fourth rushes me from behind. His knife digs into my left side lat with enough force to ignite my dulled nerve endings. The pain almost feels good.

"You'd stab me in the back, motherfucker?" I'm on him before he can move. I break his arm, take his knife, and drive it through his eye. Instant death. "Next time, just shoot me from the door. Idiot."

I find the team leader among the fallen and stomp on his head until he goes limp, then take his walkie-talkie and find a spot of fresh air.

The radio crackles. "Strike lead, come in."

I pull down my bandana. "Hey there," I say as pleasantly as I can. "Is this Dominus?"

There's a pause. "I'm here." The head of the Vesuvio family doesn't sound happy.

"Your men are dead. I hope they weren't friends of yours. Or family. You only have two sons left, correct?"

Heavy breathing on the line. Dominus is pissed. "You can't fight all of them."

"That's exactly what I'm going to do. And when this is over, Fraternitas will come for you." I toss the walkie-talkie away. Blood's trickling down my back. Pain screams in the background of my mind. I twist to check the wound, but it's not too deep. Outside, someone's shooting something. Argos must have activated the drones and the Vesuvios are returning fire. Bad idea: Argos' drones tend to explode.

I roll my shoulders and crack my neck. The blood hums under my skin, making me feel alive. As much as I love playing house with Bella, I missed this. Explosions rock the house. Shouts tell me more forces have arrived. They're pouring in from the front door.

The fight has just begun.

I stand in the safe room, watching the screen. I was pissed when Kaiser told me to stay put, but I agreed because I didn't want him to tie me up. But now I have a front row seat to the action.

On screen, Kaiser mows down row after row of armed men like they're tin soldiers.

My whole body vibrates like leaves in a storm. Watching him is like watching a hurricane destroy a beach or a tornado rip through a cornfield. He's a force of nature. No one else stands a chance.

But more men are coming. Dominus isn't holding back. He's coming to take out the Poisoner's daughter.

And it's all going according to plan. I want to decimate his army and then kill all his heirs. I hope his sons come to the fight. I can get it all done in one night. Kaiser has actual grenades now. He tosses them, and they explode, taking out chunks of the floor. We'll have to remodel after this.

He's magnificent. But he's just one man. More armed forces are coming, and they have bigger guns. Bazooka size.

It takes two of them to point the gun at a wall. What are they doing? Boom! There's a rumble and dust flies, blurring the feed. A few of the cameras go offline. My guess is that part of the house collapsed. They're willing to bring the house down around their ears to beat one man.

And it's working. I can't see Kaiser. He either escaped the destruction or he's collapsed under some drywall.

I have to go. I have to help him.

I run to the door and hit the button to open it. I'm safe as long as I stay here.

But where's the fun in that?

I head into the dank, smoky air, straight for my greenhouse. There was a huge fight in the kitchen, but I skip over the blood-smeared tiles and fallen bodies. Once I'm in my greenhouse, I slam the door loud enough to echo through the house.

I hit the lights, but they don't work, so I turn on the backup lights attached to the generator.

I'll get it nice and bright in here so I can watch the life bleed from my enemies' eyes.

They hurt Kaiser. It's time to make them pay.

## 36

K aiser
When I come too, I'm face down in a pile of rubble.

These fuckers brought a rocket launcher. What do they think they're going to do? Destroy the house until only the safe room is standing? I wipe dust from my face and crawl out from under the destroyed wall. Gotta get to Bella.

But when I get to the safe room, the door is standing open. *No!* Where could she have gotten to?

I weave through the rooms, grit crunching underneath my boots. I stop and snatch up a fallen gun. There's no time to mess around.

"What the fuck is going on?" someone shouts. I hide out of sight, barely breathing as I listen.

"Sir," the soldiers snap to attention. "We're tasked with hunting down the target, Bell—"

"The bitch. I know. And you fucked it up. Dad sent me. I'm supposed to be in New Rome, making the Poisoner choke on his own vomit."

New Rome? Dominus must have sent another strike

team to take out the Poisoner. I hope Argos still has ears here. Otherwise, I need to end this fight fast so I can alert my brothers that the Poisoner needs help.

They probably already know. If I were Dominus, I would've had the strike team hit two locations at the same time.

This newcomer is either Sal or Frankie, one of Dominus' sons. "You're telling me that it takes all of you to get one little girl?"

"She has a bodyguard."

"A bodyguard. One man? One fucking man? Fucking Fraternitas. Where is she?"

"The target is in the safe room—"

Music crackles on the loudspeakers, and the loud music Bella likes to play for her plants blasts through the house.

"What the fuck is that?"

"Sir, I believe it's from *Turandot*, an opera by Puccini—"

"I fucking know! My nonno loved this shit. I wanna know why I've suddenly got front row seats to a fucking opera."

"It's coming from the conservatory. Behind the house." A radio squawks, and the man reports. "It's the girl."

"Right, let's go get her. Remember, we want her alive."

The team lead orders the forces to split into two teams, one to go through the house, one to go around back. "We secure the safe room along the way. Let's go."

Bella isn't in the safe room. I bet she's in her greenhouse, thinking her plants will save her.

But there are dozens of men headed her way. I can't let them take her. But I don't know how I'm going to kill them all without starting a firefight that kills us both.

.   .   .

BELLA

"Nessun dorma" blasts from the speakers as I stand in the middle of my plants, spotlit by the floodlights. I'm still in my ball gown, so I'm feeling classy.

There's movement outside the greenhouse, men approaching the back door behind me. And in front of me, there are muffled voices at the kitchen entrance. I'm surrounded. Just like I planned.

The men open the doors, their guns trained on me. They move closer, advancing slowly. Their sight lights dot my back and chest.

I stand very still.

*Shhh, my flower. You have to be quiet,* my mother told me long ago, with a finger to her lips. *Remember, Mama loves you very much.*

I lie in wait, but this time I'm not trapped. I'm the bait.

The music cuts off—one of the men must have cut the line. They don't get close to me, not yet.

One of them speaks into his microphone. "Sir, we've got the target on lock... yeah, she's just standing there. Unarmed."

"Let me see this." A few moments later, a man elbows his way through the pack of armed men to the front. He's mostly bald and stocky, with a ruddy tone to his skin. He reminds me of a bull.

"Hi there," I say and give him a cheeky wave. "I'm Bella. What's your name?"

He looks me up and down, and likes what he sees. Good. I need him to let down his guard. "Name's Sal, doll."

"Salvatore Vesuvio?"

His eyes narrow. "Yeah." He motions his men to creep forward. "You're coming with us."

I don't move. I want as many men inside the house and greenhouse as possible. "Livia told me about you."

"Oh, yeah? What'd that bitch say?"

"She said you were bad." I shake my head, giving him a cute little pout. "A bad, bad man. She told me you and your brothers killed my mother. Is that true?"

"How the fuck should I know?" He's still cocky, but he's frowning, like he can't figure me out. "I killed a lotta people."

"Mmm. So have I. "

He mutters some curses. "Get her."

"Lower your guns," I say. "I'll come quietly."

Sal shrugs, and a few of his men lower their guns. "You'll come with us either way."

Then I utter the code phrase. "Shoshonna Bosco won't stand for this."

*KAISER*

I move with the soldiers to the back of the house, picking a few off on the way, dragging them into the shadows, and breaking their necks. I strip one of the corpses, grabbing a set of goggles and a flak jacket, and leave the bodies lying under the trees.

But by the time I get to the greenhouse, I'm too late. Bella's in the center of the room, lit up like she's on stage. She doesn't look afraid, but she's surrounded by gunmen. I seriously wonder about her sense of self-preservation sometimes.

I watch through the windows as she talks to Sal. I can take out a few more soldiers, but I'll never reach her in time. I'll have to wait until they grab her, and then kill them.

Why did Bella offer herself up on a silver platter?

Then Bella says loud enough that I can hear from

outside, "Shoshonna Bosco won't stand for this." Invoking her mother's name. Why?

There's a click and a whir. Some machinery turning on. The men inside look around. A second later, water rains from the ceiling. A heavy downpour from the sprinkler system.

That's when the screams begin.

I run toward the back door, using my hands or the knife to take out every soldier who stands in my way. I have the jammer on still, but it's not foolproof. I don't want people to start shooting.

When I get to the back door, I pluck out the men trying to get in. I kick out one's knee and punch the other until he goes down. More men rush toward me, screaming. But they're not coming for me. They're trying to get away.

"It burns!" they shriek. "It burns!"

I stand aside as they run past me, clawing at their faces.

What the fuck is going on?

The soldiers are down, fallen where they stood, blanketing the floor. The lucky ones die fast with mouths open in silent screams. The unlucky ones are still writhing and twitching, blisters forming on their faces.

The air feels like razor blades, slicing my throat. I cough, throwing up an arm to shield my eyes. My eyes burn like they're being seared in my skull, but I can't look away from Bella.

She's still standing in the center of the greenhouse. Her hair is soaked, plastered to her face and bare shoulders, and she has a triumphant smile on her face. She looks like the supervillain she wants to be.

Something moves behind her from the ground. It's Sal, raising his arm. He's got a gun. He's squinting through the swelling on his face, taking aim at Bella.

No!

I race toward Bella through the poison rain, praying I won't be too late.

*BELLA*

Liquid poison slicks my hair and coats my face. The compounds in the acid rain affect the lungs, skin, and heart. If I weren't immune to all of them, it would definitely burn. The shape of a man blurs in front of me.

There's a loud crack like thunder but too close. The noise shatters my hearing.

Then I see Kaiser throw himself in front of me, only to fall. The shock hits me like a bullet.

He was shot.

"No," I cry. Kaiser is face down on the ground between me and Sal. Sal is propped up on his left arm, gun in his right. Blisters bubble on his cheeks as he bares his teeth at me.

I'm screaming. I race over to Sal, snatching a pot off a worktable. The rest of the planters go flying, ceramic shattering on the stones.

Sal fires again, but I'm already on him, rage coursing through me. I smash the pot on his head, and Sal's body sags. I kick the gun away and grab his hair to pull his head back. Blood covers his face. His hands rise to defend himself, but he's too weak from the highly concentrated poison. I pull out a vial of hemlock from my pocket and rip off the top. I force it into his mouth, pouring the liquid down his throat and slamming the vial past his teeth until it shatters and he chokes on glass. I let him fall to the ground, convulsing. It won't take long for him to die. I feel like a Valkyrie.

But then I remember Kaiser.

He's still face down on the floor where he fell after being shot. He's not moving. The poison rains onto his bare arms and the back of his neck. "Oh no, no, no, no." I bend over him, blocking the rain with my body. "Stop," I scream. But the rain keeps falling.

I've got to get him out of here. I grab his right arm with both hands and start dragging him out of the greenhouse. He's so heavy, each inch takes an eternity. But I finally get him outside. Away from the poisonous rain.

He's not breathing, and his face is raw and blistered.

*Fuck, I did this.*

I rip open the vest he's wearing, my hands coming away blood-soaked. "Hecate, help me." There's so much blood. From the bullet wound? He was wearing a vest, but he must have been hit.

And if the bullet doesn't kill him, the poison will. I don't know what to do. There's a balm I can use to help his skin, but what about his lungs? The compound is designed to kill fast. Papa and I agreed we would use it as a last resort. I didn't make an antidote because I'm immune.

Kaiser coughs, and the sound stabs my ears. He groans, coming too. "Shh," I say. "Just rest easy. You're hurt."

"I'm okay." But he coughs again, and blood and sputum froth at the corner of his mouth.

"You were shot."

"No, knife. Stabbed."

I don't know what he's talking about. "I'm sorry." I lean over him. I want to touch him, but I can't. His skin looks like someone rubbed it with sandpaper. Even his eyes are bleary and red. Bloodied tears drip down his face. "It wasn't supposed to go like this," I tell him. Except that's a lie. I wanted to unleash the poison on everyone. Things went down exactly how I wanted them, too—except Kaiser got hurt. "I didn't want you to be hurt."

A shadow rears up over us. I throw myself across Kaiser. Our enemies found us, and it's all over.

But then someone calls, "Bella?" It's not the Vesuvios. It's someone in a demon mask. He pulls it off, and I recognize my future brother-in-law.

"It's okay, Bella." Jaeger crouches next to me. The light glints off his long hair. I realize I'm shaking, holding onto Kaiser like he's my lifeline. More Fraternitas members melt out of the woods. "It's okay," Jaeger repeats. "We're here. Everyone else is dead. You're safe."

The battle is over. Dominus has lost a lot of men and another son. I should feel triumphant.

But Kaiser is barely breathing. He's hurt because of me. I want to die.

*It's my fault. Don't leave. Don't leave me.*

## 37

# B *ella*

Fraternitas takes us to a safe house.

I'm huddled in a blanket in a dark corner of the room while Atticus and his team work on Kaiser. Jaeger stands next to me, guarding me even as he watches his brother fight for his life.

Everyone's been careful not to touch me.

"I'm sorry," I tell him. "He wasn't supposed to get hurt."

Jaeger glances at me but doesn't say anything.

Pain stabs my abdomen. I curl up and cover my face with my hands. I can't look at Kaiser lying in the medical bed. He's been cleaned up, his head and face swathed in white bandages. Even his eyes are covered. He looks halfway to being a mummy.

Blood stains the white sheets.

I kept thinking of him as impervious, immortal. A

demigod like Thorbjorn. I should've done more to protect him. I thought of it as a game, one I would win.

It *was* a game between us, I realize. I wanted it to be real, so he obliged. He made it fun. I didn't think through the consequences of my actions, and now Kaiser might pay the ultimate price.

I cover my mouth, stifling a moan. I can't do this. It hurts so much. Memories flash through my mind. Kaiser watching me garden in the greenhouse. Chasing me through the forest. Touching me. Taking me to the bookstore. Reading my mother's journals.

I can't imagine living one day without him by my side. My captor, my protector, the one who keeps me grounded, keeps me sane. The one who goes along with my wicked games. The one who chases me, catches me, punishes me and makes me like it. The one who soothes me. The one who hates to be touched but holds me through the night.

I need him to live. I don't want to be without him.

"Bella?" It's Atticus, standing over me with concern etched on his face. "Are you okay?"

"Fine." I sit up, hiding my wince, and wipe the wetness off my cheeks quickly. "What's up?"

"He's stable. We need to know what you poisoned him with."

"It was a lot of things mixed together. My father invented it. Distillation of sap from a manicheel tree, plus a few other compounds from lily of the valley."

"Lily of the valley? The little white flower?"

I nod sadly. "Just because it's pretty doesn't mean it won't kill you." Atticus and Jaeger murmur to each other, then turn as three more men enter the room. St. James and the Devil. They look different without their masks. I could imagine poisoning them, but I don't bother.

Father Francis walks in behind them. A priest coming to the deathbed to administer last rites.

"No." I stand up, ready to race Kaiser's side. "No, no, no—"

"Bella?" Atticus asks. Jaeger tries to stop me, but I slip away and throw myself between Kaiser and the rest.

"He's not going to die. He can't."

The men are all staring at me.

"Bella—" Atticus tries again.

"You have to help him," I scream. "Don't give up. Don't let him die."

Father Francis moves closer. I back up as if he's going to attack. "No one's giving up on Kaiser. Atticus will do everything to keep him alive."

"You have to help him."

"We are, Bella," Atticus says. "He's our brother. We're doing everything." I look around desperately. I need to do more. "Did you call my father? He might be able to figure something else out."

Father Francis looks grim. He motions to St. James, who steps forward into the light. "That's why we're here to speak to you. We need to tell you something about your father."

"Come," Father Francis beckons. I let him and St. James lead me to a side room for a private conversation. "Men went to your father's house in New Rome. Frankie Vesuvio and a force of fifty men. They busted down the door." I brace myself, waiting to hear what happened next.

"Three minutes later, the house exploded. It took out Frankie and at least half of Vesuvio's best men, as best we can tell. There are no remains." My face feels frozen.

"He set a trap." I can imagine him doing that. He lay in wait, like I did in the greenhouse, only on a bigger scale.

"He did. And it worked. But I'm sorry, there's no sign of your father."

"I understand." He was the bait. Now everyone thinks he's dead.

I think my father's smart enough to fake his death, but I don't need to tell St. James that.

"NRPD is all over the site. We have some spies who will keep us informed if they find anything. Once the cops clear out, we can try to access his underground labs—"

"Okay." They're not going to find my father. I don't believe he's dead, but I doubt I'll see him again.

I let my head droop, like I'm sad. And I am. Whether or not my father is gone, I'm on my own.

"We will honor the contract," St. James says. "Your safety is our priority. Fraternitas will stand with you against your enemies."

I don't give a fuck about the contract, so I say nothing.

*One day, I will die,* my father told me. *When that day comes, it is my final wish that you remain in an alliance with Fraternitas.*

He knew this was coming. He planned for it.

The fucker. He left me. As soon as he knew he could trust Kaiser to protect me, he left me.

I don't know whether to scream or cry, and I'm empty from everything that happened tonight, so I allow myself to feel nothing. I'll save my tears for someone who deserves it. Like Kaiser.

St. James sets a box down in front of me. "We also intercepted this package. It was sent to Club Inferno, care of Lucifer. Lucy opened it and saw the contents were addressed to you."

My father's handwriting. I don't have to fake the tears

clogging my throat. Finally, he sends me something. "Can I have a moment?"

"Take as long as you need." He and Father Francis leave.

My father didn't send me much. Inside the box is a thick envelope. As soon as I open it, a few rose petals fall out. The rest of the contents are stacks of paperwork. I skim a few documents that outline my inheritance. I now have ownership of all Bosco holdings, including a few warehouses and farms I didn't know existed.

I look for a note from my father, but there is none. Next to his signature, though, he taped a dried flower. Lily of the valley. The sweet scent clings to the paper. I page back through the packet, skimming the list of properties. One that I can't find listed is the family farm, Flowerwood. It belonged to my maternal grandparents, who farmed it and then gave it to my mother as a wedding gift. It was probably in my mother's name.

Maybe he sold it?

Or maybe... he hung onto it for himself.

A shadow falls across the doorframe. It's Jaeger. "He's waking up," he says. I stuff everything back in the box and head back to Kaiser. The room's cleared out except for me, Jaeger, and one nurse monitoring the machines.

"Bella," Kaiser rasps in a raw voice. Under the bandages, his skin is horribly blistered; I need to get some salve on it.

"Shhh, don't try to talk," I say.

"I'm here, brother," Jaeger rumbles.

Kaiser lets his head rest on the pillow. They shaved off his hair to clean him up, and the crumpled edge of his misshapen ears peeks out above the bandages. "Vesuvios?"

"Dead," Jaeger confirms. "We're dealing with the bodies. Final count is forty-three. You did good." He looks down at me. "So did she." I move closer to Kaiser, wishing with all my might that I could heal him. Why do I just have to poison people? Why can't I fix him?

I thought the only thing that mattered was being a supervillain. But I was wrong.

Kaiser reaches for me. I retreat before he touches me—my skin is still poison—and his hand falls on the box.

"What's this?" he asks. His voice sounds like his throat is sliced to ribbons. Just hearing him is painful, and I wish he would stop trying to talk.

I wrap my hands in the blanket so my skin won't touch his and cradle his hand between them. "It's from my father. He's... he's gone."

"I'm sorry."

"It's okay. He wanted this." My father may not be dead, but he's gone from my life. He finally left me. He's finally free. After making sure that Kaiser would keep me safe from blowback, he was finally able to get his revenge.

It hurts knowing he's gone, but I'm glad he finally fought for the vengeance my mother deserved.

"Dominus will pay," Kaiser vows.

"He already lost two sons in one night," Jaeger says. "He's hurting. We'll end this soon."

I want to close my eyes and sleep. I don't want to be a supervillain right now. That was a bloody battle and it was epic, but it came at too high a cost.

I never want Kaiser to be hurt. Never, ever. Everyone expects him to fight for them. But who will fight for him?

Atticus returns to speak to Kaiser. "We wrapped your ribs. You had a stab wound in your back that we treated, but we couldn't find a bullet hole. It looks like the vest protected you."

That's right, that's where all the blood came from. The stab wound. The bullet he took for me didn't penetrate.

It hits me: if Kaiser dies, it won't be from Sal's shot. It will be because of the poison.

Because of me.

"My eyes," Kaiser says. His hand raises a few inches, like he wants to touch the bandages but thinks better of it.

"Do they hurt?"

Kaiser flicks a few fingers, which I take to mean, yes, they hurt. "Manicheel sap can cause acute keratoconjunctivitis." Atticus glances at me, and I nod. "The damage may only be temporary. You weren't exposed to the full force of the sap, just a compound that included it. It seems to be specially formulated to be more toxic—"

"It was," I say. "Ten times more toxic. A hundred times." Papa made sure it would be instantly painful if not deadly.

"You may recover fully," Atticus says. "We just don't know."

We're all silent, probably imagining all the terrible ways Kaiser could die or be permanently maimed. At least, I am.

My eyes are wet again.

"Now what?" Kaiser asks.

"Your body is fighting the poison," Atticus says. "We've given you painkillers and a few of my own formulations that will boost your immune system." Jaeger and Kaiser nod as if they know what Atticus is talking about. I remember Kaiser saying that Atticus cared for them after their fights. They're used to him patching them up. They trust him.

"A little activated charcoal in case you ingested any of it." Atticus sighs, rubbing his shaved head. "But since the compound was designed to be absorbed through skin contact versus your digestive system, I don't know if it will help. We just have to wait and see."

"What about my blood?" I ask. My voice sounds almost as raw as Kaiser's. "It might hold the antidote. I'm immune to poison. There might be something you can find in my blood to save him."

"That's an idea," Atticus says, sounding thoughtful. "There was a man who developed super immunity to snake bites through repeated exposure, and he gave his blood to a lab to create a universal antivenom. We might be able to isolate an antitoxin from your blood. How many poisons did you ingest?"

"As many as I could. I'll write you a list."

"And you're immune to all of them?"

"To most poisons, yes. Some of them still cause a reaction, though."

"That's why you were in a coma for a few days."

"Yes."

"And the senator? How did you poison him?"

Atticus is prying for more information, knowing that in this desperate emotional state, I'm likely to give him anything he wants. I can hear my father warning me not to give away any proprietary formulas, but I don't care about protecting our secrets anymore. "It was a blend of several compounds mixed into a lotion I put on my palm."

"Ricin?"

"No. He would have to ingest that. I used compounds distilled from cassava and oleander, along with a compound my father invented to make it faster-acting."

Atticus's eyes narrow. "And Alfredo Vesuvio?"

Despite feeling rotten, I smile. My secrets are out. They all know I'm the Poisoner now. "Good old arsenic and belladonna. *Aqua Tofana.*"

"Nobody knows that recipe."

"My mother did."

"And what about Bella's blood?" Jaeger asks. "Can it help my brother?"

Atticus rubs his face. He's thinking about what a bad idea this is. "It's risky and it might not even work. I'd need to test it."

"Just try." I hold out my arm. "Please." Atticus waves to his team, and two nurses come to my side to prep my arm for a blood draw.

I don't even feel the bite of the needle. I don't feel anything at all. Jaeger leans over Kaiser. They speak softly to each other. Then Jaeger hovers his hand over his brother's head, not touching him. He stands frozen like this for a moment, then turns and strides out of the room without another word. If Kaiser dies, Jaeger will probably kill me.

If Kaiser dies, I'll probably beg him to.

No, it won't come to that. I'll nurse Kaiser back to health, I don't care what I have to do. I can't lose him. He's all I have. Without him, I'll be all alone.

"All done," Atticus says. He and his team now have several vials of my dark blood.

Kaiser lies still and quiet. Only the rise and fall of his chest tells me he's alive.

"We've done all we can do for him, for now." Atticus takes a deep breath, hesitates. "Except... we have a salve for his skin that should help with the blisters."

"Okay..." I say, confused.

"We want to apply it but—"

It dawns on me what Atticus is hinting at. Of course he knows Kaiser's secret weakness. "He doesn't like to be touched. I'll do it."

"Are you sure?"

I look up at Atticus, and he blurs. I'm crying again. "He's mine," I say. "My... fiancé. I'll do it."

"All right, we'll hold him down for you."

"No," I sniffle. "No. I'll be okay."

"He might fight," Atticus warns.

"He won't hurt me."

"Call out if you need us." Atticus and his team rip off their gloves and throw them in the hazmat container, leaving me and Kaiser alone.

The room feels so big and empty. Kaiser usually fills every space with his presence, but now he's small, shrunk down, confined to a bed. His beautiful eyes are under a shroud.

It's like he's lying in a tomb, ready for death.

I can't stand it. But I did this to him, so I'd better face the consequences. His head lifts when I move to his side. "Bella?"

"I'm here." I don't know what to say. "I'm... I'm so sorry."

"I'm not. I'd do it again."

I place the container of lotion close enough that his fingers can brush it. "I have to put this on your skin."

"Okay."

"I don't want to hurt you."

"It's okay. I can take the pain."

**38**

B*ella*
*I can take the pain.*

I nod, because I know it's true. Kaiser can take the pain. He's taken everything I've dished out.

I feel such despair. I've done nothing but hurt him. He had to be strong to survive me. He almost didn't.

I want to touch him. Stroke his face, cup his cheeks, kiss his lips. Caress his cauliflower ears.

I pull on a pair of latex gloves instead. "I'm going to start on your face. I'll be gentle but... tell me when to stop."

"My safeword is kumquat."

Oh no, he didn't. "Shut up," I whisper. My tears are falling again. "Shut up—" I press the back of my hand to my eyes. I don't want to lose it. But I am.

"Hey." He reaches for me, grabbing my arm, and I don't pull away. "Come here."

"I can't," I say, even as I let him pull me so I'm sitting on the bed. I don't want him to strain himself. "I'll hurt you. I'm so sorry."

"It's okay." He takes my hand and presses it to his jaw.

His skin is cracked and bubbling, an angry red ready to ooze pus.

"I'm hurting you," I say.

"It doesn't hurt. It feels like heaven."

"Liar."

"I will never lie to you."

I pull my hand to free it from his. "Let me do this. Let me help you." I scoop out the cream, a lot of it, and dab it on him.

I'm having flashbacks to when I coated myself in poison. Why did I do it? Why was I so focused on my plan? Why didn't I think it through? I glide my fingers up his cheeks, trying to reach under the loose bandages. He has blisters everywhere, even on his ears. When I get to them, he winces, and I stop, sucking in a breath. "I'm sorry."

"It's okay."

"It's not okay," I rave. "You're hurting! Because of me."

"No," he says. "I feel things... because of you."

I shake my head and realize he can't see me. I bite my lip and start coating his upper chest and arms with the lotion.

"I didn't feel anything until I found you. It was like my skin was dead. I had no feeling left in me. Couldn't reach it. Until you."

"Because I hurt you." I smear the cream over his blistered bicep.

"Because you healed me."

"I'm not a healer. I'm... I'm a fuck up." It feels so good to finally admit it. "I wanted to be so strong. I wanted to be a supervillain—"

"No," he's saying. "No—"

"I am. Will you stop being nice to me? This is all my fault."

"It's not and never will be. The Vesuvios got what they deserved."

All I can see is Kaiser face down on the floor. "I failed." My tears burn my throat, and my voice cracks. "I failed you." It hurts, it hurts. And it hurts more knowing I hurt him. This ache in my chest? It's what I deserve.

"You did what you had to do. Baby, please hear me. Just because it didn't go right, doesn't mean that you didn't do right. You're not in control of everything. No one can be in control of everything. Not even supervillains."

*Oh fuck me.* I'm sobbing now, and it hurts like my heart is ripping apart. "I'm such a fuck up. I am, I am."

His hand cups my face. The back of his hand is still raw, and my tears are falling on him—it must burn. But he just murmurs, "It's okay, baby, let it out. Let it go."

"He left me," I cry. I feel weak and useless, so I let the tears run down my face. I can't do anything else. "He's gone. He never wanted me."

"Baby."

"Don't leave me." I grip his hand, fighting the urge to scream. *Mama, don't leave!* "Everyone else is gone. I don't want you to leave. I want you to stay with me."

"I'm here. You're not getting out of this marriage so easily. We have a lifetime, remember?"

Now I'm crying because I can see it. Years and years with him. I see us walking through the orchard, holding hands, the sun glinting off his golden hair. All the moments stretching beyond our happily ever after. And I want it. I want it so bad. "Dammit, I wanted to be strong." I wipe the extra cream on the back of his hand. "I was so stupid, thinking I could be a supervillain."

"You are. You are the best villain I've ever met. You scare me."

I laugh sadly. "No, I don't."

"You do. And you're going to unleash terror on this world unlike anyone's ever known. I believe in you. But also... you're not alone. Not anymore. I'm not leaving, Bella. You're stuck with me."

I SLEEP in a chair beside him, my face planted on the bed, his hand on my head.

I wake when he groans. He shifts in the bed, making it creak. "No, stop—" he moans.

"Kaiser?" I croak. My head is pounding and woozy at the same time. I'm probably dehydrated. I wet my lips so I can speak. "I'm here."

But he's caught in a nightmare, thrashing. He's going to hurt himself. I pull back the covers, and still he fights. The blisters on his face crack and bleed, and he still doesn't stop tossing and turning. "The bars. I can feel them—" His cry turns to a roar. His veins stand out on his skin.

I back away, I can't help it. The monster in the bed is terrifying me. Where is the medical team? "Help!" I cry. "Help me!"

Machines are beeping, shrieking, and Kaiser is bellowing like he's being electrocuted.

The attendants come running. "What's happening?" one asks me.

"I don't know. He just woke up—and you have to help him!"

"Hold him down." They move to pin his arms, and he shoves them away, sending them flying.

"We need reinforcements—"

"No, you're hurting him." I hover where I stand, unable

to move closer but unable to leave. I don't know what to do. "Don't touch him."

"Bella?" Atticus appears. He's alert, but he must have been sleeping. He's shirtless, only wearing black baseball shorts and fuzzy brown slippers.

"He's having a bad dream," I say.

"His temperature is too high," an attendant says.

"His body is fighting the poison, but it's not working," Atticus says. "We need to try your blood."

"Do it," I say. "But don't hold him down," I say. "He can't stand it."

"She's right," Atticus says to his team.

"But he'll fight if we try to inject him," one attendant protests.

"We don't have time for this." Desperate, I head back to Kaiser's side. I feel like I'm entering the lion's den. "I'm here, Kaiser. Please. You're safe. You don't have to fight."

He moans but quiets.

Atticus readies the shot and nods to me.

I put my hands close to Kaiser's arm. "I'm going to touch you now. It's just me. Bella. Your fiancé."

"Now," Atticus mouths to me.

I clamp my hands on Kaiser's arm and Atticus injects him, quick as a bee sting.

Kaiser roars again, but he doesn't fight me. I keep my hands clamped on his arm. I can feel the power in the muscles. He could rip it away and strike me, hurt me, but he doesn't. "It burns," he groans.

"I'm sorry. I'm so sorry." I didn't think I had any more tears, but they come all the same and leave burning tracks down my cheeks. "Don't leave me."

Atticus dismisses the attendants. Once they leave, he

starts to back away. "Where are you going?" I ask. "He needs you."

"He's not here. He's back in his past. Dreaming." Atticus motions with his hand. "He won't want me to see him like this."

"I don't fucking care. Everybody gets sick. No one is strong all the time, for fuck's sake."

Atticus still looks unsure.

"He doesn't need a doctor. He needs a friend. You're his friend, right?"

"His oldest one." He paces forward. "Kaiser, I'm here."

Kaiser turns his head. There are bloody tracks down his cheeks.

"You're free, brother. Maestro is dead. You killed him. And we won't let anyone cage you anymore."

I feel Kaiser's body relax.

"It's helping. Thank you." I look down. "There are fuzzy bears on your slippers."

"I know." Atticus looks troubled. "Should I call Jaeger?"

"Where is he?"

"Back home with Elodie."

"No," I say. "Let him sleep. Call him in the morning. Maybe Kaiser will be awake."

Unless he doesn't live through the night.

In my darkest dreams, I'm not free. I'm back in that cage. It's too small, and I can't move. The bars press to my skin, burning them until I feel nothing. I am nothing. Helpless.

There's nowhere to go. Nowhere to run. Only the shadow of Maestro stretching over me, able to do anything he wants to me. I can't fight. My muscles bulge between the bars. I want to scream but don't want to give him the satisfaction.

If he touches Jaeger, I'll kill him. But this is all I deserve.

And then a sweet voice says, *Don't leave. Don't leave me.* I hear her. I feel her poison burning through me, waking me up, bringing me back.

It burns, but it cleanses me like holy fire. The poison she gives me destroys the darkness inside me. The bars disappear, and the shadow of Maestro fades away.

And she's there the whole time, slaying my monsters, laughing with triumph and delight, and burning with me.

I wake up with cool air on my face. I can feel everything. It hurts so much, but it's a good sort of pain. Grounding.

And she's with me. Sitting by my sickbed, slumped on it, asleep with her head resting by my leg. I take her small hand and press it to my skin.

I've been numb for so long. It wasn't safe to feel anything. But now I'm desperate for her touch. And I can feel it. I can feel everything.

I will never leave. I will never leave her. I will always be here.

Even when the dark tries to take me down, I will always come back to her.

**39**

---

# B*ella*

WHEN I WAKE UP, Kaiser is holding my hand. I try to tell him I'm toxic, but he refuses to let go.

It's possible he's toxic, too. The only person who can touch me without dying. The injection worked.

Atticus comes and runs all sorts of tests. He seems puzzled by the results, but one thing's for certain: Kaiser's still alive, and he's slowly improving.

I tend to him as if he were a sickly sapling. A half-dead bloom I rescued from the discount pile at the nursery. I nurture him and bring him back to life. His eyes still need extra care. Atticus thinks he will regain most of his sight, but he'll need to wear protective glasses for the rest of his life.

After a week in Atticus's care, we move to Kaiser's penthouse in New Rome. His brother and Elodie live in the same building. Jaeger tries to bully Kaiser into moving in with him, but Kaiser refuses. He hates being sick. Feeling weak, especially when he's around anyone else. Except me. He seems to relax when it's just us.

I still hate myself for doing this to him. Every time I see his shaved head, his dark glasses, his healing skin, I remember what I've done. It makes me feel wretched. I almost wish I believed in a merciful god, so I could go to a temple or Father Francis and atone.

We end up hanging out with Jaeger and Elodie enough that we might as well be living together. We watch endless sappy holiday movies until I put my foot down and introduce them to season one of *Vampire Varsity*. By episode five, they're hooked, as I knew they would be.

St. James and the rest of Fraternitas give us space. But I know there's contract stuff I'm supposed to know about.

I'm the Poisoner now, and the Vesuvios still want war.

I couldn't care less.

Eventually, life inserts itself into our happy interlude.

One afternoon, Jaeger and Kaiser disappear for a few hours. Elodie doesn't know where they are, and Kaiser's on crutches, so I doubt they're on a job. When they return, they both look grim.

"What's happening?" Elodie asks. She's a beautiful woman with thick, curly red hair and an explosion of freckles on her face. Right now she's twisting the ring on her finger.

"St. James and Damien finally had a call with Dominus," Kaiser says, maneuvering himself to my side on the crutches. "He's agreed to a temporary truce while we negotiate peace. In one more week, we end this once and for all."

"How?" Elodie asks.

"There will be a fight," Jaeger says. "Two men will face off in the ring. Anything goes." He looks at me. "There will be a champion representing your family and one representing the Vesuvios."

"Who will be my champion?" I ask.

Kaiser folds himself onto the couch. "Me."

I look from him to Jaeger and back again. "But you can't fight, you're hurt."

"That's what I said," Jaeger mutters. He heads to where Elodie is sitting, picks her up, and settles them both in the armchair with her in his lap. She lets him, looking worried.

Kaiser has the remote. He's cuing something up on the TV.

I put a hand on his arm. "You can't," I say. "You just got out of a wheelchair."

Kaiser shrugs.

I turn to Jaeger. "You need to stop this."

"I can't," Jaeger growls. He looks like he wants to commit murder. "It was his idea."

"What?" My mouth falls open.

"This will end things once and for all," Kaiser says and rolls his shoulders. "It's the only way." He clicks the remote, and the screen fills with a grainy, homemade-looking movie. Two shirtless men face each other in a boxing ring. One is bald and towers over the other. The bald man lumbers forward, fists swinging. Most of his shots go wild, his opponent ducking out of the way, but one hit lands, and the smaller man goes flying.

"Power, not precision," Kaiser comments. He seems to be studying the screen.

"You like to take the first punch," Jaeger muses, looking at the screen. "With him, that might not be such a good idea."

Kaiser grunts.

"Excuse me, what is this?"

"An underground fight," Elodie says, her voice tense. "They study them so they know how to beat their opponents."

I get up and point to the bald man on the screen. "Is this him? Your opponent?"

"Yes," Jaeger and Kaiser say in unison. "People call him the Giant."

"He looks like he's seven feet tall," I say, almost not believing it.

"But slow. I can beat him," Kaiser says.

Jaeger rubs his mouth, looking almost sad. Since he usually smiles too much, this is alarming. "They say he was bred from Dominus's seed. But they... did things to make him grow to that size."

"A bastard son," Kaiser says. "If Dominus was truly the sperm donor."

"Yes."

"We'll take another son from him, then."

I can't believe they're talking about this like it's normal. Kaiser has just started using crutches and now he's supposed to fight?

I stand in front of Kaiser, blocking the screen.

"You can't do this," I say to him. His face is still red from the blisters, for fuck's sake. "This is madness."

Jaeger stands up, lifting Elodie in his arms as he does. He carries her out of the room and shuts their bedroom door behind them, giving us privacy. I tense up even further.

I doubt I'm going to like what Kaiser has to say.

Kaiser reaches for me, and I let him take my hands and pull me closer so I'm standing between his knees. He's so much bigger than me, but he's still fragile. His shaved head reminds me of what he just went through.

He raises my hands, kisses them. I try to pull away. His lips are so soft.

"Shhh, Bella. Let me have this. Let me hold you."

Oh no, I'm going to cry. I let him rub his face along my fingers. His eyes are closed, as if he's memorizing how they feel.

"You can't fight, Kaiser."

"This is my role, my beautiful poison. I'm a fighter. I will fight for you."

"Fuck that," I say.

He releases me long enough to reach into his pocket and pull out a black ribbon. Then he pulls me in with a sudden move that takes my breath away. I end up with my back to his chest, secured in his arms.

"Stop," I squeak, squirming, but he's holding me fast. "I'll hurt you," I try to argue.

He clamps a hand around my neck. "Be still," he orders.

Immediately, I'm soaking wet. I close my eyes, panting with bliss. It's been so long since he's touched me like this. We sleep in an oversized bed together every night, but I'm careful to give his healing body its space. And he hasn't pushed me, even though I know he wants to. The only thing he insists on is holding hands. That feels good, but this... this is everything.

I forgot how easily I respond to him. Fuck, I'm almost crying with how good it feels.

"Belladonna. Beautiful, wild. My perfect poison." He nuzzles the back of my neck, and I relax.

Then he straightens and lifts my hair, fastening something around my neck.

The black ribbon.

"What's this?" I ask.

"This means I intend to claim you as my *elita.*"

My heart soars to the stars. He's claiming me. It's happening.

"No matter what happens to me, Fraternitas will recognize you as mine."

My heart freezes. "Wait, what? No matter what happens to you? What does that mean?"

"If I die, you will still have the protection of my brothers."

"Oh no." I start shaking. "No, no." I scratch at my neck, wanting to rip off the ribbon. He stops me, but I'm still shaking, emotion bursting out of me. I want to cry, laugh, scream. I'm hyperventilating.

*They will protect you.* This is exactly what my father said before he left me.

I wrench myself around to face Kaiser. I'm panting, leaning on him. I cling to him like he's the only thing keeping me from drowning.

"No, you promised. You promised me." I make the mistake of gazing into his ocean eyes. Suddenly, I'm drowning.

"Bella, shh." He cups the side of my face, so tender. He's so gentle with me. He doesn't let anyone see this side of him, only me. "This is how I know you will be safe. Dominus won't come after you. However the fight ends. Especially if he feels like he's won."

"But... the fight is to the death. You can't lose. You'll die. You have to win."

"No, I don't. I can do this for you. You won't have to marry me. You'll have upheld your end of the contract." He searches my eyes, making sure I understand what he's telling me.

And I do. It settles on me like a giant weight. The magnitude of what he's offering takes my breath away.

He's giving me a way out. He's fighting for me and making sure I'm safe. From everyone, even him.

"You won't have to marry me," he says. "You'll have everything you wanted. You will be free."

He's right. This is everything I once wanted. A way out. Kaiser knows his brothers will respect his claim. None of them will touch me, but they'll protect me as someone precious to him. They would consider me his widow. They wouldn't make me marry anyone else.

I won't have to marry anyone. Everything I've fought for will be mine.

Because of him. His sacrifice.

But now, I don't want freedom, not without Kaiser.

"You said you wouldn't leave me," I say. "You promised. You promised me years together! All the things we're going to do together. You promised me, and I want them. I want those years, Kaiser. I want a lifetime."

"You will have them," he says.

I thump his chest. "I want them with you, damn you."

"Bella, look at me."

"I can't," I say, sniffling. "You're too pretty. You'll convince me to do anything with that big, dumb, beautiful face."

"Hey. Come here, beautiful." He tries to lift my face, but I set my jaw and close my eyes.

"You're a butthead. I hate you. I hate you, and I want to marry you. I am going to marry you, dammit."

"No," he says. "This is your way out. I want you to be happy. And if I'm alive, you can't be happy. So I'll go."

I lean into him and cry.

He holds me.

Then someone is standing over me. Jaeger.

"Keep her safe," Kaiser says to his brother.

"What?" I wipe my eyes.

"No!" I scream. He wants a fight, I'll give him one.

But they're both too strong. Jaeger clamps his arms around me. I fight, screaming Kaiser's name, but Jaeger carries me into the bedroom.

Elodie hovers by the bed, her hand over her mouth.

As soon as Jaeger puts me down, I race for the door. He beats me to it, holding it closed as I claw and pound on it. Then I turn on him. "You fucker," I hiss. "I'll poison you, don't think I won't."

"Kaiser won't like it."

"Kaiser is an idiot!"

"I agree." Jaeger's solemn expression stops me. "This is madness. He should not fight. It's not good for him, even if he does survive." Jaeger shakes his head. "I offered to take his place in the ring, and he threatened to chop off both my legs. To save me, he said."

That's so beautiful, I could cry. "That's so like him."

"He would do it, too. He loves to sacrifice himself for the people he loves. I could kill him, but he's my brother. What can I do?" He shrugs. Then, to my surprise, he opens the door.

I rush into the living room. The TV is still playing raw footage of old fights, and the crutches are leaning against the couch.

Kaiser is gone.

"He'll go into hiding and start training. You'll see him before the fight."

"We have to stop this."

"I don't know how." Jaeger's head hangs down. Elodie comes to his side, and he clamps an arm around her, bowing his head and breathing in the scent of her hair.

"I'm sorry, Bella," Elodie says. Tears are rolling down her cheeks, too.

"This isn't happening," I say. Despair is leaking out with every tear, but my mind is flitting around from possibility to possibility. There are so many ways out of this. So many poisons.

Kaiser isn't going to die.

He's mine.

"We have to find another way," I say to Jaeger and Elodie. "You have to help me."

Jaeger shakes his head, looking hopeless. Elodie puts a hand on his chest, and he covers it with his own.

"What can we do?" she asks in a steady voice.

A plan pops into my head. I have to think through all the consequences, but if I'm right, they'll only fall on me. "I know what to do."

**40**

---

B*ella*
The night of the fight, Jaeger escorts me and Elodie into the dark underbelly of New Rome, down an elevator in Club Empire, and into a long tunnel that smells like the subway. I'm blindfolded, breathing the wretched air. Jaeger leads me to the fight space, and I hear the distant buzz of voices. The closer we get to the fight, the louder the voices become.

When he removes my blindfold, I blink, even in the dim light. We're in a vast space crowded with all sorts of people. Men in suits, smoking cigars. Bikers in leather jackets with neck tattoos and black helmets hiding their faces. Muscle men with no necks. People with sun-worn skin and unwashed clothes, their big smiles showing their black and missing teeth. Yuppies stumbling around, a drink in either hand. Too-skinny teens selling all sorts of goods—soda, peanuts, packets of white powder—to anyone who has cash to pay them. The noise—and the smell—is overwhelming.

In the center, on a sort of stage, is a roped-off ring

surrounded by blinding lights. This is where they'll hold the fight.

I look around, holding my breath, waiting for a glimpse of Kaiser. I haven't seen him since our fight in the living room. He's stayed away for over a week, working with Atticus to heal enough to be ready to fight. He's called a few times, but all I did was shout at him until tears ran down my face.

He left me. The big, beautiful idiot. He thinks he's saving me. Freeing me.

But without him, I can't be free. Look what happened to my dad when he lost my mom. He hasn't really been living. He's in prison.

I'm going to fix this, and then I will make sure Kaiser never leaves me again.

"There he is," Jaeger says, pointing across the room. Kaiser is behind a group of men in skull masks. The blond hair on his head has grown into stubble and glints in the low light.

Across the room are the Vesuvios. They're all in green and gold, with pentacles hanging on oversized chains around their necks. Some of them are in golden masks with horns like a bull. The Bulls. That's their house mascot at Unitas University.

The Giant is there in a bull mask, towering over the rest.

"This is a terrible idea," Jaeger growls. "Kaiser will never forgive me if anything happens to you."

"I'll be fine," I say, but looking at the Giant, I'm not so sure. "Is this even legal?"

"No," Elodie says. Her face is bloodless, which makes her freckles stand out even more. "But no one cares what happens down here."

I remember the fight videos Kaiser and Jaeger were reviewing. "You're like gladiators."

Jaeger doesn't confirm or deny it. He looks grim and hasn't smiled since he told me Kaiser was going to fight. I used to think he smiled too much, but now I miss it.

He leads me to Kaiser's side. I stare at him like he's a stranger. He's shirtless, with a satin robe draped over his shoulders. The picture on the back is a roaring lion.

Then he looks at me, and I feel everything. I can't stop my feet from hurrying to him. I stop in front of him, not touching him. I missed him so much. The big, beautiful idiot. I want to slap his perfect face, then cry and make him hold me.

"Bella."

I have one more chance to stop this, change his mind. My guts are twisting like I'm gonna puke. "You don't have to do this." If he's willing to listen to reason now, I won't have to go through with my plan. "You can throw the fight."

"No. The Vesuvios don't understand anything but brute force. I have to fight."

"You don't have to be willing to die for me just so I'll be happy."

"This will fix everything."

"Kaiser, please. Don't make me beg." I bite my lip. I'm not going to cry. Not here. "Please, you don't have to protect me."

"But I do. That's what a good husband does." He cups my face in his large, calloused hands. I rise to tiptoe, but he only kisses my forehead. For a long moment, he breaths in my scent.

Then he steps back. "Goodbye, little bride."

"Kaiser, no." I swallow my desperate plea. I have to be

strong. I'm wearing a long coat and clutch it around me for a second, getting myself together. "I need you to kiss me."

He freezes in the act of turning away.

"Do this one thing for me." I wet my lips, tasting the bitter lip gloss I've coated them with. "Kiss me, Kaiser. Please."

He hesitates, a tremor running through him. He knows I'm up to something, but he can't resist me.

He comes closer, and the noise and the crowd fade away. "Belladonna."

I reach up and stroke his lips. I can't stop myself.

He seizes me, pulling me close. I can feel him fighting himself, but he can't fight me.

I'm the one who's beaten him. The only one. And he knows it.

He lowers his head to mine. It feels inevitable.

Our lips brush, and he sighs, a shocked gust of air against my lips.

"Please," I barely whisper.

With his fingers tight in my hair, he kisses me.

My whole body thrills at the sensation. I feel alive.

And then it's over. He draws my head back slowly, tugging my hair hard enough to make my eyes water. Fresh pain washes through me, and I embrace it.

I take a step back, letting him put distance between us. He needs it. He's bracing himself, getting ready to leave me. "It's okay. You're only doing what you think you have to do."

"I have to…" He shakes his head. "You will be safe."

"Thank you," I whisper, stroking his face. He lets me. He can feel the resignation in me, and he thinks I'm willing to let him go. "Thank you for being willing to free me. There's just one thing," I pull him down and whisper into his mangled ear, "I don't want to be free."

He rears back to study my face when a wave of drowsiness hits him, rolling over his tense muscles and loosening them until he sways. "No—"

"Shhh. It's okay. Just go to sleep." I put enough sleeping potion on my tongue to knock out two of him. He's unsteady on his feet, but he clutches at me, fighting to stay upright.

"Bella—"

"I win." One little push and he falls like a cut tree. Jaeger catches him, staggering under his brother's weight. A few Fraternitas guys in skull masks rush to help.

"He's out. Keep him back," Jaeger tells them. "No matter what happens."

Phase one of my plan is complete.

Now for the hard part.

Jaeger turns to me. "I hope you know what you're doing."

I don't, and it doesn't matter. I'm doing it.

Jaeger glances over at the Giant, then back at me. There's at least two feet of height difference. "Don't let him hit you."

"I'll do what I have to do." I pull out hair ties and put my hair up in two high pigtails. Then I untie the sash of the big coat I'm wearing and let it fall. Underneath, I'm wearing my supervillain costume.

I wipe the soporific from my lips and pull out my extra-special lip gloss, applying a thick layer.

Then I square my shoulders and walk toward the ring. Jaeger moves ahead of me, clearing a path. More masked men fall in front and behind me, escorting me through the crowd.

I tried to get Fratneritas to allow Honey to come ringside, but they denied my request. Instead, there's a woman named Angel who will be my ring girl. She's beautiful, with a dazzling smile, and turns to greet me as I approach.

"Ready?" she asks.

I touch my hair, checking the pigtails. My roots are dark because I've had bigger things to deal with than taking the time to fully re-dye my hair. But I did put more color over the platinum. Now, both ponytails look like they've been dipped in pink paint. I'm in a black and pink bra and hot pants set, the one Kaiser didn't want me to wear out of the house the day we went to marriage counseling.

That day feels like a lifetime ago.

"You look great," Angel assures me.

I look like a cute, naive young woman out of my depth. Which is what I want. The best offense is a good disguise.

She hands me a water bottle filled with my own brew, and I drink it all, feeling it burn down my throat.

"Is that it?" Angel asks.

I shake my head. Before I can say anything more, St. James climbs into the ring to kick things off. He doesn't say anything, just stands there with a microphone in hand until everyone gets quiet. In less than a minute, a hush falls over the space.

"This is a fight to the death. The gods will decide the champion, so pray to them. Or Him. Whichever you prefer."

"To my right, representing the Bulls and Don Vesuvio, is the Giant."

The Giant enters the ring. He takes his bull mask off and throws it to the crowd. The Bulls cheer and chant, "Dominus, Dominus," over and over. In front of them, a thin man in a dark suit leans on a cane. Dominus Vesuvio, the Don of the Bulls. He looks mean and ancient, with a passing resemblance to Sal Vesuvio, his late son.

"To my left—" St. James starts and stops when Angel slips into the ring and points to me. He frowns and shakes his head, but I step forward anyway.

Jaeger comes alongside me and settles a satin robe on

my shoulders. The lion robe Kaiser was wearing. It's way too big, dragging like a train behind me.

"—representing Fraternitas and the Poisoner's family. Introducing Belladonna Bosco."

Behind me, Fraternitas breaks into a shout. "Fraternitas," their voices echo off the high ceiling. "Fraternitas."

Angel helps me out of the robe and holds the ropes while I scramble into the ring. St. James has disappeared. It's just me and the Giant and the crowd screaming around us. I wish they'd shut up, but I guess it's on me if I get distracted.

The lights are hot on my face, and I feel like I'm going to throw up.

Is this how normal people feel? Mortal? Fragile?

My heart is beating so fast, it might fly out of my chest. I grit my teeth and force my breathing to slow.

I'm doing this for Kaiser.

And my mother. And Livia.

And myself.

I'm Belladonna Bosco. The Poisoner. I've got plenty of poisons up my sleeve.

It won't be easy, but I can do it.

I just have to not die.

## 41

B*ella*

THE BELL RINGS, startling me out of my thoughts.

The Giant faces me, looming on his side of the ring. He's got two pentacles tattooed on his cheeks.

"Hi there." I bounce and give a little wave. "I'm Bella."

The Giant squints at me, confused. He looks around, as if to say, "Is this for real?"

The Bulls are screaming for my blood. "Hit her! Kill her!" And worse. There's a whole crowd of them, excited to watch me bleed. And die.

I smile at my opponent. His back stiffens automatically. He doesn't understand what's happening, and my behavior is weirding him out.

Good.

"Shake?" I hold out my hand. There's a second while he

hesitates, and I wonder if the Vesuvios figured out how I killed the senator.

But then his hand engulfs mine. I'm dripping sweat already. Shit, I hope the poison sticks.

We shake slowly. His fist is the size of my head.

*Don't let him hit you,* Jaeger said. One blow will cave my skull in.

I try to step back, but the Giant's still holding me. He looks me up and down, a bit mesmerized.

I've got a lot of skin on display.

"What happens now?" I say in a little girl's voice.

"Now you die."

Shit. Okay.

*Your best offense is a good disguise.*

I lick my lips. "I'm scared."

"It's okay, little girl. It'll be quick." He's staring at my chest.

With my free hand, I tug at my bra top. "It's hot in here."

"Take it off." The Giant leers at me.

He wants a public peep show. Gross. I don't have to fake a tremor in my voice as I ask, "What will you do to me if I do?"

He clamps a hand on the back of my neck. I stiffen, leaning back, but he draws me forward, the way Kaiser does. No, no, it's wrong. I don't want anyone else touching me like that.

I'm shaking as he grips my head in one huge palm, forcing my chin up. He lowers his face. He's going to kiss me.

No! Only Kaiser does that.

I fight, but he's already mashing his lips against mine.

So I bite his lip.

He roars, jerking back.

I spit in his face. He releases me, surprised. He wipes the spit off the bridge of his nose and scrubs at his eyes.

Then backhands me across the ring.

I go flying.

I slam into the ropes, and they snap me forward. I hit the floor, tasting metal.

Fuck.

Fuck, that hurt.

I blink, dizzy. Fuck me, why did I let him hit me first? That was a terrible idea. He didn't even punch me. Just a casual slap and he could've killed me.

Someone's shouting. I see Angel's desperate face. "Get up, Bella," she mouths the words, but there's no sound. Well, if there is, I can't hear it.

The taste of blood is overwhelming. Fuck, did he knock out a tooth? I let my jaw go lax. Blood fills my mouth, along with the bitter taint of something else—the poison I've ingested. My gift to anyone who dares to try to fight me.

But fuck, I might be in over my head.

I rise slowly, trying not to jostle my skull too much.

The Giant is strolling back and forth on his side of the ring. Glaring at me. Why didn't he finish me?

I look past him into the stands. The crowd's on its feet, screaming, but I can't hear them over the ringing in my head.

And Dominus is there, smiling. The fucker is smiling.

I have to win this.

Dominus signals to the Giant, and the big man turns and lumbers to me. I don't move; if I run, I might pass out, and my plans are for him to touch me as much as possible, anyway.

"I'm going to fuck you up, little girl," he snarls. "Gonna tear off your head and—"

"Right, I get it. Gross." It hurts to talk, but I can't help it. I don't want to hear him talk about all the awful things he wants to do with my body.

I should thank him for making it easier to kill him. But I don't know if I'm going to win.

The Giant reaches out and snatches me off my feet. The move jars my sore body, and the pain takes my breath away. His hand clamps around my throat, tightening, squeezing. Cutting off my air. I'm choking, my feet kicking in the air.

He raises me above his head. If he slams me to the floor, it's all over. I open my mouth and let a stream of blood trickle into his eyes.

He opens his mouth, roaring. He tosses me away, and by some miracle, I land on the ropes and not the platform or the concrete beyond the fighting ring. The cords cut into my side—owwwww—but I slide to the ground. Something twinges in my ankle. I'm hurting. I've probably broken something.

But I'm still in one piece. And I'm sweating. The poison's coming out of my pores.

The Giant is scrubbing at his face, covered in my blood. It's probably beginning to burn.

He spits a few times, but it's too late for him. I'm in his system now.

I step forward. He swings for me, but it goes wild. I duck it, cackling. This is fun! The Giant staggers, still rubbing at his eyes.

The crowd falters, realizing something's wrong. Their chosen champion isn't fighting like he should.

"Hurts, doesn't it?" I ask. "Hogweed and manicheel sap. It burns. Causes blindness."

Dominus is on his feet. "Finish her," he shouts in a rasping voice.

I smile at him with my mouth bloody.

The Giant wipes a hand over his mouth. His eyes are swelling up. His throat will be next.

I wipe some sweat onto my palm and run past him, slapping his arm. His left, then his right.

He swings for me out of habit but misses.

I dance in and miscalculate. His slap knocks me across the ring again. I fall to the ground, laughing. My face aches.

I spit blood into my hand. Blood and part of a tooth. So, he did break one.

But the pain is so far away. Adrenaline is my friend, keeping the pain at bay, fueling me.

The Giant is twitching, frowning. He's rubbing his skin now, trying to reach everywhere I touched him. Red handprints—my handprints—stand out on his huge muscles. The poison is working.

"Bella, no," someone bellows.

It's Kaiser. He's woken up.

He's still surrounded by a group of masked Fraternitas men, who are holding him back. He bellows, fighting. One of his arms breaks free for a second before they grab him again.

Damn, I got the dose wrong! I've got to end this before he tears across the room and tries to fight. He's swaying like he's still half-drugged.

I grin and wave, then realize I'm covered in blood, so I blow him a kiss. It only seems to rile Kaiser up more. Oops.

Jaeger punches him in the face, and he goes down.

Yikes. I wince.

I'd better end this.

The Giant is touching his face like he doesn't understand what it is.

"Does it feel numb? That's another symptom," I inform

him. "Let me tell you something. It doesn't take much poison to kill a grown man. You think you're invincible, but the bigger you are..."

He swings for me, and I easily evade him.

"The harder you fall."

I feint a punch to his dick, and he doubles over to protect his crotch. Both hands cover his groin area, so I jab my fingers into his eyes.

He shouts in pain, and I spit in his mouth.

Then I back away. It'll be over soon.

The Giant retches, but nothing comes up but air. His airways are swelling, too. I dosed him with everything I could.

His head lolls back, red-tinged tears streaming down his face. His eyes are bloody. Ooh, that looks bad.

The end is near. Which is good because I'm swaying on my feet. My head is throbbing.

But I'm still riding a wave of adrenaline, floating high above the pain.

"Let's face it, you underestimated me. But everyone did." I lean in. He tries to swat me like a fly, but his hand falters. "You thought you were stronger than me. But there are many forms of strength." Oops, I'm monologuing again. But I can't resist. "Tell me now... how does it feel to be weak?"

He groans. The poison inside must be like putting a blowtorch to his insides.

"Poor baby," I croon. "Don't worry. It'll be over soon."

He's shivering. He curls into himself. His hands stiffen into claws.

"Three, two..."

He takes a step. He tries to take another, but his foot won't move. Bloody foam pours from his mouth.

"One."

The Giant crashes to the ground.

The Bulls are on their feet, shouting foul play, but the rest of the crowd drowns them out.

Angel climbs on the ropes, pumping her arms over her head. She's leading a chant.

It takes me a second to hear what they're saying.

"Fraternitas! Fraternitas!"

Oh, hell no.

I put one foot on the fallen giant and pump my own fist into the air. "My name is Belladonna Bosco," I shout. "I am the Poisoner. And this is what I do to my enemies." I point to the fallen giant.

I notice the crowd has moved back from the sides of the ring, giving me space. Good. It's about time people know how dangerous I am.

"Bell-a-don-na," I shout my name until Angel takes up the chant. "Bell-a-don-na."

"Bella, Bella, Bella!" the crowd screams.

"That's right," I whisper. "That's me. Fear me."

The Bulls are still there, but Dominus is gone. Fled. His champion is down.

I am the champion.

I open my arms and accept the people's adoration and fear.

They know who I am. They know what I can do.

From now on, they will think twice about messing with me.

I am the greatest supervillain who ever lived.

*Kaiser*

Bella stands in the center of the fighting ring, beautiful and terrifying. The room is swimming, and my head is throbbing. She definitely poisoned me. And Jaeger punched me.

But I can't tear my eyes from her. She's got her hair up all cute again. Dyed bright pink. Her face is a bloody mask, her eyes wild. She's propped her foot on a huge fighter, who is face down in a pool of blood.

It's definitely her. That toxic combination of excitement and murderous glee.

"Let me go," I growl to my brothers.

They hesitate, but Jaeger barks at them to do it.

"Secure the room," I tell Jaeger. "Get everyone out of here."

He nods, and I turn slowly to face the ring. I take a step and stumble.

Jaeger reaches for me, and I push his arm away.

I will crawl to her if I have to.

Jaeger shouts at the people, clearing them out. The rest of Fraternitas spreads out, shoving people to get them to leave.

I limp forward like I'm moving through mud. My body has healed—Atticus made sure of that—but whatever Bella drugged me with is still in my system.

But time slows, and everything fades out of existence when I look at her. If it takes me an eternity to get to her, I will count it a blessing because it means more time to bask in her presence.

I step up to the ring, and she sees me. "What are you doing? You idiot. Let me help you."

I sag on the ropes and let her fuss over me. "You don't have to be strong all the time. You can ask for help."

She's glorious. The ring lights are hot on my skin, but she outshines them all.

"You could've died," I growl.

"No. Well, maybe. But I didn't." Her lips and chin are bright with blood. So is her chest. It might not all be her blood.

The swelling on the right side of her face, though, tells me the Giant got at least one good hit in. He hurt her. I'd kill him and desecrate his body if she hadn't already destroyed him so thoroughly.

"I could kill my brothers for allowing this—"

"I didn't give them a choice. And Jaeger and Atticus helped me. Atticus figured out a way to poison the Giant before he even set foot in the ring." She grins. "We made a plan. It was dangerous, but I had help."

My legs feel weak. I'm hanging on the ropes. She brushes her hand over my new hair growth, and goosebumps rise on my back.

"You fought for me." My throat is closing. I have to force the words out. "It was supposed to be me, but you took my place."

"Of course I did. Come here." She helps me climb through the ropes, into the ring. I'm getting stronger just by being in her presence.

Her poison hums under my skin.

"Bella," I reach for her, then remember she's poison. "I wish I could touch you."

"You can." She wipes her face, cleaning some of the blood away, but the bare skin of her arms is still slick and shiny. "I used poisons you're immune to."

"What?"

"Atticus and I talked, and we think my blood did something to you. Not the sleeping potion—we made that up special. But... you're immune to me, Kaiser. You and no one else." She grins, showing bloody teeth. "Touch me, Kaiser."

I let my fingers brush her jaw. Her cheek is red and puffy where he hit her. "He could've killed you."

"Nah. I'm a supervillain."

I fall to my knees. It feels right, being on my knees in front of her. "You fought for me. No one's ever fought for me."

She passes a hand over my head again. "You're not alone anymore, my beautiful cauliflower." Her lower lip juts out, trembling. "You were going to leave me. I couldn't let you leave. You promised me a lifetime."

"I know, baby. I'm sorry."

"I love you, dammit." She touches her throat, where she's still wearing the black ribbon. "I love you."

"You can't," I say, my throat closing. I don't know why, but it's hard for me to believe someone like her could love someone like me. "I'm not... You can't love me."

She bares her teeth at me and leans in. "Challenge accepted."

It hits me then. She really loves me. Would do anything for me. Even sacrifice herself.

"I love you," I say in a rush. Because I can't give her what she deserves, but I can give her that. I can give her all of me. "I need you, Bella."

Her hand hovers in the space between us. I can't take it anymore.

"Baby, please, please touch me. I need you, please—"

"Kaiser." She cups my face, and I gasp. Her touch doesn't hurt. It feels good.

I grip her hips, keeping her close to me. I stare into her dark eyes. "My beautiful poison. Will you marry me?"

She leans in and lets her lips brush mine. I close my eyes. Her touch is heaven.

"Yes."

## 42

------------

Bella

The fight is over. I won. And now it's time for my reward.

I hurt my ankle, but Atticus checked me over and wrapped it. It's not ideal, but it's time for the claiming ceremony. Kaiser and I don't want to wait. I'm still gross, covered in sweat and blood and poison, but Kaiser wrapped me in his red robe and insisted on sweeping me off my feet. Literally.

He carries me deeper into the underworld. Each step takes us further from the light. He seems to know these tunnels, their twists and turns, by heart. I imagine him as a boy, racing through this space, finding a home here in the darkness.

I squeeze his hand, and he squeezes mine in return. I'm his home now, and he's mine. I will never leave him or allow him to leave me.

I can tell we're close to our destination because the grimy stone gives way to polished black marble. The only sound is the echo of our shoes on the tiles. The dank smell disappears, covered up by the thick scent of heady incense. Underneath it all, though, is a scent of rot.

There's a tingle at the base of my spine, my sense of anticipation growing. I feel like I'm in a horror movie, about to come face-to-face with an evil cult.

But I'm grinning like a maniac. This is fun!

There's a crackling sound up ahead, and I gasp when we come around a bend into a nightmarish world.

The tunnel gives way to a cavernous space made of obsidian stone. Flames dance in gas fireplaces set right into the walls. The only light comes from the fire and hundreds of candles, and the reddish light glints off the rows and rows of skull masks.

Fraternitas is here. Waiting for us. The men in devil masks and skull rings stand silently in the pews, facing the front.

"This way." Kaiser carries me to the front and a small pool that reminds me of a baptismal font. The scent of incense hangs heavier in the air. Frankincense, cassia, and myrrh.

Then I realize what this place looks like.

A church. An upside-down church. A sanctuary made in hell.

There's even an altar. The Giant's body lies on it like a sacrifice. Someone cleaned him up a little, but blood still pools around him.

I almost feel sorry for him. He was Dominus's son, sent to fight for his family's honor. But in this world, it's kill or be killed. And I am a killer.

Kaiser sets me down on a chair. "Can you kneel?" he asks and helps me into a high kneeling position that won't twinge my ankle. He tucks his robe around me more tightly. It's so huge it wraps around me a few times and pools at my feet, but I appreciate it. It's chilly in here, despite the fireplace built into the walls. Or maybe I'm just feeling the aftereffects of adrenaline leaving my body. All the pain I didn't feel in the ring has arrived, and I'm living in it. My ankle and cheek ache.

Two men come forward, one wearing a black mask with devil's horns. I recognize him from my father's office a lifetime ago. The Devil is here.

The other is Father Francis. What's a priest doing in hell? *It was my idea,* he told me once. He raised these boys, founded Fraternitas. Helped hone them into a weapon.

A few more figures join us at the front. A woman in a wheelchair, with brilliant tattoo sleeves. She's holding a dagger, stroking its handle. The blood red jewels in her skull ring glint in the firelight.

"That's Lucy," Kaiser whispers to me.

Jaeger and Elodie also drift toward us, holding hands. Elodie's changed into a simple white dress that makes her look like a priestess. She looks solemn, like she's at a funeral. She and Jaeger take their place beside the altar. I notice she can't look at the body.

"It's time," Father Francis intones.

Kaiser leans down to turn my face toward him. "It's time I make you mine," he murmurs to me. "Forever. My chosen one. My *elita.*"

"This is it?"

"This is it. I'm claiming you." He cups my sore cheek. His brow furrows as he swipes his thumb gently over my swollen skin. He looks so upset by the fact that I'm hurt that I want to comfort him.

"I'm okay," I murmur. I turn my head, kissing his palm. "Let's do this."

"The sacrifice has already been made," the Devil rasps. "Blood has been spilled. You are already bound by blood and death. After this ceremony—"

"Wait," I blurt out. The sound echoes in the cavernous space. All the skull masks tilt my way, and I can feel their silent disapproval. I'm probably the only person in the world who dares interrupt the Devil. "Sorry. I know this is probably a bad time. But, uh, I have something to confess." Crap, I've messed up this beautifully sinister moment, but I have to get this off my chest. I hover my hand over Kaiser's arm. "You won't like it."

"Tell me," he rumbles. "But if it's about hunting down Dominus, I'm in. I'll do it for you. We all will."

"No, it's not about that. I actually was going to leave Dominus to my father. My father's still alive, you know."

A murmur runs through the Fraternitas's ranks. Out of the corner of my eye, I see one of the men raise his mask. It's St. James, and he's rubbing his face like he has a headache.

Kaiser kneels to take my hands. "What is it, Bella?"

"Um... so... I've been poisoning you."

"I know."

"Yeah, no, it wasn't what you think. I wasn't trying to kill you with the poison. This time." Hecate, help me, I'm making a mess of this.

Kaiser has a patient look on his face. "Is this about the candles?"

"No. Not the candles. This is a poison you don't know about." I talk faster, trying to speedrun through my feelings. "See, oxytocin can be used as a fertilizer and some samples got shipped to me by accident and I thought it would be good to make you fall in love with me. So I made a sort of aphrodisiac lotion and rubbed it into my skin and—"

"I know," Kaiser says.

"And I think it made you love me... but it's not real..." It takes me a second to hear him. "Wait, you know?"

"Yes. I figured it out. Atticus tested everything in your room when you were in a coma."

"Oh." I look around. In the front pew, a masked man raises his hand at me. "Hi, Atticus." I turn back to Kaiser. "You knew."

"Yes. You weren't exactly subtle. You labeled the lotion "Love Potion Number 9.""

"But—" I'm trying to catch up. He knew, and I didn't know, but now I do... and where does that leave us? I'm confused. "I made you love me. This isn't real." He has to understand I manipulated his feelings. This is why I had to tell him right away; I can't stand that I tricked him. "This is just what the potion made you feel—"

"Bella. No." He gathers my hands to his chest, holds them there at his heart. He takes a moment to gather his words while I try not to fidget or look away. "I want you to hear me." He waits until I meet his gaze to say, "From the beginning, you were my poison. Even before we met. It wasn't anything you used on me. You were in my system the moment I laid eyes on you."

I shake my head. I don't believe it. I can't. I did all these tricksy things to win, and now I'm devastated because what Kaiser and I have might not be real.

"Think about it," he says softly. "You haven't wanted to touch me since your coma. Any effect of the love potion wore off long ago."

Finally, I get what he's saying. He's right. I haven't used

the love potion on him in over a month. "It wore off," I repeat slowly.

"Yes."

"But... tonight you were willing to fight for me, sacrifice for me."

"I was. I am. Because I love you." He steps closer, drawing me into the circle of his strong arms. "It wasn't the aphrodisiac, Belladonna. It was always you."

It's too much. I start hyperventilating, but he rests his hands on my back. I feel him, and it feels good.

"Shhh, it's okay," he murmurs, kissing the top of my head.

"I still want to do it," I confess. "I want to keep poisoning you. I don't want you to leave."

"I know. It's okay. You can still poison me if you need to, okay? I can take it."

I sigh, half slumping against him, drinking in his delicious scent. I finally feel calm again. I could stay like this forever, but all of Fraternitas is watching us right now.

"Okay." I lean back and push my hair out of my face. I feel like my whole world has tilted on its axis, but now it's spinning smoothly. "Sorry. We can go back to your evil ceremony or whatever. I love all this by the way." I wave a hand around the sanctuary. "Very *Dante's Inferno*. Black is the new black, I think—"

Kaiser grips my hand again, and I shut up.

"You ready?" he asks.

"Yes."

The Devil clears his throat. "Usually, we hold a collaring ceremony at Club Empire first, and then there's a sacrifice. But you, Belladonna Bosco, have already killed for Fraternitas." He motions to the Giant's body. "Your place among us is secure, if you wish it."

"I do." I take a deep breath so I really feel it. "I wish it."

"Kaiser," the Devil says, "do you vow to love and honor your elita? Will you care for her and keep her, cherishing her above others? Will you fight to protect her and put her safety before all else, even your own life?"

"I so vow."

"Belladonna Bosco."

"Present." I wave a hand. Out of the corner of my eye, I see Elodie bite her lower lip to keep from laughing.

"Do you vow to submit to Kaiser and wear his collar as a sign of your loyalty and love? Will you honor and obey him and give yourself over to him in full and complete surrender?"

"I so vow." My knees have started hurting because they're pressed into the hard stone, but I embrace the discomfort. It makes me feel submissive.

Lucy rolls up. She now has a pillow in her lap, holding both the dagger and a silver collar.

Kaiser removes the black ribbon from around my neck and replaces it with the collar. The metal is cool to the touch, and I stroke it, enjoying its weight on my neck. There's something comforting about being held like this. Forever. Maybe that's why the submissives at Club Empire looked so peaceful.

Father Francis comes forward and starts intoning something solemn, speaking another language.

Kaiser leans in and whispers, "It's Latin."

"What does it mean?"

"You're one of us." He nods to the ranks of masked men. "Joined to them through me."

I close my eyes and let the words roll over me. *You are not alone.* But it's a lot to take in, so I just let myself lean into Kaiser's warmth and his scent.

Father Francis says in English, "Above all, you commit your life to the one you have chosen. You will be bound together by water, by fire, by death, and by blood. So shall you vow."

"Yes, I so vow," Kaiser says.

"Yes, I so vow," I say and shiver, because this feels huge. Like a graduation, a wedding, and a funeral all rolled into one.

*Focus, Bella!*

Together we dip the dagger into the Giant's blood, then into a goblet that Lucy holds.

Kaiser helps me up, and we join hands over a silver bowl set on the altar above the Giant's head.

"Together in life. Bound by death," Father Francis murmurs, making the sign of the cross over our hands.

The Devil pours the bloody water from the goblet over our hands. I expect it to feel cold, but it's not. It's warm, and somehow that's worse.

*I'm a killer.* I've always been, but now, taking part in a ceremony of death and communion, I get how fucked up I am. But this is natural, right? Life and death flowing in one endless circle. Everyone dies. Sometimes, I just help things along. Trim the diseased limbs and prune the vine of humanity so it bears good fruit.

Someone has to do it. It might as well be me.

Father Francis steps back. So do Lucy and the Devil. Several robed Fraternitas figures approach the altar, where they lift the Giant's body and cart him away.

I stare up at Kaiser, every nerve ending sizzling with excitement.

"Is that it?" I ask.

"That's it."

He lifts me off the chair and sets me right on the altar. Feels a little sacrilegious. I like it.

He grips my hair, pulling my head back. I gasp, and he tugs my hair harder, baring my neck to him. Dom Kaiser is back, and he's all business.

I lick my lips. "What now?"

"Now I claim you properly." And he pushes me to lie back on the altar. The silver bowl crashes to the floor, and pink water spatters everywhere. He forces me down on the stone slab, releasing my hair so he can hold me down by my throat.

I love it.

I feel alive.

My hair is soaking up the bloody liquid, and I don't care. Wash me clean. Wash me bloody.

"Kiss me," I whisper, and he does. He leans over and tastes my lips like he can't get enough of the flavor. I try to lean in, wanting more, and he pulls my hair, controlling the kiss. It feels so good to be held down, controlled. He's trapped me, and there's no escape. He will never leave. He wants me too much.

His hips grind into me, and I could cum just like this. But when he rears up and tears open my bra top, I shudder with happiness.

"Yes!" I shout. I look around. There's no one here. No more Devil or Lucy. No more Father Francis or St. James.

We're alone.

"They're gone," I say. Even the men in masks have disappeared. They left silently, and now it's as if they'd never been. I wonder if they were here at all.

"No one gets to see you like this," He skates a hand down my bare chest. "No one touches you. No one but me."

"No one," I promise. From now on, I'll poison my enemies from afar.

He drags his lips down my neck to my shoulder. I'm still covered in blood and poison, and fuck, I don't want to hurt him, but I don't want him to stop.

"I feel, I feel you," he murmurs against my skin.

"Kaiser, please, I need you." My skin is hot and too tight. I feel like I will die if he doesn't claim me now.

He drags his lips down my neck, between my breasts, to my belly. Pleasure blooms through me. I can do nothing but lie back and let him worship me. My hands are free, and I touch every part of him I can reach. His shaved head, his ears, his forehead.

He licks between my legs. Holy Hecate, yes! Heat bursts through me, and I want more. He drives the fingers of his right hand deep into my sex. It feels so good, I come up off the altar, my voice ringing out in the cathedral space. Kaiser grabs my wrists, keeping me from fighting him. He's holding me like he never wants to let go.

"I will never let anyone hurt you," he murmurs. His lips are soft, but his grip on my wrists is hard and cruel. No mercy.

"Yes, more. Touch me. Hold me down. Don't let me go."

"Have to taste you. Fuck." He pushes his whole face into me. His shoulder muscles bunch, his blue eyes flashing up to meet mine. I writhe, but he pins me, forcing me to lie here and take it.

And I. Love. It. The sight of him pressed into me, the feel of his tongue licking me, his fingers strumming my clit—it's all too much.

I come hard, with the love of my life on his knees before me, drinking me down. Then he rises up and claims me, fucking me right in the hellish sanctuary, while we're both drenched in the blood of our enemies.

It feels right. It feels like deja vu. Inevitable.

It's not normal, but we will never be normal. And that's the way I like it.

I look pretty and sweet, but inside, I am as deadly as nightshade. To love me is to court death.

Kaiser knows this. He understands. He has a kill count I aspire to. He will teach me his ways. And I will teach him mine.

Together, we will be the deadliest couple on Earth.

## 43

B*ella*

The sunlight is warm on my face as Kaiser drives me through the countryside. He holds my hand in between shifting gears.

The wedding is tomorrow. My friends are going to be my bridesmaids. Honey is excited, and so is Elodie. Raine's stepbrother agreed that she could come, as long as he was invited, too.

Kaiser and I even went to marriage counseling one last time. One thing led to another, and Kaiser and I started making out on the couch, and Father Francis had to leave the room.

We're all set for the ceremony at St. Xavier's. There's just one more thing I need to do.

"Turn here," I say, pointing to a small dirt road between overgrown fields.

Kaiser obliges, and we roll down the long, winding road. He slows the Jeep so we don't kick up too much dust.

Finally, we come to a sprawling white farmhouse with peeling paint.

"Is this it?" Kaiser asks.

"Yep." I point to a sign that's hidden behind stalks of goldenrod and half swallowed up by morning glory vines. It reads *Flowerwood.* My mother's family farm.

It should be mine now, but my father didn't include it in the inheritance paperwork. I know he's here, hiding out.

I jump out of the Jeep before Kaiser can initiate the child locks. "Be right back."

"Bella—" he shouts after me, but I'm already running down the lane.

"I'm just going to see Papa!" I shout over my shoulder. "I'll be fine." I dart off the path and take the shortcut through the orchard. Kaiser will still chase me, but this will buy me some time.

The old barn looks just like I remember. Red with a gray tin roof and Virginia creeper running up the side. But it also looks smaller. Papa is there, not inside working in the lab like I expected, but outside with a gardening hat and gloves on. Weeding the garden, like he used to do back when Mom was alive.

He straightens, plucking a handkerchief out of his pocket to wipe sweat off his face.

"Papa," I call, out of breath.

"Bella." He looks so shocked, and I can't help it. I run right up to him but stop before I can throw my arms around him. I want to. One of these days, I'm going to hug him whether he likes it or not. "You're here."

"I fought the Vesuvios. Hand-to-hand combat. I won," I say in a rush.

His eyes widen.

"It's all fine. Dominus wants war, but his forces are decimated. If he tries anything, Fraternitas can defeat him. Anyway, that's not why I'm here. I'm here because I'm getting married. To Kaiser. Because I want to. And I want Mom's ring." I bite my lip, afraid to ask. "Please say you have it. Please say you didn't throw it away."

He looks like I've struck him. Then, slowly, he reaches into his shirt and draws out a long chain. At the end are two plain gold bands. His and hers.

"You have them both," I say. "I thought..." I stop before I say *I thought you didn't want them anymore.* But obviously, he held onto them. He's been wearing them on a chain around his neck.

He undoes the chain and starts sliding the smaller ring off. He pauses a moment when it's free. I get the sense that he's reluctant to let go.

All this time, I thought he wanted to forget my mother, but her wedding ring has rested next to his heart since he took it off.

"Wait," I say. "You can keep it—"

"No," Papa says softly. He's so quiet, but there's a load of emotion in his voice if I listen closely. "She would've wanted you to have it." He holds out my mother's ring and places it onto my upturned palm. I close my fingers around it, and a tremor runs through me. I slip it into my pocket.

"So you're getting married."

"Yes. It's my choice this time." Kaiser made sure of that. I realize now that my dad was terrified of my supervillain tendencies. He did everything he could to get me under control, and when that didn't work, he made sure Fraternitas would protect me.

He did it out of love. As fucked up as that is.

Feeling bolder, I say, "I want you to walk me down the aisle. It's a private ceremony, but no one has to know you're still alive. You can wear a mask—except that Fraternitas kind of already knows you're alive..." I'm about to apologize for telling his secret when he responds.

"I don't know if I deserve that."

The sadness in his voice rocks me back on my heels.

"You don't. But I forgive you. And I want you by my side." I take a deep breath and say the magic words. "It's what Mom would've wanted."

Papa hangs his head. I've never seen him cry. Not in all those horrible years after. But tears run down his face now.

Mine too.

My arms ache to reach out and hug him, but I just sniffle and say, "I want you in my life, Papa. I know it's hard for you. I'm not the daughter you want me to be—"

"No, no. You're everything. Everything she wanted. Everything she hoped for. I look at you and I see..."

*Her.* He looks at me and sees Mom. No wonder it was hard for him to be around me.

"She's still with us, you know," I say quietly. "I can feel her helping me. Watching over me. But I need you." I take his hand. He doesn't look at me, but he grasps my hand tight. "I need a father. As long as you're still alive, I want you in my life. Will... will you hug me? Please?"

And then I'm in his arms. He's holding me tight, like he'll never let go. "My daughter, my belladonna. My flower. My beautiful flower."

I don't know how long we stand there, hugging. Long enough to release the pain of all the wasted years. When we break apart, I'm a mess of tears, and Papa's collar is wet. Some of the grass stains on his clothes transferred to me. But I feel good. Lighter.

He straightens and studies me. "I'm glad you found me."

"It wasn't very hard. This was always your favorite home." Even though we never came here after Mom died.

"It was a wedding gift. Your mother would want you to inherit it."

I pluck a stray piece of grass off his shirt sleeve. "I think you should hang onto it. It'll be good for you to live here, out of the city."

"I thought so. I want you to know, Bella, I didn't throw away anything of your mother's. Everything of hers is yours if you want it."

"Her paintings?" I remember the bare walls at the New Rome house. I was so devastated, thinking he had removed every trace of Mom from the place.

"I moved them here. All of her things, our photographs."

"The money tree?"

"Of course. All her plants."

I sigh, feeling relief. "I thought they were destroyed when you blew up the New Rome house." He must have planned ahead. I'll have to ask him to teach me to do that.

There's a rustle in the bushes beside us. Kaiser is here, but he's giving us a moment.

"Did you get the samples I sent?" my father asks in a soft voice only I can hear. I know he's talking about the oxytocin packets. I guess they weren't sent to me by accident.

"I did," I say. "Turns out I didn't need it. He loves me for me."

"You're all grown up." Papa pats my back awkwardly. Maybe he's just an awkward guy. He needs help with emotional stuff.

"Come on." I twine my arm in Papa's and lead him toward the house. "Let's show Kaiser around. Kaiser, you can come out now!"

Kaiser stalks out of the brush. He's got burs clinging to his pants and goldenrod pollen smudged on his face. There's a morning glory tucked behind his ear, though, and I'd bet anything he put it there.

Sure enough, he pulls it out and hands it to me.

He and Papa nod to each other in silent greeting.

"I just got off the phone with St. James," Kaiser says to Papa. "Someone poisoned Dominus Vesuvio."

"Oh no, that's awful," I say without a trace of sympathy. "Who would do such a thing?"

"No one knows." Both Kaiser and I look at my father.

"What a tragedy," my father says with a straight face.

"How did he die?" I ask.

"He's not dead yet. Just in incredible pain. Which is good, because we think he was about to move on us. Now he's fighting for his life and might lose everything. If Dominus doesn't defend his organization, the other families will move in."

"Good." I smile. Sounds like my father got his revenge.

"It's more than he deserves," Papa says. "Have you thought about an alliance with the Regis family?" He and Kaiser start talking strategy. Alliances and mafia families. Blah blah blah. Wake me when it's time to poison someone.

We walk through my mother's garden. The last of the summer roses are still blooming, the scent strong around us. Underneath an oak tree is a grove of lily of the valley. It's not the right time for them to be blooming, but they are. The little white flowers are so lovely and delicate. And deadly.

I stop and stand under the oak tree for a moment, breathing in the sweet scent.

I reach into my pocket and take out my mother's ring. I slip it on and it fits perfectly. I hold it up, letting it sparkle in the sunlight.

The wind picks up and rustles my hair. It swirls around me, and I smell a rich, floral perfume.

"Thanks, Mom," I whisper, and follow my father and future husband into the house.

44

---

# B<sup>ella</sup>

THE DAY of the wedding finds me in a side room at St. Xavier's. I'm wearing a white wedding dress with pink appliqué flowers and green vines decorating the skirt.

Out in the sanctuary, the organ starts playing.

"I think that's our cue," Elodie says. "I'll go check."

"I'm almost done," Honey says, brushing the finishing touches onto my face. She did all our makeup.

"You look awesome," Raine says.

"So do you." Raine, in particular, looks great in the dark purple bridesmaid gown I chose. "Thanks for doing this. I know all this was last-minute."

"Thank you for inviting us. I can't believe you're getting married the week after your house blew up," Honey says.

"It's fine. It was the New Rome house, not the one in

Metropolis next to campus. That one just needs some remodeling."

Honey shakes her head. "Girl, one day you're going to tell me the whole story."

"We need another sleepover," Raine says. "I just need to get Ransom off my back."

Ransom is her stepbrother. "Do you want me to poison him?"

"What?" Raine's startled eyes meet mine in the mirror.

"It doesn't have to be a deadly dose. Just incapacitate him a little. Make him sleep a lot."

Raine just stares at me.

Honey sighs. "Bella, we talked about this. You can't just go around poisoning people."

"It's just a little sleeping potion—" I protest.

"You could do that?" Raine interrupts.

"Don't encourage her," Honey says.

I nod. "Oh yes, I used all sorts of poisons on Kaiser, and it worked out fine."

Honey gasps. "Fine? You said he found out and chased you through the house to punish you!"

"I know." I waggle my brows at Raine, who looks more freaked out by the second. "It was great."

"Thanks for the offer," Raine says. "I'll save it for plan B."

"Anytime." I grin at her in the mirror. "I'm here if you need me. Your friendly neighborhood venefica. We're the *Villaini*, remember?"

"Right, I remember." She grins back. "Do it for the plot."

We both snicker, and then Raine heads out to wait with Elodie, leaving me alone with Honey.

"Thanks for doing this," I say to Honey. I stroke the silver collar around my throat. "I know I haven't always been a great friend."

"You're fine. I was just upset about Fraternitas banning me. They were always kinder to me than my own family, I just thought..."

I bite my lip, wondering if I should tell her what I learned. "About that. I learned something. Elodie actually told me after she figured it out. Fraternitas considers you under their protection."

Her eyes are wide in the mirror. "What does that mean?"

"I don't know. Elodie and Angel and I are going to try to find out."

Raine rushes back. "It's time. Elodie already went down the aisle. We have to go!"

Honey grabs my bouquet and hands it to me. "Ready!"

I hurry out just in time to see Angel march down the aisle. Raine and Honey line up to go next.

The only other person in the narthex is a short man in a skull mask. Papa, in disguise and waiting for me.

I notice he's wearing his wedding ring again. He also has a boutonniere made of a rose with a few sprigs of lily of the valley. It matches my bouquet, although I'm also holding some belladonna blooms, too, and spikes of *salvia divinorum*. Gotta keep the husband on his toes.

"Papa." I take his arm. "You ready?"

He sighs in a way that makes me think he'll never be ready.

"I want this," I remind him. "I want him."

"All right, little flower." We share a smile, and he escorts me to the entrance of the sanctuary. The scent of roses and lily valley hovers in the air.

The church is grand and filled with light. But all the light in the world can't make the rows and rows of masked men look normal. This has got to be the creepiest wedding ever. Everyone on the groom's side is wearing a skull mask.

I love it!

But after a few steps, all I can see is Kaiser. He's in a white tux and his hair is shining like a crown. I know his brother is beside him. And Atticus, too.

But I can't take my eyes off my betrothed.

Papa hands me off, and I face Kaiser, my head tilting back to take him in.

I never thought it'd come to this. I never thought I'd meet someone I'd want to spend my time with.

Father Francis clears his throat and starts the ceremony. Kaiser and I don't really pay attention. We're staring at each other, drinking the other in.

At one point, Father Francis has us join hands. Kaiser cups mine between his two huge palms.

"Respect," he murmurs.

"Communion," I whisper back. And we smile at each other.

"I now pronounce you husband and wife. You may kiss the bride."

I reach for Kaiser, and he lets me touch him. He cups my face and I cup his, and then our lips touch and it's amazing.

Everyone is cheering. Even Raine's stern stepbrother, who glowered at her through the whole ceremony, is clapping.

Kaiser ends the kiss and drags his lips to my ear to whisper, "Tonight. Page 269."

*Shiver.*

Father Francis spreads his arms, announcing to the audience, "It's my pleasure to introduce you to Mr. and Mrs. Belladonna Bosco." Kaiser told me he didn't have a last name. So I gave him mine.

He collared me, I claimed him. We deserve each other.

We will never be alone again.

# EPILOGUE

B *ella*

It's Halloween, and Kaiser and I are at Elodie and Jaeger's place. We're hosting our first annual rewatch of *Vampire Varsity*. Elodie is absolutely hooked. Which is good, because usually she and Jaeger only want to watch some godawful Christmas movies.

Elodie's cuddled up with Jaeger in an oversized chair, while Kaiser's stretched out on the couch with me on top of him. We all have bowls of popcorn within reach.

"I think Luna should be with Dargon, the evil twin," Jaeger says.

"No," I say. "Obviously, she should be with Nik."

"Nik is too evil," Elodie argues. "They just wrote him in to be a worse villain than Dargon. He killed his whole pack and imprisoned his entire family. He's the worst."

"She can handle him," I say. "And he's as powerful as she is. She deserves the best of the worst."

Elodie shakes her head. Both her and Jaeger's eyes are fixed on the screen.

I roll my head so my chin rests on my arm. "What do you think, Kaiser?"

He kisses my nose. "I think he's just evil enough to deserve her."

THANK *you for reading my beautiful book! I absolutely loved writing my unhinged heroine and her beautiful mafia man.*

*I put so many of my favorite things in this book. Like Bella, I was homeschooled through high school and often feel a little out of touch with pop culture... and life in general because I live so much in my head. I'm also obsessed with plants, high school vampire shows, and of course, romance novels. I'll never forget my first bodice ripper—a lovely Viking romance with a bare-chested blond on the cover. My friend Shanna H. would smuggle them from under her aunt's bed to my friend Katrina and me to read in math class. We'd hide them under the desk.*

*More is coming in the Vino Verse...whose book do you want me to write next? Email me at lee@leesavino.com and let me know!*

*<3*
*Lee*

ENTER LEE SAVINO's dark world (The VinoVerse)
Start with:

- Innocence - Hades & Persephone retelling

- Beauty's Beast - Beauty and the Beast retelling

Then. . . the Mafia Brides series

- Revenge is Sweet - as close to a rom-com as a mafia story can be
- Vengeance is Mine - the exact opposite of a rom-com. Dark with BDSM torture. Victor's story

And then. . . the Fraternitas series

- His Perfect Prey - Jaeger and Elodie. Little Red Riding Hood retelling
- His Perfect Poison - Kaiser and Belladonna Bosco.

Coming soon...

- Raine and Ransom
- Honey's story
- Damien (the Devil) and Eve's story
- Asmodeus and Sarah's story
- And of course... Sebastian St. James
- More Mafia Brides and Fraternitas

# JOIN THE VINO VILLAINI!

If you're a Booktok or Instagram influencer, I'd love you to apply to join my Influencer team.

Team members are eligible for ARCs, special edition books and other book mail, peeks behind the scenes, live launch parties and more!

Come join the fun! Become a Vino Villain today!

<3 Lee

Apply here: https://www.leesavino.com/influencers

# ALSO BY LEE SAVINO

For film and TV rights inquiries: <u>lee.savino@</u>
<u>leesavino.com</u>

Want more dark romance? Check out His Perfect Prey, book
one in the *Fraternitas* series.

*Dark and Mafia Romance*

**Mafia Brides**
Revenge is Sweet
Vengeance is Mine

**Fraternitas**
His Perfect Prey
His Perfect Poison

**His Perfect Darkness**
His Perfect Darkness
Darkest Before Dawn

**A Dark Mafia Romance** trilogy with Stasia Black
Innocence
Awakening
Queen of the Underworld

**Beauty and the Rose** trilogy with Stasia Black

Beauty's Beast
Beauty & the Thorns
Beauty & the Rose

*Contemporary Romance*

**Royally Wrong**
Royally Bad
Royally Fake Fiancé

**Bad Boy Heroes**
Her Marine Daddy
Her Dueling Daddies
Beauty & The Lumberjacks
Snowed in with the Lumberjack
Rescuing Regina

~

*Paranormal romance*

**Berserker Saga**
Sold to the Berserkers
Mated to the Berserkers
Bred by the Berserkers (FREE novella only available at
www.leesavino.com)
Taken by the Berserkers
Given to the Berserkers
Claimed by the Berserkers
Rescued by the Berserker
Captured by the Berserkers

Kidnapped by the Berserkers
Bonded to the Berserkers
Berserker Babies
Night of the Berserkers
Owned by the Berserkers
Tamed by the Berserkers
Mastered by the Berserkers
Surrendered to the Berserkers

**Berserker Warriors**
Aegir
Siebold with Ines Johnson

**Bad Boy Alphas** with Renee Rose
Alpha's Temptation
Alpha's Danger
Alpha's Prize
Alpha's Challenge
Alpha's Obsession
Alpha's Desire
Alpha's War
Alpha's Mission
Alpha's Bane
Alpha's Secret
Alpha's Prey
Alpha's Blood
Alpha's Sun

**Shifter Ops** with Renee Rose
Alpha's Moon
Alpha's Vow
Alpha's Revenge
Alpha's Fire

Alpha's Rescue
Alpha's Command

A Very Merry Alpha's Solstice

**Bad Boy Bears** with Renee Rose
Alpha's Claim

**Midnight Doms** with Renee Rose
Alpha's Blood
His Captive Mortal
The Virgin and the Vampire
(All Souls' Night anthology exclusive)

**Werewolves of Wallstreet** with Renee Rose
Big Bad Boss: Midnight
Big Bad Boss: Moon Mad
Big Bad Boss: Marked
Big Bad Boss: Mated
Big Bad Bully

*Sci fi romance*

**Planet of Kings** with Tabitha Black
Brutal Mate
Brutal Claim
Brutal Capture
Brutal Beast
Brutal Demon

**Tsenturion Warriors** with Golden Angel

Alien Captive
Alien Tribute
Alien Abduction

**Dragons in Exile** with Lili Zander
Draekon Mate
Draekon Fire
Draekon Heart
Draekon Abduction
Draekon Destiny
Daughter of Draekons
Draekon Fever
Draekon Rogue
Draekon Holiday

**Draekon Rebel Force** with Lili Zander
Draekon Warrior
Draekon Conqueror
Draekon Pirate
Draekon Warlord
Draekon Guardian

*Cowboy Romance*

**Rocky Mountain Mail Order Brides**
Rocky Mountain Dawn
Rocky Mountain Bride
Rocky Mountain Rose
Rocky Mountain Romp
Rocky Mountain Rogue
Rocky Mountain Daddy

Rocky Mountain Ride
Possessing Pearl

**Wild Whip Ranch** with Tristan River
Cowboy's Babygirl
Taming His Wild Girl

# ABOUT THE AUTHOR

USA today bestselling author Lee Savino has written over 69 steamy romance novels. Bad boys, mafia men, wolf shifters, and dragon shifters in space—her dominant, alpha-hole heroes will stop at nothing to possess their one true love. Happily-ever-after and book hangover guaranteed!

Download a free book at leesavino.com.

Connect with Lee Savino in her fabulous Goddess Group: https://www.facebook.com/groups/LeeSavino

Goodreads: http://bit.ly/2tqaH28
Bookbub: http://bit.ly/2h8N6le
TikTok: https://www.tiktok.com/@authorleesavino
Instagram: https://www.instagram.com/authorleesavino